DAVID TALLERMAN

A SAVAGE
GENERATION

This is a **FLAME TREE PRESS** book

Text copyright © 2019 David Tallerman

FLAME TREE PRESS
6 Melbray Mews, London, SW6 3NS, UK
flametreepress.com

Distribution and warehouse:
Marston Book Services Ltd
160 Eastern Avenue, Milton Park, Abingdon, Oxon, OX14 4SB
www.marston.co.uk

Thanks to the Flame Tree Press team, including:
Taylor Bentley, Frances Bodiam, Federica Ciaravella, Don D'Auria,
Chris Herbert, Josie Karani, Molly Rosevear, Mike Spender,
Cat Taylor, Maria Tissot, Nick Wells, Gillian Whitaker.

The cover is created by Flame Tree Studio with
thanks to Nik Keevil and Shutterstock.com.
The font families in this book are Avenir and Bembo.

Flame Tree Press is an imprint of Flame Tree Publishing Ltd
flametreepublishing.com

A copy of the CIP data for this book is available from the British Library.

HB ISBN: 978-1-78758-243-9
PB ISBN: 978-1-78758-242-2
ebook ISBN: 978-1-78758-244-6
Also available in FLAME TREE AUDIO

Printed in the UK at Clays, Suffolk

DAVID TALLERMAN

A SAVAGE GENERATION

FLAME TREE PRESS
London & New York

For My Father

PROLOGUE

EARLY WARNING SIGNS

Kyle Silensky is watching as the city starts to burn.

There's only a single column of smoke so far, creeping almost apologetically up the sky, but Kyle has the sense that there will be other fires soon. The night has that feeling: an intensity, as though breaths are being held. As though, when the tension finally snaps, something terrible will follow in its wake.

All it has taken is the sickness – and the Sickers. The infection, or whatever they now thought it was, had spread up the coast, before turning inward: each time a few dozen cases, then hundreds, and soon after, chaos. On the news, they mapped its spread with curves, curves that never ended well. They gave warnings, but no explanations. They showed footage of men and women made crazy, made unpredictable, just like the disease they carried in their blood. Every day they hinted that it was contained, by evening admitted it wasn't.

Here, the first sighting occurred a couple of days ago, and already the city seems on the verge of tearing apart.

Kyle knows he should be afraid. And he is, but not for himself. The window he sits half in, half out of, is on the fifth floor. Being perched on the narrow frame feels dangerous, yet the danger is exciting. In another way, his position makes him safe. The street is far below, sufficiently far to belong to a different world. The bedroom at his back, the small apartment beyond, that has been home for a year and still doesn't feel like home, is a world as well. Here he belongs to neither. In this moment, for as long as he can make it last, he has no need to worry about himself.

A good thing, because right now he doesn't have enough worry to go around. Kyle heard the argument, through a door too thin to muffle shouted words. He heard what Carlita told his dad, what his dad shouted back. Kyle has some idea where his dad has gone, and what he's about to do.

Kyle sits in his window, watching smoke crawl up an orange-bellied night sky, listening to the distant sounds of a city grown sick.

He is waiting for his father to come home.

*   *   *

She would have liked to stand up to Howard. She'd have liked to refuse this task. She's a doctor, and her job is not to run errands, nor to be a pawn in other people's games. This time, Aaronovich would dearly have liked to say no.

But the ice is thin under her feet.

Not only thin, riddled with cracks. His hold on her is strong, and Howard knows that. He has always known, and so never says it. He is, in fact, never anything except polite to her.

He can afford to be polite, she supposes, when his hold on her is so complete. Whatever the man is, he isn't petty, not one to bully or cajole for its own sake. He established the terms of her presence at White Cliff on the day she arrived, explained why she was here and precisely what his own role in that had been, and afterward there had been nothing else to be said.

Still, this time more than ever, Aaronovich would have liked to stand her ground.

She keeps her head down as she crosses the yard. She can't help feeling exposed. The angle of the gate tower hides Doyle Johnson from her view, but he'll be there, because he invariably is. As she anticipates, the door at the bottom is unlocked and open, though surely it should be neither. Aaronovich climbs the stairs beyond with quiet steps.

Coming up behind Johnson, Aaronovich follows his gaze. He's staring at the distant forest edge, one hand clenched on the parapet of the guard tower, the other balled at his side. The trees are mostly pines, a jagged fence that falls away immediately as the land begins to decline. Their shadows are deep and black. Aaronovich imagines herself amid that cool gloom, the earth at her feet stained with its litter of needles, and shivers.

Whatever the pines hide, whatever Johnson has spied, she can't see it. "Something out there?" she asks, trying to make her voice sound bright, knowing he won't like the news she brings.

Johnson turns slowly – unwillingly, it seems. She'd thought he hadn't heard her ascend the stairs, so absorbed had he been, but he doesn't appear surprised by her presence. "No," he says. "There's nothing."

Then what are you looking for? she almost replies, before thinking better of it. Johnson's business is his own, and increasingly, so is his time. His purpose has been stolen from him, and who is she to question how he chooses to occupy himself?

"Howard asked me to come and find you," she says.

A terse smile passes across his lips.

"What?" She had expected anger from him, frustration.

"Why don't you call him Plan John? Everyone else does."

Aaronovich tuts. "Because I'm not everyone else," she says. "Because nicknames are for children." *And*, she admits only to herself, *because to think that creature has a plan, and that I'm part of it, frightens the hell out of me.*

*　*　*

Doyle concentrates reluctantly on Aaronovich. He's resentful of her intrusion. Momentarily, he'd been sure he saw a figure out there, hunched, flitting between the boles of two trees. Then, an instant later, it was gone – or else had never been. A headache is coming on, one of the bad ones. He can feel the pain rising like a tide.

Sometimes they get so bad that it's hard to think straight. Sometimes he doubts what he sees.

One day he'll have to talk to Aaronovich about the headaches, to get her professional opinion. He wonders why he hasn't already. Perhaps because there's always something else to deal with.

"So what's Howard after?" Doyle inquires.

"A meeting." Aaronovich phrases the two words with care, as though nervous of his reaction. Tension bunches the lines around her eyes and mouth.

She may be in her fifties, but she rarely looks it. She has a stubborn handsomeness that has nothing to do with age, and her hair is so purely white that it makes her seem somehow younger rather than older. Now, however, Doyle feels for a moment that he is looking at an old woman. He wants to argue with her, though she's merely a messenger, and an unwilling one at that; though she is among the few people here that he trusts.

That's why Howard sent her, Doyle realises. *Because we could be allies.* The pain in his head has increased by a definite notch. He wants to ask Aaronovich who the hell Plan John Howard is to be calling meetings. He wants to ask what that man could have to say that will possibly interest him.

"All right," he agrees. "I'll be down in five."

Doyle doesn't need her to tell him. He knows what Plan John will say; he's been waiting long enough to hear it. And with the warden finally transferred out, with most of the prisoners and guards evacuated, with bribes paid and strings pulled and records amended, with nobody even giving a damn amid the crisis that's consuming the nation, what has been unofficially true for months has become an inescapable fact.

That's the message Plan John will deliver, no matter that they know already. That this is no longer a prison. That while it might resemble a prison from the outside, while it might still run something like a prison on the inside, if you thought a prison was only the routines that defined its day-to-day existence, it isn't one anymore.

It's no longer the White Cliff State Penitentiary. Now it's transformed entirely into the place they've taken to calling Funland. And it belongs to him, to Plan John.

*   *   *

"You about done in there?"

Austin's muscles freeze involuntarily. His stepfather is using his second voice, the one he never uses in front of Austin's mother. The one he reserves for Austin, which makes the pit of his stomach flip-flop. The one that makes each word a threat, and doesn't make threats it isn't willing to keep.

"This isn't the day to fuck around," Martin observes from beyond the restroom door. As if there have been other days when disobedience was cheerfully tolerated.

"I'll be out in a minute," Austin manages. His own voice is thin, turning the response into an apology without his conscious effort.

"You better be."

Austin hears footsteps, and the slap of the door to the diner. The flip-flopping eases. But not altogether; maybe there are repercussions yet to come. Martin doesn't forget quickly or easily, so there are often repercussions. Did he suspect the truth? That Austin finished using the toilet five minutes ago, that he barely needed to go anyway? That he came in here to escape, however briefly?

Austin thinks about climbing through the tiny restroom window and running, just running, wherever his feet take him. Austin thinks about killing his stepfather: with a gun, a knife, with his bare hands. Austin pulls his pants up, rinses his palms under the rusted tap, unlocks the door, and goes out.

In the diner, he expects to find his mother and Martin in the booth, as they were when he left them. He wonders if someone told them to leave. He had thought the man behind the counter would refuse to serve them, the way he'd acted. For an instant, Austin had supposed the man's reaction was down to his colour; he'd seen only white faces since they'd entered town. But of course, it wasn't that, or not solely. The sickness didn't care what colour your skin was. And right now, people were on the roads for one reason: they were fleeing from somewhere or to somewhere. If they were fleeing, there was a chance they were sick. So probably no one was staring because he was black. They were staring because at any second he might lose his shit.

And maybe they were right. As Austin picks a path along the centre of the diner toward the doors, he could so easily let it all out. These days, he feels like he's always on the verge of a scream that he needs every scrap of his strength to contain. He can see Martin's SUV parked outside, partway onto the curb as if it owns the space around it. Martin has the driver's window down. He looks impatient. Yet he waits for Austin to get close before he speaks, and when he does, it's in his other voice, his normal voice, the one that's a lie that perhaps only Austin perceives the truth of. "Holy cow, kiddo, were you giving birth in there?"

Austin has no answer. He sees the disappointment in his mother's eyes, in the moment before she glances away, her frustration at his sullen silence. That wounds him more than almost anything could. Austin climbs into the back of the SUV, and Martin tuts – as though to say, *Look at the kid, can't even speak up for himself* – and pulls onto the road with a jolt.

Austin still doesn't know where they're headed. But he knows it was Martin's suggestion. So wherever they're going, it can't be anywhere good.

PART ONE
CONTAINMENT
CHAPTER ONE

"Are you a Pole, Silensky?"

"What?" Ben doesn't take his eyes off the two men farther up the street.

"I just thought, *Silensky*," Brody says. "Maybe a Pole name or one of those places. Nice to know who I'm working with is all."

Though they're almost upon them, Brody doesn't appear to have noticed the men. His gaze is jumping about, but he doesn't seem to be taking in much at all. Ben is sure that Brody is high on something. He remembers, as if he'd ever forgotten, why he's always hated working with such assholes.

He could turn around. He could just walk away. What would Carlita say then? If he went home and explained how it's gone bad from the start, how Alvarez has fixed him up with an asshole, a liability?

"Tough bastards, Polacks," Brody suggests. "Heard they don't get it so bad. Heard they got themselves a resistance." The way Brody pronounces *resistance*, it sounds like a disease in itself.

Ben hasn't heard about anybody or anywhere not getting sick. Of course, he gave up on watching the news a couple of days ago, exhausted by its ceaseless and apparently ungrounded optimism. "I'm not a Pole," he says. "I'm not anything."

"Yeah?" Brody gives a gurgling laugh. "Then I guess you're as fucked as the rest of us."

They're passing the two men now. One is a bum, dressed in traditional bum uniform: a long, filthy coat over layered shirts and sweaters. A shopping cart behind him is tipped on its side, spilling anonymous refuse into the street. He might be past sixty behind his straggle of beard, or younger and ravaged by whatever vices and misfortunes have brought him to the streets. He is cowering from the other man, who wears a dark pinstripe suit and has his hair trimmed threateningly short.

The suit is stabbing a finger, planting it squarely in the bum's chest, punctuating each stab with a snapped word. "I. Said. Have. You. Got. A. Light?"

The bum, having retreated as far as he can toward the storefront behind him, is shaking his head furiously. Abruptly, the suit backs off a step. The bum sags with relief, eyeing his desecrated cart hopefully – until the suit shoves him with both hands, so hard that he falls against the window and the glass spiderwebs around him. The bum doesn't try to get up. After a moment, he slides down onto his rear.

The suit watches for a second longer, then turns and sees Ben and Brody on the far side of the street. He's in the region of forty; his gut swells over his belt. He doesn't appear to be in good enough shape to have pushed anyone so hard. His face is florid, glossy with sweat, and his eyes are bloodshot, not merely red but speckled black with haematomas.

Ben notices Brody's hand stray to the rise in the back of his jeans, flicking the hem of his shirt to reveal the pistol grip there. Ben recalls his own gun, which Alvarez insisted on loaning him, recalls how he carefully emptied out the bullets into the restroom bin. If things should go bad then, in his experience, guns would not make them better.

"Come on," he says, catching Brody by the arm, pulling his fingers from the pistol.

"Hey, hey," calls the suit, "I'm just hunting for a…you guys, you look like one of you would have a light."

"Let's go." Ben hauls, leading Brody, walking as fast as he dares. He doesn't glance to see if the suit is following.

"Funny thing is…." The suit's voice is glutinous, as if he's talking through a mouth full of phlegm. "I quit years ago." Yet the retching noise he makes sounds like the product of a sixty-a-day habit.

"I'd got it." Brody wrenches his arm free. Ben thinks he might go back to prove his point. Instead, he turns left, marching toward a side street. "It's this way, if we're actually doing this fucking deed."

Ben could walk away. What would Carlita say?

Only what she's said already. *God, Ben, don't you see how this is going to end for us if we stay here? What kind of man are you that you won't so much as try to get your girlfriend and your son out of this city?*

He could get them out, he'd told her. Except there's nowhere for them to go, and no money once they get there.

There must be someone you can talk to.

He'd strived to convince her that he has no one, no one but her and Kyle. That even in the bad old days it had only ever been him and a few grifters just like him, hopeless men making money by whatever means, no matter how desperate or dumb. Now, since he turned his back on that life for her, he doesn't even have them.

You must know someone.

Sure. There's Alvarez, who'll fix anybody up with anything if he gets his cut. Sure, if you don't mind what it is or how bad it can go.

Ben thinks about how scared she looked, and how beautiful Carlita is when she's scared, how beautiful she is when she's in any mood at all. She'll leave, maybe even tonight, go back to her people, not because she doesn't care but because she's scared and desperate, and they are better than he is, more able to weather the coming storm.

Ben sighs, low enough that Brody won't hear, and follows behind him.

*   *   *

The street, when they reach it, is short, dilapidated. Half a dozen buildings have been boarded and the boards are thick with graffiti. The lights are out at the farthest end, as they are out in so many parts of the city tonight. The store is on the edge of the blackout zone, making the glow that spills from its barred windows unnaturally harsh and bright. A neon sign blinks 'Open All Hours' in staccato rhythm.

"That's it?" asks Ben. "A liquor store?"

"I'm telling you," Brody says, "this place is great. We hit here, like, every six months, and the dumb old bastard never does a thing about it. He's too cheap to hire anyone. He goes right on keeping money in the register. This guy is, like, a hundred. Easiest money in town."

"Screw this," Ben announces.

"Say what?"

"I'm not knocking over a liquor store."

"Hey!" Suddenly Brody is in Ben's face, the acid reek of his breath filling Ben's nostrils. "You wanted easy money. *This* is easy money. You wanted to do it the hard way, maybe you should have trained your ass in, like, investment brokerage or something. Instead of, you know, going to Alvarez and pleading on your fucking Polack knees for a break."

Ben takes a step back, buying just enough time to consider his options. "I told you. I'm not a Pole." He pulls the .38 out of his waistband, taps open the cylinder, and makes a show of inspecting bullets that aren't there. "So what's my part in this crime of the century?"

"Hey, that's easy." Brody's tone has changed completely, as though all memory of their dispute has been erased. "You, compadre, don't have to do anything except watch my back. Hell, the Negro's probably going to remember me. So it's better if I do the talking, okay?"

Ben's heart sinks further. He could go, right now. Walking up to the first person he meets, sticking his gun in their face, and demanding their wallet is as sound a plan as this. A few hundred dollars will get them free of the city. Even with prices as they are, they can load up the car with food and fill the tank; get out, before things become truly bad.

"You coming or not?" Brody calls. He has his own gun in hand, is waving the pistol like a pennant. Not waiting for an answer, he pushes upon the glass-panelled door.

Ben catches the door on the backswing and steps in behind him.

By then, Brody is already screaming: "Nobody move! You, you antique fuck, you empty that register."

The bell above the door is jangling crazily, so Ben lets it shut. The sour electric light is equally as bright inside. There are refrigerator cabinets along the right wall, bottles of spirits displayed to the left. In between are islands of piled cans and unopened boxes of beer. Near the counter, as if to break the alcoholic tedium, stands a rotating magazine rack: pornography at the top and, in surreal contrast, superhero comics around the lowest tier.

The only customers are two Chicano kids, both wearing 'seen it before' expressions, like they could just as easily be the ones with the guns. Brody swings his piece on them and barks, "Hands where I can see them!" The Chicano kids wrap hands behind heads in a well-practised gesture, smirking all the while at the stupid *Gabacho*.

Ben turns his attention to the counter. Brody was right about one thing: the man behind it is ancient. He's stick-thin, his hair a wispy mop of white over almost blue-black skin rutted by countless lines. Ben points his .38 at the two kids instead. They grin back at him, as though pleased at the attention.

Brody takes a step toward the counter, aiming his own gun at the storekeeper. "Hurry it up."

The storekeeper has the register open, is methodically piling bills in ones and twos upon the counter. Ben finds it hard to judge if he's stalling or if this is genuinely the best he can do.

Either way, Brody is losing patience. "How's about I shoot you and do it myself?" He takes another step forward.

The bell above the door jangles.

Everyone turns to look: Ben, Brody, the storekeeper, the kids. Half through the doorway stands the suit from before. Flecks of spittle dot his lips and chin. The bloody blackness in his eyes has swallowed retinas and pupils, leaving fathomless holes.

He's sick. Really sick. Dangerously sick. Ben doesn't know where to point his gun.

The suit shudders softly and releases the door. "Has anyone get a... ah...." He staggers.

Brody, who so far has been keeping his pistol on the storekeeper, changes his mind. But he manoeuvers clumsily, trying to turn in the narrow aisle without upsetting a monolith of beer cans near his elbow. Maybe that's his mistake, or maybe it's not making his move sooner. Whatever the case, the suit goes for him – and is quicker. Catching Brody by both shoulders, he flings his own head forward, colliding his forehead with Brody's face. Beneath the impact, Brody's nose ruptures like a flung egg.

The suit pulls back, and Ben assumes he'll do the same again, but this time he snaps open his jaw and clamps his teeth on the ruin of Brody's nose. Brody roars. When he draws away, his legs go from under him. He and the suit are tangled enough that they trip together. Brody, clutching the suit's arms, has nothing to break the fall with except his head.

Ben takes his gun off the Chicano kids. Immediately they start toward him. He dodges aside and they push past, out into the street. Brody is still screaming, a strident wail that climbs and climbs. The suit is scrabbling at Brody's neck and face, as if eager to dig his way inside. Ben points the .38, attempting to work out whether shooting the suit in the back at this angle will hit Brody and how much he cares. He only remembers that his gun isn't loaded in the moment that Brody's own goes off.

One of the refrigerators haemorrhages glass and alcohol. A second shot takes out a striplight, darkening the perimeter of the store. The third and fourth demolish another fridge, turning the river of liquid and glass shards into a flood. There's a pause. Brody's scream changes in modulation, takes on a frustrated note.

His fifth shot blows a chunk off the suit's right foot.

The suit, though he hardly seems to have felt the impact, gives up on Brody's face and cranes to glare at the gun. Then he catches the neck end of a broken bottle and grinds it deep into Brody's exposed forearm. Brody's scream goes off the scale. Instead of stabbing again, the suit keeps his grip on the bottle and twists until the glass fragments. Ben can see exposed cords of muscle amid the bubbling blood.

Brody's pistol fires one last time, as though of its own accord, then clicks, clicks, clicks. The suit almost has Brody's forearm off now, and appears to be losing interest. *Go for the old guy*, Ben thinks, *the old guy. Please, not me.*

A roar that makes the earlier shots seem hushed crashes through the store. As Ben flings himself instinctively backward, his heels catch on some obstruction. He falls hard against a refrigerator cabinet. He can hear nothing but a tinny buzzing, can see the tiled floor, scuffed with tracks of dirt. When he manages to look round, the first thing he observes is the old man. He is standing in front of the magazine rack, a break-action 12-gauge jammed close to his chin. Smoke is oozing from its left barrel. The suit is still crouched over Brody, but much of his head and a chunk of his shoulder have vanished. His neck is pumping thick dark blood. Even as Ben watches, he keels sideways, tumbling into a pyramid of Coors boxes.

The old man walks forward, carefully appraising the suit. Satisfied, he turns his attention to Brody, who is twitching and jerking, apparently at random. First the remains of his bicep go, flapping the mostly off forearm. Then one foot jolts. Then his head bounces up and slams against the tiles. In that instant, Ben glimpses what's left of Brody's face, whole at the edges and mangled at the centre, nasal cavities teasing through ragged flesh.

The old man hefts the shotgun and empties the second barrel down at Brody. At such range, the effect is practically cartoonish, as if someone has dropped an anvil on him.

The old man turns toward Ben. His once-white apron resembles a butcher's castoff. He cranks open the shotgun, struggles over the spent shells, takes two fresh ones from a pocket, and slips them into the barrels. Tucking the stock under one armpit, he snaps the action shut. Thrusting the shotgun at Ben, he asks, "You sick?" His speech is low and breathless.

Ben shakes his head. "No, no, I'm not sick. Brody wasn't sick." Or conceivably he had been, and drugs weren't what had been making him crazy. Anyway, didn't they say the infection got passed quickest via blood? The old man did the right thing, taking Brody out like that. "We were just…I'm sorry. I wanted to get my girl and kid out. I didn't want this."

Ben is dizzy. He's never in his life seen so much blood. Perhaps he banged his head, too, as he fell. He craves to throw up, but he feels certain that, if he does, the old man will shoot him. Maybe not even for being sick, maybe for making a worse mess of his already messed-up store.

Yet when he looks, the old man is walking away. He navigates the gap in the counter and disappears again, through a door in the back. A few seconds later, Ben hears, faintly, the old man speaking, in short, muffled bursts.

After that, there's a long silence. Ben expects the old man to reappear, but he doesn't. Though he ought to get up, should get out of there, Ben can't convince his legs to work. Blood is pooling in the centre of the room. By scrunching his knees, he can keep his feet clear, but the moment he stands he'll have to step in it. He doesn't know if he can do that. The pain in his head is a throb broken by sudden, shuddering stabs. The nausea rises and falls in waves.

"You! Put your hands on your head." The voice comes from his left. "We're coming in. Jesus, what a mess…."

Ben laces his fingers behind his head, feels wetness stickying his hair. He hadn't heard the cop car arrive. There are two of them, in uniform.

The first – white, not young, eyes shadowed and wild with sleeplessness – is holding the door open with one hand, using the other to train a .38 much like the one Ben has lost. The first cop waits while the second cop – olive-skinned and younger than her partner – enters and scans the room.

"Where are the guns?" the first cop asks.

"One there, near the bodies," the second notes.

The first cop aims a kick at Ben's leg that doesn't quite connect. "Hey, asshole, you have a gun? Nod if you have a gun."

Ben shakes his head. "It's not loaded."

"Was that the question? Where's your gun?"

"I dropped it."

"You better have."

"It's over there," says the second cop.

Ben looks where she's pointing, and sees his gun lodged half under a rack of Corona bottles.

The first cop looks too. "Well, that didn't do all this."

"I'm coming out," the storekeeper wheezes from the back of the store. When nobody contradicts him, he steps slowly through the door behind the counter, the shotgun gripped above his head in both fists.

"Yeah, that's more like," the first cop acknowledges. "Put it down on the counter."

The storekeeper lowers the shotgun, to lay the weapon beside the cash register.

"This your store? These trying to rob it?"

"Not the well-dressed one. He was sick."

"Yeah? What a fucking mess."

"Are we going to take him in?" The second cop indicates the old man with a wave of her gun.

"Are you kidding? Way things are going, the whole city's going to be like this by the end of the week."

"What about that one?" This time she points her gun at Ben.

"Hey, old man. Sure you don't want to do this one into the bargain? Save us a trip? Got my word we won't write you up."

The storekeeper shakes his grizzled head. "Nah. I'm done."

"Shame." The first cop sounds authentically aggrieved.

Ben holds up his wrists. "Look, I'm sorry," he says. "The gun isn't even loaded."

"What's he doing?" the first cop asks his partner, as though Ben's behaviour is a new phenomenon to him.

"I think he wants you to cuff him."

"Yeah? Do I work for him?"

The first cop holsters his gun and unclips the baton at his belt. He flicks it free and swings in one neat gesture. Ben hardly has the opportunity to register the motion, let alone to get his hands in the way, before the baton strikes his head with a crack like bottled thunder.

CHAPTER TWO

Right then, Austin can't say who he hates more.

All he's managed to conclude is that it comes down to different kinds of hate. What he feels for his mother is something brief and blazing that will burn out eventually, leaving pain behind. Not like his hatred of Martin, which is hot coals, hot embers – too hot to touch, and capable of smouldering forever.

His father? Different again. Austin doesn't know yet how that hate feels, not entirely, but there'll be time enough to discover it. For they've finally told him where they're going, and he sees now that he should have guessed, because it's the single worst thing Martin could have done to him.

Austin Carter, born Austin Johnson, gazes out through tinted glass at the trees whipping by, stiff pines crowding the road's edge. They seem to go on interminably. He is already homesick, a dull ache in the pit of his stomach that's very much like actual sickness. There's nothing out here, nothing for him.

Then, without having thinned at all, the trees are gone, and to either side is an expanse of dead earth, the SUV's tyres rousing plumes of desiccated dirt. Ahead, he can see their destination: grey-white concrete walls, a gate of reinforced mesh, and the shadowy impression of low buildings beyond.

His mother has rung ahead, she told him. They're expected. Sure enough, the gate is sliding aside. Austin can hear its monotonous rattle even at such a distance. In the gap is a uniformed figure. His dark skin is indistinguishable from the navy blue of his shirt; amid the brightness and the grime, he's all of one shade. As they draw closer, the figure begins to resolve into a human being: tall, broad-shouldered, head clean-shaven except for an oblong of stubble around the jaw. His eyes are narrowed and his face tense, an expression Austin recalls too well.

His father isn't a man who relaxes easily. Nor can Austin ever remember seeing him smile.

He has a first instinct, then, of what form this particular hatred will take, of how he will feel toward the father who walked out of his life all those years ago with such apparent ease.

Martin pulls up the SUV just before the prison gate. Austin's mother rolls down the passenger-side window, and his father walks round to it. "Hello, Rachel," he says. He glances into the back seat. "Austin." Martin he ignores.

"Hello, Doyle." His mother's voice is careful, precise. She takes this tone with Austin sometimes, on the occasions when she predicts conflict and is readying for it. "Austin, say hello to your father."

Rather than look at Doyle, Austin glares at the back of his mother's head. "Hello."

"Like I told you on the phone," she says, speaking to his father once more, "we're going to Martin's parents. But they don't have much space. And I don't—"

"This is a prison," his father cuts her off, emphasising each word.

"So he'll be safe here."

"That's crazy."

"Have you seen what it's like out there?" She shudders. "You have walls. You can keep them out."

"It's a disease, not a—"

She silences him, in turn, with a glare. "You haven't seen." Then, almost pleadingly, "You *know* this is the safest place for him."

"What I know is, you wanted the responsibility and now you don't." Austin's father looks with undisguised disgust at Martin, who still has his hands on the steering wheel, drumming fingers impatiently upon its leather arch. "What I know is, it doesn't suit you anymore."

"That isn't fair." Austin's mother sounds genuinely wounded.

"Fine. It isn't fair."

"And you don't have a choice." Her voice has grown hard. "He's staying here. You deal with it."

Austin's father sighs, brushing a palm across his eyes. "Have you asked Austin what *he* wants?"

"It doesn't matter what he wants. We can't keep him safe. You can. There's nothing to discuss."

Austin can bear no more. The sense of betrayal is like a point working its way up through his innards. "I don't want to go with you," he tells his mother. "I'd rather be anywhere else."

She shivers again, as though the car has suddenly grown cold. But rather than answer, she says to his father, "You see?"

Austin thinks his father will keep arguing, is sure that he will argue for as long as it takes. So he's surprised when Doyle responds, "This is temporary. Until things calm down. Until you work something else out."

"Yes."

"All right. Austin, get out please."

Too eager to be free of the car to resent his father's order, Austin does as he's told. His mother reaches a hand through the open window, clutching for his. He moves aside, out of reach.

"I know this is hard for you," she says. "I know you didn't mean what you said."

"You don't know," he insists, not looking at her but away, toward the forest.

"It's just for a while."

"Bye," he says.

"I love you." He can tell that she's close to crying.

He won't meet her eye, won't let himself. When he does look up, it's because the SUV's engine, which Martin had left idling, has revved back into life. Austin catches only a glimpse of his mother, before the vehicle's abrupt arc and the swirling shroud of dust snatch her from sight.

Austin understands then, with a certainty he can't explain, that he will never see her again. He turns to his father, not knowing what to say, not knowing if there are words for such a sensation. But surely saying anything is unnecessary. It's impossible that he should feel like this, like he's falling into a gaping hole inside himself, and his father won't notice.

Yet there's nothing in his father's face, no sympathy, no recognition. "Come on," he says, "let's get you inside."

*　　*　　*

"I realise this must be tough for you," Doyle tries.

It isn't true. He has no insight into what might be going through his son's mind. But Austin lets the comment go without acknowledgement.

"It's not forever." Doyle wishes he could think of something to say that isn't a lie.

He has already decided he'll go to Aaronovich. He has no idea what to do with Austin, no idea how to keep him safe. While the doctor might not either, at least she will appreciate the problem for what it is.

Except that between him and Aaronovich is the whole of Funland. *White Cliff*, a part of him contends – but it's hopeless. He only has to look around to see that there's no such thing as White Cliff Penitentiary anymore. Its existence has been tenuous for years now, decades: its original incarnation, the White Cliff Prison Farm, had been deemed uneconomical ten years ago or more; then the fences came down and the walls went up, cutting off most of its estate. What remained hung on in its reincarnated form for a few years, as a low-security prison mostly taking overflow from the larger state penitentiary fifty miles east. Then a wave of cutbacks saw it flagged for winding down, and so its lifespan would have ended, but for the intervention of one man.

Plan John Howard is sitting on the balcony of the Big House, contemplating his domain. He'll have watched Doyle go out to meet the SUV, have watched him reenter with Austin, Doyle knows. He knows because Plan John watches everything.

"Come on," Doyle tells his son.

The administrative wing, where Aaronovich's office is, runs to their right, a long, squat building, innocuous compared to the aggressive bulk of the cellblocks opposite. Separating them is the yard, a desert of blanched concrete. The Big House, which closes off the farther, northern perimeter, is out of their way. It doesn't matter. Plan John watches everything, and what he sees, he controls – or tries to. So there's no chance of this ending without a confrontation.

"When did you last eat?" Doyle asks Austin.

"We stopped in a diner. But all they had was fries." Austin makes each word sound like a trial.

"I'll fix you something," Doyle promises. At least they still have food, for now.

To his left, a small group are stubbornly working out in the weights pile, despite the summer's heat. He identifies Farmer and Cousins, Landser and Silas from the white skinheads, and keeping slightly apart,

Torres and Soto. Anywhere else, that little crowd – black, white, and Latino within a few square feet – would be a powder keg waiting for a match. Not here. There probably isn't a prison on Earth as integrated as White Cliff. Plan John wouldn't allow it any other way.

He'd spelled that out when he'd spoken to them the day before, though it had hardly needed saying: "You'll put aside your differences," he'd declared, "because the only meaningful difference is the one between us in here and them out there."

Doyle wonders belatedly which *them* he was referring to. Had he meant the great mass of humanity, the vast everyone-else, or merely the sick? Rumour has it that Plan John, true to his name, has been preparing this current arrangement for a very long time. Even before the sickness became an epidemic, when the outbreak was confined to a few isolated cases in a country most people barely recognised the name of, Plan John had been avidly following its advance.

Now, however, it's Doyle's and Austin's progress that commands his attention. They are almost upon the Big House.

"Are you listening to me?" Doyle asks, not turning his head.

Austin makes a noise of vague assent.

"Unless he questions you directly, whatever he says, you keep quiet. Do you hear?"

Austin gives another noncommittal grunt.

"Do you hear me?" Doyle growls.

"I heard you."

Doyle stops, squinting up at the balcony and the ice-blue sky. Plan John, silhouetted, is Humpty Dumpty-like, his colossal mass scarcely contained by the chair he's ensconced in. As Doyle struggles to bring his shape into focus, Plan John toys with the rim of his sun visor, squinting through its green plastic crescent.

"Who's your young friend, Mr. Johnson?"

"This is my son," Doyle answers. "Name's Austin."

"Your son? What an auspicious occasion." Plan John lays his palms flat on his vast stomach and smiles, with apparently genuine pleasure.

"It's just for a few days," Doyle says, trying not to sound apologetic. "Until his mother gets things sorted."

"A sort of holiday for the boy," agrees Plan John.

"I guess you could look at it like that." Doyle gives a shallow nod goodbye and begins to turn away, knowing all the while that Howard isn't done.

Indeed, he hasn't taken a step before Plan John's voice comes again. "Do you see this?"

When Doyle turns, Howard has a hand raised to indicate the sun visor he's wearing.

"One of my most treasured possessions. It cost me two dollars in a booth outside the beach resort I was then staying in."

"Yeah?" Doyle says. "It suits you."

"Thank you. Some men wear three-thousand-dollar suits identical to ones that can be bought in a department store. They spend hundreds on watches that do nothing any watch wouldn't do." Plan John takes off the visor, wipes sweat from the elastic band with the hem of his Hawaiian shirt, puts it back on, and wriggles it until he's satisfied with the angle. "Most people have no understanding of the value of things."

"It's a nice hat," Doyle says.

Plan John's smile broadens. "Well. I'll let you get on with your business. I'm sure we'll all be seeing each other again soon enough."

*   *   *

Aaronovich looks the boy up and down. He's lighter skinned than his father, smaller of build, slightly plump with baby fat he hasn't quite grown out of. The only familiar features are those eyes, which have the same brooding quality as Doyle Johnson's, and the mouth, set hard as a scratch in concrete. He already has his father's intensity, that sense of pent-up tension kept on a short leash.

She'd like to say something to reassure him, but all she's felt since the moment Doyle introduced his son to her is horror. *A child. A child in Funland.* As if things weren't bad enough. As if one loose spark wouldn't suffice to bring Howard's entire madhouse down in flames.

"You must be tired," Aaronovich suggests.

"I'm fine." Austin grinds the syllables together as though even this simple greeting is an intrusion.

"All right. That's good."

He doesn't sound or look fine. He looks tired and on edge, more so even than the circumstances demand. But the fact is that she has no clue how to deal with this angry, brooding boy, no more than Johnson evidently has himself.

"Austin," she says, "would you mind if I talked to your father on his own? There's a settee in the outer office. Why don't you make yourself comfortable?"

He raises his eyes then, transparently unsure whether he should glare at her or whether this is some limited kindness. Evidently the quandary isn't important enough to pursue, for he drops his gaze and slouches out without a word, pulling the door closed behind him.

Aaronovich releases the breath she hadn't realised she's been holding. "All right," she says once more.

Johnson is leaning against her filing cabinet. He hardly appears aware that Austin has gone. She tries to catch his eye, gives up. "I'm not an expert," she says, "but frankly, the boy seems traumatised."

"It's been a tough day for him."

"I mean, more than that. I mean, he seems *traumatised*. How acquainted are you with his home life? Has he been under stress lately?"

"*Everyone's* been under stress," Johnson snaps. "You know what's going on out there."

Aaronovich sighs. She's seen Johnson like this before. Any conversation regarding his son is going to have to wait. "You've been talking to Howard."

"Howard's been talking to me."

"He knows about Austin."

"Yes," says Johnson, "he knows about Austin."

On occasions, Aaronovich has heard Howard refer to White Cliff as a machine. She understands that he intends something specific by this. A machine works in precise ways, which are the ways in which it was designed to work by its creator. Its elements act in unison, or else get replaced.

Still, when he'd first said it, the metaphor struck her as clumsy, a thoughtless comment from a man of limited education. Nothing made from flesh and blood components could possibly function as Howard conceived. She had needed time to comprehend that Howard had said exactly what he'd meant, had found a simple and exact model to convey his perception of the place he called Funland.

There's one more thing about machines, it occurs to Aaronovich now. They have no use for excess parts.

"So Howard has made your son his business. What are you going to do about that?"

Doyle's expression reminds her forcibly of Austin's from a minute before. There's that same uncertainty: is this provocation or help, and how much does he care to differentiate between the two?

Just like his son, Johnson doesn't reach any conclusion. "That," he says, "is definitely the question."

CHAPTER THREE

When Carlita comes into his room, Kyle pretends to be sleeping.

He can't say why, but he doesn't want her to know that he's been lying awake, staring at the ceiling and the minor galaxy of glow stars he stuck there, listening to the discordant sounds of the nighttime city and hoping for the rattle of the apartment door.

"Kyle, wake up," she says. Then, louder, "Kyle!"

"What is it?" His heart is beating hard.

"Your father's been arrested." Carlita speaks the words with forced calm, as someone else might say, *Your father's going to be late from work.* "Uncle Nando is going to pick us up, even though he's on duty and he shouldn't. I need you to get dressed. And put some clothes in a bag."

As soon as she's out of the room, Kyle does as he's been told, feeling all the while only a hollow sense of anticipation. He stuffs a second pair of jeans and a few T-shirts into a backpack, and then underwear, books, his MP3 player. When he can't think of anything else, he sits on the bed, waiting.

A car horn bellows from the street. Looking out of the window, Kyle sees a police cruiser directly below, engine idling. Kyle shoulders his backpack, hurries out. In the hallway, Carlita is wrestling with a large suitcase and an overstuffed sports bag. Taking the bag, Kyle follows her out the door and down the central staircase. Even for the time of night, the building is quieter than he's ever heard it.

Behind the wheel, Nando appears nervous. Yet there's no one in the street, certainly no sign of what the TV has taken to calling Sickers, when it became clear that the infected were not dying but finding new ways to grow more and more sick. Nando has the window down. When he spies the bags and case he says approvingly, "Good, good. You did like I said."

They get into the back and Nando pulls away from the curb. Normally, Carlita's cousin is friendly and cheerful, full of jokes for Kyle.

Tonight he says nothing. Kyle wants to ask what his father has done, but he knows they'll tell him when they're ready, or else not at all. He can't escape the feeling that their silence is aimed at him, as though he's guilty by association.

Kyle has been to the police station once before, with Carlita. The route Nando takes is different, longer, and seems to consist entirely of diversions. Twice they have to reverse because roads are closed. On the first occasion, the obstruction is another cop car pulled across the street; on the second, half a dozen grim-faced soldiers gathered around a parked Humvee.

When they reach the station, finally, Nando pulls into an underground garage and leads them up a back staircase. The first room they pass through is huge and chaotic, with panic tangible in the air.

Catching Kyle's expression, Nando leans close. "Your papi's in my office," he says. "Don't worry, he's okay."

Sure enough, when they get to his dad, Ben isn't even handcuffed. He's sipping coffee from a Styrofoam cup. He glances up as they enter, and his eyes are bleak. Kyle wishes he could smile, to try and reassure his father, but he finds he can't convince his mouth.

"Hey," Ben says.

"Hi," Kyle replies. Carlita says nothing, not even looking at Ben.

"Okay," Nando begins, starting to talk the moment he's shut the door behind them. "Here's the thing. I think I can get you out of the city, but you have to listen to me."

"All of us?" Ben asks.

Nando scowls, not looking his way either. But he says only, "Yes, all of us."

"Then where do we go?" Carlita wonders.

"There's a place. A place called Funland."

"Like Disneyland?" Kyle puts in, faintly hopeful.

Nando shakes his head. "Funland is a kind of prison. They just took to calling it that. Its real name is White Cliff."

"A *prison*?" Carlita's voice has grown jagged.

"We'd be safe. It's all but abandoned. Do you remember my Uncle Tito? He's a guard there and we write each other sometimes. The last time, he said that if things got really bad then I should go."

"So he doesn't know about this plan of yours?" she asks. "Nando, I see that you mean well, but this is no good."

"It isn't like that. Anyway, I'd warn Tito and he'd arrange something. It's cut off; he says they haven't had even a trace of sickness. We would stay with the guards."

Carlita's exasperation is obvious. "You seriously want to take a woman and a child into a prison?"

"Baby," Ben says, "you're missing the point."

Carlita stands so quickly that her chair goes tumbling backward. She closes the gap to Ben with a single pace, leans forward until her face almost touches his, and screams, "Shut up!" She raises one hand, as though she'll slap him. Instead, she spins away and strikes her palm upon the window. Then she folds her arms against the glass, sinks her forehead onto them, and gives a choked sob.

When she turns back, her eyes are dry, and sharp as nails. "This is your fault. All you had to do was find enough money for a full tank of gas. And now what? You're going to prison, so I have to come too?"

"I know it seems bad," Nando tells her. "But we don't have much time. So will you listen to what I have to say? I wouldn't suggest this if I didn't believe it was the right course. I'm trying to help you because you're my cousin, and so I'm helping Ben, because he's your boyfriend. The way things are, he might not even make it to jail in one piece."

"Can't you just let him go?" Carlita asks, not quite pleading.

"It's going to be hard enough to arrange this. I think I can; they're desperate for drivers. But——"

"For drivers?"

"They're sending the sick out in trucks. The ones that get arrested."

Her eyes widen. "Oh no."

"Nobody knows what else to do. The commander is saying they have to be treated as normal until somebody tells him differently. It's crazy, but there it is. Martial law will come soon, and then no one will give a damn about locking them up."

"Fernando, you can't really be serious."

"They're letting the trucks through as priority. No cars are getting out at all. There isn't any other choice. If we don't hurry, even this will be gone."

"I've heard what they're like," Carlita says. "I saw an old woman who had it. She was out of her mind, screaming about nothing. And then she chased a man, for no reason. She was so old, she could barely run, and people laughed at her. But I could see how badly she wanted to hurt him."

"That was what happened last night," Ben mumbles. "I mean, one of them, the sick. It was the worst thing I've seen."

"So you understand? We can't go to this Funland place."

"No, you've got it backward." Ben's voice is still hushed. "The cities are the worst bet. Somewhere like that, out in the middle of nowhere—"

"That's it," Nando agrees. "Tito says Funland used to be a farm prison. They have their own water, supplies, everything. What could be better?"

"I think it's a good idea," Kyle puts in, partly because he wants them to acknowledge him, for someone to care about his opinion, and partly because he has an image, firm in his imagination, not of a prison but of a farm, and he and Nando and his father and Carlita there and getting on again, as they hardly ever seem to do these days.

But Carlita doesn't look at Kyle. She's staring at Nando, holding him with her gaze, as though she can weigh him and his plan both together. Finally, she looks away, releases him. "You're a good cousin, Fernando. You have a good heart. I hope for all our sakes that you're right about this."

★   ★   ★

Since Fernando went out, saying only that he needed to clear some things, Ben has wanted urgently to talk to Carlita, to assuage her anger somehow. However, he knows her expression, and that she'll cool down on her own, an hour, three hours, a day from now. Ben thinks then of speaking to Kyle, of telling him what happened. Carlita has probably given him a distorted account of why they're here, of what his father has been up to in the night. Ben feels ashamed at the thought, and frustrated at his shame. Hadn't he tried to do the right thing? Nevertheless, he isn't sure how his version would sound any better.

When Nando returns, he's even more on edge. "Okay," he says. "Come, quick."

He marches them through the main office, down three flights to the garage in the basement. There, he leads the way to a white van parked near the exit ramp. A prison service decal has been hastily stencilled on the side; the paint is visibly wet. A mechanic in filthy overalls is just finishing sealing the back doors with an acetylene torch, having welded sheets of metal entirely over the rear windows.

"Wait," Ben says, realisation dawning. "That's an ambulance."

"We've been requisitioning them," Fernando tells him.

"You're kidding me."

"We still have a couple of squad cars," the mechanic offers, "if you'd rather share one of those with half a dozen Sickers."

"They're already in there?" Ben says.

The mechanic hefts the acetylene torch, gives him a look of contempt. "They're chained up?"

"Sure. I went in and did it myself, while they were napping."

"How are they going to get them out at the other end?" asks Carlita.

"Honestly, I hadn't thought that far." The mechanic fishes in his pocket, pulls out a key on a metal fob, and hands it to Nando. "The hospital let us take her because she was down for repairs. They're morons, all she needed was new plugs. The tyres are pretty raw and she could do with an oil change, but you said you were in a hurry, right? Anyway, you have problems, you know who to call."

Nando manages a weary smile. "Anyone but you?"

"Fuck yes."

With that, the mechanic goes off to scream at two younger guys working on the belly of a jacked-up black-and-white. When Ben listens, he can hear the Sickers within the ambulance, hammering against the ceiling and sides. "This is insane," he mutters.

Nando throws him a glare, as if to say, *You have a better idea?*

No, Ben has no better ideas. He has no ideas at all.

Fernando takes the driver's seat. Carlita sits in the middle, with Kyle crushed next to her, and Ben struggles to wedge himself in at the end. Then, without a word, they're off.

Outside the garage, the city is a different place from the one Ben walked just hours before. It's coming apart so quickly, like it was always primed to do so. Last night, there'd been a definite craziness in the air, but almost no one had been out, as though they were hoping en masse that perhaps the nightmare could yet blow over. Today, with any such hope gone, it seems that everyone has taken to the streets. Traffic clogs every road. Cars fill the sidewalks, jostling those limited to their own two feet. There are cops, and men in army uniforms, probably National Guard. It's difficult to tell what they're trying to achieve, if anything.

And there are the Sickers. Whatever its actual presence, the effect of the sickness has been to escalate the general madness, so that each jostle or shouted insult is misread as a sign of infection. Maybe one in ten of those involved is actually infected, Ben guesses, but no one appears to care. The cops and guardsmen only step in when blood is shed, and frequently not even then.

Nando has understood the situation far better than Ben himself. If he'd pulled off the robbery, he, Carlita, and Kyle would be out amid this chaos. It isn't going to get better. It can't be contained, not even by martial law. In all likelihood, the infection really is spreading invisibly through the boundless crowds. Ben doesn't know much about diseases, but surely this isn't the way to stamp one out.

Fortunately, the modifications on the ambulance haven't extended to removing the lights and siren. Fernando flicks a switch and the familiar wail sounds from outside. Even now, people retain a little of their social programming; they move aside grudgingly, often with screams of abuse, but they move.

Fernando hits the first roadblock as they turn onto Twelfth Street. It consists of two black-and-whites parked crosswise, a harassed cop, and a soldier with an assault rifle. The soldier looks about sixteen, and Ben can read in his face how near he is to losing his shit altogether. That end of the street is packed with cars, all honking their horns, and any gaps are mortared with struggling bodies, their combined antagonism directed at the cop and soldier.

It takes twenty minutes just to navigate as far as the roadblock, even with the siren screeching. When they finally get close, the cop scowls at Nando's uniform, then at the flashing lights above, and yells, "Will you shut that thing off?"

Nando turns off the lights and siren with an apologetic grin. When he's manoeuvered them into the narrow fissure between the parked police cars, he holds out his badge for the cop to see.

The cop barely glances at it. "What's in the back?"

"Prisoners," Nando says.

"Prisoners?"

"Sick."

The cop nods. "I can ask the kid there to put a few rounds through the side if you want. He's getting awful twitchy; it might calm him down some. And better for you…better than hauling them alive."

Nando makes a show of considering. "Thanks, but he'd be as likely to shoot his own feet off."

"Yeah. There's that. Well, good luck." The cop sounds like he means it.

Once they're past, Carlita says softly, "Maybe you should have let him."

"And provoke a riot?" Nando replies. "Do you think that mob behind us needs anything to set them off?"

She doesn't argue.

After that, the going gets easier. The official response seems to be a clear zone round the edge of the city, allowing a degree of control over the migration. Whether the purpose is to maintain a steady current of refugees or to strangle the flow altogether, Ben can't say. Is the city in quarantine? As far as he knows, nowhere else is doing any better. Either way, within the buffer there's almost no vehicle traffic, though still plenty of pedestrians. They begin to see military transports too, Hummers and at one point an Armoured Personnel Carrier completely blocking a side street. From the roof, four soldiers aim their weapons in line with the APC's turret, down into the road beyond.

Ben starts to wonder what's on the other side and then catches himself. Those kinds of questions will help nothing.

Eventually, they make it to the edge of the city. Doing so has taken all morning and the early afternoon. Ben's whole body aches from being motionless so long. Nando had the foresight to bring two bottles of water and a few packs of cookies, and everyone except him has eaten a pitiful lunch. No one, not even Kyle, has been talking.

The army's presence is more concentrated around the entrance to the freeway. They even have a tank, which sits close to the on-ramp with no discernible purpose, its cannon menacing the city. There are soldiers everywhere, some of them making efforts to steer the civilian traffic, most just milling. They're allowing those on foot out in ones and twos, letting them walk along the verges and the central reservation.

The ambulance is the only non-military vehicle to be seen, and draws stares from the troops and the waiting lines.

It's as they join the ramp that Ben is struck by an epiphany. The soldiers have no plan at all. They aren't following orders, or if they are, they're orders vague enough to circumvent any later apportioning of blame. There are pedestrians but no vehicles because, in the absence of anything better, the troops on the ground have settled for an arbitrary compromise.

It's insane. What will happen if the soldiers get sick? Or, not if but when.

A sergeant stops them and asks what they're moving, though it must be obvious from the hammering coming from the rear. When Fernando tells him, he says, "Go as far as the first exit. They'll give you further instructions there. Keep your speed down below twenty or you may be fired upon."

There's something unreal about leaving the city, all eight lanes devoid of traffic but bordered by the interminable queue of those on foot. More even than the havoc he witnessed that morning, the vacant highway brings home how utterly everything is breaking down. Ben wants to share his revelation with Fernando, until he sees in his face that he's reached the same conclusion by himself. Then Ben thinks about the sergeant's words. What do they need instructions for?

The soldiers aren't just going to let them drive out. In the absence of a plan, they'll settle for the illusion of one. They'll herd people like sheep simply to feel as if they're doing something.

Nando does as instructed, holding their speed at barely fifteen miles an hour. It's hard to determine who'd be doing the threatened shooting, since there's no one to be seen except the refugees, who, having made it this far, are now spreading aimlessly. Snipers, maybe; it makes sense that there would be snipers posted.

Even crawling at fifteen, it doesn't take them long to come upon the junction. Access roads lead off to left and right, the one on the opposite side curling to meet the overpass there. The refugees are being directed by a party of troops onto the overpass, perhaps to keep the outbound lanes clear for military traffic. On this side, there's only another armoured personnel carrier blocking the leftmost lane, and around it, half a dozen soldiers. In front of the APC is an arrow sign pointing left and a set of blinking amber lights.

"Nando," Ben snaps.

"I know."

"If we go where they say, they won't just let us leave."

"I *know*."

Nando drifts over to the right-hand lane, without accelerating. All of the soldiers are looking at them. When they're almost within spitting distance, Nando gives a nod, and a gesture half wave and half salute. One of the soldiers returns it.

None of them take their eyes off the ambulance as it pulls alongside, and then as it slides past. None of them makes any move to stop it. Whatever mandate the soldiers have been given, their orders apparently don't stretch to such a situation.

Nando begins to pick up speed. The APC is diminishing in the side mirror; there's nothing but open highway ahead of them. And just like that, Ben realises, they're free.

CHAPTER FOUR

Doyle has to think this through. He has to think it through before Plan John does.

But that's impossible. Plan John is smarter than him, or at any rate more devious. And even *that* doesn't matter, not really. What's important is that he enjoys this. Plan John will be figuring out right now how he can screw Doyle Johnson, not because there's real enmity between them but because that's how his mind works, and because this is a game to him and Plan John isn't the kind of man who loses.

"He has to stay here," Doyle says.

Aaronovich, as absorbed in her own thoughts as he has been, looks up. "What?"

"Austin. He needs to stay here."

She couldn't appear more shocked if he'd slapped her. "Don't be ridiculous."

"There's nowhere else."

"There has to be. I'm not taking care of your boy. I'm a doctor, not a nursemaid. Anyway, where do you imagine he'll sleep?"

"You have the infirmary downstairs," Doyle says. "It has a lock, a good lock. It's intended to be a bolt-hole."

"How do you know about that?" Aaronovich asks, with apparently genuine surprise.

"I know a lot of things. Am I wrong?"

"No," she admits. "It's designed to be locked down in case of a riot. But the point is not whether he'd be safe here, it's that he's *your* son and you have to take responsibility for him."

"I *am* taking responsibility." Doyle is careful not to let impatience into his tone. "And I need to be sure he's somewhere safe until it's clear which way this is going to go."

"Look," Aaronovich says – and he can see that she, too, is endeavouring to be reasonable – "I can't have a teenage boy living here.

It's completely inappropriate. You need to hear me on this, Johnson."

There's a note to her voice, practically of desperation, that almost persuades him. In any other circumstances, he would give in. But now, just now, this is the only choice. To expose Austin to the other guards, let alone the inmates, is to expose him to Plan John, which would be to allow him to become a pawn in Plan John's schemes, and that isn't an option.

"I'm sorry," Doyle says. "This is how it has to be…for a few days, until I think of something better." And even as he speaks, he remembers how he said similar words to his ex-wife, not an hour before.

When Aaronovich doesn't answer straight away, he registers that, instead of him, she's watching a spot behind his left shoulder. Doyle turns, to see Austin standing in the doorway.

"Hello, Austin," Aaronovich says.

"How much did you hear?" Doyle asks.

"Enough," Austin replies.

"Okay. Then you know you're going to live with the doctor for a little while."

"You don't want me to stay with you?" There's no emotion in the inquiry. It's phrased entirely as a test, one Doyle has failed.

"I want you to be where you're safe. So does the doctor." Doyle turns on Aaronovich. "Isn't that true?"

She holds his eyes, and hers are fierce. Then she says, "Of course."

"All right." Doyle doesn't dare look at either of them. He feels wretched, and angry too, bent out of shape by frustration. He'll need to vent that soon, and it shouldn't be here. "I'm going to talk to Howard. Before this gets out of hand."

But it's already out of hand, Doyle thinks. The question is which way it falls out, and who gets hurt first.

*   *   *

Outside, the heat is growing punishing. The group working out in the weights pile have surrendered, and are lounging about on the benches. Glancing behind him, Doyle sees that another of the guards, Houseman, has set himself up on the flat roof of the administrative wing. He's acquired a folding chair from somewhere and is lolling, a can of beer in hand.

There are only four of them left now. Four guards to twenty-three prisoners; those aren't great odds. Contreras is on the verge of a medical retirement, while Foster gave up any pretence of not working for Plan John long ago. That leaves Doyle and Houseman, and looking at him, sprawled up there with his beer perched on his gut, Doyle feels he knows everything he could ever need to know about the man.

Doyle presses on toward the Big House: the building, mostly fallen into disuse, which held most of White Cliff's communal facilities in its original, long-abandoned design. The Big House makes him think of a faded Southern mansion, though there's nothing about the place, except perhaps the balcony that Plan John favours, that particularly warrants the comparison. There are three entrances: the double doors that open onto the yard, a second at the farther end near to the stores, and the one that Doyle chooses, which should be locked and isn't.

The corridors within are monotonous and gloomy. Doyle can't help but hurry through them. He only pauses when he reaches the bottom of the staircase that leads up to Plan John's apartment, which was until recently the warden's apartment. There he takes a deep breath, briefly grateful that the migraine that dogged him all day yesterday has finally cleared. Then he climbs the stairs, marches down the short corridor at their summit, and hammers upon the door at the end.

There are footsteps from the other side. "Who's there?"

"CO Johnson," Doyle replies, trying to make the title sound like it means something.

He hears the rattle of locks. The man who opens the door is definitely not Plan John; Doyle recognises the imposing figure of Baptiste. Plan John chooses his bodyguards apparently at random, and always in pairs.

Doyle nods a greeting and says, "How's it going, Baptiste?"

"Can't complain," Baptiste rumbles. "'Cept it's damn hot."

"Yeah, it is that."

"Going to have to frisk you, Johnson."

"Baptiste...."

"Rules are rules."

"Hell." Doyle spins round and slams his palms against the wall.

Baptiste pats Doyle down carefully, though with no great skill.

There are a dozen places Doyle could have hidden a blade that he'd have missed. But then, that's the virtue of Plan John's rotating security; on another day it might be Landser or Oxendine or Soto that opened the door.

Satisfied, Baptiste leads the way into the space that Plan John refers to as his office. Near where a second door gives onto Plan John's private bathroom and bedroom, a heavy desk cordons the far corner. Apart from that, the only furnishings are a few metal chairs and a table opposite the desk. Nguyen, sitting at the table, looks up when Doyle enters and, seeing who it is, goes back to the magazine unfolded before him.

Plan John himself is sitting behind his desk. "Ah, Mr. Johnson. It's so rare I get the better class of visitors." To Nguyen and Baptiste he says, "Gentlemen, please wait outside."

Nguyen scowls at Doyle as he goes by. Doyle hears the door close and feels momentary panic, panic to be trapped in there with Plan John. The man is massive, and it's hard to figure out what's fat, what's muscle. He carries himself with such confidence, like a prizefighter. There's no way to judge what he might be physically capable of.

Plan John lays rubbery forearms on the glass-panelled surface of his desk and says, "Why don't you pull up a chair, Mr. Johnson?"

Doyle walks to the middle of the room, but no farther. "I don't want to take that much of your time."

"No? All right then. Shall I start us off? You're here to discuss the issue of your son."

"It needs discussing," Doyle agrees.

"You know I can make things easy for you or I can make them difficult. You understand *how* difficult I can make things, the many and varied ways in which I could do so. Which civilises the matter for both of us, since I won't need to do anything as crass as make threats."

"No," Doyle says. "You don't need to threaten me."

"Nor would I wish to. Threats are for violent, stupid people. I'm a businessman, and I make business arrangements. Like this place, like my presence here: all business."

Doyle should let it go, but he can't. "Is that right?"

Plan John smiles. "Oh, not my incarceration in itself. I've made my share of mistakes, I admit. But things worked out in the end, and I choose to believe that's what's important. Freedom is overrated, especially these days. Security, on the other hand—"

"Which is what I came to talk about," Doyle cuts him off.

Plan John's smile widens, revealing more teeth, until it's barely a smile at all. "Excellent. I've always felt we'd gotten off on the wrong footing."

Doyle has heard enough from the other guards, and in overheard conversations between the cons, to know how Plan John's meetings go. Plan John pushes hard or in just the right way, and people break. Here is the moment when that push begins. Give an inch and it will be inexorable.

"I'm not going to work for you, Howard," Doyle says.

Plan John's smile freezes. "Is that so?"

"That's what I came to tell you. I'm not Foster. I'm not Houseman. I won't work for you. But I won't screw with you either. I'm not kidding myself that you don't run this place, at least for as long as it takes the world out there to put itself back together. So you do what you need to do, however you need to do it, as long as you don't expect me to help."

"That sounds a lot like the arrangement we currently have," Plan John observes. He seems perfectly unflustered.

"It is. That's *exactly* what it is. Except now, it's formal. You get my word that I'll keep out of your business if you keep out of mine."

Plan John gives a thunderous chuckle, from deep in his throat. "Oh, I do like you, Johnson. We should have more of these little talks." He leans back in his chair and closes his eyes. Sleepily, he declares, "You know, everyone left in Funland is here for a reason."

"So I've heard." Rumour says that when the warden and most of the prisoners and guards were bussed out, it was Plan John and Plan John's money that determined who stayed and who went.

"And those reasons are my reasons. Civic responsibility is such a rarity these days. It falls to men like me to craft our communities where we can. Everyone here is here because they have a quality that I believed would prove useful in the times ahead." Plan John looks at Doyle then, with a directness that makes his knees weaken. There is conviction in the man's scrutiny. "Have you asked yourself why *you're* here, Mr. Johnson?"

"I haven't given the question much thought," Doyle says truthfully.

"But you accept that there is a reason?"

"If that's what you're telling me."

"Perhaps," suggests Plan John, "I just wanted someone honest to keep me on my toes." He draws a handkerchief from a desk drawer and wipes the square of cloth across his brow, then slowly, delicately, between the gaps of his fingers. "Whatever the case, I like you, Mr. Johnson. Would you care to hear why?"

"Not overly."

"I like you because you're a crazy son of a bitch, and you don't even know it. You haven't the faintest notion of how crazy you are."

"I guess not," Doyle concurs.

"Also, you have the balls of a bull elephant." Plan John chuckles once more, a rich and fluid sound, as if struck by his own image. "So, yes, we have an understanding – for the moment."

CHAPTER FIVE

Fernando's hands are shaking so much that, even though the interstate is empty, Ben worries he'll manage to crash into something. The constant noise from behind them can't be helping. The metal panel welded over the dividing window doesn't do more than muffle the screams and banging.

"You did good back there," Ben says eventually, feeling that someone has to speak up.

Nando glances his way. His eyes are round with suppressed tension.

"You saved our asses," Ben informs him, willing Nando to return his gaze to the road.

Then, just as Ben has convinced himself that Nando's in shock, he asks, "Is there water left?"

Carlita passes him a bottle and Nando takes a long swig. "I was sure they were going to shoot," he says.

Ben can tell he means it, that in those moments he'd believed they were all going to die. "Well, they didn't," he says futilely.

"No, they didn't."

Apparently, that's all Nando has to say on the subject. At least his shaking has subsided. Ben checks his watch, sees that it's past three. They lost the greater part of the day in getting out of the city. After a few minutes, when they haven't passed any vehicles, military or otherwise, Nando starts to speed up. The road is empty in both directions. Ben presumes the army has also shut the highway off ahead, and hopes that barricade is past their turnoff. It's too much to expect that they'll get so lucky a second time.

After keeping to the speed limit for a while, Nando dips the gas pedal farther. Ben watches the dial creep toward a hundred. Without traffic, a hundred miles an hour doesn't seem fast. Nando's hands are perfectly still on the wheel now. Either he's calmed down or the shock has taken a different turn; so long as he keeps them on the road, Ben doesn't much care. He'd have thought Carlita might protest, but she says nothing. She's staring straight ahead, one hand clenched in her lap, the other draped around Kyle's shoulders. Kyle himself is asleep, or maybe pretending to be. He shut his eyes after they passed the APC and hasn't opened them since.

Nando slows when they pass two army transports. They're on the wrong side of the highway, but Nando is in the inner lane and the transports keep to the outer, passing with plenty of space. The other vehicles are travelling almost as fast as they have been. Ben wonders if something's happening back in the city.

Then he thinks, *Of course something's happening.* The question is what – or perhaps just, how bad.

For the first time, Ben lets himself feel relieved. They're out. Whatever happens, it can't be worse than the catastrophe they've escaped.

At some point, Ben drifts into sleep. He was up most of the night, and only nerves have kept him going, but the empty road is lulling and even the hammering and cries from behind aren't enough to keep him awake. He's roused by a sharp jolt that freezes him with panic, to realise Nando has stopped the ambulance and is reversing. "Shit, Fernando," he says.

"Nearly missed the turn," Nando mumbles.

Ben sighs and stretches numbed muscles. "Why don't we take a break?"

"A break?" Nando echoes, as if he hasn't considered the possibility.

"Are we going to make it there today?"

"I don't think so," Nando admits. "Maybe it's not a good idea to drive through the night."

"So we'll need to stop?" Carlita asks. She's had her eyes closed and sounds muzzy, as though she too has been sleeping.

"Sure we will," Ben says. "You're right, Nando, it's a lousy idea to do this drive at night. Which means there's no harm in taking a break, yeah?"

"I guess," Nando agrees. "Okay. Let me find somewhere."

True to his word, he pulls up a few minutes later. The men take turns to go piss among the scrub trees that border the road, Ben escorting Kyle like a bodyguard, waiting at a distance for the hiss of urine splashing loam to finish. Then they pick out a place to sit, choosing by unspoken consent a spot sufficiently far from the ambulance to mute the noises from within. Nando is last to join them. He stands apart with his phone to his ear, and in the end mutters a curse.

"No reception," he says, lowering himself onto the dry earth.

"So Tito doesn't know we're coming?"

Ben decides he catches a hint of accusation in Carlita's voice, and is pleased. He's already tired of playing the screwup to Nando's upright cop act.

"I'll try again once we're closer to a town," Nando says. Then, changing the subject, "If we're stopping for the night, we should aim to get some food and more water. I think there's enough gas in the tank, but it wouldn't hurt to fill her up."

"We could lose the ambulance," Ben says. "Leave it somewhere. Find a car."

"We're not stealing."

"I didn't say steal."

"And I'm not abandoning my duty." Nando scowls back toward the ambulance. "We're not making *that* anyone else's problem."

"Okay then. You've got your gun," Ben says, not prepared to let this go. "You put a few rounds through the side. Like that cop in the city was talking about."

"What? Wait a minute—"

"Come on, Nando. What's going to happen? You know there's no cure. Those people in there…they're sick and they're only going to get worse. Without a cutting torch, we can't even get them out of that thing. You think you're doing them a kindness keeping them alive another day or two?" Looking to Carlita for support, Ben sees her expression. "Hey, I'm just saying," he mutters.

"He has a point, Nando," Carlita ventures, which frustrates Ben all the more, because the way she'd glared at him, you'd suppose he'd argued for setting fire to a busload of school kids.

"Sure," Nando concedes, refusing to meet her eyes.

"If we're going by a town anyway," she adds, "maybe we should stop. Maybe we'll find a car someone's abandoned. If not, we can buy food, as you say, and some gas."

"Sure," Nando repeats. He sounds distant now. "Can't hurt to try."

"And the towns are safer? Not like the city?" There's an edge to Carlita's question, almost of pleading.

This time, Nando doesn't answer. Ben suspects he knows why. Before he'd given up on the news, they had been mapping outbreaks everywhere, dots blooming like algae in the cities, meeting up to form what they'd called 'infection bands'. Even then, though, great swathes of the US – in contrast to Europe, say – were merely spattered in a rash of isolated specks. However, the anchors had taken pains to stress that this reflected nothing except population densities. Where there was no trace of sickness, generally it meant only that there were no people.

"The odds are better than in the city," Ben cuts in. "But I think we need to assume that nowhere's exactly safe."

★   ★   ★

They see a little traffic: cars full of grim-faced families, trucks, and the occasional weathered pickup. A light rain falls as evening draws near, and the air, heavy and leaden prior to then, releases the worst of its tension.

Kyle, who has felt withdrawn and out of sorts ever since they left the police station, finally begins to relax. He hadn't wanted to admit how scared he'd been in the city, not even to himself. When his dad and Carlita start tentatively talking, he joins in. He makes a dumb joke and they laugh and suddenly things seem better. He and Carlita even play 'I Spy' for a while, until the monotony of endless pine forest defeats their imaginations.

They spot a sign for a town, which his dad manages to pinpoint on a sheaf of printed-out maps that Nando hands to him. The place looks tiny, barely more than a main street. Nando says that's for the best, that the smaller the place, the less hard it will have been hit.

Then they crest a rise and there it is, far down the road ahead, mostly hidden amid the trees.

"We can't drive this thing in there," Ben points out.

"We'll get closer," Nando says, "and see if anyone's about."

They pass a couple of houses before the town proper, wood and brick two-storeys set well back from the road. Kyle notices that there aren't vehicles on the driveways. Just past the second house, a trail leads into the forest, cut off by a high mesh gate. There's space on the roadside, and Nando pulls up there.

"We'll be hidden from view," he announces.

They all get out, eager to be free of the cab's confines. Kyle walks back and forth a while, staring at the nearby house, attempting to catch a glimpse of someone at the windows. He can't say how, but some unnamed sense tells him the house is empty.

"Kyle," Carlita calls. "We're going into town. You stay here."

"What?" He's genuinely shocked.

"We need you to guard the ambulance," Nando says.

That's bullshit, Kyle almost snaps back. He tries to devise a more reasoned argument. He doesn't want to be alone here. He can hear hammering, sobbing, and shouting from inside the ambulance; it hasn't let up for a moment. But neither does he want his argument to be that he's afraid.

"It might be good to have the kid along," Ben says. He gives Carlita a look Kyle can't decipher.

Carlita throws her arms up, a gesture of mock surrender. "All right. Then I'll stay."

Kyle thinks he gets it. Two men and a child are less threatening than three adults. Not that he's a child, but at fourteen he looks young for his age, he's pale and skinny, no one is ever going to take him for a threat. And ultimately, the reasons don't matter. He's glad to not be the one left out.

The three of them, Kyle, his dad, and Nando, walk in single file on the roadside to where the sidewalk starts. The wide main street stretches to perhaps forty buildings, with an intersection before the halfway point and presumably more houses in the other directions. The buildings match those they passed coming in, brick and wood, all much the same. There are a few empty lots, and in general an air of run-downness. No one's around. The first shops are closed and of no use anyway: a hairdressers, a pharmacy, a place that appears to sell nothing except ride-on lawnmowers. However, farther up Kyle spies what looks like a general store.

"There's a gas station," says Nando, indicating the intersection. "I'll see if anybody's there. Why don't you two try the store?" He moves off without waiting for an answer, crossing to the far sidewalk.

Kyle and his dad walk in parallel with Nando as far as the store entrance. The sign behind the glass is turned to 'Open', but Kyle is doubtful. Even under normal circumstances, it's late for anywhere to be serving, let alone in a dead-end burg like this. He's surprised when his dad pushes the door and it gives.

The inside is roomier than is necessary for the two wide aisles. The shelves are stacked mostly with boxed and canned groceries, while, near the entrance, candy, magazines, cheap paperbacks, and greeting cards are mounted in rotating stands. The counter runs along the rear wall; behind it sits a middle-aged woman. She resembles a fourth-grade teacher Kyle had once: dyed hair piled in a bundle, narrow glasses perched on her nose, and a sour look, as though she's tasted the world and found it not to her liking. She is eyeing them with open suspicion.

"We're not open."

"We don't want to bother you," Ben says. "Just hoping to buy a little food and some bottled water. Or soft drinks. Whatever you might have."

"Like I said. We're not open."

"Okay. But since you're here. If you can spare us a minute."

"I've been told not to sell. Due to the emergency."

"We don't mean to cause any trouble," Ben says. "You can see, I've got my son with me. He hasn't eaten all day. If we can just get some water—"

"Are you sick?" the woman asks abruptly.

"I'm not sick. None of us are sick. We're just tired and hungry."

"You need to get out." There's an edge of panic in the woman's voice. "I can't sell to you and I don't want you in here."

Kyle puts a hand on his father's arm. "Come on, Dad. It's okay. It's only one night."

"Sure. Yeah. Let's all go hungry."

"It'll be okay," Kyle repeats. There's something in the woman's face that worries him.

"It's people like you..." Ben says to the woman, and then, "ah, fuck it." He spins away and, in his anger, nearly sends a rack of candy bars toppling. He looks as if he might shove the stand over altogether, and pauses, instead, to right it. "Sorry to have taken up your time," he tells the woman, sounding not sorry at all. He pushes through the door and Kyle hurries to keep up, careful not to look back at the storekeeper.

In the street, Kyle glances around for Nando. He can't see him. But far along the road, in the opposite direction from which they came, a figure is walking toward them. He's wearing a hunting jacket and a wide-brimmed hat, and is keeping close to the centre. Kyle can make out clearly the rifle slung over one shoulder.

"Go back to the ambulance," Ben says.

Kyle wants to, but he can't bring himself to move. He can't take his eyes off the man and the rifle.

Then he does see Nando. He's stepped into view across from them, where the gas station forecourt is. The man with the rifle has marked him also, and has adjusted his course slightly to maintain the distance between them. He isn't looking at Ben and Kyle. Nando walks slowly, deliberately, across the forecourt. He stops when he reaches the road. The man, only a few feet from him now, stops too.

"I was checking if anybody was serving," Nando tells the man.

The man unslings his rifle. Even from a distance, it's expensive-looking, all black wood and polished metal. The man doesn't aim, just holds the rifle in the crook of his arm, the way a hunter would.

"But there isn't," Nando continues. "So I guess I'll be leaving, try somewhere else."

"Where's your vehicle?" The man's voice is low and throaty. Stubble darkens his jaw, and what's visible of his face is all hard angles. His eyes are hidden in the shade of his hat.

Is that deliberate, Kyle wonders; *is he deliberately hiding his eyes?*

"It's outside of town," Nando says. "We didn't intend to alarm anyone."

"What's so alarming about it?"

"I'm a prison driver. I'm transporting prisoners."

Another voice comes from close behind Kyle. "That you, Holland?" It's the woman from the store.

"Louisa," the man acknowledges her.

"That one took something." Though he can't see, Kyle can feel her accusing finger jabbing at his father's back. "He was acting real aggressive. I think he might be sick."

The rifle snaps up. The man doesn't use the scope, merely sights along the barrel. "That right?"

"I'm not sick," Ben says. "I didn't take anything."

"They're looters," the store woman moans. "Like you warned about."

"We just want to leave," says Nando. There's a forcefulness to the words that draws everyone's attention. Sure enough, Nando has a revolver in his hands, pointed squarely at the man's body. "I'm a police officer. We're not looters."

The man, Holland, keeps the rifle on Ben, not acknowledging in any way the gun aimed at him. "You said you're a prison driver."

"Right now, I'm both." Nando has begun to back toward Kyle and Ben, with slow deliberate steps, never once letting the barrel of the revolver drift from the man's body. "I can show you my badge. But you'll need to lower your weapon."

"You tell your friend," the man says, "to return what he stole."

"I didn't steal anything," Ben insists. But the man doesn't appear to be listening, though he still has the rifle trained on them.

"We're leaving," says Nando.

"I reckon they're sick, Holland." The store woman is practically wailing.

"We're not sick. Nobody's sick." To Ben and Kyle, Nando hisses, "*Come on.*"

"You don't think we've seen enough of it?" There's a new note in the man's voice, an edge of desperation.

Ben starts walking backward, in step with Nando. Kyle keeps close. The tip of the rifle barrel clings to them like an angry insect.

"You don't think we've had enough?" asks the man.

"We're sorry," Fernando tells him. "I'm sorry." As they pass the woman, Louisa, she retreats into the doorway of her store, as if their very proximity is a threat.

Finally, the man lowers the rifle. He gets down on his knees, oblivious of the store woman. He lays the rifle on the asphalt and puts his forearms up over his face. His shoulders begin to heave.

It might be a symptom of the sickness. But Kyle's pretty sure that he's just crying.

CHAPTER SIX

He's striving to hold onto the anger. If he isn't angry then he'll be scared, and Austin isn't willing to be scared. He can feel the fear waiting, lapping like dark water. If he lets that current rise, even for a moment, it might drown him.

Anyway, the anger is still coming freely. First his mother dumps him here, choosing Martin over him once and for all. Then his father can't be around him for more than ten minutes without rushing away. It seems to Austin that everything he needs to know about his life can be found right there, between the poles of two parents who can't so much as tolerate his existence.

Now he's alone with this nurse, doctor, or whatever she is, and he can tell that she's trying to be kind. But it doesn't come easily to her, and in any case, Austin isn't ready to trust her. She has the edge of a strange accent: something European, Russian perhaps. She looks old, with her gaunt face and stark white hair, but she doesn't handle herself like an old woman or talk like one. She's brought him coffee from another room that leads off her office, and is staying close, as though afraid he might run.

As Austin sips the coffee, she attempts a few hesitant inquiries.

"Did it take you long to get here?"

He shrugs.

"You had to travel by night?"

No, they'd stayed in a motel. Austin had lain awake, at first listening through the wall to the angry-animal noises that counted in his stepfather's case for passion, and then, in the silence afterward, observing the merciless passage of his own racing thoughts. "Yeah," he says.

"Is it bad out there? As bad as they've been claiming?"

Austin hears a note of trepidation in her voice, but also genuine curiosity. *It's pretty bad*, he almost says. He remembers things he saw on the way here. People fighting, over anything or nothing. Some of them visibly sick, many not. Rather than answer, he nods instead.

The doctor asks him no more after that. Austin has finished his coffee, and the silence between them has stretched tight like shrink-wrap by the time his father returns. His face, too, is taut.

"Will you give us a minute, Austin," his father says, not phrasing it as a question.

Is this how it's going to be? Pushed out of every conversation, even when it's about him? "No," Austin replies.

His father looks at him then, the first proper attention he's shown since entering the office. "No?"

"I've a right to know what's going on."

Austin thinks his father will argue. But all Doyle says is, "Fine." He turns back to the doctor, dismissing Austin from existence. "It's settled. For the moment."

The doctor considers him doubtfully. "Settled?"

"For the moment," Doyle repeats.

The doctor's response is to glance at Austin out of the corner of her eye, as though calculating how much she can say with him there.

Austin wants to tell her, *You can just talk.* There's no need for this bullshit. He gets that his dad went to speak to the man on the balcony about him, and that he's made some kind of a deal, one that perhaps puts his dad in danger. Austin should be grateful, yet their evasiveness makes that impossible. A part of him longs to trust these people, the parent he barely knows and the strange doctor, stern and considerate both at once. Only they won't trust him, so he can't.

"What did you promise?" the doctor asks finally.

"Nothing," his father says. "Nothing he hasn't got already."

"That doesn't sound like him," she notes.

"I guess not."

The doctor sighs. "I hope you haven't done anything you'll regret."

"If I have, I suppose I'll find out soon enough," Austin's father says, and there's something in his voice that makes a lie out of that *if.*

*　　*　　*

There is, for today at least, just one problem left to deal with.

You faced down Plan John, Doyle tells himself. *Surely you can talk to your own son.*

Yet somehow, Austin frightens him more than Plan John does. Doyle can feel the anger coming off the boy, a radiation that taints the air. He has no argument to oppose it; he knows that it's earned. He has let his son down. Whatever the reasons why Doyle's marriage failed, so entirely and so mercilessly, they don't matter in Austin's eyes. Austin thinks his father abandoned him, and he's right.

So much damage to undo. Too much, maybe. But Doyle has to start somewhere. "Come on," he says to Austin, "I'll show you where you'll be sleeping."

Doyle leads the way through the door to the infirmary stairwell, and Austin falls in grudgingly. As Doyle discussed with Aaronovich, the infirmary was designed to double as a safe room in case of trouble; injured prison guards would make for easy hostages. The upper door is a solid, windowless slab of metal. The stairwell walls are a grimy yellow, a colour intimate with sickness.

The door at the bottom – this one merely plastic – does have a window, of frosted glass. The room beyond is tiled to waist height and scathingly white under the fluorescent striplights. There are three gurney beds, an operating table against one wall, and locked cabinets for instruments and drugs. A lift like a coffin-length dumbwaiter is set into the far wall, there for moving patients. The infirmary hasn't been used in weeks, but Aaronovich has kept it scrupulously clean. As a living space, that's about all there is to recommend it.

"I'll bring you down a mattress from the guardroom," Doyle promises. "Some books and magazines. And a lamp."

"Great." Austin is considering the room with frank disgust. "It'll be exactly like home."

His reaction is understandable. Given the limitations of what Doyle has to offer, small gestures can't hope to penetrate the shell of Austin's antagonism. Perhaps Doyle was wrong to push the boy out of his conversation with Aaronovich.

"The man you saw before," he says, "the man I went to talk to just now, his name is John Howard. He runs this place, and he's dangerous. I needed to make sure he isn't going to try and hurt you."

The look Austin gives him suggests grave doubt that anything Plan John threatens could be worse than this.

You have no idea, Doyle thinks. But all he says is, "Hopefully I've fixed things so that he'll leave you alone."

Something darts through Austin's expression then, a flicker of meaning that Doyle can't parse. "Did you make a deal?" Austin asks.

It seems to Doyle that there's a specific answer his son wants, but he hasn't a clue what that might be. "No," he says. "Not really."

Austin pulls up a chair and sits, looking away, as if to indicate that any slight interest he's had in the conversation is over.

Doyle fights back a sigh of frustration. *I don't know how to do this.* Even when he and Rachel had been together, fatherhood had not come easily or naturally, but the Austin he remembers from then was nothing like this taciturn, anger-filled adolescent. In desperation, Doyle says, "I'm going to go do my rounds. Why don't you come with me? I'll give you a tour of the place."

"I'm fine here," Austin mutters, in a tone that makes clear that he isn't, and how could anyone be?

"Okay." What can Doyle do, force the boy? Still, he feels like a coward as he says, "You settle in. I'll be back to check on you in a while."

CHAPTER SEVEN

Nando drives for a couple more hours. No one says a word, not even when it starts to get dark and they're still on the road. Just as the last light is failing, Kyle points out a barn, half tumbled down and obviously derelict. Without a discussion, Nando pulls off the road, into the long grass.

Kyle is glad to be out of the ambulance. He thinks he's never been so glad of anything. The sounds from the back are getting worse. Mixed in with the banging and yelling there have been other noises: sobs, retching, for a while laughter that seemed like it was never going to stop. And he aches all over, all through; he hasn't ever been on a journey this long. Then there's the atmosphere. Since the town, it's felt as if a storm was about to break in the cramped cab. Kyle can't even say why. What happened had been scary, but they'd got out okay, hadn't they?

Kyle scales an intervening fence and heads for the barn, wanting to be first to reach it. The double doors are standing open; one of them is rotted half off its hinges. Inside, the back wall is caved in, and most of the roof. The space is empty besides a little damp straw in one corner. At least they'll be out of the wind, though, and not sleeping in the open.

Carlita comes next. She gives Kyle a fragile smile, but he doesn't miss the revulsion she's trying to hide, the tension in her features that says, *So this is how we live now?* Nando enters after her, and Carlita gives him the smile too. "It's just one night, right?"

When Kyle's dad follows behind Nando, he doesn't bother to look around, and no one except Kyle looks at him. Ben sits on his own, in the far corner near the doors, and closes his eyes as if he's settling down to sleep.

Nando begins gathering scraps of wood, breaking off planks that appear rotten, and Kyle joins in. Carlita, who still smokes occasionally despite having quit the year before, produces a lighter from her purse, and with it Nando manages to get a fire burning. The three of them sit about the small blaze, sharing the last of the bottled water and the few remaining cookies. Kyle wants to know why his dad doesn't come over, and why neither Carlita nor Nando invite him to, but somehow he doesn't dare put either question into words.

"Are we safe here?" Carlita asks.

"No reason we shouldn't be," Nando says. He'd dragged the heavy doors closed while he was gathering their firewood.

"And how far do we have left to go?"

"I'm not sure," Nando admits. "Maybe another five hours, if the roads are clear."

"Do we have enough gas left?"

Even Kyle has noticed how the needle is drifting steadily toward the red. But all Nando says is, "Maybe." Abruptly, with no apparent break in the conversation, he gets to his feet. He paces halfway to where Kyle's dad is sitting and spits, "So what did you take?"

Ben looks up, and there's resentment in his eyes. Kyle wants to say something, to defend his father. *Tell him he's wrong*, he thinks, willing the assertion into his dad's mouth.

Then Ben empties out his left-hand pocket. There are eight candy bars, crumpled and broken within their wrappers. He lays them out on the dirt before him. "Best I could do."

"I should have let him shoot you," Nando says. Disregarding Ben, he returns to the fire.

Ben grins at Kyle and holds up two of the candy bars. Kyle returns the grin, though hesitantly. He doesn't fully get why Nando is so mad. Sure, stealing is bad, but they're hungry, and the woman in the store had refused to sell to them, so doesn't that make it practically okay? He climbs to his feet and goes over to his father. Ben piles up six of the bars and tips them into Kyle's hands. "Share them with Carlita and your Uncle Nando, okay?"

Kyle carries the bars back with care and proffers his cupped hands to Carlita, who plucks two from the heap. He continues to Nando and offers him half of the remainder.

Nando looks as if he'll refuse. Instead, he takes the bars, puts one in his pocket, and starts to unwrap the other. "One of these days, you selfish son of a bitch," he says, not looking at Ben but loud enough that he can't fail to hear, "you are going to get somebody killed."

★   ★   ★

They set out earlier than Ben would like.

Still numbed and exhausted from Brody's screw-up attempt at a liquor store robbery, his head smarting from where the cop slugged him, he would have slept half the day if they'd let him. But he has no say. The first time Nando tries to wake him, Ben ignores it, rolling over on the hard-packed earth. The second time, Nando shoves him with a foot, and there's no ignoring that. Ben bites down on his anger. The way things are going, he and Nando are going to have words and perhaps worse, but there'll be a right moment and now isn't it.

There's scant comfort in the fact that the others haven't had much rest either, that none of them have anything to eat. Though Nando starts out driving, he looks exhausted, and when at one point a back wheel clips the edge of the road, Carlita insists she take over. By then, the sun is fully up. After an hour, even with the air-con on full and the windows open, it's getting clammy inside the cab. The heat seems to rile the Sickers behind them to new heights of frenzy – or maybe it's only that they, too, are fed up with being hungry.

They pass through the first town around noon. There are two bodies in the street. One is lying face down, half on and half off the sidewalk, in a pool of caked blood. The other is crumpled in a doorway. There has been a fire, half a dozen houses reduced to chitinous wreckage; those on the edges are still smouldering. There are no signs of life.

Soon after, the road begins to climb. Nando, poring over his maps, says they're not far off. The day gets hotter.

The second town is larger. There are indications of an ordered evacuation: all the vehicles gone and no bodies to be seen. Ben spies one person, a man, white, not young. He's at the end of a side street, head tilted forward, barely looking their way. He takes a few half-running steps toward the ambulance and then darts for an alley. Something in the manner in which he moves leaves no doubt in Ben's mind that he's sick.

Eventually they turn onto a narrow road marked with 'PRIVATE' signs that winds up into the hills. Nando says that this is it. The worst of the day's heat has finally retreated, masked by clouds whose greying borders hint at impending rain. The road is not well maintained. The forest is thicker than elsewhere, dense and unwelcoming.

Twenty or so minutes after they turn onto the private road, they come across the SUV. The vehicle must have been coming from the other direction and has crashed into a tree, hard enough that the trunk has shorn off much of the right side of its hood. To Ben, the accident appears recent. A woman is lying in the road, except for one leg that's snagged inside the passenger door. Her face is bloody, what's visible of it.

"We have to stop," Carlita says.

"I don't think we should," Ben tells her.

"We *have* to."

Nando offers no opinion. But as they pass the shattered SUV, he slows further, and then pulls up a little way beyond.

The decision has been made. Once again, Ben has no say.

★   ★   ★

Kyle has never been near a dead body before.

The woman looks as if she'd been trying to climb out of the car, or perhaps as if she was dragged out. Her leg is snared, but he can't see what by. Nor can he see her face, and for that he's glad. There's blood sprayed in a loose star, across the asphalt and up the wheel arch of the SUV. It seems to Kyle that someone must have done that to her, hammered her face into the road like that.

Nando is already crouching beside the woman's body. He stays that way for a few seconds, eyes roving, absorbing details.

Ben is leaning against the back of the ambulance, heedless of the blows from its inside. "Come on," he says to Nando. "I don't like this."

Kyle moves nearer. It isn't as though he wants to see the body, and yet he feels drawn, as if here is something he needs to observe whether he wishes to or not.

Nando raises his gaze to inspect the interior of the SUV. "I think her neck's broken," he says.

"So what?" Ben asks. Then, hastily, "I mean…okay, her neck's broken. I'm sorry. But this isn't on us."

Nando doesn't look at him. "Someone could be hurt." He stands. "She was the passenger, and there's no sign of the driver.

The keys are still in the ignition. We should have a hunt around."

"I'll look," Kyle proposes. But he says it softly, and neither of them pays him any notice.

"If you're going to get us into someone else's problem," Ben tells Nando, "we ought to deal with our own first." He has pushed away from the ambulance and is indicating its flank with one outstretched hand.

"*Deal* with it?" Nando's tone is cold, though not quite hostile. For once he sounds unsure.

"You know what I mean."

"I'm going to go check," Kyle says. He expects someone to contradict him, but Ben's and Nando's attention is entirely on each other, and Carlita is watching them too.

Kyle trips down the shallow embankment, breaching the edge of the forest. He's tense, frustrated. The sight of the dead woman has rattled him badly. And then there's this conflict between his dad and Nando, which makes no sense to him and seems to have no end. Why can't they put their selfish bullshit aside? He feels less alone here in the dark beneath the trees than he had with them.

Kyle pauses to let his eyes adjust. The sky above is darkening fast. The air is weighty and pregnant. What light filters through has a greasy, vague quality. It's a long while before he makes out the two figures in the clearing ahead.

Kyle's skin prickles. His heartbeat, suddenly, is thunderous. He should go back. But he can still hear the current of Ben and Nando's argument, murkily penetrating the underbrush. This will be another thing for them to fight over, and in the meantime Kyle could be helping. He can see now that the figures are a man and a woman, and that the man is crouched in front of the woman, who is resting with her back to a tree and probably hurt.

Kyle edges closer, flinching at every rustle of the foliage around his feet. By the time he's drawn near the edge of the clearing, rain is beginning to fall. Fat drops rattle among the treetops and spatter unregarded upon the man's jacket. Yes, the woman is hurt, and the man is kneeling, trying to help her.

Then Kyle realises, as if the image has refocused: that isn't it at all. The girl is in her late teens, wearing a white strapped top and jeans.

Much of the left side of her face is smeared across the tree, a mulch of fractured bark and crusted gobs of red and pink. The man is just staring at her, his face adjacent to hers.

Hearing Kyle, he looks up. "She made me crash," he says. "And the crazy bitch bit me. Can you believe that?" He holds up his arm to display the lacerated meat between his elbow and wrist. "It doesn't hurt. You'd think it would hurt."

Kyle starts to back away.

The man stands up. "Did you see my wife? Is my wife okay?" He pauses, scrutinising his own hands.

Kyle takes another backward step, another.

The man doesn't move to follow. "She was making such a fucking noise," he says, "and...I think, maybe I...." The man holds his bloodied hands toward Kyle, as though in supplication.

Then the shots ring out. Six, in rapid succession.

Kyle turns and bolts.

The man – *not a man, sick, he's sick* – is running as well. Kyle can't see him, but he doesn't need to.

"Dad!" he screams. "Get inside!"

The words come out garbled. They're incomprehensible, even to him. Kyle breaks through the edge of the trees. His dad isn't getting into the ambulance. He's standing there, staring. Nando, beside him, is first to spot the man. In an instant, he's pointed his gun and pulled the trigger, and even from a distance, Kyle distinctly perceives its stubborn *click*. Kyle can distinguish the line of neatly spaced bullet holes in the side of the ambulance, where Nando has expended an entire cartridge.

As he flings himself up the embankment, Kyle is certain the man must be right behind him, ready to drag him back. But seconds later he's on the road, and when he looks round, the man has stopped, arrested awkwardly in mid-motion in a way that makes him appear more animal than human.

Then Ben has Kyle's arm and is dragging him, almost lifting him, and before he knows it he's in the cab of the ambulance, being shoved into a seat like luggage. Carlita is beside him, and she's shouting, though he can't pick out words. As if he's been deaf and the deafness has abruptly passed, other sounds flood in. He hears the slam of the driver's door and the choke of the ignition. In a moment they're moving, gravel churning beneath their wheels.

But something's wrong. His dad is yelling; even now, his dad's yelling. Kyle doesn't want to look, can't not. The clamour seems to clutch his head and wrench it.

He can't fathom what he sees at first. Ben is flailing, still shouting, and there are too many limbs. Then Kyle understands.

The Sicker has hooked his arm inside the open window. His forearm is wedged into the opening. And his hand is clamped around Ben's wrist.

CHAPTER EIGHT

Doyle lets himself out through Aaronovich's front office, without saying goodbye to the doctor. He feels uncertain, aimless. His routine has been disrupted, first by Rachel's arrival, then by trying to find somewhere to lodge his son and the encounter with Plan John. And his routine is broken enough. These days, now that he's only playacting the role of prison guard, it takes all of Doyle's strength of will not to abandon the part altogether, as the others have.

There are shadows in the yard and the sky has clouded over, reducing the heat of earlier to warmth that clings around the buildings and to the concrete beneath his feet. The weights pile has been abandoned, Houseman has given up his perch on the administrative wing roof, and Doyle is glad to note that Plan John isn't on his balcony. A couple of the Latinos are smoking at the far end of the cellblock. He can't make out their faces, but he guesses it will be Torres and Soto, since, despite Plan John's regime, they rarely seem to have much better to do.

Doyle heads for the south tower, the one overlooking the gate. He spends all the time he can there; of everything he could be doing, being on watch still feels useful. If there's trouble in the yard or near the cellblock entrance then he wants to know, even if he's helpless to intervene. And if anyone or anything should threaten Funland from the outside, Doyle wants to know that too. The fact that he has no real reason to fear such a threat does nothing to diminish the way the worry gnaws at him.

Doyle lets himself into the tower and climbs the steps. The air is definitely cooling. When he gets up to the deck, the sky is painted mostly in oppressive shades of grey and dirtied white. The stripe of blue just above the treetops looks artificial and excessively bright. The forest itself is a single block of darkness, trimmed into untidy outlines by a careless hand.

Then Doyle notices the bloom of dust there, followed a moment later by a glint of silver or white where the road is visible briefly through the forest.

Is it possible Rachel is coming back? That she's changed her mind? Perhaps, but it's not likely. Yet no one has come near White Cliff in days, and what are the odds of two visitors in such close succession?

Doyle picks up his radio, which he'd left on the parapet. He thumbs the switch and says, "This is Johnson. I'm up in the tower. Anybody waiting on visitors?"

The response is silence, layered upon queasy static. What had he expected? Is anyone else even still using the radios?

The vehicle finally breaks free of the forest edge, and Doyle recognises that it's an ambulance. Why would an ambulance be coming here? As the driver approaches the gate, they're picking up speed. And they're all over the road, travelling a snake's path between the edges, even clipping the dirt beyond the gravelled surface. What the hell do they think they're doing?

Then Doyle sees.

He thumbs the radio button, roars into it, "I need help at the gate."

No answer. Doyle flings the useless radio aside, catches up his shotgun, and throws himself down the short flight of steps. The ambulance had already crossed half the distance from the forest edge; Doyle takes mere seconds to get down the stairs and out, but by then the vehicle has halved the remaining distance again. It isn't slowing even slightly, and still the driver is hurling it from side to side, trying to dislodge the man clinging to the passenger-side door.

Doyle hesitates. Should he open the gate? But there's no time.

The driver swerves again, yet harder. An explosion rends the air, so loud and unanticipated that at first Doyle supposes it's a gunshot and catches himself ducking. Then he comprehends. Not a gunshot. A tire. The ambulance, travelling at an impossible angle in defiance of its own wheels, heaves over like some dying prehistoric beast. It covers the final distance on its side, with a roar of grating metal. When it strikes the wall, Doyle feels the transmitted impact via the soles of his feet.

The ambulance had left the road at the last, or else it would probably have sundered the gate from its frame. Doyle can see it through the wire, through the driving rain. The vehicle lies felled on one side, warped and buckled, smoke belching from its crumpled engine.

No way is anyone walking out of that.

Almost as the thought crosses his mind, the driver's door jerks open. The man who struggles to clamber free is wearing a cop's uniform. He hasn't spied Doyle. Having wedged himself in the door casing, he's reaching back into the cab, presumably to help someone else.

Doyle hurries to unlock the gatehouse booth, dashes inside, and jabs the button for the gate. By the time he's outside again, the gate is half-open and the cop has someone else up there with him, both of them perched on the side – now the top – of the overturned ambulance cab.

Oh hell, Doyle thinks. *Oh hell no.*

To the woman he calls, "Jump down. I'll catch you." He lays the shotgun against the exposed roof of the ambulance and reaches toward her.

She's evidently afraid, of him or conceivably of everything. "It's okay," the cop tells her. He seems remarkably calm.

The woman slides to sit on the edge of the cab and, when she's persuaded herself that Doyle really means to catch her, pushes off and into his arms. She's light; he catches her effortlessly. When her feet first touch the ground, she staggers slightly. Doyle holds her arm until she's steady and then lets go.

To the cop he shouts up, "I have to get her inside, do you understand? Before she's seen. Before anyone sees her. Do you *understand?*"

The rain is coming hard, driven by a wind that has risen out of nowhere. The cop looks like he hasn't heard. Then his expression focuses. "I understand. But just wait."

The cop reaches for someone else, bending half double to thrust his arms back into the cab. When he straightens, he's hauling a boy, a skinny white kid in jeans and a cotton shirt. Blood is pouring freely from a wide cut in the boy's forehead, and one arm of the shirt is dark with blackish red. The kid is very pale, and his eyes are huge. He's mouthing words at the cop but Doyle can't catch them.

"Pass him down," Doyle calls against the wind and the rain.

The cop says something to the kid and he edges over. When he swings his legs round, Doyle catches hold of them and lifts him down, taking care not to knock the bloodied arm. His mind is working fast. There's no one in the yard yet. Perhaps the storm has masked the sound of the crash. Perhaps the rain will be enough to keep everyone else inside, maybe even Plan John. But Doyle can't take that chance. He has to get them into the administrative wing, and it has to be now.

"Your turn," he tells the cop.

"No. There's another. He's trapped."

"I'll come back," Doyle yells. Then to the woman and boy, "Can you run?"

She nods. After a moment's hesitation, the boy does too.

"All right. Stay with me."

Not even pausing to be sure that they're with him, Doyle turns and sprints toward the distant entrance.

*   *   *

"Oh god, Johnson, don't tell me...."

Aaronovich has had only a second to register what's happening, no opportunity at all to prepare herself. One minute she'd been working at her desk, distracted by the drum of the rain. The next her door was being dashed open, Johnson was shouting her name, and there he is with a woman and child, two strangers, both of them scratched and bloody.

Aaronovich can't quite explain the terror that's choking her, but if anything it's growing worse, threatening to strangle her breathing.

"Not now," Johnson tells her. To the woman and child he says, "You'll be safe here."

"Did anybody see them?" A calm part of Aaronovich is assessing their injuries: in the woman's case, nothing except a few nicks and bruises; in the boy's, a head wound, bleeding plentifully but not deep – though it might mean a concussion – and an injury to his left arm, potentially a fracture. "If someone saw...."

"No one saw."

"If someone *did*." She wants to grab Johnson and shake him. Why is he refusing to recognise what's so plainly apparent? "That woman? *Here?* Look at her!"

The dangerous sense of calm that Johnson has, Aaronovich has never witnessed it so focused. "These are *injured* people," he tells her, and each word seems immovable.

"And I'll treat them, obviously, but you can't be thinking—"

"Doctor." He steps up to her, holds her shoulder with one hand.

"Settle down. Do your job."

He's right. Of course he's right. She's a doctor; these people need her help. All of her training, all her years of experience, returns like air exploding into a vacuum. Yet she knows, also, that he's absolutely wrong. Not because he's brought these people here, but because of what's going to come next.

He wants her to treat them, but this won't end there. She glimpsed the truth in his eyes, from the moment the three of them burst through the door. When she's patched them up, when the time comes to send them out into the world, Doyle Johnson will not do it.

He's already gone. The door is slamming at his back. He's made this problem hers, and the tiny window she had in which to change that fate is closed.

"Come on," Aaronovich tells the woman and the boy, her mind still oscillating between seeing them as two hurt human beings and as the terrible dilemma they represent. "Hurry, we have to get you hidden."

★   ★   ★

He has been partly thinking, partly trying not to think. He's been staring at the wall as though staring could make it dissolve. Austin has never felt homesick before, but now that ache is a knot in his stomach, cold as a stone. Then the door bursts open, the doctor is rushing in, and behind her – to his astonishment – follow a woman, and a boy about his own age.

"What's going on?" Austin asks. The words come out choked.

The doctor shakes her head. "I've no idea. An accident, I imagine."

The woman is Latina, not tall, younger than his dad and not old enough, Austin decides, to be the boy's mother. She's strikingly attractive. Even with her face scratched and bruised, even with her eyes wide and bright with fear, Austin finds it hard for an instant to look at anything else.

Then she glances his way, and shyness drives Austin's gaze to the boy instead. The boy is covered in blood. His face is bleeding and terribly pale, the same artificial white as the furnishings. One arm is bleeding too, and he's carrying it with the other. When he moves slightly, blood patters from his fingers to the tiles.

"Where's my dad?" Austin says. He isn't even certain why he wants to know.

The look the doctor gives him conveys that she has better and infinitely more important things to be dealing with in this moment. "Outside," she says.

She leads the boy to a gurney and helps him climb onto it. The woman, hovering close, is unsure, almost skittish. With the doctor's attention focused elsewhere, she seems peculiarly helpless. Austin thinks she might start crying, but she only watches as the doctor begins to cut the boy's shirt away.

Austin gets up, trying to move quietly. They've hardly noticed him; he'd rather not draw their attention. He can't be here. He can't rationalise his instincts further than that. It's as if his loneliness and his isolation have reached a critical threshold, beyond which he's helpless. Every muscle in his body insists he has to get out.

He knows there's nowhere to go, that his home and his friends and anything that mattered have been severed from him forever. He knows that what's left to him is this place and these terrified, terrifying people. He knows his father can't help.

Yet he's all Austin has now, and nothing could be worse than this white-walled, blood-spattered cell.

CHAPTER NINE

"I can't move," Ben tells Nando, for what feels like the twentieth time.

Ben remembers each moment: getting into the ambulance; the grip on his arm, so tight that it seemed the fingers were welded in a ring of flesh and bone; the way he couldn't tear free, no matter how he wrestled, no matter how crazily Nando flung the ambulance back and forth. Then the explosion – a gunshot? And the world had canted, its angles abruptly wrong.

After that comes a patch he *doesn't* remember, a sliver of unconsciousness. It can only have been a sliver because, the next he knew, Kyle was being hauled out and was calling for him, calling for his dad.

That was when Ben had tried to move his legs and discovered he couldn't.

Now everything is clear: very clear and very bright. Despite the storm clouds above, despite the rain slanting through the open driver's door above him, he can see every detail of the cab precisely, as though its edges have been emphasised with luminous paint. Except he can't figure out why he can't move.

He isn't hurt, that he can tell, or not badly. A dozen parts of him ache and stab and shiver with pain, but nothing refuses to work. He can flex his fingers and toes. What he can't do is get his legs free. With the passenger door beneath his right side and flat to the ground, the sole way out is upward, through the cab. An easy climb, if his body would comply.

Ben attempts to explain this to Nando: "I can't move." He repeats the words patiently, though a part of him doubts whether Nando is hearing him at all. Ben tries to raise his voice, but his chest is one of the parts that aches most, and the effort sets him choking. "I can't move," he whispers, willing Nando to understand.

Perhaps, finally, Nando does. For he vanishes from view, and moments later Ben detects the scrabble of boots descending the cab roof behind his head, the sound fuzzed by the thrash of the rain. Ben begins to panic then, fearful that Nando might simply be leaving – can he hate him that much? – but seconds later he reappears, now before the windshield. He's holding something in his hand, a torn-off side mirror. From Ben's perspective, Nando seems giant, elongated by the angle. The rain is churning off his head and uniform, which it has dyed a slick black shade.

Nando wields the side mirror like brass knuckles, twining his fingers in its shattered innards. He brings it down on the windshield, already a labyrinth of cracks. Afraid the glass will shatter over him, Ben drags an arm up to shield himself.

When he lowers his arm, the windshield is still intact, and someone is standing behind Nando.

And they're sick. Ben knows it in the instant he sees them. From the deeply bloodshot eyes, the gaunt face, and the filthy clothes, but mostly from the wound – the *bullet* wound – in their shoulder. It has torn muscle and splintered bone, half severing the left arm, yet they're moving as if it's nothing.

That injury, and the man's obliviousness, tells Ben all he needs to know. That this is one of the Sickers they brought from the city. That he survived the hail of bullets Nando fired into the ambulance's side. That the doors have not endured the crash; maybe a hinge popped, maybe the clumsy welding didn't do its job. That he's angry. That he's mad.

Perhaps Nando follows Ben's gaze, because he's turning his head when the man catches hold of it. Nando has a moment in which to resist, which he wastes reaching for an empty gun, before the Sicker drives his face into the windshield.

He draws Nando back, as though he's weightless. Nando's nose is smashed almost flat, split at its tip and pumping blood. His mouth is open so wide that it's like he's yawning. His eyes are frantic.

Then the man does it again. Again, again, again.

Ben watches Nando, dying blow by blow. His face, already unrecognisable, is coming apart a little more with each impact. Still the Sicker beats his head against the window, over and over, seemingly tireless.

Ben wants this slow murder to stop. He knows that if it does, he'll be next. Knowing that, he wills it to continue, hates himself. Hates his fear. Hates the Sicker. Most of all hates Nando, for not diverting him longer.

The Sicker gets bored so suddenly that it's like a switch has been flicked. He shoves Nando aside, lets him flop in the dirt. He squats to stare into the cab. He's smiling, a crooked twist of the lips. He mouths something, but if it's words, Ben can't hear them. Then he bunches his fists and starts hammering the glass, at the weakened point, the spot where Nando's face ruptured.

There's a roar, a blast of light so bright that Ben is certain he can feel the heat of it. When he can see again, the Sicker is gone. The windshield is misted and dripping with red.

Another figure ducks into view, distorted by the smears of blood and brain matter filthying the window, smoke still coiling around the barrel of his shotgun. A black man in dark trousers and grey shirt, not a cop though; remembering where they are, Ben distinguishes the prison guard uniform. The guard raises his shotgun and brings the butt down hard on the cobwebbed, blood-smeared windshield, once, twice, three times, until at last it comes loose from its frame. He lays down the shotgun and sets to pulling the entire pane loose.

Ben does what he can from his side. Somehow, unexpectedly, he works a leg free, and with that done, the other comes. He applies both feet to a corner and exerts all his strength. With a creak, the buckled windshield tears from its frame.

The guard reaches in, catches hold of Ben's forearm, and draws him upward. "Come on," he says, his voice a drawl that seems channelled down to Ben by walls of pain, "let's get you on your feet."

★　　★　　★

The room is distant. Ever since the doctor gave him the injection, Kyle has been somewhere else, though never far away. He's conscious of her presence nearby. He comprehends that she's been working on his injuries, for he's suffered through brief fever dreams of spiders spinning webs on and in his flesh, their touch no more than a whisper.

Now he's partly awake. He's in a room, a white room. The striplights are unpleasantly bright. He wishes he could move an arm to shade his eyes. He wishes he could move at all. His body is heavy with a weight of lassitude, yet at the same time buoyant, like he's floating. But already both the heaviness and the buoyancy are starting to evaporate, and with their passing his mind is growing clearer.

Kyle manages to tilt his head. The light is less dazzling, or else he's growing accustomed to it. Shapes resolve into people. A man lies on a gurney against the opposite wall, and Kyle sees that it's his father, asleep or unconscious. His head is bandaged, and Kyle is afraid, until he realises Ben's chest is rising and falling. That insight steadies him. His father is alive at least.

Kyle's scrutiny roves on. Carlita is sitting in a plastic chair, and she's crying, racking sobs that shake her like little earthquakes. There's a man beside her, the prison guard who led them here, and she's leaning her head on his chest, his body muffling the sounds she's making. He has his arm around her shoulders, and Carlita's right arm is curled across her body. Her fingers are clasped upon her own left shoulder, the guard's large hand cupped over her smaller one.

It's that which Kyle can't bear. The rest he can accept, but that – there's something in the way their hands connect that makes him want to scream.

Leave her alone, he thinks. *Leave her alone!* The second time he means to say it, but no words come.

Kyle closes his eyes. When he opens them again, his head is clear and his body his own once more. The man, the guard, is gone. Carlita is sitting near to Ben's bedside, watching him as he sleeps. She seems composed now.

But I saw what I saw, Kyle thinks. It had been real. And though he didn't entirely understand it, he won't easily forget.

*   *   *

Austin has no idea how long he's been up on the guard tower.

The rain is starting to slacken, rigid beams of sunlight breaking the crust of the cloud. However, his clothes are already soaked through, adhering like a second skin. He's beginning to shiver, or maybe has been shivering for a while. But he feels no impulse to do something about it.

By the time he'd got outside and across the yard, his dad had been hauling another man, a white guy in faded jeans and a T-shirt, out of the wreckage of the ambulance's cab. There were two bodies at their feet, and there was blood everywhere, in great splashes that were streaking and dissolving under the storm's onslaught.

But Austin hadn't cared about that. Because there had been a third figure: out past the gate and the overturned ambulance, far up the road toward the forest's verge. Someone he recognised, even at such a distance. Someone who, no matter how bad everything else might be, he'd thought that at least he would never have to see again.

Austin had watched, frozen. He had barely noticed as his dad passed him, supporting the wounded man, leading him in the direction of the doctor's office.

"Austin," his dad had called, "what are you doing here? Get inside."

Austin hadn't been able to answer. He couldn't have begun to explain. Even thinking was beyond him. And acknowledging that he wasn't about to speak, let alone move, his dad had said, "I'll come back for you." He'd sounded angry, and immensely tired.

More time had passed. Austin didn't know how long. Then the figure moved, out of his line of sight. In a frenzy, Austin had looked around for somewhere he could get a better view. There was the guard tower, its door standing open. He'd covered the distance and the stairs inside at a run. Still, he'd been too late. He'd thought he saw a trace of movement in the shadows at the forest's edge, but hadn't been sure. It had been hard to make out anything through the downpour.

His gaze remains on that spot. He blinks rain from his eyes and wonders if he's been crying. How are you supposed to tell the difference? Distantly he hears footsteps, first slapping upon the drenched concrete of the yard and then jangling on the metal staircase under his feet. From behind him comes his father's voice, at once irritable and concerned. "Austin, what are you doing up here?"

He can't say. He can't. That his stepfather, the man he hates above all others, is out there. That he's sick. That Austin can imagine no explanation of that fact that doesn't mean his mother is dead.

"Are you all right?" Doyle asks, but the irritation is winning over the concern.

Austin can't put those realisations into words. If he did, he feels certain they'd tear his throat open, like scorpions clambering into the air.

"Austin?" Now, finally, his father sounds nothing but impatient.

And with that, something breaks inside Austin – something that has been drawing taut throughout the day, and for much longer, longer than he can remember. Austin turns and pushes past his father, wishing he had the strength to shove him to the ground, wishing for so many reasons that he was stronger than he is.

"Leave me the fuck alone," he snarls.

Before his father can react, he is out of the tower and storming across the yard. He doesn't know where he's going, but everything else is perfectly, painfully lucid.

Austin sees the future ahead of him, unavoidable. He knows what he'll have to do.

He knows that, when the time comes, he'll do it alone.

PART TWO
RESISTANCE
CHAPTER TEN

"We can't keep on like this."

Ben, not wanting to be drawn, grunts noncommittally.

Foster slides back the mirrored door of a walk-in wardrobe and starts rummaging through its contents: first the neat row of women's clothes on hangers and then the boxes, mostly shoeboxes, arranged beneath. "Two of us killed. Not including the thing at the beginning, because okay, no one's saying that was Plan John's fault."

No, they say it was Ben's fault. Nando, after all, can hardly be held to blame for his own death.

"But everything since. What happened with Cooper and Dallas." From where he's kneeling before the wardrobe, Foster regards Ben warily.

Ben walks to a bedside cabinet and opens the drawer. There's a tattered paperback, on the cover a firefighter with his jacket open to reveal his bare chest, holding a woman in a negligee. There are some hairclips, a small flashlight, a pair of reading glasses, and two packets of tablets, one of painkillers and the other some drug Ben's never heard of. Ben takes the glasses and flashlight and stuffs them into the bag he carries. The tablets he slips into his own pocket, having made sure that Foster is no longer watching him.

Ben knows what's going on. At least, he hopes he does, hopes this is merely Foster desiring an in with Plan John. He's been angling for a share of the pie for weeks, setting himself up as leadership material – playing hero.

Yet Foster doesn't have the look of a hero. His jaw is weak and patterned with grey-tinged stubble, not clean-shaven and square like the firefighter's on the paperback cover. He's too close to forty and too out of shape to boast such flawless musculature. His eyes may have a certain steely quality, but that resolve tends to get lost in the sneer that hangs around the corners of his mouth.

Foster abandons the wardrobe. "Nothing in here. What are we going to turn up that we haven't already?"

"What do you suggest?" Ben asks carefully.

Foster doesn't reply. Instead, he walks to the window and stares down into the street.

He has a point, Ben thinks, but only halfway. There's no pinning Cooper's and Dallas's deaths on Plan John. Probably they got sloppy. No one knows, since all they found were the bodies. But the violence of their deaths, the way they'd been bitten and bludgeoned, *that* said Sickers, and so far the Sickers have proved an avoidable threat. Alone, they tend to run. In packs, which increasingly is how they travel, they're conspicuous enough to steer around. A couple of near run-ins have ended the moment a gun was fired.

These days, they're not what frightens Ben the most.

As for the growing redundancy of these interminable search parties, if it's hard to see the purpose in ransacking a town for the third time then the pills, flashlight, and glasses, and the other pieces in Ben's bag, raise doubts over how thorough the efforts were the first two times. As long as their supplies are holding out – and the stocks Plan John managed to accumulate in the run-up to the outbreak were considerable – it's difficult to imagine anyone taking these expeditions entirely seriously.

"The thing with a situation like this," says Foster, just as Ben has given up expecting a response, "is that everyone needs to know where everyone else stands. Or else assumptions get made."

"Maybe we should be looking farther afield," Ben ventures, since it's clear he needs to say something and he isn't ready to answer Foster's unspoken query.

"You talking about going into the city?" But that isn't what Foster's asking. What he means is: *Is Plan John talking about going into the city?*

"I'm just saying," Ben tells him.

Foster scrutinises him closely. Expanding the range of their looting is one of the pillars of his campaign. Foster's main reason seems to be that Plan John opposes it, no doubt because he fears that the army or some other vestige of government remains there and will be disinclined to turn a blind eye to a looting colony of former convicts.

A shout from the street saves Ben from trying to wriggle out of the question. "You pricks done up there?" It sounds like Landser.

Foster, still by the window, counters, "Unless you want a nice new dress."

"You keep it, Foster. Look nice for Plan John the next time he fucks your fat ass."

Foster, flushing, is evidently prepared to escalate the shouting contest. Getting a grip on himself, he instead stamps out of the room, calling back, "You fucking coming, Silensky?"

Ben, grinning at Foster's discomfort, pauses a moment to snatch up an item unearthed by his rummaging. He stuffs it into a pocket and hurries after. Outside, the other search parties are gathered around the two trucks, three groups of two men each. Aside from Foster, the only guard along is Houseman – though that differentiation, *guard*, is becoming less meaningful with each passing day.

Or so Ben had thought. He perceives now that Foster has gravitated toward Houseman and a couple of the older cons, Art Green and the English cook everyone calls Porridge. Everybody knows Houseman is on side with Foster, and likely the cons are too, both of them temperamentally unsuited to life under Plan John's rule. At any rate, if Foster is recruiting, they're where he would start.

Plan John won't tolerate factions. If Foster is getting away with anything, it's because Plan John intends to make an example of him. However this dissent shakes out, it will lead to trouble. And trouble has a way of exposing secrets. Ben has an excess of those; it seems to him that secrets are about all he has. The situation with Carlita can't go on forever, or even for much longer.

Foster and his little group have already occupied one of the trucks, with Houseman and Foster in the cab. Oxendine has settled into the driver's seat of the second vehicle. Ben clambers over the tailboard, joining Stokes and Silas in the back, and tries to make himself comfortable. Then they're off.

The worst of the summer heat is behind them, and the days are cooling rapidly. The wind whipping across the open rear of the truck has a particular chill, a premature taste of autumn. Ben tucks his parka round him, pulls the hood up, and leans against the corner where the tailboard meets the low sidewall. He closes his eyes.

He doesn't want to be drawn into conversation, or even to overhear. If something is going down, if sides are being picked, he doesn't want to be forced to choose.

Yet Plan John has chosen for him, and in so doing, has set the trap that's closing on him day by day. If Ben can't find a way to escape then sooner or later it will snap shut, and when it does, it won't be just him it tears apart. Carlita, Johnson, perhaps Aaronovich, even Kyle and Contreras, all of them are within its radius.

So could it be Foster? Could Foster be his chance, his route out?

Conceivably. If he plays things right. But the risk appalls him. This isn't a decision he dares make alone.

★   ★   ★

Doyle happens to be crossing the yard when the search parties come back. He is crossing from nowhere to nowhere. These days he has less and less to do, and feels the weight of inactivity more keenly than ever. Plan John doesn't send him out on the search parties. Plan John doesn't ask him, or tell him, to do anything.

I won't work for you. But I won't screw with you either.

Is this Doyle's punishment for standing up to the man? To get his wish? Because the price of not working for Plan John is not working, and these days not working is too close to not existing. Is that the message Plan John had intended to send through Doyle, by giving him his way?

Maybe, or maybe Doyle is overthinking it. As their de facto leader in a world grown generally and unignorably hostile, Plan John has a lot on his plate, and for that matter, a lot of plates in the air. So maybe Doyle just isn't as important to the man's schemes as he believes he is.

"Hey, wait up."

Recognising Ben Silensky's voice, Doyle hesitates before he slows. "What is it?" he inquires, not turning.

Catching up, Silensky delays until he can be sure no one is in earshot. "I need to see her, Johnson."

Doyle picks up his pace again, and Silensky falls into step behind him. "What the hell?" Doyle growls. "Have you forgotten what I said?"

"Look, I'm sorry. But I need to talk to her."

"There's no way."

"Hey, I mean it, I'm sorry, but—"

"I can take a message for you."

"*Johnson….*"

Doyle stops then and turns on him, suddenly not caring who might be watching. "What do you *want*, Silensky? Questions being asked? Because that's what will happen. Everything I do with this looks suspicious. And no one trusts anyone at the best of times."

"That's *why* I need to talk to her."

That gives Doyle pause. "How so?"

"I think there's something going on," Silensky says. He's pleading now, and his body language wills Doyle to start moving again. "And fuck, Johnson, anyway, it's been over a week since I last saw her. I mean, I appreciate all that you've done, but this is my girlfriend we're talking about. If someone notices, we'll tell them I needed to talk to Aaronovich." Silensky takes a deep breath. "I'm serious, I appreciate how you've helped us. I know how it could have been for Carlita if you hadn't done what you've done. I won't ask again, not like this."

Doyle glances rapidly around the yard. His eyes stray up to Plan John's balcony. He doesn't want to have this conversation. He doesn't want to examine his own motives. Hearing the sound of doors opening, he looks downward, toward the entrance of the Big House. Colton, one of the white skinheads who tend to hang together, is standing there waving, at Silensky rather than himself, Doyle realises.

Colton calls, "Hey Silensky, get your ass over here. Boss is asking for you."

"You better go," Doyle says.

"Yeah. Okay." Silensky looks disconsolate.

And what did you expect when you agreed to work for Plan John? Doyle thinks, knowing he's being unfair, that *agreed* implies the option of saying no.

He turns away. "I'll talk to her, all right? But I'm not promising. It's her risk, so it's her call. Come find me after dark."

★   ★   ★

Kyle is leaving the administrative wing as Johnson enters.

He's been given one of the bunk rooms reserved for the guards. There are plenty vacant. It's bleak, the walls of painted cinder blocks, the furniture metal and plastic, nothing like the home he's given up. But it's far better than sleeping in the cellblock, a possibility that fills him with dread. Right now, he's heading back to his job on the farm. As he understands it, the assignment was Plan John's suggestion, though Singh, who acts as farm supervisor, was the one to tell him. Kyle is fourteen years old; he can hardly go out on the search parties as his father does. He has no useful skills, no specialist knowledge, not in the way the others seem to have. At least farm work is something he can do.

"Are you going to see her?" Kyle asks, his voice hushed.

For a moment he thinks Johnson will ignore him, or deny it. Then he says, "Yes. You want to come?"

"Sure," Kyle agrees. If he's quick, he won't be missed from the farm.

More and more, he worries about Carlita. Of the three of them, she has come off worst. Kyle is constantly afraid, surrounded by men who ignore and intimidate him in equal measure, but he also has greater freedom than he's ever experienced. His father fell straight away into a position with Plan John, one everyone appears to envy. Carlita, though? Through no fault of her own, Carlita has found herself Funland's final prisoner.

Aaronovich isn't in her office, and Johnson doesn't look for her. He opens the upper door to the infirmary; Kyle knows he holds one key to it, the doctor the other. Johnson descends the stairs and Kyle follows. He knows as well that Carlita is supposed to keep the lower door locked from the inside, but when Johnson tries the handle, it opens.

When they enter, Carlita is sitting on her bed in the corner, knees tucked up to rest a book against, headphones on. Seeing them, her eyes light. She pauses her battered old CD player, lays the book facedown, and says, "Hello, Doyle. Hi, Kyle."

"Hi," Kyle responds, feeling suddenly out of place. Something about the extremity of Carlita's solitude makes any visit an intrusion.

"Carlita," Johnson greets her. He too seems uncomfortable.

Carlita swings her knees round, ending in a sitting position at the wall end of the bed. "You look worried, Doyle," she says. And then, "It's not about Ben is it?"

Johnson almost answers, and the answer he's about to give is clear on his face, but at the last moment he remembers Kyle, and says, "Can you wait outside a minute?"

"Okay," Kyle replies, hiding his irritation. What can Johnson say about his father to his father's girlfriend that he shouldn't hear? He knows how badly his dad misses Carlita, because Ben tells him, often. He knows he wants to spend more time with her than Johnson is ready to allow, and that Johnson blames the risks of those clandestine visits. The fact that he's probably right doesn't make his dad feel better about it, and so neither does Kyle.

Kyle watches them through the frosted glass, two distorted and inhuman-seeming shapes. Yet their flickering movements give them away: a blur of darkness when Johnson gestures; a streak of lighter brown when Carlita moves a hand; a shimmer when she nods, as she does frequently. She will try and look as though she's weighing the risk of discovery against the brief diversion of seeing her boyfriend. It's a sham. Her desperation is impossible to miss. Even if she thinks they'd be exposed, she'd say the same thing, simply because time with Ben offers a break from the unbearable monotony of her life.

Still, Kyle doesn't like how close she is to Johnson. There's no need for her to get that close. Absurdly, he feels relieved when they move apart, and when Johnson crosses the room to reopen the door.

Behind him, Carlita says, "I know you want to be careful, Doyle."

"I'll see how things look." Does something in his tone admit that her answer was not the one he'd hoped for? "If it seems safe...."

"Of course. You shouldn't put yourself at risk."

To Kyle, Johnson says, "I need to go talk to the doctor. Don't be too long, okay?"

"Sure." Kyle slips past him, blinking beneath the harsh electric light. Carlita turns her smile on him. He's known people to have different smiles for different circumstances, but Carlita has one, for everybody and any occasion. Warm, eager, indelicate, it always unsettles him. "Hey, Kyle," she says. "It's good of you to come."

Kyle shrugs. "I just ran into Johnson."

He's waited, but now he has nothing to say to her. Back before, they'd got on okay, had never been close. Why would they have been? Carlita is his dad's girlfriend. That doesn't make them anything to each other.

"What have you been up to?" Carlita asks, the smile hovering about her mouth. "Still working on the farm?"

She isn't really interested. She's merely bored – going crazy with boredom. She doesn't care who she talks to, whether it's Johnson or Kyle or his dad. Anyone is better than being alone.

Nevertheless, she *sounds* interested. And Carlita isn't unique in being lonely. Apart from his father, who he sees less these days than he ever has before, the only person Kyle has to talk to is Nando's uncle, Tito Contreras. And all Tito wants to talk about, sometimes tearfully, is Nando. Kyle has tried with Johnson's son, Austin, assuming at first that being almost the same age should be a bond between them, but Austin barely acknowledges his existence, and something about him frightens Kyle.

So he tells Carlita about the farm. He tells her about Tito, about Singh, who had been a farm supervisor for a while in his old life, and Torres who grew up on his family's farm in Mexico, and Art Green, the oldest of the cons, who knows nothing about farming and claims he was an architect back in the day, but seems to enjoy the work. Kyle tells her how he gets all the shitty jobs, how he doesn't mind so much, how they're already getting beans and potatoes and onions from the hard ground and hope for better next year.

"God," Carlita says, "I wish I could see it."

"It's no big deal."

"But to be in the open."

There's such desperation in her voice, such hunger. Through her manner more than the words, Kyle feels her claustrophobia, and it's unbearable. It raises the doubt that he might never be able to leave. "I need to get back," he says.

If she's hurt, if she realises she's driven him away, Carlita hides the fact well. "Okay. Hey, it's been nice talking to you, Kyle."

"Yeah," he agrees. "Only, I don't want to get into trouble...."

"No," Carlita says. "But come again, maybe? Sometime. If you can."

CHAPTER ELEVEN

"Do I have a choice?" Aaronovich inquires.

Johnson considers. "You have a say."

"You know my say," she tells him. "That woman is a ticking bomb. You should have sent them away the second I'd patched them up."

"I can't believe you mean that."

And do I? Aaronovich asks herself. *Do I mean it? Do I believe I do?* "You and I have the same job," she says. "To keep the inmates of White Cliff Penitentiary safe. Even if it's not White Cliff anymore, even if it's calling itself Funland. If word gets out that that woman is here – and word *will* get out, sooner or later – then this place is going to tear itself apart. It will burn to the ground. You'll be lucky if anyone survives that."

"You're a woman," Johnson says, "and I don't see anything burning." He only manages to weather the look of scorn she gives him for a moment. "All right. Fine. But if I'd sent them out of those gates, there isn't a chance they'd be alive now."

"There must be other groups. Other safe zones."

Though he can't possibly be certain, Johnson shakes his head. "Anyway, there's no point in debating this. What's done is done. The question is what happens next."

"You know my opinion on that too," Aaronovich says.

"That we keep her like a prisoner? That we treat her worse than the inmates were ever treated?"

"That whenever you let Ben Silensky in here, you bring them both a step closer to being discovered." Aaronovich sighs. "Johnson, you know what I think and I know you won't listen, so why don't we stop wasting our time?"

She's surprised by the aggrievement in Johnson's eyes. Is he frustrated that she won't agree with him, or is she doing him a disservice? Before Carlita's chaotic arrival, she would never have taken him for a man who'd play the authoritarian like this. Maybe he regards himself as a victim of circumstance, and maybe he's justified in doing so. Then again, doesn't that describe every last one of them?

"There's something else," Johnson says. "I'm worried about Austin."

Ah. So that's it. "Yes," Aaronovich assents, "you're right to be."

"Oh?"

"I tried to tell you when I first met him. The boy is traumatised. He's been through some ordeal."

"Has he spoken to you?" Johnson asks.

"No. I don't believe he will, and I don't need him to. It's there in everything he does. You know what I'm talking about, Johnson."

She wasn't intending to hurt him. She's genuinely surprised by the flicker of pain that twists his mouth. Johnson's face is normally so impassive that strong emotion completely deforms it, in a way he seems helpless to control.

"He won't talk to me," Johnson admits. He says the words with finality, as though he's already accepted a situation beyond his ability to repair. "I can't get through to him. I've no idea where he is most of the time."

He's scared of the boy, she can see that, or at any rate, scared of what he represents. In that, Aaronovich can sympathise. Even knowing that Austin is essentially a child, that trauma is what's locked him inside his sullenness and anger, she still finds reaching out to him difficult. Working in a prison doesn't encourage such instincts. Her job has taught her that boundaries are there for a reason, that while what's beneath the facade might be different, it isn't necessarily an improvement.

Anyway, Austin may be a child, but he isn't *her* child. "Well, you need to try harder," she says.

Doyle nods, weightily. The gesture doesn't persuade her that he will, only that he can't fail to recognise the need.

★   ★   ★

Austin doesn't think of what he does as hiding.

He doesn't think about it at all. Thinking implies choices, choices would mean options, and those are something he has none of. He does whatever he has to do.

Austin has a bunk room in the administrative wing, but he doesn't feel safe there. He can't sleep; he's hardly slept for more than a couple of hours a night since that first day. He isn't sure what he's afraid of. He doesn't think in terms of being afraid.

Kyle is working on the farm, but Austin has been given nothing to do. To Plan John, he seems not to exist. Which is okay; he doesn't *want* to exist. Not here. Not like this. If he could make himself invisible then he would, without hesitation.

So he explores. Funland was built to be somewhere else, to be White Cliff. And even White Cliff has been repurposed and reimagined time and again, shedding skins and growing new ones. Now, he doubts that a third of the place is used regularly. Maybe a quarter hasn't been touched in years. Instinct, more than any plan, tells him that those lost regions can be his: that there are two Funlands, one within the other, and that the closest he can get to disappearing would be to inhabit that second, shadow Funland.

But the buildings are dangerous. The cellblock, especially; nothing would convince him to set foot in there. Though he's made attempts to reconnoitre the administrative wing, it isn't large and he has no way to predict the movements of the former guards. His father, in particular, seems almost as lost and aimless as Austin himself. Of the three blocks, the one they call the Big House is least used. Whole sections have been given over to decay and dust. Yet the Big House is Plan John's, and the handful of incursions Austin has made left him terrified.

So he moved his exploration, more and more, to the walls, and the few smaller buildings nestling in their shade – and from the walls he made the discovery that has defined his efforts ever since. For it was there that he learned how the roofs of Funland were within his reach.

There's a ladder in a cage, halfway up the west wall of the Big House, nestled in the crook where it meets the cellblock. Working out a way to get that ladder down, let alone quietly, has become a mission in itself. Clearly there should be a pole, but that could be anywhere. Fortunately, stealing in Funland is easy, so long as you don't want things that others deem valuable, which means food, ammunition, fuel, and whatever small luxuries can be found. All the items Austin has stolen are worthless to anyone except him, and none of them will be missed.

Austin considers the results of his handiwork. The twine came from the farm store, which isn't even kept locked. The same source furnished the broken hand fork he's bent into something like a grappling hook. The sponges he's taped tight around the prongs to deaden the sound came from the kitchens, where there are literally hundreds, packed in boxes. No one comes round here, and the adjacent end of the cellblock is long abandoned, probably this portion of the Big House too, but Austin isn't about to take risks. There's no possible explanation for what he's doing.

His initial try strikes off the wall with a dull *chink* that makes him wince. The second catches the ladder, only to deflect, as does the third. The fourth, however, snares a rung and holds. He isn't certain how the mechanism works, or whether brute force will achieve anything. Still, Austin puts all his weight upon his homemade rope. At first, there's no result, but a shift of footing rewards him with a sudden click, and a rattle like a freight train in miniature. An instant later and the lowest rung is near enough to the ground that, with a jump, he can just reach it.

Austin's heart is hammering. Sweat glazes his brow. It's a good kind of excitement, though, maybe even a good kind of fear. He's *done* something. This belongs to him.

He climbs quickly more than carefully. But at the top he makes an effort to keep low, as he flops through the gap in the parapet that rings the roof of the Big House. Beside the ladder is a crank, and when he turns it, the ladder retreats complainingly into its housing. With that done, still crouched on hands and knees, Austin surveys his new kingdom.

The landscape is an inhuman one, like somewhere manufactured by giant insects and then deserted. The floor is layered in chipped gravel. Pipes and ductwork rise, dip, and intertwine without apparent logic. Ahead, a low shack juts, with a metal door imbedded in its front. Altogether, the rooftop gives the impression of being unfinished, as perhaps it is. Every part of Funland, after all, has the air of an experiment abandoned before reaching its intended conclusion.

Regardless, this place appeals to some craving deep in Austin. This, he knows, is what he's been looking for these recent weeks. This is what he's sought in Funland's abandoned corners. He makes a circuit, crouching so as to be hidden from the yard below, committing each feature to memory. When he arrives back at the ladder, he sets out again, even more slowly, pausing often to tease out some feature or judge its relation to the building below.

By the end of the second circuit, one feature above all others is gripping his attention, filling him with sickly excitement. At half a dozen points, wire gratings cover orifices into the building's sinews and cavities. Three of them are large enough for him to get inside. He's checked the screws, and he thinks they'll come off.

Austin had wanted a place of his own and he's found one. What if, close by, is somewhere even better? Somewhere he can't ever be reached? Yet it feels hazardous to press ahead now, as if, after what he's ventured today, anything more would be a danger too far.

Then again, perhaps he doesn't need to. Time is on Austin's side. Because the ladder, the rooftop, the vents, and whatever lies beyond them — all of this is his and his alone.

CHAPTER TWELVE

Doyle tries to calculate the risk he's about to take, and what the cutoff will be, at what point he will say no to Silensky.

Except that, if he's honest with himself, that isn't the question. So, at what point will he say no to Carlita?

If he hasn't got there yet, perhaps he never will.

He's been up on the gate tower all evening, as he was on that day when everything changed. From here he'd watched the ambulance swerve, tumble, and slide, staring uncomprehendingly as it delivered a world of problems right into his lap. Since neither the cons nor the guards ever come up here, apparently not caring what happens outside Funland's walls, the tower is the one place Doyle is guaranteed privacy.

Despite two deaths at their hands, no one much seems to consider the Sickers a threat anymore. Dallas and Cooper died, the reasoning goes, because they got stupid. Their deaths have served to make everyone a little more vigilant, and that's all well and good. Thanks to them, the problem has essentially solved itself.

Doyle believes differently. From his perspective, there are two possibilities: you regard the Sickers as still being people, in which case they're dangerous; or else they are something different, something worse, and then they're both dangerous and unquantified. So he keeps to his tower and looks out and wonders what might be occurring beyond that distant line of timber.

Or so he tells himself. Today, at any rate, Doyle has hardly been seeing anything. Had Sickers advanced in droves upon the walls, he could easily have missed the spectacle. Instead, he's been thinking: about Silensky, about Carlita, about what Aaronovich said to him, what Plan John may be up to – the entire damned mess. And now it's too dark to see, and a day's thinking has got him nowhere.

He hears a sound, shockingly loud amid the silence, and it takes Doyle a moment to realise it's merely the rattle of a throat being cleared.

When he looks down, Ben Silensky is just an outline in the darkness. Doyle hadn't noticed his approach. They're all getting pretty good at navigating the yard without light; funny how quickly the mind adapts, how eagerly it slews off the habits of civilisation. Or maybe, Doyle thinks, not remotely funny.

"Thought I might find you here," Silensky calls up.

"Keep your voice down," Doyle hisses. He descends the tower stairs, resisting the urge to lock the door behind him out of habit.

"Sorry," Silensky says once they're beside each other. He's lowered his voice to a whisper. Doyle can make out his features: the thin, down-turned mouth, the sleepy-lidded eyes perpetually on the verge of squinting, his whole face posed for an inquiry that never quite comes.

The only lights are the ones above the doors of the cellblock and the Big House. One of the more surprising things they salvaged early on was a wind turbine, which Nguyen has rigged in the grounds of the farm and managed to cable into White Cliff's existing grid. It's taken some strain off the gas generator, but not enough, and electric lighting has rapidly become yet another resource to ration. Nonetheless, Plan John has prohibited absolute darkness as well, perhaps wary of what it might breed.

That caution, however, does not extend to the administrative wing. It can be recognised solely by its absence, as a solid rectangle of blackness. Doyle leads the way toward it.

"So?" Silensky says, his voice still muted.

"So, what?"

"So, we're on? I can see her?"

Doyle feels no need to reply. Their direction should be sufficient answer. A query of his own has been eating at him all day, and though he doesn't expect Silensky to tell him the truth, he asks anyway. "Before, you said you thought something might be going down. Were you talking about Foster?"

"That was a dumb thing to say." Silensky sounds uncomfortable.

"Because it was true?"

"Because I don't know anything. Foster was just talking, the way he does. He was talking and I was worrying about Carlita and I got spooked."

"So you *don't* think something's happening?"

"Jesus, Johnson, how would I know? I'm not anyone."

"Keep your voice down," Doyle reminds him.

You're scared, he decides. *More than you were a few hours ago.* Some encounter has rattled Silensky, rattled him badly. If it wasn't Foster then it's Plan John. Doyle nearly says, *You're someone enough to be Plan John's bodyguard of choice*, for that's the role it was decreed Silensky should occupy, almost as soon as he arrived. Plan John's reasoning has been a matter of conjecture, since he isn't a man to share his motives.

Doyle has his own theories. Silensky is an outsider, and the manner of his arrival, even in the redacted version Doyle himself has circulated, has meant that status will stay with him for a long time. Carlita, of course, has been erased from the official history, and, to keep anybody from asking the wrong questions, it seemed useful to emphasise Silensky's responsibility for the disastrous events he's now the only adult survivor of. That in turn has made him vulnerable, and vulnerability is what Plan John thrives on. This way, Silensky is both beholden to him and useful.

Does that make Silensky loyal? Doyle is still working that one out. If nothing else, he's loyal enough to keep himself covered. Doyle could press, but there's no point. Silensky will simply clam up.

"I've known Foster longer than you have," Doyle says. "If there *is* something going down, don't be so sure he can protect you. Don't be so sure he'll even try."

Or Plan John, either, Doyle thinks. *He'll look out for you for exactly as long as you're useful and not a second more.* Especially given that Ben Silensky has one further virtue. He's disposable.

Envisioning Plan John, Doyle looks up instinctively, as he has a dozen times since they set out across the yard. Howard, however, isn't on his balcony tonight. A good thing, except that there are plenty of routes by which this assignation can reach his ear. Silensky's absence alone, in the hermetically sealed environs of Funland, might be enough to spark rumours.

Too late to worry. Too late, at least, to do anything that would assuage his worries. Doyle has a bad vibe about this, but then he has bad vibes about so many things these days. Really, what cause is there for any other kind? As he pushes through double doors into the administrative wing, he can feel the first stirrings of a headache coming on. Though rationally he knows that superstition is a privilege he can't allow himself, Doyle has grown to associate his headaches with trouble, like a buildup of pressure before a storm.

It's not a sign, he thinks. *Damn you, a headache is not some portent.*

But he can't quite make himself believe.

★   ★   ★

At the last instant, Ben feels almost uncontrollably nervous. On top of the bubbling unease he's already suffering, that anxiety makes acid rise perilously toward his gullet. Is he scared of his own girlfriend now? Yet, in that moment, he's afraid of everything.

Johnson regards him without concern or interest, but with distant impatience. "I'll wait upstairs," he says. "Don't be long."

"Sure." Ben can't stop his mind returning to the meeting with Plan John, and as soon as it does, he begins to panic.

Time we find out what's going on.

Plan John talks at Ben sometimes, never to him, but sometimes, not often, at him. When he does, his monologues have the air of free-flowing thought, jazzlike in the way they set up ideas and roll them around and test them against each other, drifting from subject to subject before looping back to try a seemingly abandoned concept in a new light. At first, Ben felt he was being invited to share an intimate secret, a special, threatening feeling. By the third time, he'd come to understand that Plan John tells him nothing, not one syllable, that he doesn't want him to hear.

Now, Ben has no desire to ever be taken into Plan John's confidence. Whatever Plan John tells him, it's not intended for his benefit. It doesn't raise him up. Or if it does, it's only because – step by step, word by word – he's ascending the gallows stairs.

Time we find out what's going on, wouldn't you say, Mr. Silensky?

Ben shudders, and lets himself into the infirmary.

Carlita is sitting on her bed. "Hey baby," she croons. She's made an effort for him: worn a skirt and a clean blouse, a skimpy, semitranslucent thing, and neatened her hair, pinning glossy strands into some kind of order. Yet up close, her skin smells sour. When he moves to kiss her, so does her breath.

There's a tub in one corner, for washing. On those rare occasions when their strictly rationed power is used to pump water from the well, Aaronovich will let Carlita shower briefly in her apartment. Neither can emulate the standards of hygiene they both took for granted mere weeks ago. Ben has had to grow used to irregular bucket baths, and likely he doesn't smell a great deal better. But at least he hasn't been sealed in one room until its odours began to permeate his clothes, his hair, his very flesh.

"It's good to see you," Carlita says, almost hesitantly. "These last few days...it's been so bad."

"I know," he replies – and he does. In that moment, he appreciates the nature of her existence with painful clarity.

"But, Ben—"

"I know, okay?" he repeats, his helplessness turning to vexation. "I know how this is for you. But what do you want me to do? Either we try to get out of here, and if somehow we make it, all we'll have to worry about is no food and Sickers and drinking infected water and a million other things, or we stay and deal. It's not like any of this was my idea."

Suddenly Carlita is on her feet. "Don't you *dare*."

"What?"

"Fernando. You don't criticise him. Not a word. He was a good man, he did his best for us, and maybe if he hadn't...if he hadn't, then—"

"What? This would all be different if he hadn't died? Plan John would have set us up with a nice little place in the Big House?" Ben slams a hand against the wall, not marking the tiles but jolting needles through his fingers. "Hell," he mutters over the pain. "I didn't come here to argue."

Carlita sits again, crosses her legs, and tests the edge of a nail with her teeth. "Just, please, don't badmouth Fernando," she says, with a touch less anger. "He did his best for us."

I wonder if he'd have gone to such trouble if his cousin had been some fat old sow? Ben thinks, but this time he has the sense to keep his mouth shut.

After a minute, Carlita says, "Okay. You didn't come here to argue." She teases at the nail again, and then lets her hands flop in her lap. "So... Doyle said you're worried about something."

Ben nods, trying to arrange his thoughts. He's worried about so much. It's hard to recall what apprehension first tipped him over into deciding the risk of coming was worth taking. That would be Foster, but Foster has already been superseded, and by an entire order of magnitude.

"I think Plan John is going to talk to one of the guards," he says. "I mean, *talk* to. Whoever he picks, he might hurt them if he doesn't get the answers he wants. It won't be Foster, because that would be a declaration of war. That leaves three candidates."

Carlita's eyes go wide. "Oh no."

"Look, it's okay. Probably he'll go for Houseman. But if he doesn't...."

If he doesn't, that leaves the only other two men in Funland who know you exist.

He realises how thoughtless he's been. The fear remains there in her eyes, making them deeper, darker. "It's okay," Ben says again. "Whatever happens, I'll be there. I'll keep it in check."

Still feeling her tension, endeavouring to press it down, Ben sits beside Carlita, straddling the narrow gurney-cum-bed to face her. He brushes a hand over her knee. "Baby. Really. It's okay." Liking the tautness of the skin there, he leaves his hand on the inside of her leg, where knee meets thigh, and massages with the tips of his fingers. She gives him a faint smile.

"I'm just worried, is all," he says. "I wanted to warn you to be extra cautious. I should be able to keep a check on the Plan John situation. But on top of that, I'm pretty sure Foster's planning some kind of a move. He's not even being careful anymore."

"Perhaps he thinks it's too late to be careful."

Ben tries to judge whether there's something disparaging in the statement. "Well, it's easy for Foster. He's not having to play nice with Plan John every day." He wishes she'd understand his predicament, and is forced to accept that her own circumstances preclude any possibility of empathy. So instead, he says, "But I wanted to see you, too. This is hard for me, you know? I miss you. I have to keep up this pretence, walk this line. I don't know what the right thing to do is sometimes."

He's still massaging Carlita's inner thigh, and he discovers, almost with shock, that he's starting to get aroused. How long has it been? Two weeks or more. "What do I do without my *bomboncita* to look out for me?"

Carlita smiles at the pet name, genuinely this time, and places one hand on his cheek. "What have you said to Foster?"

"Nothing. I didn't want to commit to anything I can't get out of."

She strokes his cheek with her fingertips. "I think you should talk to him. Maybe he'll help us, if things go his way."

"Foster's an asshole." Moving his own hand farther up the inside of her thigh, Ben leans in closer. "We can't trust him."

"Worse than Plan John?"

He shakes his head, not so much disagreeing as not knowing. Such men, the dangers they pose, are beyond his ability to compare. Eager to change the subject, he remembers what's in his pocket. With the hand that isn't on her thigh, he draws out the bright crimson panties he unearthed during the search. "Hey," he says. "I saw these and thought of you."

Carlita gives a small, fragile laugh. "I'm not sure they're my size."

He hadn't considered that. "I guess not," he agrees, and tilts his fingers, so that the panties – absurd-seeming now, not at all sexy – slide free and to the floor. Then, lust and frustration flowing abruptly together, he edges nearer and kisses her hard on the mouth. At the same time, his fingers stray farther, brushing cotton and the tight coils around her pubis. He's pleased to find that both are warmly damp, more pleased when she presses into the kiss and groans softly. With his right hand, he cups her breast, outside her blouse to begin with and then sliding his fingers up within. He marvels at how small and perfect it is, how adamantine the nipple beneath his thumb.

She breaks the kiss first. "So you'll talk to him?"

There's a note to the question, yet in that moment, he can't even remember who *him* is. Ben stays exactly where he is, Carlita's face close enough for him to feel the stale wash of her breath. His right hand still envelops her breast. The fingers of his left are pressed in the tangle of her pubic hair, the tips just barely inside her. "Sure," he says, struggling to make the word sound normal. "I'll talk to Foster."

"Mm. Good." Then her mouth is over his again, her tongue hunting, and simultaneously she edges forward against his fingers. Her own hand fumbles at his jeans. She tries to open his belt, fails, and settles for dragging down the zipper. She shuffles forward, so that his fingers are partly inside her and partly between the cheeks of her ass. She draws his cock out, not gently.

"Oh. Fuck." Ben frees his left hand, and uses both together to work clumsily at the buttons of her blouse. She doesn't help him. Her hand is still around the root of his cock, her face still pushed into his, her kisses so furious that they're nearly bites. He finally gets the blouse off and reaches for her, a thumb on the underside of each breast. Like that, he lifts her. She claws up her skirt and puts both hands in his lap, so as to guide him.

When he enters her, she sobs. He feels the noise before he hears it, battling to liberate itself from the cage of her ribs.

Ben slides to get the wall at his back, bringing her with him. She's already moving against him, quickly, violently, her breath coming in fierce explosions. He thrusts to meet her, but he can't find any rhythm to her sudden passion.

The gurney creaks. He's afraid it will pull away from the wall. There's something alarming in the unpredictability of the pleasure hammering from his groin. He wonders if he can slow Carlita somehow, calm her. Ben slides his hands down to her ass and clasps it. But he has no purchase. Her ass and the small of her back are clammy with sweat. He attempts to edge his arms up, to cradle her.

Then she's pulling out of his grip, retreating into the corner where she was when he entered, legs once more tucked up, struggling into her blouse. When he catches her eye, she looks as if she's about to cry.

"I'm sorry," Carlita says.

"What?" He doesn't understand.

"I'm sorry, I'm just…."

"Just *what?*"

"It's…here, like this. This place. Like a dungeon."

It seems to Ben as though his emotions are so many and so jumbled that picking one out and interpreting how he's feeling would be impossible. Then he recognises that, stronger than the anger or confusion or the curious impression of loss, is embarrassment. His erection, the fact that it's still there, strikes him as shameful. He tucks his cock back inside his jeans and emulates her posture, hauling his knees against his chest.

"Shit, Carlita." He doesn't know what he means, whether it's a complaint or an apology. He feels ridiculous.

"How can I be here, all day long," she whispers. "All day, alone, no one to talk to and nothing to do, and then want to fuck? I try and think about it. To feel excited. But it's like something out of another world. Afterward, I can't even wash. I'm sick of sweat and filth."

Ben gets down from the gurney. "Look," he says, "I only came to tell you to be careful." His voice sounds small to his own ears. "I'll talk to Foster. Maybe I can get on his good side."

Carlita nods. "I'm sorry, baby. If I can just get out of here...."

She pauses to fix her skirt and the last two buttons of her blouse. The gesture seems to Ben like a door slamming shut.

"If I could get out," she finishes softly, "it would all be different."

CHAPTER THIRTEEN

The headache has come, as Doyle knew it would.

Except that headache is so small a word. Rachel had claimed sometimes that she got migraines. That's closer, but not much. What Doyle needs is a word that conveys the unfeasible weight, as though his head has been occupied by some alien matter that the space of his skull is too narrow to contain. The pain is almost secondary to that sheer sense of wrongness, as if his cranium should split like a rotted fruit at any moment. Still, the pain is bad enough, a roving drill bit churning at the tender meat of his cerebrum.

It doesn't mean anything, he thinks.

He can't persuade himself. If nothing else, the headaches mean he isn't coping, not as he's used to believing he can cope. They started around when Plan John's regime began in earnest, when Doyle had gone from being a guard, at least nominally, to whatever this tenuous new existence is. So at the very least they mean that this is how his brain chooses to deal with stress, the sort of stress that there's no way out from under.

Perhaps all it means is you're falling apart.

Yet Doyle has spent a lot of time observing Funland, maybe more than anyone apart from Plan John himself. There are others who comprehend its individual components far better than he does: Foster understands the cons more than Doyle can or wants to, and Plan John has his files, his secret histories, all the information he's stolen and extorted to build his little commune. In those terms, most of the men here aren't much to Doyle beside names.

But as an organism, an entity, on that level he understands Funland. And today, something is off.

He knows it, but knowing isn't enough. Doyle isn't about to give in to a hunch, or to a headache either. All the same, those two ingredients together make rational analysis difficult. If he stares at a spot, the headache kicks like a horse. If he tries to think rather than feel, his intuition plays havoc with his nerves.

For some reason, also, Doyle's mind keeps going back to Rachel. Seeing his ex-wife again all those weeks ago has shaken him, stirring recollections that haven't quite settled. On a gut level, watching her drive away, leaving their son behind, had made real their separation in a manner that nothing before ever had.

Unsought, memories float up. Often during the months of bile and recrimination that ushered in their divorce, she had accused him of being aloof, withdrawn. What was the phrase she'd used? *Emotionally autistic.* Then it had seemed to him that she had enough emotion for the both of them. Now? Here he is, keeping to his tower – of ugly white concrete rather than ivory, but perhaps the spirit is the same – and observing, always observing, always keeping inside his head.

Could that be why it aches so violently? Is the reason his skull feels like it's splintering, sending shards through the pulp of his brain, that he knows the only way he'll find the answers he seeks is to get involved? To stop pretending he's still a prison guard on the walls of White Cliff State Penitentiary. To step down, once and for all, into Funland.

Maybe, somewhere along the line, he has already made that decision. Maybe, without realising it, Doyle has accepted that he might have to get his hands dirty.

*   *   *

After Carlita, it's probably his Uncle Tito that Kyle feels most sorry for.

Tito Contreras seems so lost. It's there in the way he talks, the way he moves, as if he's found himself in the wrong place and nothing he does will put him back on track. While he's never said as much, Kyle has a feeling that Tito blames himself for what happened to Nando. In fact, when he speaks of his nephew, it's generally Nando as a child, Nando as a teenager, not the adult who died a horrifying death a few dozen feet from where they now stand.

But then, no one mentions *that* Nando. So little time has passed, and yet he's virtually ceased to exist. Kyle can barely remember what he looked like.

Of course, Tito isn't really Kyle's uncle. But that's how he refers to himself, and the prospect of family, even illusory family, is not something Kyle would willingly turn down. It would be too much to say they've grown close; that lost quality of Tito's makes any real familiarity impossible. Nevertheless, Kyle is glad that they're both working the farm. Tito's presence makes him feel safer, though rationally he appreciates that Contreras – the oldest of the guards by a decade at least, and looking older for his deep wrinkles and shockingly white hair – is in no position to protect him, or even himself.

That truth strikes Kyle forcibly when he sees his dad appear around the distant corner of the cellblock: the corner near the Big House, the direction no one ever comes from. Kyle knows, without knowing how, that something is wrong. What he recognises can't be in Ben's face, because that's only a blur at such a distance. Maybe it's some subtly off-kilter property of his movement.

"Hi, Dad," Kyle says uncertainly, as Ben threads a course among discarded tools, beds of ragged crops, and piled rocks emptied from the bitter black earth.

"Kyle," Ben acknowledges, not looking at him. To Tito he says, "Contreras, you mind coming with me?"

"Yes, I mind." Tito doesn't sound scared, exactly. "I have work to do."

"Don't make this difficult," Ben says. "Plan John wants to talk to you. Don't make it into a thing."

"Howard has no reason to talk to me."

Ben's face contorts. "Fuck, Contreras! That's not your call. Are you coming or not?"

On sudden impulse, Kyle steps forward, inserting himself between the two men. "Dad," he says, "what's going on?"

The glare Ben throws Kyle's way roots him to the spot; it's so filled with resentment and rage. "Nothing."

It's not nothing, Kyle thinks – desires urgently to say. He's frightened of his dad, more so than Tito himself seems to be. That unnerves him all the more because he's rarely been frightened of his father. His dad hasn't hit him often, or lost his temper often, or got mean drunk often. This new persona is unprecedented and so much worse for that.

"All right," Tito says, "I'll come."

Kyle is struck by a sickening revelation: Tito is going along for his sake. Tito is trying to protect Kyle from his dad. Kyle's stomach clenches at the thought, and he wants to argue with both of them, to tell his father to leave Tito alone and to tell Tito that his father won't hurt him, that whatever he's doing, this isn't the person he is.

It's too late. Ben has already reached the upper edge of the farm, and Tito Contreras is trailing behind him, something defeated in how he drags his feet. And neither of them would have listened to Kyle in any case.

★   ★   ★

When he hears voices approaching from the direction of the farm, Austin's first reaction is to hide. This entire corner is waste ground, littered with the debris of White Cliff's last round of redesign: broken scabs of concrete, fences of rebar probing through the desiccated earth. No one goes by this way. Now they are, and they will notice his ladder, they'll come up and turf him out of this place he's called his own. How could he have been so stupid? Nowhere is safe; nowhere can be his.

He has it wrong. He sees that quickly. It's easier to think clearly on the rooftop, as if the air is different up there, not laced with those terrors and suspicions that hang close to the ground, which everybody but him seems to thrive on without ever perceiving.

The men approaching aren't talking about him. They have no idea he's here. They'll walk past the ladder and never notice it, because that's what everyone except Austin has done. They'll never consider that there's another world, so nearby, just waiting to be claimed.

There are two speakers, and with effort Austin can identify them both. There aren't many people in Funland he knows by name. No one has exactly introduced themselves, and what Austin has learned he's learned like this, by overhearing. But he's familiar with the name Ben Silensky. He's always spoken of with contempt, and usually with outright hatred. Silensky crashed his way into Funland, literally, and his punishment has been a coveted position at Plan John's side.

The other man, Austin knows him as well. The Mexican, the guard with the white hair. He stands out. He's related to the man who died in that same accident, whose name Austin can't remember or has never heard.

It's the first man, Silensky, the one who works for Plan John, who's in control. Austin can discern that from their voices, even before he makes out words. He presses close to the parapet, forehead against the flaking brick. He distinguishes the moment they round the end of the cellblock from how the sound changes and the words become abruptly clear.

"Look," Silensky snaps, "be careful what you say."

"About what?" the guard asks. "Why don't you just tell me what this is?"

They're passing right beneath the ladder. As sure as he'd initially been that they'd look up and spot it, Austin is now utterly convinced that they won't. He could stand, watch them walk by, and they would never see him.

"Because if you don't know anything—" The end of Silensky's reply is sliced away by the corner of the Big House.

"Is this about—" the guard says, and there's a name Austin can't catch. Carlos? Alberto? No, Carlita. The name of the woman who came on the night of the storm, the one Austin's father is hiding.

"No, of course not," Silensky says, "and don't you—"

But they're practically whispering, moving up the flank of the Big House, and however hard he strains, Austin can't catch the last words. Moments later, there's the opening and closing of a door, then only silence, weighty and unnatural.

Regardless, Austin has heard enough. Not to make sense of, for Austin knows so little of Funland's inner workings that he can't imagine any subject they'd discussed having much importance to him. But it's enough to teach him a lesson: that there's power in having a place nobody's aware of. There's power in secrets; power, even, in hiding, if hiding means he sees and hears things he's not intended to. And power is a currency. Maybe it can buy him what he needs.

If he told Plan John about the woman, Carlita, would Plan John help him? No, Austin is too afraid. And what would his dad do, what would Plan John do to his dad? There must be more to find out, though. This doesn't need to end here. If he tried, really tried, what else might he learn?

But not from a rooftop. Austin's eyes hang on the ductwork, the silvery conduits, the latticed grilles, the barely visible indents of screw heads, so easy to remove.

Inside the Big House – that would be a different story.

CHAPTER FOURTEEN

Ben attempts to read Plan John's face and fails. His expressions are all in code; they don't mean the same as other people's do. Currently he's smiling. Ben has learned that Plan John's smiles are dangerous. When he's genuinely happy, he laughs, a roaring, reverberating blare. When he smiles, that can mean anything.

There are just the three of them in the room: Plan John, Ben, and Contreras. Ben has rarely been in here without one of the cons present; it isn't in Plan John's way of doing things to entrust his life to one bodyguard. Does this suggest that Plan John trusts him? Perhaps he merely distrusts Ben less. Of everybody in Funland, he's had the least opportunity to fall under Foster's disruptive influence. To Plan John, who knows nothing of Carlita, it must seem like he has the least motive too.

An advantage of sorts, Ben thinks. But not much of one in the end. Because his secrets aren't a strength, they're a thousand needling weaknesses, and right now he feels each of them keenly.

"You took your time," Plan John says. There's no apparent judgement in the observation, only curiosity. "I hope you didn't give our young friend any trouble, Mr. Contreras?"

Contreras appears to consider. Is his nerve slipping? Maybe he's finally realised what Ben understood intuitively: that bravery has no value in this room. If Plan John wants you hurt, then you get hurt. "No," Contreras insists. "No trouble."

"Well," says Plan John, "I've managed to keep myself amused. I've been having a thumb through your file. Not exactly a distinguished career, but points due, I suppose, for tenacity. What qualities keep a man like you in such a job?"

"You've got my file?" Contreras asks. For the first time, he sounds really nervous.

"Of course. I have everyone's file. Is this not my prison?"

It's clear in Contreras's countenance that he would dearly love to argue that claim. What *did* bring him here, Ben wonders; what's kept him here? Tito Contreras is not a young or a healthy man. They would surely have had to retire him out soon. There are easier ways to make a living than prison guard, even in the relatively safe environment that White Cliff had been.

"I guess," Contreras says, "I just don't get on so well with change."

"Indeed," Plan John agrees. "Tenacity, like I said. Your perseverance must have been particularly tested in these last few weeks."

"I suppose it hasn't been easy for anyone."

"So true. And everyone reacts to adversity differently. Some choose to push against it. Some, like yourself, sit quietly and hope it will go away. Which reminds me." Plan John slaps a palm to his forehead in exaggerated recollection. "Mr. Silensky, shouldn't you show our guest to a seat?"

Plan John's expressions are a code, but he has others. This is one of them. They have half a dozen of these phrases, which Ben has been made to memorise.

Ben grabs Contreras by one sleeve and his collar and, relying on surprise to supplement his strength, flings him hard to the ground. Contreras lets out a pained gasp.

"Stay down," Ben says. "It'll go easier."

Plan John gets to his feet. He is huge, not only fat-big but tall, well in excess of six feet. "I'd like to think that Funland is something special," he says. "Outside our walls, the world is falling apart… what's even left. In here, there's order. We have food and water. The lights stay on. All of that is me, my doing."

Plan John moves free of his desk. There's barely room for him to pass. He steps around its edge, props himself upon one corner. Ben is sure he hears the lacquered wood complain.

"We have a good thing here. But there are those who can't appreciate it. I understand that; it takes all kinds. In fact, I designed Funland that way. A little adversity is beneficial. Nevertheless, I can't allow dissent to get out of check. So your role, Mr. Contreras, is to tell me who they are and what they are doing."

Contreras is endeavouring to hoist himself up against the wall, but stops when Ben takes a pace toward him. "I don't...I'm sorry, I don't...who *who* is? I don't know what you mean."

Plan John picks up the cardboard folder he'd been holding when they came in, gives it one more glance, and returns it to the desk. "I also have your medical records. Your file says you suffer from arthritis in the joints of your hands."

Contreras manages to nod despite his posture. "Yes. But I can still work."

"Put your left hand out," Plan John tells him.

"I...what? I don't know...."

"Your left hand. Flat on the floor."

"I'm sorry, I just, I don't...."

With a sigh, Plan John beckons Ben. No need for subterfuge this time, his implication is clear. Ben kneels beside Contreras, pins his left arm under one knee, and holds the wrist out flat, splaying Contreras's fingers on the greasy carpet. Contreras hardly resists, and his flesh, where Ben grips it, feels like moist putty.

"Now," says Plan John. "What's happening in my prison that I should be cognisant of? A vague question, I admit, but a straightforward one. Tell me whatever comes to mind. You needn't worry about boring me."

"The f-fact is," Contreras stutters, "if there was something, if there was, I wouldn't be told because I'm nobody, and I'm not...they don't talk to me. They don't tell me what's going on. Why would they? So how would I know?"

Plan John places the flat of his heel on the arch of Contreras's hand, directly upon the knuckles.

"Oh god, I don't...ah...."

His contribution no longer needed, Ben lets go and steps aside. "Contreras," he warns.

"I'm nobody!"

"Everyone sees things," Plan John observes. "Everyone hears things. Sometimes they don't even realise they've done so. That is, by the way, a mere portion of my weight. About, oh, a quarter, I'd say."

"*Please....*"

"Your file also notes that you're Catholic. I have at least two traits in common with your god, Mr. Contreras: your fate lies wholly in my grasp, and I help only those who help themselves." Plan John wriggles his heel, and Contreras gasps, and then sobs. "Concentrate. Calm down. Tell me something I want to hear."

Don't say it, Ben thinks. *Don't say anything. Keep your damned mouth shut.* Even Foster's little rebellion seems too dangerous a topic. There are so many threads, and in Funland's close confines, who can judge which ones might lead back to Ben himself? He is behind Plan John now, out of his view, and so he tries to catch Contreras's gaze, to mouth a warning. But Contreras's entire attention is focused on his own hand.

"Carlita," he whispers, through clenched teeth. "Is that it? What you want? I don't know...."

With no conscious impetus, Ben's eyes jolt to Plan John. Ben feels as though his heart has stopped beating, or perhaps he's caught in the moment between beats, a moment that refuses to end. He can't see Plan John's face, but there's some new property in his posture, an incredible alertness.

"Repeat what you just said," Plan John directs. "Speak clearly."

Ben's absent heartbeat comes then, a sorry, ineffectual flutter.

"Nothing." Contreras's enunciation is marginally more audible. "No, nothing. I'm sorry."

Plan John raises his foot and dashes it hard upon Contreras's fingers. Contreras screams.

"Don't lie to me," Plan John says.

Contreras whimpers. He tries to inspect his fingers, but Plan John's foot, wrapped in the crisp leather of his ginormous shoe, is pinning his hand so completely as to hide it from view.

"A woman," Contreras sobs. "Hiding. A woman."

Plan John removes his foot. "Good," he says. "That's good. Keep cooperating, Tito. Where? Who's behind this?"

"The infirmary." Contreras's voice is like something broken and crudely pieced together. "She's in the infirmary."

"Yes. Good. And who?"

Finally, Ben manages to catch Contreras's eyes. They are startlingly white, the pupils contracted to pinpricks. *Johnson*, Ben mouths. *Doyle Johnson.* He makes the words again and again, not even caring anymore if Plan John should turn and see. *Johnson. Doyle. Johnson. Doyle....*

"Johnson," Contreras whispers. "It's Johnson."

*   *   *

Kyle knows his dad has made mistakes. He knows his dad has done some bad things.

You can do bad things and not be a bad person. That's the truth. And doesn't everybody get it wrong occasionally? His dad hasn't had an easy time. Still, he's done his best. And in the end, he turned his back on the mistakes, for Carlita and, Kyle hopes, for the sake of his son.

His dad wouldn't have chosen to work for Plan John. That hadn't been his choice. If it had been, Ben would have turned the job down, for Carlita and for Kyle. Or maybe he'd have said yes, but only so that he could protect them better. Maybe he had a choice and he said yes and that was why.

Maybe it was a choice that's just gone really, really wrong.

His dad isn't a bad man. But he's made mistakes, and sometimes he still makes mistakes, and this, this is one of them.

Because Tito Contreras knows about Carlita. It had all come out on the first night. Tito had been asking too many questions, and too many of the *wrong* questions. There had been him and Kyle and Ben, together in the early hours of the morning, and Tito had been in a bad state, sick with grief. He knew enough to know that Nando had a cousin on his mother's side that he was fond of, that her name was Carlita, and that Carlita was dating a man named Ben. Why would Ben be here and not Carlita? So Ben had let him in on the truth, and made him understand what that truth signified, and Kyle had done his best also, to force a degree of sense through Tito's distraught exterior.

Perhaps none of it means anything. Perhaps Plan John is talking to everyone, or he wants to discuss some inconsequential matter, a subject Kyle can't even guess at. Only, he knows his dad, as well as anyone does, and he knows when his dad is scared. His dad had been scared just now. And it's when he's scared that he makes his worst mistakes.

Kyle has been trying to work, or give the impression of working, since his dad and Tito left. He'd rather not have Singh interrogating him. He's been digging the same patch of ground for a quarter of an hour, while the tension cramped his hands and made his thoughts race. In that quarter hour, he's come to some conclusions.

Maybe everything's all right. But maybe it isn't. The way his stomach flip-flops tells him it isn't. And if his fears are grounded then there's nothing he can do on his own. He'll need help.

He can get around Singh. Singh is basically okay. They're losing the light anyway; they'll have to stop soon.

There's one person who will help him, the person whose help he wants least. Because Kyle has never quite overcome his suspicion of Doyle Johnson, not since that first night. Still, it's a fact that much of what makes Johnson tough to like makes him the one person who can, perhaps, be trusted. He's not afraid of Plan John. He doesn't appear to be afraid of anybody. He keeps on the outside, looking in, and doesn't seem to care about any of it.

Except, he cares about Carlita. Enough to have put his life on the line for her.

So that when Johnson comes into view, hunching his shoulders against the wind that whips around the far end of the cellblock, Kyle doesn't feel as if he's making a decision. He crushes the blade of his spade into the hard earth, leaves it standing there, and starts toward Johnson almost without a thought.

★   ★   ★

Plan John makes him leave Contreras outside in the corridor. There's no chance that he'll run. Ben has never seen anyone look so broken. It isn't, of course, the pain alone, though he doubts the pain is helping. But guilt is what has snapped Contreras's spirit like a reed, guilt at his own weakness and what it has wrought.

"I'm sorry," he whispers, as Ben hauls him out and dumps him heftily against the wall.

"You fucking should be," Ben tells him.

He has no time to feel bad for Contreras. He has no time to question his own role in events. He helped Plan John torture Contreras because he had to. And all Contreras needed to do was keep his mouth shut, to hold out a little longer. Contreras's weakness has probably killed them both, not to mention Carlita.

Carlita.

Ben pushes the thought aside. No time for that either. "Stay here," he orders Contreras, and goes back inside, closing the door behind him.

Plan John is once more behind his desk. He is delicately mopping his brow with a handkerchief, a process he performs fastidiously and apparently takes some pleasure from. His eyes are half-closed, his fleshy lips pursed. He doesn't look up at the sound of the door.

Ben sits, not on the other side of the desk but in the metal chair near the doors to the balcony. He leans back to stare at the ceiling, hoping that this way Plan John won't be able to see his face. But Plan John barely seems aware of his presence. The silence stretches.

Then Plan John says, "A woman."

Unable to judge if Plan John is speaking to him or to himself, Ben chooses not to answer.

"A woman," Plan John repeats. "A real woman. I mean no respect to the good Doctor Aaronovich when I say that I'd rather be castrated than fuck her dry old bones." Plan John chuckles softly. "Anyway, the doctor is valuable. Best to be circumspect with that one."

Plan John stands. He walks to the balcony doors and brushes the blinds aside, peering out through the gap he's created.

"It's getting dark," he says. "Here's what you're going to do. First, talk to Nguyen and tell him to shut off the outside lights. Then you'll go to the infirmary. Speak to the doctor; explain the situation. Try not to ruffle her feathers too much. Find the woman and bring her to me."

The woman. Ben has to keep reminding himself that Plan John is talking about Carlita. He feels as if he's been clumsily bisected into two people, two separate lives. He's felt like that ever since he came to Funland. It's even been okay. But now those dual lives are tumbling together, those two identities are being brought face to face, and he's powerless to stop their collision.

"Sure," Ben manages. His throat is tight, exactly as though there are hands around it. "What about Contreras?"

Plan John's perplexity suggests he's already forgotten the existence of Tito Contreras. "What about him?"

"I mean," Ben says, "should I let him go?"

"Ah." Plan John nods cumbersomely. "Yes, we're all done with Mr. Contreras. Make certain he understands to keep his mouth shut, or the next time will be very much worse."

"I think he understands," Ben says.

"Yes. Good." Plan John is looking at him, is actually considering him. "And you, Mr. Silensky?"

Under the focus of those deep-set, purposeful eyes, Ben finds it hard not to squirm. Even concentrating is difficult. There have been two of him, and suddenly there's only space for one. What will happen when they meet?

"Me?" Ben asks.

Plan John's gaze holds him. "Do *you* understand?"

"Yes," Ben says, "I do."

He stands, because it seems to be what Plan John expects. His walk, the motion of his arms, is entirely mechanical. It's the walk of a man with something, everything, to hide. Ben can't believe Plan John won't notice. His fingers feel numb and bloated around the door handle, but he gets it open. He closes the door behind him, hears the lock click, and experiences no relief.

Contreras is curled in the corridor, knees drawn up, his damaged hand propped carefully upon them. He can't be fifty, but pain and shame and fear have piled two decades onto that, making an old man of him. There are tears in his eyes.

"Get up," Ben says. "We're going."

Contreras looks at him in puzzlement.

"Get up," Ben repeats.

Contreras struggles to his feet.

"Come on." Ben leads the way down the stairs and through the passages beyond. Most of the striplights have been ripped out to save the generator, leaving milky funnels of illumination that make the surrounding darkness thicken. He walks until he has no doubt that they're out of Plan John's earshot and then keeps going, because there's no knowing what Plan John can or can't do. Only when there are two sets of doors between them and Plan John's office does Ben pause. Contreras, who's been staring at the ground as he shuffles along, almost bumps into him. He's cradling his hand and his eyes are glazed.

"*Contreras,*" Ben growls. "Are you with me?"

Contreras looks up. "I'm sorry," he says again. "Carlita. I'm sorry."

Ben wants to hit him. The urge is nearly overwhelming, and the fact that it's wholly unreasonable barely makes it easier to restrain. "That doesn't matter now," he says. "I need you to get Foster for me. Tell him

it's urgent, that it's life and death. Do you understand? I'll meet him...."
Ben considers. "I'll meet him at the north end of the admin block, in
fifteen minutes. Can you do that?"

"Yes," Contreras says. "I'll get it done."

"Okay. Then you need to go talk to Nguyen and tell him to kill the
outside lights. Make sure he knows the order came from Plan John."

"I understand," Contreras says.

Does he? But Ben has so little time, and no choice except to trust
him. It feels like the wrong call, even as he's making it. Ben has never
been a quick thinker, and everything's coming apart, so damn fast, faster
than he can begin to keep up with. He's making decisions with no
idea if they're the right ones, putting his faith in men like Contreras
and Foster. He should be coming up with something better, something
that might get him through this night in one piece – yet Ben knows
he won't.

He's fucked up. He will keep fucking up. This, he sees with awful
clarity, is how it has always been. And now, as a part of his mind screams
at him to pause and think, he will go and get Carlita for Plan John.

★   ★   ★

Doyle can't say what dragged his feet toward the farm, except that
he had to go somewhere and there were so few places he could go.
He'd been willing to brave the cellblock if that was what it took, but
to do so involved any number of risks, not least that his presence was
bound to hint at his suspicions.

His plan, in so much as he'd had one, had been to talk to Singh.
Doyle had had a notion of volunteering to work the farm and maybe
getting some insight out of Singh that way. From what he's observed
of the man, he might be Funland's least intimidating inmate: quiet,
withdrawn, glad of the role he's been given. It's hard to imagine
him being in deep with Foster. Then again, he's in charge of one
of Funland's most valued resources, so it's just as hard to believe he
wouldn't have been approached.

Whatever Doyle had been pondering, it changes when he sees
Kyle Silensky. It isn't that the boy is scared, though he is; it's
more than that. Even from a distance, there's much going on in

his face: thoughts twitching past like a film sped up, doubts and conflicts colliding.

Kyle spies Johnson before Singh does. And only when Kyle calls out, "Hey Johnson," does Singh turn. His expression is judiciously impassive.

"Listen," Kyle says to Singh as Doyle draws close, "is it okay if I finish up? I need to speak with Johnson." There's an unmistakable tremor in his voice, one that Singh must surely hear.

But all he does is contemplate the darkening sky, edged into premature dusk by bands of cloud. "Get going," he agrees. If he thinks it's strange that Kyle Silensky should want to talk to Doyle Johnson, that Doyle Johnson should want to talk to anyone at all, the sentiment doesn't reach those two words.

Doyle lets the Silensky boy lead. He's heading toward the well house, the shapeless concrete edifice that supplies their fresh water. It crosses Doyle's mind that he could be walking into a trap. But if someone intends to hurt him, there are easier ways than this.

When they're out of earshot, Kyle slows. "My dad was here," he says. "He made Contreras go with him."

"To Howard?" Doyle asks, knowing the answer.

Kyle frowns at the unfamiliar name. "Yeah. To Plan John."

"Hell." Doyle feels suddenly cold, colder than the evening chill can warrant. This isn't at all what he'd been expecting, and yet is perfectly attuned to the ramping pain inside his cranium, like a key turning in a lock.

So this is what Silensky had meant the day before. This is what had got him so worked up. If Plan John has chosen to question Contreras, there can only be one reason, because there's just one thing Contreras knows that isn't common knowledge. Doyle doesn't pause to wonder what Plan John has already found out, or suspects. If his conjectures led him to Contreras then there's every chance they've led him to Carlita.

"Johnson, don't hurt my dad," Kyle pleads.

"It might not come to that."

"That's not an answer."

Dishonesty has never come easily to Doyle. "What do you want me to say? I'm not looking to see anyone get hurt here."

Except that isn't the truth either. He's prepared to see Plan John hurt, if that's what it takes. And if protecting Carlita means harming

Silensky, he's ready to do that too. Doyle is, in fact, shocked by how ready he is, how willing.

"I'll do my best to keep your dad safe," Doyle says, and is surprised by how effortlessly the lie comes this time.

CHAPTER FIFTEEN

It's maddening; there's so little for her to do. Back before, Aaronovich would have counted herself lucky to have a mere two dozen patients. Now it's only a frustration, to feel useless when everyone should be needed.

With no worthwhile business to occupy her time, with her office tidied beyond the fantasies of any obsessive-compulsive, Aaronovich worries. And there's so much to worry about. Mostly, she troubles herself over the woman living beneath her, if that existence can justifiably be described as living. Sometimes she thinks about the sickness, trying to make sense of it, trying to rationalise, as so many others have strived and failed to do. Or maybe they've succeeded. Maybe somewhere people are working productively, perhaps there are cures or antidotes being developed at this very moment. Aaronovich's specialist knowledge of such matters is as limited as her resources; there's nothing she could have done. Yet that doesn't still her curiosity. The Sickers are out there, so close that there are days when she imagines she can feel them, exerting a pressure like the gathering of storm clouds.

Today, though, has been a day of numbing, centreless anxiety, and she's glad to hear the rattle of the outer office door. It's a perverse position for a physician to find herself in, to be eager for injuries and disease, but these are not by any means good men, and if their discomfort offers her a modicum of professional satisfaction, she can't feel entirely guilty.

However, Aaronovich is halfway to her feet when the door to her office slams open, in disregard of the 'PRIVATE' sign on its opposite side, and that intrusion is her first signal that something is badly wrong here. If it hadn't been, Ben Silensky's face would leave no doubt.

"I need to see Carlita," he says.

"Have you cleared this with Johnson?"

"Have I cleared with Johnson that I can see my fucking girlfriend?"

"Yes," Aaronovich says. "Have you?" Then she recognises the truth. It's all there in his eyes. "Oh god."

Silensky is still trying to hide it, though he must have realised by now that she understands. For an answer, he scowls at her.

"It's Plan John, isn't it?" Aaronovich asks. "I'm not opening that door." She hopes there's no hesitation in her voice. Certainly she feels none.

"Don't make me hurt you," Silensky says.

"You know," she tells him, "I despise that phrase. If you mean to hurt me, I'm sure you'll do it, but I definitely won't be making you."

Silensky heaves a sigh and sags, as though he's beginning to deflate. "Look," he says, "she's my girlfriend. Do you think I want anything to happen to her? If I go back to Plan John without her, then he'll have me killed and send someone else."

"Can you guarantee me that woman down there won't be mistreated?"

Silensky slumps farther, more fight draining out of him. "I guarantee I'll do whatever I can. Jesus...of course I will! But every moment we fuck around here is just making things worse."

Silensky has no knack for hiding his emotions. The truth of what he says, or at least his belief in it, is written across his face. It's astonishing, really, that he's managed to keep Carlita's existence from Plan John all this time.

But Aaronovich has no desire to consider Plan John. Of everybody in Funland, she has perhaps seen the man at his best. Howard has always been polite to her. Even when he's threatened, even when he's controlled, he's never been less than polite – and she's heard enough, and has enough sense, to know that he's not polite to everyone. Were it not abundantly clear that no one could reach the unique position he occupies without getting their hands copiously bloody, the man wears his misdeeds like old clothes.

Plan John takes what he wants. Carlita will not be an exception to that rule. She will be the furthest thing imaginable to an exception. And if this is his way of asking politely, then it isn't something that will be repeated. Aaronovich can't stop Silensky, only delay him, and as much as she hates to admit it, he's right about what that will achieve.

Aaronovich goes to her filing cabinet, unlocks the top drawer with the key in her pocket, and takes out the second, sturdier key secreted behind the final separator. She presses it into Silensky's palm. "Damn you," she says.

Silensky closes his fingers round the key. "Yeah, damn me," he agrees.

* * *

Carlita comes without much argument; less, at any rate, than the doctor made on her behalf. But once they reach the room above, she holds back for the first time. Maybe it's Aaronovich's presence. The doctor is standing against one wall, still and pale as an alabaster statue, her mouth pursed into a brittle line.

"We could run," Carlita says. "We could just run."

And go where? Ben thinks. *And do what?* But under those questions is another: who is he trying to protect? Ben shrugs that misgiving aside. Protecting himself is protecting Carlita. "We're not running," he says. "I'm going to figure this out. You've got to trust me."

She doesn't trust him. He can see her utter lack of faith. She doesn't trust him, and she's afraid of him. "Okay," Carlita allows.

"There's one other thing. You have to say it was Johnson." He scowls toward Aaronovich, wishing she wasn't here as audience to yet more of his shame. "Do you hear me? Johnson was the one who brought you. Who hid you."

He assumes Carlita will debate it, but the argument never gets past her eyes. "All right."

"You don't have to go," Aaronovich says softly.

"Shut up," Ben orders. He doesn't look at either woman. "Come on," he tells Carlita. He's relieved when she follows with no resistance.

Close to the double doors that lead onto the yard, Ben stops again. "Wait here." He hasn't planned this far, except to think that he can't leave her in the doctor's offices. The slender risk of someone coming in and discovering Carlita seems less than the danger of letting Aaronovich work doubts into her mind. "Carlita, promise me you'll wait."

"I promise," she says.

"Because if you run off...."

"I promise."

She's taking this well, better than he is. Then again, maybe she's simply in shock. There in the dim moonlight that trickles through frosted inset windows, her copper skin is as pale as his own. The only detail he can discern clearly is the brighter white of her eyes. If she gets scared, if she runs....

"I won't be long," Ben says, and pushes out the doors into the yard.

By then, another apprehension is already dragging at him. What if Foster doesn't show? But as Ben rounds the corner of the administrative wing, he sees the figure in the darkness immediately, its subtle threat diminished by the listless way that Foster lounges against the concrete.

"'Matter of life and death,' huh? This better be good. That old spic Contreras was in a hell of a state."

"Plan John knows everything," Ben announces, caught between keeping the panic from his voice and letting it flood in completely.

If he'd expected to shock Foster, he's disappointed. "Everything? What's everything?"

"Listen, I'm just warning you. He's on to you. I don't give a fuck what you're up to; whatever you're going to do, this is the time to do it."

"I'm not going to do anything," Foster says. "If Plan John thinks I am, he can come talk to me."

"You know it won't go down like that."

Foster leans in, and there is sudden menace in his tone. "Don't tell me what I know or don't know, Silensky." Then he relaxes once more. "If you're really so worried about Plan John, I'll do you a favour. Hold your hand out."

Ben does as he's commanded. A moment later, Foster is placing some object in his palm, and closing Ben's fingers around cold, hard plastic.

He comprehends, even before he looks. A shiv, a con weapon, strangely anachronistic now that White Cliff is no longer White Cliff. Nice craftsmanship, too, Ben observes distantly. What was originally a screwdriver has been filed into something more like a needle.

"I don't know what you think I'm going to do with this," he says. But he doesn't try to give it back.

Foster's grin shows white teeth to the darkness. "Before you get any ideas, Silensky, I can guess what's going on in that head of yours. *Look at this asshole Foster, putting his life in my hands.* All you have to do is blab to Plan John, right? *Hey, boss man, see this blade Foster gave me. Problem solved.*"

Ben tucks the shiv into the back pocket of his jeans and pulls his shirt out over the handle. "Never crossed my thoughts."

Foster ignores him. "But that's not what's happening here. You don't own me. That's the opposite of what this is. Want to hear why? Because you don't know shit. You work for Plan John, but he doesn't confide in you. Me? I know plenty. I know you work for Plan John, and who else works for him. But he doesn't know who works for me, and even if he did, he wouldn't let you in on it. So you can tell him about this, and sure, that might be me in some trouble. But however things fall out, Silensky, I promise you, however bad this goes for me, it'll go twice as bad for you. Ten times. A hundred. For you, your boy...."

"Keep Kyle out of this," Ben says. But his mind is partly elsewhere, and he came awfully close to saying something different. He'd almost said *Carlita*, almost cut his own throat with five words.

This is so badly out of control. One mistake could get him killed. Or maybe the mistake has already been made, and all that's left is watching how events transpire.

"I will absolutely keep your son out of this," Foster agrees. "Hey, he's a nice kid. Good little worker. No one wants to see him hurt. Let's face it, there's only one person who needs hurting."

"You don't understand what you're asking."

"You know I do."

"I mean...fuck, Foster, Plan John's paranoid as hell. Do you think I get near him? Because I work with the guy? If that's what you think then—"

"Silensky," Foster cuts him off, "I do not give a shit how you get it done. But we're not standing here debating."

And with that, Foster is gone, moving off into the darkness, swallowed by it as though he's never been, leaving Ben with just his thoughts and the cold presence of the shiv goose-bumping the flesh around his spine.

★   ★   ★

At first he decides the generator must have failed. The yard is so suddenly pitch-black that looking in that direction is like going blind.

It takes Austin a few moments to notice how a glow still spills from isolated windows of the Big House, and from parts of the cellblock and administrative wing. Not all of the lights have been extinguished, merely the external ones: the great spots in front of the Big House and cellblock.

His racing heartbeat gradually steadies. In that initial instant, when the world had grown darker, he'd assumed the worst, without knowing what the worst might mean. Now, satisfied that no answers will be forthcoming, that the questions don't affect him, Austin ducks from the low parapet and crawls toward the larger of the two vents. He finds his way easily by touch; this space he's claimed is growing familiar, its details ground like grit into the surface of his memory.

Austin has gathered everything he needs. He's already removed the vent, defeating through sheer, violent effort the resistance of long-rusted screw heads. He'd sat staring into the depths until fireworks popped and fizzed on the edges of his vision. Before the lights went out, he'd been pacing the rooftop, dragged by conflicting emotions.

Some part of him is resisting. *Maybe*, it says, *there are other solutions.* Maybe, if he hides too deeply, there'll be no path back.

Back to where? To what? Prior to Funland, his life had been nothing worth fighting for, and even that is gone. His mother is likely dead. His father might as well be. His stepfather is alive and out there, and perhaps that's the worst of it. Austin needs somewhere to think, to plan. He needs a place that's safe.

There's no way back, he argues.

I don't want to go back, he insists.

Now Austin is ready for a sign. And he's ready to take anything as a sign. Something is happening: lights don't just go out by themselves. His blood is rushing. There's a charge in the air, akin to the static before lightning. And he appreciates somehow that, if he lets it, this sensation will control him, will free him from the responsibility of choice.

Austin moves closer to the exposed opening. He lays his hands on its edges. He'd expected the metal to be cold, but it holds the faintest recollection of the day's warmth. The gap is narrow. If he was any bigger, if he was any older, he could barely fit at all. Really, that's everything he needs to know.

He pushes the flashlight in first, and watches its beam dance crazily around the silver-skinned walls. Then he hoists himself inside, and the very difficulty of doing so, the claustrophobia, is only further reassurance.

This is the right choice. There's no way to back out. And there's no way for anyone to follow.

CHAPTER SIXTEEN

He's never been aware before of how Plan John's office smells. Yet now it's all Ben can concentrate on: the rankness of old sweat, old food, and pent-up air, and under that another scent he can't identify, though it makes his stomach flop helplessly. Perhaps it's fear – maybe his own.

Or maybe Carlita's. She's staying close to him, but close as a prisoner would hang to a guard, not as a frightened woman might try to shelter behind her lover. It's good acting on her part, or else it isn't.

Plan John has tidied himself up. That's the second thing Ben notices. He's wearing a crisp black suit that, if not fit to the impossible demand of disguising his size, at least gives definition to that bulk. He has shaved off the two days of stubble that formed a dirty crescent around his jaw, has even applied something to his thinning, dirt-brown hair, slicking it into a semblance of order.

He makes Ben think of the middle-aged businessmen who thronged the city's better class of bars. They knew they'd end the night with a rushed fuck or a blow job in the back room of a club, and they knew they'd have to pay for it in cash. They made an effort, not in spite of that fact but because. Whores were still women to impress, and if they weren't impressed, they would fake it. That, indeed, was high upon the list of favours being bought.

"Good evening." Plan John has slicked his voice down, too. "They tell me your name is Carlita."

"Yes," Carlita says. The word is not much more than a whisper.

"Come. Take a seat." Plan John motions toward the chair set ready in front of his desk and waits until she sits. "Don't be shy. This is the beginning of a long acquaintance. The sooner you start making the best of the situation, the better for everyone."

Ben doesn't know where to look. He can't look at Plan John and doesn't want to look at Carlita. Unlike with Contreras, he has no idea how to influence her, no idea what's the right thing for her to say, if anything could be. *I should have listened to her,* Ben realises, with abrupt horror. *We should have just run. That was the one chance we had.*

"I'm not a man who finds the notion of rape palatable," Plan John says. "I'm clarifying this to put your mind at rest, and because I want you to pay attention. You've probably heard unpleasant stories about me, and I dare say most of them are true. However, I'd prefer not to be reduced to the status of rapist."

"Then let me go." Carlita's voice is stronger. She's trying hard to keep the fear from it.

"Yes. Good. Let's get that out of the way. If I found you out, sooner or later someone else will. This is simple fact. I'm likely the only person here, with the possible exception of Mr. Johnson, who will treat you with the barest scrap of respect. Many of the men here would make you long for a fate as straightforward as rape. Moreover, I am categorically the only person who can protect you. You see now that Doyle Johnson can't."

This time, Carlita doesn't answer. That unexpected silence makes Ben give in and look at her. It's difficult even to recognise the small, dishevelled woman perched on the chair as the Carlita he once knew, out there in the world, before all this. Her eyes are not quite on Plan John; she's sitting perfectly still, except for her hands, which are constantly folding and unfolding in her lap.

"Here's what I have to offer," Plan John continues, having let the silence draw to its uncomfortable limit and beyond. "You will come to live with me. You'll give me what I want, when I want it, but besides that you'll live as you like and no one, *no one*, will interfere with you. This will be my preferred solution."

Ben is positive Carlita will say something. Her body tenses, her shoulders bunch. Yet the tension drains from her, and she slides her face into her cupped hands.

"Then there's option two. In option two, I send Silensky and some of my boys to cut off Doyle Johnson's feet, drive him out into the forest, and leave him for the Sickers. Perhaps poor Tito as well, why not? And you pleasure me and anyone else I feel deserves a reward until the day you're utterly dried up."

Carlita, finally, looks straight at Plan John. "I'd rather be dead than let you touch me."

"That's a kneejerk reaction," Plan John says, entirely unruffled, "so I'll forgive it. The point I'm making is that these are your only two options. Neither includes your death, or any other form of escape, but one will certainly make you responsible for the demise of people you care about. Once you've had time to consider, you'll see the virtues of the deal I'm offering – and not merely for yourself."

Plan John contemplates his watch.

"Silensky will take you back now. You have nine hours to think this over…the rest of the night to return by your own volition. You can send a message via the good doctor. She and I need to have a conversation anyway, it would seem. If you don't, if you try to leave, we default to option two."

He nods to Ben.

"Go on. Get her out of here."

Ben isn't sure that Carlita will stand on her own, but when he takes a step toward her, she does, and waits, staring back at him without expression. He begins in the direction of the door and she trails after.

He's halfway there when he hears the knocking.

Ben freezes. Since there's nobody who can save him, it follows that whoever is on the opposite side of the door can only make this terrible situation somehow worse.

"We have another guest," Plan John says, without apparent concern. "Can you handle this, Mr. Silensky?"

The spittle has dried in Ben's mouth, leaving it barren as a desert rock. Ben licks his lips, coughs – to test that his throat is still capable of making sounds – and calls, "Who's there?"

The voice from outside the door is muffled. Nevertheless, Ben recognises it immediately, from the very first syllable.

"It's Doyle Johnson," comes the reply. "I heard Plan John wants to see me."

*   *   *

He'd gone to Aaronovich first, and the doctor had told him the essential details. Hell, the look on her face had told him virtually everything. Yet she was composed, and that had impressed Doyle and unsettled him in equal measure. This wasn't a situation that seemed to warrant calm.

Regardless, he needs calm now. He's never needed it so badly. And as the door opens like a precipice yawning, it comes without any effort on his part. He has no plan, no clue what he's doing here, and yet his mind is serene. Words from his childhood drift up: his mother's, Bible-borrowed. Something to do with having on the breastplate of righteousness. He's never believed in that, but the thought feels fitting.

Silensky isn't calm. He's about as far from being so as Doyle has seen anyone. He's keeping his panic inside, though, barely. That means Plan John doesn't know. Ben Silensky and Carlita's relationship remains a secret, something Doyle is aware of that Plan John isn't, and that's as close to an advantage as he has.

"Get inside," Silensky says. The next thing Doyle notes, the thing that perhaps he should have observed first, is that Silensky has a gun. It isn't his, therefore it's Plan John's. It gives Silensky a little more authority, but not much. Doyle pushes past him, making a point of not looking at the gun.

"Howard," he says. He doesn't look at Carlita either, though he can feel her presence.

"Mr. Johnson," Plan John acknowledges. His tone gives nothing away.

"I thought it would be better if I came to talk to you. Save you the hassle of sending someone to find me."

"We had a deal," Plan John says.

"I haven't broken our deal."

Plan John chuckles, but there's no humour in the sound, as if it's more a tic than a legitimate response. "Balls of an elephant," he declares, apparently to himself. Then, "I have a clear memory of you telling me you wouldn't screw with me. And this? Hiding this lovely lady right under my nose? I think *that*, by any definition of the phrase, would have to be regarded as screwing with me."

"I guess it's a matter of perspective," Doyle says. If anything, his inner peace is growing, in proportion to how obviously discomposed Plan John is becoming.

"Oh?"

He's not in control, Doyle comprehends. *Before I walked through that door he was, and now he isn't.* "I just felt like it was none of your damn business."

Plan John's face contorts. "You'll watch your fucking manners, Johnson."

"No disrespect intended." Doyle is almost smiling, and has to stop himself. He's figured out why he has authority and Plan John doesn't. It's to do with information, who possesses it and who doesn't. He knows, in essence, what Plan John is thinking, and Plan John has no idea what's going through Doyle's mind.

Plan John chuckles once more, the exact same sound, and this time it's so transparently a nervous reaction that Doyle wonders how he could never have divined the fact. "I have so many questions for you. Who *is* she? How did you smuggle her in here? How on earth did you suppose you could keep this up without my noticing?" Plan John sighs, a fluttering note of disappointment, and that at least seem unfeigned. "But there'll be plenty of opportunity for Carlita to answer my questions, and I suspect that I'll like the answers a lot more coming from her lips."

"It won't be much of a story, whoever tells it," Doyle says. And he looks directly at Silensky, who shrivels beneath his gaze.

If Plan John detects their brief communion, he gives no indication. "I promised the young lady that if she complied then I'd let you live. But honestly – and I hope you won't esteem me any the less for this, Carlita – I was going to have you killed whatever she said. I was just curious as to whether she'd come here of her own volition. If I'm being *absolutely* honest, I would have to admit that I'd have liked to keep you around. There's something about you that makes me laugh. I think it's your complete inability to see the things about yourself that should be staring you in the face. But Johnson, you've taken that choice out of my hands. This can't stand."

"I know that," Doyle says. "Yeah." He considers. "But Howard, you took the choice out of my hands first."

"Is that true?" Plan John asks. There's genuine interest in the inquiry.

"You could have kept her out of it. You could have left well alone. But it's not in your nature."

"No," Plan John agrees. "I could never be a weak man. I take what I want."

"Right." Doyle nods, thoughtful. On some level, he feels that everything makes sense. "Give me the gun, Silensky."

Plan John watches him with clear amusement. "Is that your

idea? While I don't wish to be critical, I doubt Mr. Silensky is likely to comply."

"Silensky," Doyle says, "this has gone on long enough." Might he have misjudged the situation? Ben Silensky is a foetid little shit of a human being, but Doyle doesn't believe he would let his girlfriend be used by a creature like Plan John, if only because, sooner or later, the truth of his own involvement would be bound to come out. "Give the gun to me now."

He allows Silensky not quite a second to comply, sufficient that Doyle feels in his gut that he won't. Then he moves.

Doyle has always been quick. Silensky hardly seems to have caught on by the time Doyle has a hand wrapped round his wrist. As Doyle steps back and wrenches Silensky's arm, he's beginning to react.

Maybe that reaction would be to pull the trigger. Maybe Silensky doesn't know himself – in which case, he never will. Because by then his shoulder is coming out of joint, with a *crack* like splintering ice, the gun is falling toward the floor, and Silensky is screaming.

★   ★   ★

What Austin imagined had come from video games, movies, and this is nothing like it. Outside of the flashlight's illumination, the blackness is absolute, and it has weight. Nor had he appreciated how narrow the shaft would be. Seeing the opening from the outside was one thing, being within and feeling smooth metal pressing on every side is entirely another.

He barely negotiates the first bend, the one that takes him downward and inward. Only thanks to protruding joints between sections, scarcely wider than a pencil, can he descend. Even then, his attempts to be silent when everything about the situation works against him bring him close to slipping more than once. As his feet graze the bottom, his nerves are stretched to breaking point. It's all Austin can do not to climb straight back up again and flop, sobbing, into the night.

He doesn't. Instead, he waits until his heart has ceased its drumming. And bit by bit, moment by moment, his anxiety turns again to exhilaration. He's done it. It can be done. And solely by him.

Austin crawls farther, on his back, shuffling on elbows and butt, flashlight gripped in one hand. He goes far enough to grasp, fully, that he had no concept of what he was getting himself into. The ductwork is a maze of pitfalls, ninety-degree turns, and inoperative machinery. If the air-con wasn't defunct, long since become an impossible luxury, these claustrophobic tubes would be a death trap. To make this work will take time and tools and effort.

Which means it's possible. Simple, even.

Those dangers aren't what make Austin stop. He halts when he hears the voices. They're distant at first, but the more still he becomes, the louder they grow, as if the shaft is a conductor and he's becoming an instrument designed to receive. Suddenly they're quite distinct, and Austin switches the flashlight off, irrationally anxious that someone might be close enough to see its glow. He lies unmoving in the blackness, listening with all his attention.

Yet he isn't scared. That's strange in a way, because he's been so scared for so long that he's come to view his fear as basically a part of him. Its absence is like an itch going away, or like the opposite of noticing a sound you've been perceiving forever but never registered, such as the insect buzz of a refrigerator.

He's only heard Plan John speak once or twice, bellowing orders from his balcony, but the man is unmistakable. The woman, Carlita, he knows by default; there are two women in Funland, and she certainly isn't the doctor. What does it mean that they're talking together? Bad news for the woman, surely, and bad news for Austin's father. Now the conversation he eavesdropped, the guard and Silensky, makes perfect sense.

Since he's already envisaging Silensky, he identifies his voice immediately, though the words are brief and muffled. The fourth man, after the opening and shutting of a door, takes him the longest to recognise, which makes the shock all the greater when he realises it's someone he's known his whole life.

Austin has been avoiding his dad. It's too hard to forgive him, so much easier to stay clear. He thinks maybe his dad is avoiding him as well; at any rate, he hasn't tried very determinedly to find him. But Austin has never considered the possibility of losing his father for good. While his dad was okay, there'd been the chance at least that a day would come when he'd talk to Austin and Austin would respond, and that would be the beginning of something. Austin could never have admitted the hope, not until this moment, not until he knew it couldn't happen.

Because his dad is in there with Plan John: Plan John who's learned about Carlita, who must have discovered that his dad helped to hide her. And Plan John hurts people. Kills people. Even Austin knows that.

He'd thought he couldn't lie any more motionless. Yet when the screaming starts, Austin still manages to freeze, every muscle locking like old gears. He's hardly breathing, encapsulated by darkness, and for that reason, the gunshot that follows is all the more inordinately loud.

*   *   *

The pistol's roar is colossal. Doyle had intended a warning shot, but he's never fired a handgun while walking before. Plan John screeches and clutches the wound that's blossoming in his fleshy bicep. He tumbles out of his chair and goes after the second gun, the one he'd been clawing from his desk drawer, which has clattered to the floor.

"Stop it, Howard," Doyle says. He has to speak up because Silensky is still howling. "Just stop. Or the next one goes in your head."

By that time, Doyle is close enough to pause and aim, so that both of them can understand that the threat isn't empty. Plan John stops moving. His eyes cling lovingly to the gun, which has come to rest beside a wastepaper basket in the corner.

Doyle doesn't look at Carlita. But he glimpsed her when he went for Silensky, knows that she's abandoned her chair and has backed against the doors to the balcony. "Carlita, get out of here," he says. He feels, somehow, that if he sees her, really sees her, he won't be able to do this. "Run. Go back to Aaronovich. Lock yourself in from the inside."

"Ben...." Her voice is a tight ball of fear.

"Go on. He'll be fine. But run."

"You won't get away with this," Plan John says.

"Shut up. Go, Carlita."

This time, she obeys. Doyle waits until he hears her footsteps clattering upon the stairs outside. Then he retrieves Plan John's second gun from beside the basket. Silensky is sobbing now: loud, gushing noises of pain.

"Don't move," Doyle tells Plan John.

Doyle withdraws to where Silensky kneels, tentatively supporting his dislocated arm with his other hand as tears stream down his cheeks. Doyle hurriedly empties Plan John's gun and places it on the table in the corner, then drops the gun he took from Silensky and the loose bullets into his pocket. "Hold still," he commands Silensky. "Grit your teeth. Try to relax."

Silensky looks at him with horror, and maybe he would resist, but again Doyle is too quick for him. In an instant he has one hand on Silensky's back, another round his shoulder, and is wrenching. It's easier than he'd thought it might be, like the bone wants to slide into joint. It can't have felt good from the inside, though, for Silensky's roar is an exhalation of pure agony.

Doyle takes the gun from his jacket pocket and returns his attention to Plan John. Plan John is sitting with his back to the wall and his legs outstretched, one huge hand holding a crumpled handkerchief to his bleeding arm. He is watching Doyle with bitter contempt.

"What do you think you've done?" he says. "I am not a man you toy with, Johnson. I am certainly not a man you fucking *shoot*." The last word comes out in a hiss that is nothing like his usual speech. "I was contemplating letting you live, even after everything, but this…*this*…." He looks at where his palm clasps his bicep. "Shot me," he finishes, with stupefied disbelief.

"Get up," Doyle tells him. A course of action has formed in his mind, unbidden, and he has no argument to challenge it with. "You're going outside."

"And if I don't?"

"Then I'll kill you here. Get up, Howard."

For a protracted moment, Plan John's eyes hold Doyle's own. Whatever he finds there, it's enough, in the end, to make him heft himself to his feet. "Let's deal then. That's what this is about, isn't it?"

"Move. Over there." Doyle motions toward the balcony.

Plan John looks as if he's readying to say something else. Reconsidering, he does as instructed, though ponderously, like an unwilling beast of burden.

"Don't move a muscle," Doyle orders. "Or I'll shoot you in the kneecap."

Plan John watches the gun greedily, but doesn't shift from where he's standing, half in the room and half on the balcony, fingers still clasped around his bleeding arm.

Walking backward so as to keep Plan John in his line of sight, Doyle retreats to the door. There, relying on touch alone, he drops the latch and slides a thick bolt into place. "There we are," he says. "Just you, me, and Silensky."

"What do you think you're going to achieve? You have nothing to bargain with. You won't kill me. You have nothing to offer."

"I've thought about that," Doyle acknowledges.

"Not clearly you haven't. If you hadn't shot me then maybe, *maybe*, I could have found a way to spare you. But this? This is too far."

Doyle gestures with the pistol. "Go on."

Plan John seems genuinely surprised. "Are you hearing me, Johnson?"

"Are you hearing *me*? I said, on the balcony."

"My Lord," says Plan John, in the tone of one appealing to a third party in the face of impossible unreasonableness. Nonetheless, he goes. Doyle follows behind, waiting inside the doorway, out of arm's reach.

"I'll make you one offer." Plan John is speaking slowly, emphasising each syllable. "The only offer I can make. Leave now. Take one of the trucks. Take your boy. But *not* the woman, you get me? The two of you are gone within an hour and no one will pursue you."

"We wouldn't last a week."

"If you did, it would be a week longer than you have here."

Doyle steps onto the balcony and takes a position at the far end, away from Plan John. He's tired; he wishes this was all over. He leans against the railing, trying discreetly to take some of the strain off his adrenalin-exhausted body.

"This isn't about me or my son," Doyle says. "It's not about you. It's not even about Carlita — though, I tell you, you should have left her alone." Doyle discerns a strangled note in his own voice, and understands that he's talking purely for his own benefit. Is he trying to justify himself or solely to buy time? He motions with the pistol toward the cellblock. "It's about them. You're like ivy on a dying tree, Howard, and sooner or later someone's going to have to hack you down."

Plan John is looking at him with undisguised confusion. "So? You were getting by, Johnson. If you don't want the woman, why didn't you cut her loose? A man such as you…if this revolution of yours were to arrive, you'd still come out in one piece. I've been honest with you, Johnson. I like you. Whatever Foster's offered you, I'd have bettered it."

Foster? That throws Doyle momentarily. He does his best to hide his confusion. "And then? If I let things run their course, your legacy's going to be a pile of corpses on a heap of bricks."

Doyle runs his free hand across his face, rubs tiredly at his eyes. Plan John can keep this up all night, and if he lets himself, Doyle will go along with him, just to put off what needs to be done.

"This can't be a dictatorship. It can't be your personal little empire. What the hell good is that to anyone?" Doyle hefts the pistol. "So stop talking," he says, "and start yelling. As loud as you can."

"What? Don't be ridiculous."

In a single swift motion, Doyle flips the gun, steps forward, and smashes the grip with all his might into Plan John's mouth.

"Aargh! You, you fuck!"

"Louder." Doyle twists the pistol back around and points the muzzle at Plan John's forehead. "I said, louder."

This time, Plan John does as he's told. He's every bit as loud as Doyle could have asked for.

CHAPTER SEVENTEEN

The pain is indescribable. Ben had always assumed, somehow, that beyond a certain point you would pass out, your brain would switch off: a tiny, inbuilt act of mercy. Ben's brain has no mercy. The pain is such that it should kill him, he should die to stop it, but he can't pass out and he can't die and it won't stop.

Yet he has to do something. While Plan John and Johnson are out of his sight, he can hear their voices clearly. Ben knows there are very few ways in which their conversation will conclude, and he can't imagine an outcome that won't be the end of him.

Clenching his teeth, Ben reaches his good left hand behind his back and feels for the plastic handle tucked under his shirt, which bruised his spine when he went down, a minor hurt beneath the greater. He draws the shiv out carefully. He inspects the blade, though concentration is practically inconceivable. Everything, even his own hand, seems at a distance.

It's all going to be decided this night. Plan John will find a way to come out on top, or Johnson will, or Foster will make his move. But the outcome will be tonight, and here's a chance, Ben's only chance, to get on the inside. Whichever side wins, he could be on it. He could even be the one to make that choice.

Ben hates Doyle Johnson enough just now that the prospect of driving a blade up into his guts is altogether fine. But not the thought of moving, every motion that would lead to that moment strikes him as impossible. If Ben can save Plan John, won't he be grateful? Maybe, until he learns who Carlita really is, as he surely will. All right, so Foster; if Ben can get the gun off Johnson, use it to do what Foster demanded of him—

But the pain...god, the pain. Ben rehearses the chain of actions in his mind: standing up, crossing the room, then out the double doors, and the movements he'd have to make with his one good arm, which is linked inextricably to his useless arm, so that each slight flinch jolts excruciatingly through his shoulder blades. And now Plan John is shouting, or rather bellowing, and Ben knows there's no more time. He weighs in an instant all the things he might do and what the pain will allow, all the ways in which anything he might attempt could go wrong.

Ben tosses the shiv away, skipping it across the floor until it comes to rest in the shadows beneath Plan John's desk, where it's out of sight. Where, if it should ever be found, it can never be traced to him.

Then he lies back. Ben gives himself up to the pain, to the helplessness, and waits with something like acceptance for the night to play itself out.

★   ★   ★

They come in ones and twos, at first. Then there are shouts from around the cellblock, and suddenly it's everyone. They gather in the yard below, and Doyle can hear the back-and-forth of low conversation, of questions being asked. He thinks that surely someone will tell him to stop; one of them will try to stop him. But no one does.

Doyle has never felt comfortable with crowds. He looks down at the faces below, lighter patches in the darkness like dead fish bobbing to the surface of a still sea, and forces his tongue not to cleave to the roof of his mouth. With an audience, this feels like a show. Is that how it is? Gather enough people, enough sets of eyes, and any transgression becomes entertainment?

Plan John has stopped yelling. Doyle lets it go without comment. A few last stragglers are hurrying across the yard, black shapes drifting half-visibly through the darkness, gaining definition as they draw nearer to the light spilling from the balcony. Doyle hasn't a clue what he's going to say to them. He's started something he can't finish. It will cost him his life.

"You'll have to kill me." Plan John's voice is perfectly steady. "Kill me or kill yourself."

Doyle winces. He understands with abrupt clarity that what Plan John said is true, and that he's known it from the moment he entered his office, if not before. Had he been honest earlier, when he told Plan John this wasn't about them, not even about Carlita? The words had sounded grand. But under his rule, Funland has worked. Doyle has nothing to offer in return, nor any interest. Those men down there, those anonymous faces, they have never been more than a job, and now they aren't even that.

"You're right," Doyle says, and points the pistol.

Instantly, all of Plan John's calm is gone. "Jesus Christ, Johnson, I didn't mean…not like this!"

"There's no other way." Doyle feels furiously calm. Not as when he entered Plan John's office; this is how he imagines an out-of-body experience might be. He can be calm because this isn't him. He's only a spectator, one more face in the crowd.

"Wait. Wait! There are things…." Plan John's voice has diminished to a whisper, as though they are two conspirators and not one man threatening another. "I *know* things. Damn you, Johnson, I made this place! I own you all. The things I know…."

Doyle hesitates, not so much due to what Plan John is saying as because he wants to. It seems to him that each additional moment is one in which this decision might, by some miracle, be taken out of his hands.

"I'll tell you the best one, Johnson. A taster. Something you'll like." Plan John's voice drops further. Against his instincts, Doyle steps closer. If this is a trap, it's a suicidal one, for he still has the pistol pointed squarely at Plan John's temple.

He's a pace away when Plan John speaks again. Yet although the words are the barest murmur, Doyle hears each with perfect clarity. Some void inside him is clenched then, as if his ribcage has become a fist and the fist has squeezed hard.

His fingers contract, as though in sympathy.

He doesn't even realise the gun has gone off until the recoil hammers his forearm.

*   *   *

The way the second shot comes to him, perfectly loud, perfectly clear, it's as if the noise is electricity and the ductwork a wire, transmitting that deathly crack up and along via the cavities in ceilings and walls and deep into his head. It's like the gun has discharged right beside his ear, like it's Austin himself who has been shot.

He's heard everything. He knew that his father and Plan John had gone out onto the balcony because of how the sounds changed. Whenever they spoke up, their voices were lucid, and Austin could piece the scene together in his mind's eye. Plan John begging. His father with the gun, pointed at an unarmed man, a man pleading for his life. And Austin had been certain through every instant that his father would never pull the trigger, through every instant until the one when he did.

The first shot, which had come out of nowhere, he'd thought that had been aimed at his dad. And Austin had endured seconds of grieving that felt like an eternity, trying to make sense of all that had occurred – childhood memories, his parents seemingly happy and then quarrelling day in, day out, their final, wrenching separation – before he'd fathomed that it wasn't his dad who'd been shot after all. With that comprehension, he had been filled with pure, crazy love for his father, such as he'd never experienced. He had vowed to stop the hiding, to give up his secrets, to strip off this shell of anger he'd kept himself safe inside. His dad was alive and everything could be okay.

But still he listened, here in the darkness. There was nothing to do except listen. And, like a dream shading by degrees into nightmare, it had all gone bad. Because there are things you don't do, Austin knows that, lines you don't cross for whatever the reason.

You don't shoot an unarmed man who's begging for his life. If you do that, there's no coming back. If you do that, you become something else.

Suddenly Austin is dragging himself backward, shuffling on his ass heedless of sharp edges, panic rising out of his throat and bleeding through his skin, filling the darkness like smog. He doesn't care how much noise he makes. The fear has him again; it's found him even here, in his safe place. Now it's larger, alive in the blackness around him. Now the choking terror he feels is of his father.

CHAPTER EIGHTEEN

Aaronovich flinches when she hears the gunshot, not because it's a surprise but because she's been anticipating it for so long. She'd thought she heard a shot earlier, but that had been muffled, ambiguous. Since then, she's been sitting in absolute and perfect tension, and the sound that just reached her was clear beyond the possibility of doubt.

Aaronovich waits for another report. She failed to note the time of the first, and her own internal chronometer seems unreliable. Have seconds passed? A minute? More?

Eventually, she decides that enough time has gone by. No further shots are coming. But she has no idea what to make of that fact. At least Funland hasn't erupted into war – or if it has, it isn't a shooting war. It occurs to her that she should go out, that someone might be hurt and in need of her help. The thought is overwhelming in its logic, and still Aaronovich doesn't move.

She hears the outer doors open. There are footsteps along the corridor, two sets, one lagging behind the other. They march closer, closer. The slower steps fall out of synch and stop. Brief words are spoken, too low for her to identify voices. Then the door to her reception room is flung open, hard enough to rebound against the wall.

On some level, Aaronovich has been expecting Johnson, but his appearance alarms her nonetheless. Spattered blood paints a triangle across his uniform, beginning above his left knee and ending beneath his right armpit. He stops in the doorway, immobile as a monolith. "Is she safe?"

"She's in the infirmary," Aaronovich says. "The door's locked from the inside."

Johnson nods, but doesn't relax. "Ben Silensky is outside. He's going to need treatment. His arm got…I dislocated his arm. And he said something about Tito Contreras on the way over here. I think he's going to need you. I'll try and find him."

In all the months she's worked with Doyle Johnson, Aaronovich has never before known him to ramble. "And Plan John?" she inquires.

"There's nothing you can do for Plan John."

"And everyone else?"

He takes a moment to understand the question. "It's in hand," he says. "If that's what you mean. They're not fighting. It looks like Foster has enough backing to keep a lid on things."

Normally, Johnson is unreadable. Now it seems to Aaronovich that an impalpable layer has been peeled from his face, leaving no obstruction to hide his thoughts. "Johnson," she keeps her tone level, for she has no doubt that he's in shock," if there's an injured man outside, I'd like to treat him as soon as possible. So whatever you want to say to me, please, just say it."

His eyes narrow, as though with suspicion, as though he thinks she might somehow have read his mind. "Is it true?" he asks.

Aaronovich stands. Some quality in Johnson's voice demands that she should. "Is *what* true?"

"That you killed your son."

The feeling is exactly as if someone has tipped the entire room, the entire world, off-kilter, so much so that she almost staggers. "What?"

"Is it true that Howard used his contacts to get the charges quashed? That he pulled strings to have you moved here?" Johnson pauses, manifestly unwilling to go on. Then he says, "Did you kill your son?"

Aaronovich hangs her head, not able to look at him, unsure if the reason for that is shame or rage. "If that's the word you want to use."

"There's another?"

"He was dying. He was in too much pain. I did what I had to."

"And you made a deal with Howard?"

"I didn't *make a deal.* I didn't even know his name until it was all over. And he didn't have me moved anywhere. After everything that had happened, I couldn't find work. He arranged for me to receive an offer. He said I was exactly what he was looking for. He…made certain, veiled threats." *But*, she thinks, *there was no need for threats. By then, I had nothing left to lose.*

"You should have told me," Johnson says.

"I couldn't."

"If you'd really wanted to, you would have."

"Then I didn't want to," she says. "Then it was never any of your damn business."

They stand in silence. Aaronovich no longer feels angry, no longer feels anything. And Johnson's face has closed, the membrane of secrecy regrown, so that he is himself once more. It's as though all emotion has been drawn from the world, and they abide in a void where feeling is impossible.

Aaronovich waits until the air seems breathable again. "That shot. It was Howard, I take it?"

Johnson nods. Suddenly he looks tired, as if whatever has been sustaining him has been leaking out, drop by drop. Rubbing a palm distractedly on his trouser leg, he appears surprised when it comes back bloody.

"And *you* shot him." She speaks the words harshly. There is, apparently, a little anger left in her after all.

"It was the only way," Johnson says.

She can tell he believes it, or at least that he wishes her to think he does. "So what now?" Aaronovich asks, more gently.

Johnson looks down at his hand, inspecting the stained palm with distant interest. The expression in his eyes suggests it's something he's never seen before. "Now?" he echoes. "I'm damned if I know."

PART THREE
INCUBATION
CHAPTER NINETEEN

Whatever had emptied the town had done so fast.

Nothing strange in that, Ben figures. Plenty of these smaller places had been evacuated, plenty of others had been willingly abandoned, as it became clear that the crisis wasn't about to just blow over, that isolation might be more curse than blessing. He remembers the promises of medical care, the rumours of vaccination that had come to naught. High on any list of what spread the sickness would have to be misinformation, the official lies meant to keep the peace. Or maybe, Ben thinks, that panoply of wrong advice had simply been concocted by men too afraid to admit their own helplessness in the face of the truth.

All the signs here, however, point to an orderly, though hurried, exodus. Clothes and small valuables have been taken, as has a good proportion of the food and – to Ben's relief, with Landser poking around – any guns. There are a couple of stores, and both have been meticulously picked clean. Nevertheless, they've managed to siphon gas from a couple of cars and a run-down pickup; the pickup's tank had been full to brimming. They've turned up canned goods, sacks of flour, rice, and beans in cupboards and pantries, and best of all, a dozen bottles of half-decent whiskey. The food will justify the risk of coming out so far. The gas will more than replenish what they've used to get here.

Now, they've gathered about the prison truck, which is pulled up across the main street, its dust-streaked decals a stark reminder of who and what and why they are. It only occurs to Ben then to ponder why no one has thought to replace their battered vehicles, and so erase this souvenir of their old existence. Houseman has the shotgun up on his shoulder, like it's so much dead weight, and Landser is eyeing the weapon hungrily. From what Ben has pieced together, Landser is ex-military. But the tattoos peeping from collar and sleeves, ink Landser has shown off in all its ugly glory often enough when he works out in the weights pile, speaks of more recent allegiances: particularly the swastika spread between his shoulders. It's a testament to Plan John's tenacity, Ben supposes, that he found ways to make use of men like Landser, and to keep them in check.

"We've done good," Houseman says, squinting over the boxes and fuel cans heaped in the truck's exposed rear.

What he means is, *I've done good*. Houseman's star has risen since Foster began running things. No, not running, Foster doesn't have anything like the respect he'd need for that; but organising, Plan John's responsibilities with little of the power. Regardless, that gets Houseman more trust than he's ever known before – such as the duty of being leader of this expedition, and the weapon he holds and clearly has insufficient notion of how to use.

No wonder, really, that Landser covets the shotgun. Yet Ben finds that he prefers the situation just as it is.

This pause has been for Landser to finish the cigarette he's smoking, and Ben had been about to suggest that they start back. But their success and Houseman's gloating have sparked a memory. On the journey in, he'd noticed a few houses and a farm scattered loosely in the woodland to the west. He wouldn't expect that they'd turn up much in the houses; the farm, though, might be different. It's the kind of place where people were used to getting by on their own for days or weeks at a time. Also, there might be supplies that Singh can make use of on their own farm, that ragged stretch of dirt that looks more and more like their only hope for the future.

"This isn't bad," Ben says, "but we can do better."

"What're you thinking?" Houseman queries, immediately anxious.

"The farm. Remember? On the way here. Got to be worth a try."

He'd predicted an argument, but Landser is quick to say, "Fuck it, why not?"

"Isn't it begging for trouble?" asks Houseman. "We got a good haul, no Sickers sniffing about."

"You chickenshit," drawls Landser, without much rancour. The cigarette finally done, he twists its butt to shreds beneath a boot heel. "Could be they've died out."

They all know this isn't true. They saw a couple of the sick as they passed through a town they'd stripped bare back in the Plan John days, another an hour up the road. In both cases, they'd been in the distance and moving fast – but, from their evident malnourishment and the not-quite-human manner in which they'd darted for cover, unmistakably infected.

"It's worth the risk," Ben says. "We've got the gun."

"Yeah." Landser's gaze turns openly ravenous. "We've got the gun."

"I don't know," Houseman says. Maybe Landser's stare is making him nervous. "We've made a good haul."

"It's okay. We can do better." Ben tries to sound reasonable.

He has more to say, but Landser cuts him off. "Man the fuck up, Houseman."

His tone is implacable, the sentiment beyond argument. Just like that, the matter is settled.

★   ★   ★

They come to the farm by a long dirt track that runs carelessly through woods grown overbearing on either side. There is the main house, a small barn in front and off the road, and, some distance to their left, a corrugated metal shed like an old aircraft hangar. Outside the barn, an antique tractor sits on concrete blocks, its wheels removed, its engine open to the elements, which have rusted its innards into a single, molten mass of brown.

Ben feels sure that the place had grown dilapidated long before it was abandoned. The windowsills of the house are a decade at least past the point of needing fresh paint. A couple of panes have been shattered and covered with flattened cardboard boxes. There's an air of hopeless impoverishment, that unapologetic kind of poverty that has long since given up hope of ever being otherwise.

Houseman pulls up on the broad oval of dirt ahead of the buildings, kills the engine, and rolls down the window. He makes a show of appraising the scene, scratches thoughtfully at his nose, and says, "I don't see how we're going to find anything."

Ben expects Landser to take another shot at Houseman for cowardice, but instead he announces, "There's never been anything here. These dirt-poor fucks probably starved out years ago."

Since the diversion was Ben's idea, he reads their observations as criticisms of him, as doubtless they are. These days, after his utter failure to protect Plan John, with his arm in a sling and still practically useless, with so much failure to his name, criticism scares him as it never used to. It leads quickly to ridicule, and Ben feels instinctively that from there a short step would be needed before someone decided that Funland could benefit from one less mouth to feed. Ben knows he's sent out on these supply runs because he's disposable, in the same way that Landser is sent because he's too dangerous not to keep busy and Houseman because he's a worthless sack of shit that no one would miss.

And there is Ben's out. "For fuck's sake, Houseman," he says, ignoring the fact that Landser has just now, clear as day, agreed with him, "it's nothing to be a pussy about. If you're so worried, stay in the truck."

"Yeah," Landser concurs, his allegiance switching in a heartbeat against the softer target, as Ben had known it would. "You stay here. Make sure no one takes off with our wheels or some fucking thing. You give me that shotgun and we'll go get the job done."

Houseman shrinks away. "I can't do that."

"It's not much good in here," Landser points out.

"I'll wait outside," Houseman decides. "In case there's trouble."

"Come on," Ben says to Landser. He's growing increasingly anxious over the prospect of the two of them fighting for the weapon in the enclosed space of the truck. Ben opens the passenger door and steps out, willing Landser to follow, and is infinitely relieved when he hears the slap of Landser's boots in the dirt.

The house is surely empty. Both the front door and the screen door have been left open, displaying a shallow hallway. Yet even as he climbs the weatherworn steps, Ben feels a sense of disquiet that hadn't been there in the town. He tries to reassure himself; it's just that the place has been allowed to go to seed so badly. The carpet is scuffed to threads, and scars of plaster are revealed where faded wallpaper has rotted.

Ben considers suggesting that Landser check upstairs on his own. One look at his face cuts the words off in Ben's throat. It isn't fear he sees there, exactly, Landser probably couldn't appear frightened if he wanted to, but there's definite unease in his eyes.

So they search together, not speaking, falling unconsciously into a rhythm, Ben tapping doors open and peeking in while Landser keeps watch. It's apparent after a couple of rooms that they won't uncover anything of value; each is as shabby as the hallway. Ben keeps going partly from morbid curiosity, partly from a refusal to admit how wrong he'd been about coming here.

They go through the downstairs more quickly. It's much the same. The living room is particularly destitute, nothing in there but an ancient television and a settee with fat gobs of stuffing slopping from tears in the age-greyed fabric. A stink like warmed garbage hastens Ben's steps. They go on via a dining room into the kitchen, to find the cupboards stripped bare.

They leave the house by another door off the kitchen, also left open. A strip of what was once a vegetable garden is hemmed by a low, tumbledown fence. Ben's first thought is optimistic. Again it occurs to him that they'll unearth some supplies for the farm: fertiliser, pesticide, any prize to redeem this extra effort. But it's something else that gives Ben pause and keeps him staring at the small plot, though initially he can't say what.

Then he realises. Overturned dirt. Patches have been dug through recently, rifled for subterranean produce. *Animals*, he thinks. *Wild dogs.* There must be dogs all over, armies of them. Yet that doesn't explain the quiet. Ben hadn't noticed before, not in the house or the front yard, but there's a stillness in the air that doesn't feel normal. There are trees off to their right, and shouldn't there be birdsong? All he can hear is the sough of the wind and a distant, repetitive creak, a loose window or the front screen door, maybe. Ben glances at Landser. Does he feel it, that wrongness? But Landser only seems impatient.

Ben leads the way around the side of the house. The ground is overgrown there, the grass and nettles waist-high in places, up to where they wash like a sea against the flank of the metal shed. The path of cracked earth is already half overwhelmed.

The house hides the truck and Houseman until Ben and Landser are almost at its corner. Houseman is standing guard, as he said he would. However, even from a distance, his face is visibly stricken. Houseman isn't looking at them. Yet he must have heard their advance; he releases the shotgun's stock and ushers them forward. He's looking at the metal shed, at its front. Ben's angle of approach cuts it off from his view. Since Houseman is staring intently, Ben can't resist looking too, waiting for that moment when his perspective shifts. Moving so slowly – because Houseman is moving slowly – is like floating through a nightmare.

Then Ben is past the corner and can see, obliquely. The shed's twin doors of corrugated iron are open. Ben can't remember if they were open when they got here. The space beyond is lightless, blotted with shadow.

It's dark enough to hide whatever lies within, but not the figure standing inside the entrance.

CHAPTER TWENTY

He should be doing something. There must be something he can do that isn't sitting here, tying himself into knots.

Day by day, Doyle finds it more difficult to know what his function is. Things are expected of him, he feels. But he can't – or maybe simply doesn't want to – say what they are. He doubts he can meet anyone's expectations, even his own. It's growing harder and harder just to get out the door.

If Doyle had imagined Plan John's death would end his pariah status within Funland, then he'd have been disappointed. Not that he had; such a thought had never crossed his mind. Looking back, Doyle questions if any had, or if he'd only acted, putting one foot in front of the other until suddenly he was ankle deep in blood. That's how he remembers that night. It's the sole way he can arrange the memories that withstands the test of logic.

There were those who'd supposed he would try and run the place. But it had taken Doyle a day to recognise even that. Throughout that time, he'd distantly anticipated them coming for him, without knowing for certain who *they* were. Surely someone had been loyal enough to Plan John to avenge his death. If not, Foster had ample reason to want Doyle out of the picture. Doyle had used what he'd assumed to be his last day to make sure Carlita was safe and might stay safe, and to hunt for his son, uselessly. The prospect of death hadn't frightened him. He'd been exhausted, eyes raw from sleeplessness, brain raw from all that he wasn't ready to contemplate, and fear had been beyond him.

It had been Foster who'd tracked him down, late in the evening, as Doyle was eating in what had been the guards' canteen. *This is it*, Doyle had thought dully, and wondered if, when the moment came, he would find the will to fight back.

"Someone needs to sort Plan John's things," Foster had said without preamble. "All those files of his, whatever else. And I'm busy, frankly, keeping this shitstorm you've made from ripping the roof off. So I was thinking that person should be you."

Therefore, Doyle had gone through Plan John's possessions. The personal files he had burned without reading, glancing at them just long enough to appreciate how comprehensive they were. The only ones that gave him pause were Aaronovich's and his own. In the end, he'd thrown them into the flames with the rest. Everything else Doyle had catalogued, in so much as he could comprehend it. There'd been two file cabinets full of paper records, as well as various notebooks, and the codified logbook he'd discovered with the two-way radio in Plan John's bedroom. There was also a laptop computer, but it had little on its hard drive besides pornography. Plan John's record keeping had been deeply old-fashioned and utterly obsessive; it was an insight into the man Doyle had neither wished for nor been able to fathom.

Determined to do a thorough job, not because he'd expected anything to come of it but because he urgently needed the distraction, Doyle had spent the better part of a week scrutinising all that he'd excavated. After the first day, he had opened the windows and patio doors, hauled out Plan John's bed, dumped it over the balcony, and dragged up his own wire-frame bed from the guardroom. Doyle hadn't paused to examine how crazy doing so might seem, or what message he sent when from then on he slept in the apartment. He hadn't stopped to ask what it said about him that he was inclined to sleep mere feet from where he'd put a bullet in Plan John's head.

Through Foster, Doyle had called a meeting, and he'd given his report, as if they were the directors of some corporation instead of ex-cons mixed up with their former guards, readying to brave their first winter in this new and infinitely hostile world. No one had cared, of course; no one had cared about any of it. Only Silensky's kid had shown the slightest interest, and then only in the coded logbook, like it was something out of a spy story. They hadn't even found the situation funny, though surely it was. Doyle had realised belatedly just how afraid everyone was, even the hardest of them. No one had liked Plan John, but, as his name implied, he had been prepared for the worst, he'd made the tough calls, and now – thanks to Doyle Johnson – he was gone.

Afterward, Doyle had stayed where he was. Foster had been making the administrative wing his headquarters, and somehow Doyle didn't feel right being there. Again, he'd resisted considering why it *did* feel right for him to be in Plan John's old rooms, of all places. Doyle had told himself, sometimes, that he was trying to understand, to tease out the shape of Howard's scheme, and whatever had made him so certain they could endure here when the rest of the world, conceivably, was gone. Doyle had read over and over files, records, logbooks, and lists. But none of it made sense.

If he'd had a real motive, perhaps that came into focus a week later. He'd begun to explore the Big House, which, true to its name, seemed to contain more rooms than was reasonable, and so few of them used. Many were entirely empty. Others contained piled chairs and beds. One was full of mouldering uniforms and fluttering clouds of moths. Then Doyle had found the apartments. There were three, surfaces thick with dust, each with its own small washroom and now-defunct shower. Probably they'd been intended for guests, though the idea of anyone visiting White Cliff in anything but its formal capacity struck Doyle as hard to reconcile.

That night, under cover of darkness, he'd moved Carlita into one of them.

When she'd first seen the room, she'd wept. Doyle had stood awkwardly, watching her relief and pain well out in floods. When she'd quieted finally, he'd said, "You'll be safer here."

"Oh my god, Doyle." She'd sounded almost delirious.

"I've blacked out the windows. All the same, use the candles sparingly. If you want daylight, you'll have to leave the door to the corridor open. There's a second door that closes off this whole section; between here and there, you can go anywhere you like."

Her expression had been childlike, gratitude stripped of pretence. It had only made him more uncomfortable.

"I've got to go," he'd said. In truth, he'd had nowhere to go and nothing at all to do. "I'll come back tomorrow to check on you. You should have everything you need to get through the night."

"Thank you," she'd whispered.

So much meaning in those two words. The weight of her emotion had seemed like a physical force, pressing upon Doyle as he paced out of the room. It disturbed him, for it was disproportionate to such a small kindness, exceeding anything he might have earned.

Nevertheless, he had returned the next day, and the next. Doyle had gone every day, some days twice. He is thinking, in fact, of going now, though it's light outside and so theoretically more risky. But even freed of the infirmary, Carlita still gets bored, crazy bored. She'd be glad of the company.

And there's little real danger of being seen, less of questions being asked when no one cares what he does. Aside from Aaronovich, Doyle has told only Ben Silensky and his boy, Kyle. Contreras, he reasons, doesn't need to know. Doyle doesn't blame him for his failure to resist Plan John, but not blaming is a different thing from risking another such moment of weakness.

Contreras. Damn it. Yes, there *is* something Doyle needs to do. Orders from Foster the day before last: "Johnson, you've got to talk to that useless shitsack Contreras. If you want him running the stores then he needs to run them, not just let everyone take whatever the fuck they like."

Doyle hadn't wanted Contreras running the stores that he remembers. However, he does want Contreras safe, and Foster knows that. Putting someone Doyle is willing to protect in that position makes it halfway to being Doyle's responsibility.

So he'll go to Contreras and listen to his news. It will be bad, because there's no other kind. Perhaps Doyle will offer advice he doesn't believe himself. Perhaps even that will be beyond him. Either way, he'll get it over with.

And then – Carlita? Yes, maybe then.

*   *   *

"What're you doing?"

Kyle starts so hard that he drops the pencil he's been busily spinning in his fingers. It clatters from the edge of the desk.

Austin has come up behind him without a sound. He's wearing a white T-shirt and a pair of baggy blue prison trousers, sizes too big, tied at the waist with string and tucked up around the ankles. His head is shaved to the skull, a job so messy that Kyle suspects he did it himself. This is closer than they've been to each other in weeks, and Kyle can't help noticing, with a thrill of awe, how muscled Austin's arms and torso have become. There can't be more than a year between them, and yet Austin, with his wiry frame and the studied blankness in his face, now looks far older.

Kyle struggles to keep a quaver out of his voice. "You remember how your dad found that radio set in Plan John's rooms?"

Austin shakes his head, with no apparent interest.

"After he...." *After he shot Plan John.* "He found a two-way radio. For if the phone lines ever got cut off. Turns out Plan John had been keeping it in his rooms. This" – he indicates the book spread on the desk with a tilt of his head – "was there with it."

Austin's expression hasn't changed one iota during anything Kyle has said. To Kyle, the thought that there might be someone out there, someone they could talk to and maybe meet, even kids his own age, sends a shiver through him every time. If he's honest, he knows that what he's imagining is his old life, the world before, yet that knowledge does nothing to make the feeling go away.

"So what're you doing with it?" Austin asks.

"It's in this weird code," Kyle explains. "Your dad told me I can try and figure it out."

"Why?"

Kyle considers. "I guess because no one else cares."

"No," Austin says, with abrupt and disproportionate irritation, "I mean, why do you want to do that?"

The reality would take too long to explain, and Kyle is sure Austin isn't interested anyway. Kyle is the only one who's shown any curiosity regarding the coded logbook, and even the prospect of other survivors. He settles for the most simplified version. "Just bored, I suppose."

"Yeah?"

"Yeah."

Austin's face cracks for the first time, the briefest glimpse that a mental process is occurring. "If you're that bored, why don't you come with me?"

Kyle's heart jolts. Since his arrival at Funland, he and Austin have scarcely spoken, as though some intangible conflict sprang up between them at the outset. For a while it didn't seem to matter, but as the days and months have slipped by, as his dad has grown more distant, as he's come to comprehend the scope of his aloneness, Kyle has begun to wonder: how would it be if he and Austin were friends? Is such a thing possible? He barely recalls what having a friend is like.

"Okay," Kyle says. "Where are we going?"

"I'll show you," Austin tells him, already turning to leave.

Kyle gives the logbook one more quick look, marvelling as he always does at the neat, unintelligible rows of text. Then he snaps it shut, slips it into a pocket, and falls in behind Austin.

★　★　★

On her third attempt, Aaronovich gets as far as the outer door before she turns back.

Each time she's promised herself she will go outside. She'll find someone to help, something to do. There must be ways in which she could be useful. And each time she's faced the same conclusion: Funland has only one place for her, and this is it.

Indecisiveness isn't like her. Neither is cowardice. Nor is the sudden upwelling of frustration that makes her slam her office door far harder than she needs to. Aaronovich sinks into a chair, releasing the sigh that's been building within her. She understands her own turmoil and these bursts of useless energy that propel her nowhere. But understanding doesn't help.

The truth is that she misses Carlita.

Through every moment, her presence felt like a weight around Aaronovich's neck. Knowing the woman was down there, literally beneath her feet and yet beyond her ability to help, had corrupted her perception of herself by slow degrees. For, even after everything – Micha's death, the trial, the grey months of total numbness that could reductively be described as grief – she had clung to the belief that, above all else, she was someone who helped people. Doctor had never been merely a title to her. As far back as medical school, it had seemed a part of who she was, essential as a first love.

Now Carlita is gone and Aaronovich misses her. Or perhaps not Carlita herself; how can she miss someone she hardly spoke to? Their entire association had been conducted in the briefest of snatches, and whenever they'd spoken, the gulf between them had been vast. No, what Aaronovich misses and all she misses is the sense of worth

Carlita's presence gave her. The absence of having a patient of sorts is actually worse than the insidious guilt that Carlita's irremediable helplessness forced upon her.

Now there's nothing. Aaronovich has one job to do and she can't do it. She's come close to requesting that Doyle Johnson allocate her a new role, but after Plan John's death and the conversation that followed she feels less and less sure she can trust him, or that she wants to. She's thought of speaking to Foster, but she's never found anything to like about the man. And what would be the point? Her age, her gender, everything about her keeps her apart from the wider world of Funland. Fortunate, really, that her function makes her invaluable, or the price of her current uselessness might be infinitely more severe.

But oh, how she hates *being* useless. Few torments could injure her so deeply. There are times when it's all she can do not to pray to a god she long ago relinquished any faith in: *Make them sick, make them hurt each other, just give me something I can do.* Blasphemous thoughts if she still believed, mere ugly fantasies since she doesn't.

Aaronovich's mind turns then, as it frequently does, to the one person in Funland she could have truly helped.

She wishes she'd tried harder to get through to Doyle's boy, Austin. And she asks herself why she's already rendered that possibility into the past tense. Is he so beyond her aid? Or his father's, for that matter? But she almost never sees him; he's become a ghost. Anyway, Aaronovich is no psychiatrist. She can do no more than anyone else could.

Except, perhaps, that she would care. Aaronovich reflects on why she hasn't at least tried, and doesn't at all like where the question threatens to lead her. *Maybe it's not too late*, she thinks – knowing that of course it is. For if Austin had been so damaged when he came here, what must the boy be like now?

*   *   *

Austin doesn't speak as they cross the yard.

He's said more consecutive words in one day than he has in the last month, or so it seems. The effort is exhausting. He resents it, and resents Kyle for making it necessary. He resents his own need.

Resentment doesn't make the need go away. He's gone as far as he can go alone. He requires an ally, and his choices are few.

As they reach the Big House, Austin glances at Kyle – trailing behind, striving to keep pace – and observes all the curiosity and confusion he's attempting to hide. Theoretically, the Big House is open to everyone these days. In fact, though that may be true of the lower floor, which houses the library, laundry, workshops, and other facilities, the top floor belongs to Austin's father, who prowls around up there like a monster in a movie. Austin hears him often, steps echoing and magnified by conduits of dull metal, hears too the woman Carlita, and sometimes overhears their conversations. No one knows she's there, no one even knows she exists, and Austin thinks about what would happen if they should learn. But doing so leads him in a tight circle back to the night of the gunshot, to blind terror and gashing his flesh on rough-cut steel in the darkness, wanting only to escape. So Austin keeps his father's secret, for now.

Passing the main entrance, Austin steals another glance at Kyle. Reading people is easier for him these days. Get far enough on the outside and certain things make a different kind of sense. Faces are one of them. Nobody is that good at hiding their thoughts, not when you see them how they really are. Kyle is confused, yes, and eager, and afraid, all of those at once. But mainly he's curious; *Where are they going?*

They round a second corner, to where Big House and cellblock abut, brick the white of a snake's belly meeting grey concrete: a place grown so familiar to Austin yet probably new to Kyle. Austin takes a couple of steps back and runs toward the wall. At the final instant, he leaps, taps the wall with his toes, and throws an arm up. From above comes a metallic groan and then a frantic rattling. When Austin lands, he has the lowest rung of the ladder clutched in one hand. It's a technique he's been refining, day in and day out, for the last month. He allows himself just a moment to enjoy Kyle's awestruck expression, and says, "You don't leave it down, or anyone can find it."

Kyle nods, though clearly he doesn't understand why someone discovering the ladder should matter. He'll get it soon – or else, and Austin's chest tightens at the thought, he won't. What then? Something terrible, possibilities he doesn't want to imagine. Austin forces the doubt aside. He can only deal with one dilemma at a time.

Austin hauls the ladder the remaining distance to the ground and starts up. He climbs with easy grace these days; swinging up the rungs is no harder than walking. He's at the top before Kyle begins his own ascent. It's satisfying how he struggles, taking the rungs one by one, barely able to use arms and legs in concert. Austin leaves him to it, gazing instead toward the distant centre of the roof.

He waits for Kyle to reach the summit, his hands and feet scrabbling, his breathing heavy with exertion. Austin gives him space to drag himself over the lip of the wall and then works the crank that retracts the ladder. It rises with a complaining rattle, and as always Austin tenses until he's done and he's sure no curious footsteps have followed that unique, inexplicable noise.

When he turns back to Kyle, Austin studies his face once more, and finds there everything he'd hoped for. He recognises all the anxiety and excitement of before, the same confusion too. But now, lighting him like an electrical charge from within, making those other emotions dull by comparison, there's wonder.

"Come on," Austin says, feeling as good as he has in days or weeks, not letting his pleasure show even slightly, "you haven't seen anything yet."

CHAPTER TWENTY-ONE

The man hasn't moved one inch in the seconds since Ben first spotted him. Nor does he do so when Landser arrives to stand next to Ben, muttering, "What the fuck?" beneath his breath. Houseman also stays perfectly motionless, the shotgun threatening empty air.

The man is wearing blue overalls, or overalls that once were blue. They're faded almost white at the knees and elbows, stained in dark patches across the front, and in many places scuffed and torn. His face is covered with a thicket of beard. What skin is visible is deeply lined and tanned. It's hard to say what reveals him as sick, since he's stood so still the whole time. But then, isn't that precisely it? Anyone else, even if they were frightened, even if they were plain dumb, would have moved by now. His immobility is inhuman.

"Sicker," growls Landser, as though to confirm Ben's thoughts. Yet Landser doesn't seem unsettled at the prospect, more like intrigued.

Ben takes a few more shallow steps toward Houseman. From the corner of his mouth, Houseman says, "He turned up out of nowhere."

"Out of nowhere?"

"I mean, from in the shed, I guess."

"And that's all he's done? Just stand there?"

"Well, I guess."

They could get into the truck and drive away. But the Sicker might come after them, and shooting from within the cab will be far more difficult.

"You need to get closer," Landser tells Houseman.

Houseman shakes his head in fierce jerks. "No way."

"Then give me the gun."

"I can't."

"I'd bet good money you can."

"He's right, Houseman," Ben mumbles. "You need to get near to him."

"I *can't*," Houseman repeats.

"Then," Landser hisses, "give me the fucking—"

"No. Okay." Houseman takes a step forward.

The Sicker doesn't flinch. Houseman takes another step. He keeps moving, inching forward, still pointing the shotgun at nothing other than sky. The closer he gets, the shorter his steps become, the longer the pauses between. Ben wants to scream at him that he's only making this worse.

Then the Sicker bolts into the shed. Houseman's shotgun explodes. Most of the shot peppers the side of the doorway, tiny craters imploding in unison. A few stray pellets are consumed by the blackness. Into the Sicker? No, the angle had been entirely wrong.

"Hell, Houseman," Ben mutters, the words made faint by the ringing in his eardrums.

Landser mutters something under his breath that might easily be *useless fuck*. "Now you get to go in after him," he says aloud.

Houseman's eyes have gone wide as saucers. He looks to Ben, his expression pleading. What does he think is going to happen? They've come too far. "You'll be fine," Ben assures him.

Houseman holds Ben's gaze a moment more, no longer begging but just stunned. Finally, he starts moving again. To Ben's surprise, Landser stays behind him. Ben's first thought is that the big skinhead is backing Houseman up. His second is that Landser probably intends to ensure Houseman doesn't bolt.

Ben sets off after them. He knows he'll be useless in a fight with one arm in a sling, but to hang back will be to lose face, and leaves him dangerously alone. Closer and he can see that through the doors is a narrow walkway between railed enclosures. There's no sign of the Sicker. The shed is windowless, so that the only light is what's gathered around the entrance. A few feet in, the grey fades to blackness.

Houseman is outside the doorway. He is trembling visibly, causing the shotgun barrel to bob and weave. Landser is almost at his back, Ben perhaps ten paces behind. He wants to move nearer, but his feet have grown stubborn.

"You see anything?" Ben's voice sounds thick to his own ears.

"It's real dark. I think there's another level." Houseman squints upward. "Christ but it stinks."

Ben can smell it too, a chemical sickly-sweetness like slurry, and some odour behind that, a submerged perfume of rotting meat.

"Go on," Landser says. He taps Houseman's shoulder.

"What?"

"Go. On."

Houseman shuffles over the concrete lip of the doorway. "Can't see shit." He dips the shotgun into the left stall, then the right. He shakes his head. "This is crazy."

Just as something drops onto him.

No, not something, someone. They must have leaped from the upper tier. Houseman has time to squeal before the impact flattens him to the ground. The body on top of his is a woman. She's wearing jeans and a sweater, both black with filth. She clings to Houseman, gripping with hands and knees, and Houseman lies there like a passive lover. His arm is pinned beneath her knee, and the shotgun slides out of his fingers. In that same moment, a second figure falls from above: a man, younger than the first. He clamps himself over what little of Houseman is uncovered.

An ambush, Ben realises. This is an ambush.

Landser starts forward. Ben assumes that he's attempting to help Houseman, until Landser veers toward the shotgun. At that range, he's as likely to kill Houseman as the Sickers. But what can Ben do, with one good arm? Indecision turns his thoughts to glue.

As Landser clutches and pumps the shotgun, a shape barrels out of the darkness, the first male Sicker. It's like watching a car crash into a wall. Landser nearly stays upright, would have if not for Houseman, whose legs are thrashing behind him. As it is, Landser staggers, and the shotgun belches fire.

Whatever the shot hits, it isn't the Sicker. He's gained a hold of the stock and is trying to wrest the weapon free. Landser, already scrabbling to his feet, responds by pounding the man's nose with a bony fist, every blow drawing sprays of blood.

Houseman, meanwhile, is no longer moving, except for the occasional twitch. Abruptly, the female Sicker gives up on him and dashes at Landser. She attacks like a mad dog, leading with her head, driving her skull hard against his ribcage and only afterward thinking to wrap skinny arms around his thighs. Her momentum wrests the shotgun

152 • DAVID TALLERMAN

free of the male Sicker's grip, and Landser seizes the opportunity. In a moment, he has the gun back in both hands. He's on the ground, though, by the time he's pumped it, the woman snapping at his wrists. Landser drives the toe of the stock into her jaw prior to firing, and that's his mistake: he's ruined a clean shot.

Still, the damage is catastrophic. The blast gouges a crescent in the man's side, peeling strips of flesh and cloth from his left arm. He reels, to collide with the shed door. He shouldn't be standing, let alone walking; Ben can clearly identify jagged extrusions of bone amid the dripping horror of his side. Yet he manages half a dozen steps before he flops onto Landser, trapping the shotgun under his own flayed body.

Only then does it hit Ben that he's just watching this, like here he is at the Super Bowl or something. He doesn't dare to run, so instead he risks a step backward. The two on Landser, busy scrabbling their way inside him, don't look up. The second male, however, is crouched in the open doorway, and – as though intuiting the movement – he glances in Ben's direction.

If Ben runs, the second male will be on him. Ben knows without the slightest doubt. He can't outrun these things, which look like people and behave like wild beasts. Ben takes another step backward. The young male cocks his head. Ben takes a third step, and still he doesn't follow.

Slowly, so slowly, keeping his eyes on the second male, Ben retreats toward the truck. He tries not to see what's left of Houseman, on the edge of his view. He tries not to hear as, just as slowly, it seems, the other two tear Landser apart.

*   *   *

The rooftop is a world of its own.

That's the appeal. It makes sense to Kyle. He considers the structures of ductwork that rise like a futuristic city in miniature, clustered about the skyscraper of the shack that stands near the far end. All of it makes perfect sense.

Austin is already trotting around the edge, with a loping stride that Kyle can barely keep pace with. Every so often, Austin stops to indicate some detail, monosyllabically or simply with a gesture. When he goes close to the edge and looks over – something he does with care, having made certain no one is observing from below – Kyle feels obliged to join him. Only in those moments does he suffer from an awareness of height. Though the Big House and cellblock are of a lowly two storeys, their high ceilings make that seem more like three.

The altitude doesn't appear to trouble Austin. "See?" He points. "You can get up on the admin wing the same way."

Kyle traces the line of Austin's finger to another ladder suspended from the administrative wing's north wall.

A few paces later, Austin adds, "There're ways onto the walls as well."

When they've finished a full circumnavigation, Austin continues to the corner and leans over the parapet again. Below, two right angles join: the junction where Big House and cellblock meet. The cellblock roof is maybe four feet lower, and has no wall around it, just metal guttering. There's no ductwork, either, merely an expanse of tarpaper layered with grit, like a desert highway leading nowhere.

"You can walk on it," Austin says. Obviously restless, he abandons the parapet to take a seat on a tube of segmented metal, which burrows through the roof like some huge, misshapen worm. "But I don't in the day. Too easy to be seen."

Kyle nods. Of course they can't be seen. No one can know this secret, *their* secret. Kyle thinks he recognises the faintest satisfaction in Austin's eyes then. Have they reached an understanding?

"There's something else," Austin says.

Austin swings over the silver worm and ducks beneath a pipe. Kyle follows hurriedly, as though the ductwork is a maze and he might lose Austin for good. Yet he finds him immediately, leaning now against the wall of the shack. Kyle scrutinises the small shelter. There's nothing obviously interesting about it; he guesses it must provide access from below. Or is that what Austin means to show off, a back route inside?

"You keep a secret?" asks Austin.

Kyle nods once more. Yes, he can keep a secret. He has no one to tell.

Austin kneels beside one of the ducts. There's a panel there, a framed mesh of knitted wire. As Austin grips one edge, Kyle notices how the screws are missing. There are only the holes, shiny and scratched. The panel comes off easily, and *thunks* onto the roof. The cavity it concealed extends in either direction.

"Where does it lead?" Kyle says, suddenly breathless.

"Everywhere. If you're careful."

So this is how Austin spends his days. He's dug into the cracks of Funland, burrowing like a tick into its underbelly. Or maybe there's more to be revealed. If Austin has spent weeks this way, who knows how vast the borders of his hidden world might be?

It doesn't even occur to Kyle to ask why. Being on the roof for this short time has given him a sense of security he'd practically forgotten. There's none of the subdued threat that runs so thickly through Funland as to seem a quality of the air. Kyle has been lucky to find a place in the farm, where he's spared the worst, but the farm has its own tensions. It isn't safe, not as this is safe.

"Are we going inside?" Kyle's voice, of its own accord, has hushed to a reverential whisper.

Austin looks at him. Something has shifted in his face. "Why?"

The question throws Kyle. "I don't know. To see."

"What makes you think I trust you?" There's no aggression in the inquiry. On the contrary, Austin appears genuinely curious.

"I said. I promised."

Austin tilts his head. "So?"

"I thought—"

"You thought what?"

"I just—"

Quicker than Kyle can register, Austin's face is close to his, Austin's arm is pinning his shoulder, and there's something sharp and cold held to Kyle's throat.

"You listen," Austin hisses. "This is mine. You don't come up here unless I agree. You don't tell anyone. You don't *think* about it. Or else...."

But there's no need for Austin to say what else. It's there in his eyes, in the ocean of rage swelling behind them. Kyle wants to nod, can't for the blade against his Adam's apple. He hopes that his own eyes, the fear surely betrayed there, will answer for him.

As abruptly as Austin jumped him, he backs off. Kyle has the briefest glimpse of his weapon vanishing into a pocket. It looks like a vegetable peeler, though the edge glints cruelly. Austin gives him one more glance, and Kyle is surprised at how entirely his anger is gone. There's only the hint of some unspoken reconciliation, as if this has been no more than a handshake.

Austin picks up the vent cover and hammers it back in place with the heel of a fist. Then he swings up into the ductwork and disappears. Seconds later, Kyle hears the patter of his soles on the ladder, the thud as he drops the last couple of feet.

Kyle touches two fingers to his throat, confirming that the skin is unbroken. Now that his shock has abated, he feels sure that even Austin's abrupt violence is another step in his befriending, a necessary stage. Austin will come to him again. Whatever has adjusted in his brain to make him seek out companionship after all this time won't simply shift back.

He's enjoyed this, Kyle comprehends, all of it, the fear included. It's different from the kind he's grown used to, thrilling where that's only numbing. Kyle sinks to the ground, his spine against the cool metal of the duct.

He'll have to go down soon, he knows. But, for a while at least, he can be here and feel safe.

★　　★　　★

Before he leaves, Doyle goes out onto the balcony. He considers the stains on the concrete, almost scoured to invisibility now. One more heavy rainfall will do it. *You're a murderer*, he tells himself, and wishes he could find something within him that felt like a correct response to that word.

After going back inside, Doyle washes his face and upper body in the bowl of water he keeps near the bed, studies his features in the small mirror above – without knowing what he expects to discover there – and then pulls on a shirt and leaves the apartment, not locking the door behind him.

The last time Foster tried to delegate responsibility to him, Doyle's job had been to talk to Nguyen about the generator. Nguyen, the young American-Vietnamese whose breadth of engineering knowledge and inexplicable presence in Funland baffle Doyle utterly, had ranted for an hour and more. The gist seemed to be that the generator had developed a fault, or would do so imminently, and that, when it went wrong, it would keep going wrong until it was beyond his ability to fix.

"What can we do?" Doyle had asked in the end, when Nguyen's verbal energy had finally unwound into sullen frustration.

Nguyen had shrugged. "Fuck, I know. It's entropy, man. Everything breaks eventually."

Obviously there's an agenda in the tasks Foster doles out to Doyle, and it's not one that's difficult to see. Foster is creating an illusion in which they share authority for Funland's survival, while pushing anything that can go wrong, that inescapably *will* go wrong, in Doyle's direction. When the generator fails, that will be on Nguyen and on Doyle, but Foster's hands will be spotless.

Maybe that should bother Doyle more. Maybe it should bother him at all. He lets Foster order him because it's easier than figuring things out for himself, and because he needs the diversion. Doyle doesn't worry too much about the future; he believes less and less that there'll be one. The generator will fail. The stores will run out. Or something else. There are any number of resources on which their survival depends that, sooner or later, will inevitably be exhausted, and there's nothing that he, Doyle Johnson, can do about the fact. Perhaps a smarter man, a man like Plan John, but not him, and not Foster either.

When Doyle knocks at the door of the storeroom, there's a moment of silence, then Contreras's thin voice replies, "Who is it?"

"It's Johnson."

A pad of footsteps, and the door swings open. Contreras is wearing just a pair of blue prison trousers, leaving his skinny chest exposed to the autumn chill. He looks concerned, though his expression has been set that way since his nephew's death and it's hard to determine if it's grown any worse.

"Good afternoon, Doyle." Clearly he longs to say more, but the question never gets further than his eyes. *What have I done*? they entreat, with quiet desperation.

"Are you busy?" Doyle asks. "I can come back."

"No, no. You want coffee?"

"Sure," says Doyle. "I can use coffee."

Bare soles whispering against the concrete floor, Contreras walks to the diminutive gas camp stove he keeps. He takes the tin pot resting there, pours some of its contents into a cracked mug, and hands the results to Doyle. Contreras's coffee looks like molasses and smells like gas, but when Doyle takes a sip he immediately feels the cobwebs that have hung around him all day start to dissolve.

Of course, the coffee and stove are luxuries Contreras has no particular right to, small abuses of his office. Doyle doesn't begrudge him them, and no one else would be half as honest. No, that isn't why he's here.

"I went over the last inventory," he says. This isn't true, but Foster has, and passed on to Doyle the relevant details as part of his abbreviated mission briefing.

"Yes?" Contreras is already looking furtive.

"We're still going through supplies too fast. And not just a little. There's hardly a sign of the rationing plan being used."

"No," says Contreras, "I use the plan."

"Then where's it all going, Tito?"

"You know, Doyle. You must know how things are."

"Yeah." Doyle shakes his head wearily. "I know. You let them in here and they take whatever they want."

"What can I do?" Contreras holds up his hands like a penitent. "They push me. They threaten. I have to go out sometimes. You tell me, what do I do?"

"You give me names and I make it stop." Doyle recognises as he speaks the words that he means them. It's the kind of job he's ready for; not like this, not interrogating a weak and broken man.

"Names?" Contreras says. "It's everyone."

"I don't believe that."

"Everyone," Contreras repeats. He shudders. "So what am I to do, Doyle, you tell me." He crumples into a folding lawn chair beside the packing crate that bears his makeshift stove and cups his face in his hands.

Doyle sips from his coffee, feeling distantly nauseated. Despite what he said, he doesn't doubt Contreras's version of events. They would all sooner starve in a few months than go hungry now. Except nobody is considering that far ahead, not Foster, not anyone. It's like they still expect to wake one day and find everything returned to normal, the supply trucks rolling in again, the horror of taking responsibility for their own existence nothing but a memory.

Doyle realises Contreras is crying, thick sobs that travel visibly through his gaunt frame and bubble out against his hands. Doyle thinks about trying to comfort him, but he has no comfort to give. In a few months they'll likely both be dead, at the end of a long, slow suicide.

Doyle feels like he's on a train chugging sluggishly toward a cliff edge. All he has to do is step off. Why can't he do that? Just step off and walk away.

Doyle thinks of Carlita, and then pushes the thought aside, barely.

"I'll figure something out," he says. He drains the last of his molasses coffee and sets the cup on Contreras's crate-cum-table. "Make sure you lock the door behind me."

But Doyle can't judge whether Contreras hears through the muffled sounds of his own grief.

⋆　　⋆　　⋆

Only when Ben reaches the truck does it dawn on him that Houseman will have the key. His heart turns to stone in his chest. A perfectly clear image of him searching Houseman's shattered remains slides into his mind, though how Ben would reach him with three Sickers in the way is beyond the scope of his imagination.

However, when he squints within the cab, the key is already there in the ignition. Ben climbs inside, turns it, and for all that he'd been certain it wouldn't, the engine rumbles into life on the first try. His instincts tell him to drive, as fast as he dares. Yet some small, contrary impulse drags his scrutiny from the dirt road, insisting he look behind. Ben anticipates the three Sickers finally turning their attention to him. Instead, his gaze is drawn to a shape, not much larger than a sack of potatoes, in the back of the truck.

As he watches, it moves – turns its head.

Hardly thinking, Ben climbs out of the cab. It's the wrong thing to do, precisely the wrong thing. He knows without question, yet his body appears to have other ideas. Keeping his distance, Ben walks around to peer into the truck's bed.

The creature there looks back at him. A girl, stick-thin beneath a dress over sweatpants, both torn and black with dirt. She can't be more than six or seven. Her hair was once blond, but now is darker and tangled into dreadlocks. She's cowering, pushed up against the cab of the truck, cartons of rice and split peas leaking where her bare feet have trampled them. Her eyes are bright with fear; her cracked lips are curled about an animal snarl.

"It's okay," Ben says.

He doesn't know what he means. Clearly nothing is okay. If he could drag her off and cast her aside and leap into the cab and drive away, he would. But if he does, she'll struggle, and if she bites him, scratches him, spits at him even.... There's blood on her dress, in crusted smudges, and if that blood somehow mixed with his own then it would all be over.

Ben clambers back inside the cab. His mind is still providing nothing useful. Except that it occurs to him that the rear window will be toughened glass; he doubts she can break through.

He releases the hand brake and sets off slowly, fearful of startling her. Five minutes later he's on a proper road, and half an hour after that on a major highway, the one they followed down here. Ben hopes he can remember the route back. He imagines being lost, and eventually running out of gas, with that creature so close behind him.

The more he considers the girl, the more curious Ben grows. At first there had been small noises to remind him of her presence, scratching and the patter of her movements among their laboriously gathered supplies. Now she's quietened, or else the sounds of her presence have been drowned by the drone of wheels on tarmac. Ben allows himself a few miles, until he finds a straight stretch. Then he slows to a crawl and glances over his shoulder.

He's half expecting the girl's face to be pressed against the glass, jaws wide. Rather, she has curled up, almost out of view. It's hard to tell, but he thinks she might be sleeping.

CHAPTER TWENTY-TWO

Evening is falling by the time Doyle leaves Contreras, the sun just beginning to tip beneath the rugged outline of the mountains to the west.

He'd planned to go back to his room briefly and then continue to check on Carlita. It's an urge he can't place that carries Doyle's feet to the south doors, the ones that open onto the yard. Maybe he has some unconscious thought of discussing with Foster what Contreras said. Or maybe his old instincts aren't quite as dulled as he's come to believe.

The crowd isn't big by the standards of a year ago. But given Funland's current population, the gathering near the main gate is sizable, more than a dozen men huddled close together. They're encircling the truck that went out early that morning. Tension hangs around them like midges about a stagnant pond, and yet, what's strangest, no one is shouting, nor even speaking.

In Funland, the vocabulary for expressing discontent isn't wide or subtle. Certainly, silence has never figured into it. He's had a headache building all day, though, and from the way the pain shudders to new and violent life the moment he sees that mute gathering, Doyle knows it signifies nothing good. The headaches are sufficiently regular now that he should have given up interpreting them as omens of trouble. Still, he does. There's trouble enough in Funland to warrant the conviction.

Doyle thinks about going back inside. Instead, he crosses the yard, not hurrying, trying to read the scene in the dimming light. But there are just the close-crowded bodies, a barricade concealing the near side of the truck. Doyle will have to join the end of the tail if he's to learn what has them all transfixed, and so he does, sidling in beside a white con he recognises as a man named Colton.

Doyle looks at the truck. He observes Silensky, hunched in the cab, gripping the wheel as though he's half set on driving straight back out again. He notes the boxes and bags of supplies piled haphazardly in the bed. And only then does he spy what he takes to be a canvas sack, until it turns wide eyes his way.

"Shit," Doyle says. He can't believe it, he truly can't. The child is like something from another world.

"Shit is right," mutters Colton from beside him.

Then Doyle understands. This child *is* from another world. He can see her eyes more clearly now, the speckles of haematoma. "She's sick," he says.

"Fuck yes she's sick," Colton concurs.

Foster is nowhere in sight. Anger warms Doyle's belly; isn't that convenient? Foster is absent, and no one is doing anything. That means this falls to him.

He doesn't have his gun. Doyle never carries it on him, it's back in Plan John's apartment. Then he thinks, *Could you shoot a child?* And he's shocked that is his second rather than his first thought.

"Johnson."

Doyle starts. Aaronovich is standing beside him. He hadn't noticed her approach. Her presence adds to the strangeness of the scene, for she so rarely leaves her office these days.

"What is this?" she asks.

The question doesn't strike Doyle as requiring an answer. Nevertheless, he says, "A problem."

"That's a *child*." Her voice is hushed, full of wonder.

Doyle rounds on her. "Don't play stupid," he snaps. "You know exactly what that is."

"Yes," Aaronovich says calmly. "I just told you."

He catches her arm and drags her a few paces aside, not quite able to explain his behaviour. Everyone can still hear, and all he's doing is making a scene. "Listen to me. That thing is a menace. I'm going inside, I'm going to get a gun, and then—"

"Johnson," Aaronovich says, "don't do this."

He freezes. Something in her manner has paralysed him, tearing his thoughts asunder.

"Don't do it. Let me take her. It's my responsibility. It will be on me."

"On you?" he says. He can't make sense of her words. "What happens when she goes crazy? When you get sick? That will be on you?"

"Yes," Aaronovich says. Her composure is absolute. He can feel it pressing against his anger like the cool from an open freezer. "I'm the doctor here. This is my choice to make. That's a child. Let me look after her."

Doyle stares at her in horror. She's absolutely serious. Worse, she won't back down. And he still doesn't know if he can do what he said he'd do, if he's capable of pointing a gun at that ragged creature and pulling the trigger.

But Aaronovich is already taking the choice out of his hands. She's edged closer to the rear of the truck, her palms out before her as though in supplication. She's speaking softly, making gentle noises that sound to Doyle like nonsense. He tenses, readying for he knows not what. If the girl attacks then maybe, just maybe, he might move fast enough to restrain her in time.

The girl makes a vibration at the bottom of her throat, a low trilling of fear and aggression. *This is it*, Doyle thinks. But Aaronovich doesn't seem concerned. At the tailgate now, she lets it down, and stands once more with her hands out flat, perfectly passive and receptive.

The girl moves. Yet her motion isn't the rush Doyle's been bracing for. She crawls clumsily to the middle of the truck bed, heedful to keep to the side away from the audience of gathered cons.

"Back up," Doyle says as quietly as he can. "Everyone. Get back."

They do as they're told. He hadn't thought they would but they do. *These hard, dangerous men must look pretty funny*, Doyle thinks distantly, *shuffling to stay clear of a little girl*.

Aaronovich is retreating also, palms still flat, still murmuring wordlessly. The girl pauses in front of the tailgate, pushing up on her haunches to stare at the woman before her.

Then she lollops down onto the concrete and begins to follow.

★   ★   ★

For all her brave words, Aaronovich doesn't dare to touch the girl.

She would like to lead her by the hand, to do something that might assuage her fear. The risk is too great. Fortunately, the child seems eager to accompany her. She walks in a curiously animal fashion, in sudden, jittery bursts, and her posture suggests that at any instant she might drop to all fours. She will only trail after Aaronovich; she's careful not to go ahead. Aaronovich has to hold each door open so that they can slip through together. In those moments of proximity, she's most conscious of the peril she's brought upon herself. What would it take to tip this frightened creature into anger?

When they get to the infirmary stairwell, the girl stalls. She sniffs the air and regards Aaronovich with unveiled suspicion. Then she backs off a few steps. Aaronovich's heartbeat is thunderous, but the girl merely clambers onto the faded couch in the corner and scrunches herself small, as she had in the truck. She stares at Aaronovich, one eye peeking through the ropy tendrils of her hair.

Aaronovich enters her apartment, which adjoins her workspace via a door in her office. By long-standing agreement, she is allowed to keep a limited stock of foodstuffs for use in her own small kitchen. Last night's dinner was a crude attempt at chili; Aaronovich warms the leftovers, slops them into a bowl, and secretes beneath the surface two tablets from the emergency medical kit she keeps packed. She fills a glass of water and carries bowl and glass back into the outer room.

She had half expected the girl to have vanished, but she's exactly as Aaronovich left her. Putting the water to one side, moving slowly, Aaronovich draws closer and proffers the bowl. The girl catches the odour first, before she sees. Her head jolts up and she makes a tremulous, throaty sound. With astonishing speed, she snatches the bowl from Aaronovich and scoots along the seat with it clutched in both hands. Only when she's satisfied that Aaronovich isn't about to pursue does she set to eating, scooping chili with one filthy hand and smearing it into her mouth.

When she's finished, she licks at the bowl and drops it to the floor. Aaronovich contemplates offering her the water, but by then it's clear that the sedatives are beginning to take hold. It strikes Aaronovich that she needn't have hidden the tablets. The girl would probably have eaten them anyway, so hungry was she and so apparently indifferent to what she was consuming.

As soon as the girl is unconscious, Aaronovich pulls on latex gloves and carries her down to the infirmary. She seems almost weightless. Aaronovich lays her on the trolley bed that had been Carlita's and sets to cutting off her clothing. The dirt has worn its way into the fibres and set like concrete, making them stiff and hardly recognisable as fabric. In places, Aaronovich barely needs to cut before the garments come apart, shredding in rotted tufts. Aaronovich bundles the discarded clothes into a scarlet biohazard bag and, because the smell is distracting, carries it upstairs and outside.

Back in the infirmary, Aaronovich sets to cleaning the girl. She works methodically, treating cuts and abrasions – of which there are many – as she goes. The girl is terribly thin, her chest sunken, her ribs prominent. Aaronovich can easily circle fingers around her wrist and even her ankle. Yet while she's certainly malnourished, in other ways she appears reasonably healthy. The swelling muscles of her arms and legs, for instance, show no signs of wastage.

Aaronovich cuts the rat's nest of her hair, hacking it away in snarled strands that go into another of the red biohazard bags. She shaves the remainder, sweeps up every scrap, and bags that too. The girl's underarms and groin are hairless; Aaronovich decides that she can be no older than seven. She pares the girl's nails, as close as she dares. Then, with extreme diligence, Aaronovich cleans her teeth. She's grateful to find them in relatively good condition. Half a dozen are missing and a couple decayed, but given how the child must have been living for the last few months, she'd anticipated far worse.

When she's finished, Aaronovich steps back and considers the girl, as though she's an artist evaluating her canvas. Naked, skinny, and bald, the girl looks less human than when Aaronovich first saw her; she seems, in fact, quite alien. Satisfied that she's done all she can to manage the risk of infection – all she can *humanely* do – Aaronovich drapes a blanket over the girl. She'll have to ask Doyle or Foster to have an expedition bring back some children's clothing. In the meantime, she settles for shortening and adjusting one of the small stock of smocks she keeps. She's never had much interest in sewing, and the result is more like a sack than the dress she'd intended. She succeeds with difficulty in getting it onto the girl. Then Aaronovich carries her upstairs and tucks her into her own bed.

It only occurs to Aaronovich as she sits, for what seems the first time in an age, and lets the tension start to ebb out of her, that she can't keep referring to the girl as *the girl*. She's going to have to come up with a name.

★   ★   ★

Ben's hands are shaking. Something has allowed him to drive back here, something sustained him through all those long hours. He can't say now what it was. His hands are shaking, but he can no more control them than he could control any of these grim-faced men gathered about the truck. Ben knows that soon the shaking will get worse, perhaps much worse, but he feels no accountability.

However, he has to make use of his body before it fails him. Ben works the handle, shoves the door, and climbs out. He knows what he has to do, what he needs if he's going to survive this. He knows exactly what he's looking for, and thanks to that insight, the shaking is gone and his body is his own again, muscles working in happy unity to fulfil this most crucial of tasks. Ben reaches into the back of the truck, finds what he seeks, and slips it within the inside pocket of his jacket.

Then the truck is a dizzying blur and pain explodes in his nose. Tumbling, he's kept from the ground by hard hands and his torso being slapped across the hood. By the time Ben has rationalised what's happened and got around to wondering who, fingers are pinning his shoulder, an elbow is driving into his ribs.

"So what the fuck happened, Silensky? You feeble little shit? Where's Landser, man?"

Curtis Colton: six-three and most of that polished slabs of muscle, rarely less than angry and now full-blown enraged. He and Landser had hung together, a friendship that seemed to predate Funland. Colton has Ben pinned effortlessly to the hood of the truck, just as he effortlessly bounced his face off its roof, just as he will effortlessly tear Ben's arms off if he feels that needs to happen. And all Ben can think of is the object in his pocket and whether it remains in one piece.

"Jumped," he manages. "We got jumped."

"What?" Colton slaps the back of Ben's head, rebounding his jaw from the still-warm hood. "You what?"

"He's dead," Ben mumbles.

"What? *What?*"

"He's *dead.*"

Then Colton has his arm, his bad arm, has dragged it free of the sling, and Ben knows that in a moment he'll start to twist, contorting the already damaged muscle, and he won't stop. "*You're* fucking dead."

"Get off him, Colton."

Colton doesn't release Ben's arm, but the pressure relaxes, ever so slightly.

"Seriously. Back down." It's Foster. Hardly the saviour Ben might have hoped for, had he dared to hope.

Yet Colton lets go, taking care to do so with one last wrench, which sends pulses of pain deep into Ben's shoulder. "If he got Landser killed—"

"I get it," Foster says. "But there's a time and a place."

"You just better—"

"Hey!" Foster snaps. "Don't push your luck. Go on, get out of here."

Ben, half expecting the sound of Colton's fist connecting with Foster's jaw, is dimly taken aback to hear the scuff of his retreating footsteps instead. What is it with people listening to Foster these days, Foster who no one likes or respects? But then, obedience has nothing to do with that. Currently the population of Funland is glad for anyone to tell them what to do. And though Colton might be dumb, he isn't so dumb that he doesn't know that there'll be other, better opportunities, if revenge turns out to be called for.

Feeling Foster's eyes on him, Ben flops over onto his back. Finding that his legs won't keep him up, he slides until he's propped against the nearest wheel. He gulps dusty evening air and tries not to throw up.

Foster is regarding him with steady contempt. "So, I just heard what happened. Landser and Houseman dead, you here and very much alive. Not a great trade, is it? But oh, it gets better. Because you brought us a pet…a little murderous pet to keep us company. That about the size of it, Silensky? Or you got more surprises hidden up your sleeve?"

Massaging his bad arm, Ben succeeds only in spreading the pain. "No," he says, "that's all of it."

"Jesus." Fleetingly, Foster's contempt almost strays to pity. "Get your shit together, Silensky. Tomorrow, you and me are going to have a talk. Since you're the one that came back, you're the one who gets to be responsible."

Ben nods. Yes, he's responsible. He made a call, a bad call. And somehow he's going to have to deal with that, but not right now. Right now he's not sure he can deal with standing up.

"Tomorrow," Foster repeats. He starts to walk away. Then he

hesitates to call back at the gathered cons, "And someone get this fucking truck unloaded, will you? Jesus."

Ben crawls to his feet. He had forgotten about the others, those who crowded round when he first returned. They're still standing there, bored, riled, some of them smiling without humour, but all watching him. Ben Silensky. Silensky, with two more corpses to his tally.

He turns and stumbles off. He thinks someone will shout after him or follow. None of them do. Only when he nears the spot where the southern edge of the administrative wing runs close to the wall does he dare reach inside his coat. Ben feels warily for the bottle, ready to flinch from shards of glass and the antiseptic stink of whiskey.

It's in one piece. Oh god, it's in one piece.

And despite everything, despite Colton and Foster and Houseman and Landser and the memories threatening at every moment to crash in like a wave and scour his mind red, Ben breathes a sigh of relief.

CHAPTER TWENTY-THREE

Doyle gives Aaronovich an hour, conscious that the time is more for his benefit than hers. His thoughts are like clouds scudding ahead of a gale, and he needs them to settle at least fractionally before he confronts the doctor again. Rationally, he knows he should be there, that *someone* should be. How far have they fallen that anybody would consider leaving her alone with a Sicker, even if that Sicker is also a child?

Yet Doyle saw how that small creature went to Aaronovich, and how she followed her. Maybe his presence will do more harm than good. Doyle tries to convince himself of that as he sits on his bed, watching the far wall turn through deepening shades of grey.

Finally, he shakes himself. He thinks about checking in with Carlita before he sets out. Shouldn't she know what's happened? No, he's making excuses, and this needs to be dealt with. He's already left it too long. Doyle forces himself up and out the door before the lethargy can retake its hold on him.

The yard is empty now. The truck is gone. The sky is black and starless.

Doyle finds Aaronovich in her outer office, sitting in one of the shapeless plastic chairs. She looks up when he enters.

"Doctor," he says.

"She's in my apartment," Aaronovich responds. "Sedated."

Straight to the point, then. "Good. Make sure she stays that way."

"Don't be ridiculous," she snaps, abruptly angry. "I've told you. That's a little girl in there."

"And I told you. Whatever else she might be, she's dangerously sick."

"Sick?" Aaronovich says. "That's undeniable. But dangerous? There's no evidence of that, and until Abigail—"

He doesn't let her get any further. "Doctor, what the hell?"

"She has to have a name," Aaronovich replies sullenly.

"*It* doesn't have to have anything. *It* is at best an infectious carrier of a disease, at worst a crazed monster that will turn on you the first time its rabid brain decides you're looking at it wrong. Every minute you treat it like a human being is another minute you put yourself and everyone here at risk."

But Doyle isn't used to making speeches. He's surprised by how quickly he's burned through his stock of anger. He takes a deep breath, which immediately dissolves into a groan. He won't be able to hold his own in an argument with Aaronovich. That leaves him two options: act now and do what he originally intended to do, or give in.

"Why Abigail?" Doyle asks.

Aaronovich scrutinises him, no doubt measuring whether the question is genuine or only a fresh line of attack. "Before Micha – before my son got sick, Daniel and I were talking about trying for a second child. We both wanted a daughter. It's just one of the names we discussed. I suppose the one I liked the most."

On some level, it's the answer Doyle had been expecting. "Doctor—"

"Johnson," she says, "I'm not a fool. I'm not delusional. I'm not imagining that little girl is the daughter I never had. But she *is* a little girl. You saw what she was like out there. She was scared, but she wasn't aggressive. Maybe it's different in children, who knows? And that's another thing, mightn't our chances be better if we had the slightest comprehension of what's happening outside our walls? These people have been infected for months and clearly they're not dying. If the girl isn't violent, don't you think this is an opportunity to learn something? Or—"

Doyle holds up his hands, as if her stream of arguments is some physical current he can hope to dam. "Calm down," he says.

Aaronovich takes a deep, fluttering breath. "I'm perfectly calm."

"You're telling me you're going to study her."

"I'm not telling you anything."

"You should be," Doyle says.

"What? Telling you or studying a sick child? What exactly—" Then she catches hold of herself. "Yes, if that's the price. Or even if it isn't. I'm a doctor, and I'm tired of living in the dark." Her eyes flicker about the candlelit office, as though her double meaning has only now occurred to her. "Yes, I'll study her, and if we're all so ready to cast our humanity aside, that alone should be reason enough to keep her alive."

"It's not my decision," Doyle says. "It will be up to Foster. Or else he'll want to have some kind of a vote."

"Foster's an idiot," Aaronovich notes tiredly.

There's an implication to her words beyond the obvious. "He's been here," Doyle realises aloud.

She nods. "He left just before you arrived."

"And he says…?"

"I wouldn't give him the key. I told him I'd hidden it. He said, *You've got until tomorrow to make the right decision*. The right decision! That presumptuous—" Aaronovich sighs. "I'm a doctor. I took an oath. More than ever, that seems to mean something."

"I'll do what I can," Doyle assures her. In truth, he has no idea what he can do. Foster, perhaps, can be talked round, especially if the result can be made to look like his decision. But how much authority does Foster really have?

"Thank you." Aaronovich's gratitude appears to be earnest.

"I can't make guarantees. You know what this place is, Doctor. They may come here after her. We lost two men today to Sickers, and at least one of them had friends."

"I hate that word," she says.

"What?"

"*Sickers*. So stupid. Why do we have to pin a label on everything that isn't exactly like us?"

"They're nothing like us," Doyle says. His mind has returned, without his control, to the night Carlita and Silensky arrived, to the death of that cop, Fernando, and how his body looked afterward. "Whatever's happened to them, there's no good thinking of them as people anymore."

"Maybe that's it," Aaronovich says. "Maybe that's *exactly* it. Maybe we'll only ever understand if we start thinking of them as people."

Doyle considers that. It's true they've all been quick to accept the Sickers as less than human. Then again, did the word determine that choice or was it simply the extremity of their behaviour? A greater leap of imagination is required to believe that the sick are still people than that they aren't.

The train of thought reminds Doyle of the other reason he came here. He reaches into his back pocket and draws out the gun, which was once Plan John's gun. Aaronovich flinches and her eyes darken with suspicion.

"Do you know how to use this?" Doyle asks.

"Why would I want to?"

"In case." He proffers the weapon. "Can you use it?"

"Yes." Aaronovich checks the safety and then flips out the cylinder. Having established that it's fully loaded, she closes it and places the revolver on the chair beside her.

"This is the only way," Doyle says. "I'll talk to Foster. I'll back you. But only if I'm sure you're not putting Funland and yourself in danger."

Except it's not Funland you're trying to keep safe. But for once Doyle finds it easy to push the thought aside. In this instance, Funland and Carlita are one and the same.

"Fine," Aaronovich agrees. She retrieves the revolver and cradles it carefully, barrel aiming at the floor. "I know I'm right."

"If you're right then it won't be an issue. And if you're not...."

He doesn't press the point. For beneath her unshakeable confidence, Doyle can see that she understands, every bit as well as he does and maybe even better.

★   ★   ★

Whatever has been going on in the yard, whatever the distant noise of raised voices was about, Kyle has ignored it. Raised voices never mean anything good in Funland, and he feels like he has enough to deal with, enough thoughts clamouring across the space within his skull. He's gone back to Plan John's logbook instead, though he's increasingly aware that he's no longer making any real effort to translate it. Rather, Kyle stares at the tight handwritten rows while letting his mind wander.

He's jolted by the door opening, the more so when he sees who's there. If life has all but erased the old distinctions between Kyle and those older than him, there remains something about Doctor Aaronovich that marks her definitely as *adult*. Perhaps it's just that she's the only one who still recognises his youth and adjusts her expectations accordingly.

Of everyone in Funland, he likes her more than most. At the same time, there's a remoteness about the doctor that has always seemed to curtail any chance of friendship between them. Certainly Kyle wouldn't have predicted her coming to his room, and she looks entirely uncomfortable to be here.

"Hello, Kyle," she says. "What's that?"

Kyle flips the book so that she can read the neat bars of text. "Plan John's logbook. It's in code."

"And you're trying to make sense of it?"

Kyle nods.

"Interesting." Yet she doesn't sound interested. "Kyle," she says, "I was hoping I might ask you a favour."

He closes the logbook. "Sure."

Again the doctor looks discomforted, as though she hasn't planned this far into the conversation. Eventually she announces, "Your father brought back a little girl today."

For a moment, Kyle imagines she's referring to someone his own age, in the way older people will lump all younger people into a single category. But the doctor isn't like that. She says exactly what she intends.

"I think she's six or seven," Aaronovich clarifies.

"Oh." Kyle does his best to hide his disappointment.

"I'm going to look after her," she explains. "But I'm not sure I can do it on my own. I've been pondering who might be able to help, and who'd be willing to. And in the end I came to you."

She wants him to babysit? Strange how that prospect, which not long ago would have filled him with disgust, now seems so appealing. Yet there's something else: the request hardly warrants the sombreness, almost dread, with which she's made it. Kyle waits, assuming she'll tell him in her own time.

"The thing is," Aaronovich says, "she's sick. Infected."

"What?" He can scarcely believe it. He's seen the sick. To be in the same room with one would be suicide. What is she asking of him? Anger rises at the thought, as though the doctor is deliberately seeking to harm him.

"I don't think she's dangerous," Aaronovich says. "I have reason to suppose she isn't. What I mean is, she hasn't shown signs so far of being aggressive. But yes, there's a risk, absolutely there is. I don't want to mislead you, Kyle."

He sits, struggling to comprehend what she's said, while Aaronovich stands in silence. Her proposal raises so many questions, all at once, and it's hard to know where to begin. Why should Kyle put his life in jeopardy? Why would she come to him? Shouldn't he simply say no? However, the very fact that it's him she's approached is appealing. At the farm, he's just a pair of hands, given neither responsibility nor credit. If he should vanish one day, then he doubts they would care, except that there'd be more work to go around.

"What if she attacks me?" Kyle queries at last.

"The infection is transmitted through blood and saliva," Aaronovich says. "So if she bites you, it's highly likely you'll be infected." She relates this calmly, as a teacher in front of a class might. "If she scratches you, it's conceivable the result would be the same, but I've pared her nails to make sure that can't happen. Aside from pulling out her teeth, which is an option I'm not prepared to consider, all we can do to mitigate the risk of biting is to keep her calm and maintain a safe distance. There may be other possibilities I haven't identified yet. But as I said, there's definite danger in what I'm asking and I won't hide that from you."

Kyle likes how she talks to him, that she treats him with the respect she'd afford an adult, while at the same time not pretending he isn't in many ways still a child. It isn't so much that she's got the balance right as that she acknowledges there *is* a balance.

"Okay," he says. "I'll do it."

Aaronovich looks surprised, and hides her reaction badly. Kyle only realises then that she hadn't expected him to say yes.

"Why don't you come and meet her tomorrow morning?" she suggests. "The sooner she starts to get used to your presence the better."

"Sure," Kyle agrees. "I'd like that."

★   ★   ★

It's late when Ben sets out to find Carlita.

He can't say exactly how late. He's been drinking in the library. If the place has probably never been well used, now it's one of the few in Funland where solitude is all but guaranteed. The fragile light outside the window faded fast, and after that Ben was sitting in the dark. Since then, he's been drinking steadily, endeavouring to make the whiskey last. He's drunk enough to know he's drunk, too drunk to judge how badly.

Ben understands that part of what he's feeling is traditional inebriated self-pity. Underneath, he's distantly conscious that he's suffering genuine trauma. What he was forced to witness at the farmhouse was horrible; but it isn't what's stayed with him, what blooms into life when he shuts his eyes. Then he's aware again of that girl, that thing that looked like a child, so close to him, never more than a couple of feet away all through the drive. In every moment, he could feel her nearness. She's left icy knots of fear in the back of his mind that refuse to melt under the whiskey's hot breath.

He's been thinking about going to Carlita for a while. Yet something has restrained him. Ben doesn't have the words to explain to her why, now more than ever, he needs her, needs her to love him or just to pretend, until the fear shrinks to a size he can contain.

At some point he starts, as if from a shallow sleep, though he knows he hasn't slept. The bottle is still gripped firmly in his good hand, and when he shakes it, he hears the whiskey sloshing in its base. Ben attempts to estimate how much is left from the sound, but the concentrated thought makes the room wobble. It's so long since he's been drunk, hard drunk.

The night is completely dark. The generator is reserved for emergencies, and they get by with candles, battery flashlights, lanterns, and in a couple of the big rooms, braziers. Ben has none of those. He stumbles to his feet, nearly falls, thrusts out a hand, and by pure luck finds a table edge. He gasps with relief. He'd been terrified of breaking the bottle. Then Ben recalls that it has a cap, and fishes in his pocket. After considerable effort, he manages to screw the cap in place, and returns the bottle to the inside of his jacket.

Ben tries to remember his reservations about visiting Carlita and can't. There's even a little whiskey left for them to share. He tries to remember if Carlita drinks whiskey. Regardless, beggars can't be choosers. And aren't they all beggars now? Hasn't he spent the day fumbling in the wreckage of other people's lives? So Carlita can make do.

Ben can just see the doorway. He makes his way there, arms outstretched. Its angles are wrong, but when he teeters into it, the frame takes his weight. Outside in the passage, the going is easier. Ben lets his subconscious navigate and concentrates on keeping his footing.

Eventually, a turning brings him out at the staircase that leads up to Carlita's rooms. The stairs look steep. Ben closes his eyes, and the dizziness subsides to a mild swirling, like he's sitting in a hot tub. He takes the steps one by one.

Halfway along the corridor at their summit is the door that splits Carlita's small empire from the rest of the Big House. There's the faintest suggestion of light at its base; he'd never have noticed had he not been looking for it. That band of amber-grey fills him with both hope and trepidation.

Ben doesn't bother to analyse either sensation. If he did, he's sure the whiskey would wash him away again. Instead, he stumbles toward the light.

CHAPTER TWENTY-FOUR

Austin enters Kyle's room without him hearing. He's got good at moving quietly these last few weeks. There are tricks, he's discovered; a lot of it is in your head. Like the world is paper and he can cut himself out, can vanish into his own space.

Austin stands waiting for a while. When finally he grows bored, he scuffs a heel, and Kyle looks up, startled – though not so startled as Austin might have anticipated.

"Come on," Austin says, "I want to show you something." That's all he's prepared to give. He's already decided that he'll make no reference to what happened before, no apology. If Kyle expects one, he isn't worth wasting energy on.

Yet whatever Kyle's thinking, it isn't that. Now that he's over his initial shock, he doesn't even seem that interested in Austin's presence. In the light of his single candle, he looks worried, or at least distracted. Has he been reading at all or only deep in thought?

Austin is out of the habit of caring what anyone else thinks, but in that moment, curiosity gets the better of him. "What's up?"

Kyle catches himself immediately. "Nothing."

So that's how it is. Austin is readying to expose his deepest secret, but it's okay for Kyle to hold onto his. Maybe it's to do with that stupid code book, in which case Austin couldn't care less. He feels like walking away, has to remind himself that this isn't about Kyle. Having conceded that he can't do what he needs to do alone, there can be no turning back.

"So are you coming?" Austin asks, fastidiously blanking any trace of emotion from his voice.

"Sure." This time Kyle makes an effort to sound enthusiastic, recognising his mistake too late. He tucks down the corner of the page and follows Austin out the door, through the corridors, into the yard. Though Kyle keeps a respectful distance as they cross to the Big House, he must have guessed where they're going. He knows to stand well clear when Austin leaps for the ladder. Nor is he as nervous climbing up; the muted chime of his shoes upon the rungs is steadier.

On the roof, Austin leads Kyle into the maze of piping and ductwork, stopping once more at the loosened vent cover. He feels better now, the earlier slight almost forgotten. Kyle is doing okay. He's passing the tests. "You didn't tell anyone," he says, and it's a statement rather than a question.

Kyle shakes his head, the motion barely perceptible in the darkness.

"I'd have got to you," Austin says, "if you had. Even if they'd locked me up or something. I'd have figured a way."

He can sense that Kyle believes him. Austin wishes he had the same faith in his own abilities. The truth is that the prospect of his secrets being exposed, his hidden places taken away, fills him with such numbing, unreasoning terror that he hardly dares put it into thought. He has a weapon. He has his anger. In Funland, those things don't make him special, or even dangerous. Kyle is more of a threat to him than Austin can ever be to Kyle.

His brief good mood already beginning to fracture, Austin focuses on removing the vent cover. Immediately beyond the cube of grey around the opening, the inside shades into utter darkness. Taking out a small flashlight, Austin shines it within. "You scared?"

"No," Kyle says.

"If you get scared," Austin tells him, "don't freak out. If you freak out, I might have to hurt you."

He has thought over the possibilities carefully. If Kyle starts losing his shit in the ventilation shafts, which conduct sound so perfectly, Austin will have to shut him up as quickly as he can. A part of him isn't sure he'll be able to do it. Another part knows that, given the choices, he'll act without hesitation.

Even for Austin, though, the duct will be a close fit. The muscle he's built in the last weeks, much of it from doing exactly this, has in some ways actually made his exploration harder. Kyle, however, is lightly built. His farm work has done little to change that, adding definition rather than bulk. Kyle should be able to get through just fine, more easily, perhaps, than Austin himself can.

"I'm going first," he says. "So you'll be in the dark. You scared of the dark?"

"I told you," Kyle says. "I'm not going to get scared."

Austin is surprised by the resolve in his voice. "Shit," he says. "Don't get cocky." Has he underestimated Kyle? The notion disturbs him. "Keep me in sight. Don't go slow or you might lose me. You got it?"

"I think so."

"I'm going to go headfirst, but that takes practice. You won't be able to manage it this time. Put your feet in and shuffle on your back."

Austin hitches his arms within the vent mouth, its lip vaguely silvered by moon and stars. He shimmies forward, braces, and draws his legs after him. He knows that all Kyle will be able to see of him will be the flashlight's faint backwash.

Austin lies motionless. Even after so long, and so many expeditions into the depths of the pipes, he still finds their silence strange. Something about the look of them, the hard lines, the metallic sheen, seems to require a background noise of machinery. Nothing in the ductwork serves any function, and much of what previously did he has disabled and dismantled, working in fearful quiet to expand his claustrophobic territory.

This is how it should be. He understands that now. It's right that he should have claimed these passages, turning them to a new function. It's part of a natural cycle, like bugs occupying a discarded beer can. Only, he's the bug. The thought horrified him at first, and ever since has been a source of comfort. Yes, he's becoming a cockroach. You stomp on a cockroach and it just skitters away. He saw on TV once that cockroaches can survive anything, even an atomic bomb. They can live through the end of the world.

Austin resumes his crawling, and is glad when he hears the accompanying rattle of movement from behind him.

He's learned to survive as a cockroach. Is it possible Kyle can do the same?

*   *   *

Ben knocks on the door that cuts off Carlita's small portion of the Big House. He'd intended a gentle rap, but he misjudges the first attempt and overcompensates on the second, and the result is three sharp blows that echo back along the passage. His immediate instinct is to run, as if he's a naughty child playing a game. It takes effort to stand his ground.

Initially there's silence, deep in the vacuum left by his thunderous knocking. Then, as Ben's wondering if he dares to knock again, Carlita's voice comes. "Who is it?"

Who does she think it is? Well, he has an idea. In his mind, he imitates Johnson's taciturn baritone: *It's Doyle, baby, come to tuck you in.* The thought is nowhere near as funny as he'd imagined it would be. It must be late, he rationalises to himself, so of course she would ask. "Ben," he says, striving to enunciate.

The lock clicks. "Come in," Carlita says. Ben can't see her. The only light is coming from her room at the end of the passage, cast in diminishing reflections across the walls. Ben, walking with the utmost concentration, follows her dark shape.

Carlita's apartment had presumably been meant to lodge visitors. There's the small bedroom, and a shower room with a toilet, all of it utilitarian and nondescript. When Johnson told him about the move – and that memory riles Ben now, that Doyle Johnson had the balls to tell *him* what was happening to his girlfriend – Ben had been almost dizzy with anticipation. With Carlita free of the infirmary, they could start seeing each other again; no more bi-weekly visits, no more begging for Johnson's permission.

She'll be safe there, Johnson had assured him. *But not if you draw attention.*

So Ben had kept his distance, sure that soon Carlita would talk Johnson around. This latest separation would be temporary, and then things would go back to...not normality, he wasn't fool enough to hope for that, but a shadow of normality that might serve some of the same needs. A foundation, if nothing else, a place from which to begin rebuilding their relationship, and from there his life in Funland, which had grown so frighteningly tenuous.

Had he believed that? Maybe he'd known, even then, that he'd let something happen that couldn't be reversed. Maybe he'd understood that he'd given up more than he would ever be able to take back, and had done so easily.

Ben follows Carlita into her room, closing the door. There's little furniture: the bed and a chest of drawers beside it, a small folding table, a chair, and a set of shelves. Two candles are burning, a cracked dinner plate and tatty hardback book serving as stands, stubs of fresh wax jutting from the remnants of countless forebears. Carlita has gone straight to the bed, where she sits with her knees laid to one side, watching him steadily.

Ben waits while she assesses him, seeing the process work itself out over her features. He finds no affection there, only distrust at first and then distaste, a curling of the lip and hardening behind the eyes as she recognises his drunkenness. He wants to appeal against her judgement, to explain his reasons. Instead, he collapses onto the chair in the corner. Ben starts to put his head in his hands and thinks better of it, if only because his sling would make doing so difficult.

In an instinct of rebelliousness, he takes the bottle out. "Brought us a nightcap." His voice is ridiculous to his own ears, like the yapping of a dog. There's less whiskey left than he'd recalled: a half inch of piss-yellow fluid. "You can have it," he says. He offers her the bottle.

Carlita doesn't move to take it, and after a few seconds, Ben withdraws his hand and places the bottle delicately beside the chair.

"The trip out today went all to shit," he says. "We got jumped. So quick, from nowhere, like they'd planned it. Maybe you heard."

"How would I have heard?"

"I thought maybe Johnson—"

"No," Carlita says.

Ben can't decide whether he believes her. "It was bad. Seriously bad. I didn't know they could be smart like that. I think, in a way…I think it was my fault."

"Your fault?" For the first time, she sounds genuinely curious.

"We could have just come back. Houseman wanted to. We'd got a good haul, that's what he said. I figured he was chicken. I mean, he was. But we could have just walked away and he wouldn't be…. It's as if they *knew*."

"That's not your fault," Carlita says.

"No?" He's glad. If Carlita deems him innocent then perhaps it's even true.

"You shouldn't have got so drunk," she adds. Her tone, though, is fractionally softer. "You should have come here and talked to me."

Ben wants to explain about what Houseman's body looked like in the last glimpse he'd had, about how methodically they'd worked at Landser, like hunters gutting a downed deer. He wants to tell her about the little girl and the journey back and how in every moment he'd thought she would start trying to break into the cab. He wants Carlita to see how the whiskey is the only thing keeping all of that down.

Ben wishes she'd taken the bottle from him, that she'd made that small concession. He remembers what she was like when they met, how wild she was. At the time, he'd been struggling to bring Kyle up on his own, contemplating finding an honest living, always too much in need of ready cash. They'd been good for each other. Carlita, it turned out, had been seeking a way to balance out her own life, tired of getting drunk and stoned with girlfriends and of one-night stands and of not having her own place. She was happy to help look after Kyle if it allowed Ben to hunt for regular work, regular enough for them to get a decent apartment between them. Things had been good, really good, and the sex had been…well, she'd learned some tricks in the wild years, he'd discovered that quickly.

Where did they go wrong? Has it simply been the sickness? Has it infected their happiness? That's the only plausible explanation. It seems unfair and incomprehensible and cruel, cruel most of all.

Ben realises that he's crying, viscous streaks struggling down his cheeks. Carlita is watching him, with concern that he can't mistake for affection. That just makes the tears flow harder. He doesn't want her pity. He wants her to regard him with that bright, hot passion he recollects from certain summer mornings, when he'd come out of the shower to find her waiting, bedcovers cast aside, sweat beading across her flawless copper skin.

"Come here," Carlita says softly.

Do the words mean what he craves for them to mean? His mind has snagged on the image of her naked in their small bedroom, the lime-green curtains parted, casting soft shadows over her torso and legs and a band of glaring white from her thighs up to her belly button. The memory makes him ache, deep in his heart and in his groin. Ben stands, knocking the chair as he does so. Something goes *thunk* and whirrs as it rolls across the floor.

The bottle has come to rest against the shelves. Thank god it hasn't broken. Ben reaches, staggers, and ends up on all fours.

He looks at Carlita. The moment, if moment there had been, is past. He's lost it for a shot of whiskey. He sits awkwardly on the end of the bed, so near to her that she has to shuffle her feet round. Overcome with self-disgust, Ben murmurs a noise that might be, "Sorry."

Carlita half strokes, half pats his shoulder. "It must have been pretty bad."

"It was fucking awful."

Ben shuffles closer, so that he's sitting beside her legs. Sure enough, Carlita drapes an arm around his shoulders. Suddenly, although he's still horny, Ben also feels immensely tired, and there's nothing pleasant about how the two sensations mingle.

"Can I stay here tonight?" he asks softly.

A long silence. He's already convinced himself the answer will be no when she says, "Okay. This once. And you've got to go before dawn." A further silence, and then, "So long as it's just to sleep."

Ben jerks up. He's surprised by how angry he feels. The tiredness is gone, and even the drunkenness has subsided. "What?"

"Oh, Ben. Stop."

Now he's on his feet. "Stop what?"

"You're drunk! You stink of whiskey! Do you think I want to—"

"To what?"

"To fuck you!" Carlita is fighting not to shout, self-preservation struggling against her mounting frustration. "Is that what you want to hear? I'm not going to fuck you, Ben, because you're drunk and you stink."

Ben's hand lashes out. Afterward, he has difficulty putting the moment together. There's a mingled emotion of rage and pain and disgust, a red stain heaving from the edges of his consciousness. He thought he'd intended to slap her: not hard, just enough to stop the words. Yet the result is not a slap. It takes him a second to absorb, as if an obscuring fog has rolled in and then dissolved as abruptly. What the fog leaves behind is his hand outstretched and Carlita somehow off the bed and on the floor, red flowing from her split lip, her face bloodless behind. Her eyes are fixed on his, and he can see nothing in their black pits but hate.

His mind says, *Carly, I'm sorry. I'm so sorry. I never meant to hurt you.*

His voice, a choked rasp he hardly recognises, says, "I know who you want to fuck. You want nigger in you. That's right, isn't it? You want a man who can take care of you."

She doesn't make a sound. The hatred in her eyes is like a furnace. It makes Ben terribly afraid. He's lost her, and with her, everything. He can't take back what he's done. It's as if he's come out unexpectedly on some vertiginous edge, and now the only way on is down.

Still, a part of him would like to hurl curses at her, and that part will keep hitting her if he lets it, hit until her face resembles hamburger meat and those awful eyes have to let him go. It would be so easy, a million times easier than trying to repair the damage he's done. And doesn't she deserve to be punished? For not loving him? For killing their love?

Ben doesn't have that in him. He isn't even strong enough to be a monster. He certainly isn't strong enough to do what needs doing: to beg forgiveness, to swear this will never happen again so hard that the promise would have to be true.

What *can* he do? If he's too weak to hurt her more, too weak to try and make things right? What is he strong enough for?

Ben turns and stumbles toward the door. He's strong enough to run away.

CHAPTER TWENTY-FIVE

Kyle had really believed he wouldn't get scared.

He continued to believe with utter faith, up to the moment when the shaft turned downward, at a ninety-degree angle he knows without question he can't navigate. Then his heart bobs into his throat, solid and sharp-edged as broken concrete, and it's all he can do to breathe, let alone move.

Austin has already made it down, clambering headfirst into the blackness. The only sign of his presence is splinters of torchlight, flitting nightmarishly. Every nerve in Kyle's body is screaming at him to go back. Except, he isn't sure he can do that either; the possibility is equally bad.

Instead, Kyle forces himself forward, slithering until his legs are dangling over the edge. When his feet brush the far side, he can detect that there are slender ledges in the descending vent, where segments of tube meet, enough that they could serve as handholds. He can't judge the shaft's depth, but realistically it can't be far, though the fear insists the descent goes on forever.

If you don't do this, he tells himself, *you might as well give up. Just give up on everything.*

With care, Kyle rolls onto his front. Then he slides, painfully aware of how his legs are supported by nothing. His fingers and upper arms are greasy with sweat. He walks his feet down until he's in a standing position. The flashlight's luminance is the faintest glow from beneath.

He's scarcely started his descent before his feet touch the bottom. It wasn't far at all. Kyle's almost disappointed. Yet there's also no reassurance. He's come to rest in an awkward squat and still can't see where the light is coming from, or what's ahead. The darkness seems to be closing around him, his fear expanding to meet it. When he attempts to shift onto his back, he dashes his forehead hard against metal.

Kyle bites his tongue to keep from sobbing. He won't let Austin know he's scared. If this is a test, he isn't about to fail. Six months ago, maybe he'd have buckled, but that was then. He's braver now. He's grown tougher.

Kyle tries again to lie flat, scrunching small to negotiate the bend, stretching his legs and supporting himself with palms flat upon cool metal, lowering his head only when he's sure there's space. When he's certain he can move without scraping the rim of the vertical shaft, he begins to edge forward, hurrying to catch the light.

He turns a slight angle, grazing his shoulder, and there it is, breaking this time from a gap in the tube. The orifice isn't a junction, Kyle observes as he shuffles closer, but another point where a panel has been levered away. Beyond is a narrow space between cinder-block walls, pipes and cables bunched above. Kyle slides out into the gap, leading with his legs, and discovers that he's able to stand upright. He can walk in side steps, though the rough walls sting his hands. He keeps going and the light grows stronger.

Suddenly there's nothing behind him. He's come out in a room, or something like a room. Austin sits on the floor in the far corner, staring back. The flashlight is propped on its base beside him, creating a weird funnel of illumination. Austin is sitting on a rolled quilt, and the space is just long and wide enough for someone to sleep in. Beside him, a block has been levered out to create a shelf, and books, a bundle of candles, food wrappers, and other assorted junk are heaped within.

Kyle's rapid breathing subsides. His heart's pounding grows steady. He's made it. He sinks into a squat, careful to maintain the distance between them.

"You've got to be quiet," says Austin, his voice barely a whisper.

Kyle, who's hardly made a noise since they left the administrative wing, merely nods.

"I sleep here sometimes," continues Austin redundantly. Now that they've arrived, he seems unfocused, like he's concentrating on a sound he can't quite distinguish.

Kyle's excitement is quickly spoiling, tainted by a nagging claustrophobia that makes it hard to stay still. He'd envisaged so much, yet here he is and this is only strange and frightening. Austin's behaviour had made sense out there in Funland; in this cramped aperture, at such close proximity, it makes Kyle's skin creep. What if Austin really is crazy, crazy like the Sickers outside, and Kyle has blindly followed him down to this den?

"You can get all over," Austin says. "There are gaps into the walls, into the ceilings. I've a way into the stores that no one knows about. I can get near to my dad's room."

That's better, more like what Kyle wants to hear. He can ignore the craziness if only the results are worthwhile. He needs someone, a friend, because otherwise this may be how he'll end up, broken and alone. Probably he can't help Austin, but with Austin on his side he might at least avoid becoming him.

"If I had some help I could go everywhere," Austin adds.

Yes. Even if Kyle doesn't entirely believe, still, that sounds right. Two friends, keeping safe from the world outside by reshaping it from within, going where they like and taking what they want. How messed up Austin is won't matter, so long as he's on Kyle's side.

"I could get to *anyone*," Austin says.

There's a new edge to his voice, not anger but dreaminess. At the same time, his face contorts. It's a fracture in Austin's surface, a glimpse at what lies beneath: the ugliness, the desperation, the spiralling pain.

It's too deep an insight. Kyle understands then that, just as they've crawled like worms into this tiny space deep within Funland, so there's some similar cavity within Austin, hidden at his very core. It's been revealed for an instant, and if they're to be friends, Kyle will have to see it again.

Kyle had promised himself he wouldn't get scared. But he hadn't expected this, though he should have. And now he *is* scared, maybe more than he's ever been, and he can't, mustn't, show it.

So Kyle sits still, clenching his hands, digging fingernails into palms, and he listens to what Austin has to tell him.

*　　*　　*

Doyle knows who's knocking at his door. There's something in the agitated rhythm that identifies Carlita uniquely, even though she's never come to his rooms before. His first reaction is a rush of anticipation, so intoxicating that it could almost be called joy. His second is an unaccountable trepidation that roots him halfway between the chair where he'd been sitting and the door.

It's late, perhaps even early, and the only illumination is a rigid trapezoid of moonlight sprawled upon the floor. Doyle hurriedly lights a candle, and is snuffing the match as the knocking resumes, now more rapid and insistent. This time, he goes straight to the door and opens it. The corridor beyond is absolutely dark, and Carlita is nothing more than an outline until she steps into the room. She's wearing dark blue jeans and a grey sweatshirt. Her hair, which normally she keeps tied back, is loose and tousled across her face.

Doyle closes the door, easing it gently though it's absurd to imagine anyone might hear. "What's wrong?" he says. "You know how dangerous—"

Then he takes in the dark line tracing its way up her chin, and his gaze follows it to the ragged dint in her lower lip.

What ensues cannot be called thinking. His brain acknowledges the details – the streak of crusted blood, the torn and puffy lip – and collates other facts, like the slackness in her posture, the distant expression. It produces a theory, and from the theory a course, all without conscious intent on Doyle's part. The next he knows, he's pushing past her and wrenching the door back open, with no doubt in his mind of what he has to do.

A hand catches his arm. Doyle tries to resist. "I'll kill him," he says, without emotion. Trying again to pull free, he realises that only roughness will liberate him.

"Please, Doyle. Will you just stop?"

The swelling makes her voice fuzzy and lisping. That merely enrages him more.

"He shouldn't get away with this," Doyle growls.

"I know. But you need to calm down."

"Calm down?"

"Doyle!" Carlita says sharply. "Please. Stop. This isn't why I came here. If you do this, it's not for me."

She's right. Of course she's right. But he can't simply let the rage go; instead he drives it down, stashing it in that dead place where so much of him seems to be stored these days. He leads her into the bedroom, sits her on the bed, dips a facecloth in the bowl of water he keeps for washing, and begins to dab at her lip. Though Carlita winces, she lets him continue. Soon he can see that the damage isn't so bad, really little more than a scratch.

The fact that Silensky throws a lousy punch when he hits a woman does not do much to assuage Doyle's caged anger.

"It's not how you think," Carlita says.

"This wasn't Silensky? He didn't hit you?"

"No, he did. But never before. He was drunk. He's in a bad way over what happened today. Those men who died. I didn't get it at first; I've never seen him like that. I said some things…I don't know…they were the wrong things. I made it worse."

"Don't you dare make excuses for him," Doyle says.

"I'm not. I just need you to understand. And I need you to keep this between us. He's not a bad man, Doyle. He's not strong, but he's not a bad man."

Doyle goes to the first aid kit he keeps under his bed, a prize inherited from Plan John, and, taking out the antiseptic cream, tries to read the use-by date in the wavering candlelight. How long before all their drugs and medicines, all the pharmaceuticals stashed in Aaronovich's lair, become useless? Sitting also, he squeezes a drop of amber gunk onto his fingertip and says, "Open your mouth."

Carlita parts her lips and Doyle leans in to better see the cut, balancing himself with a hand on her shoulder. He dabs with his index finger. His other fingers lie on her jaw and cheek, and he finds himself unable to shut out the texture of her skin. He has to drive himself to remove his hand.

"I don't love him anymore," Carlita says. "Maybe I did once, I don't know. But I don't now. I don't feel anything for him."

Doyle has an urge to back away. There's nothing he wants to know about Ben and Carlita's relationship. But he has nowhere to escape to. "I'm not the person you should be telling this to."

"You are. You're all I have. I'm sorry, but I can't be alone."

She's clearly upset. He should be comforting her. Doyle's mind darts to that first night, beneath the overly bright striplights of the infirmary, and how he gripped Carlita until her sobs receded. He recalls her hair against his cheek, the heat of her breath on his neck, so vividly that for a moment he actually feels the sensations. "Carlita…I'm tired. I'll come in the morning. We can talk then."

She nods, despite the disappointment evident in her face. She half rises. Softly enough that he barely catches the words, she says, "After he hit me, Ben told me it was because I wanted to be with you."

Doyle freezes: every inch of him, he thinks, down to the last drop of blood. "He was making excuses," he manages, though speaking is like working the muscles of a corpse.

"No," Carlita says, "he was right."

Then he's alive again, and the urge to reach out to her floods molten through him, screaming incoherence in his brain. She looks beautiful and perfect in the candlelight, perilous too, the shadows outlining each curve of her and every detail of her face, making them sharp and graceful and threatening. Doyle fights not to move. He's on the verge of something he knows to be wrong, but he can no longer remember how he knows, as if the details have been swept from his thoughts.

"Carlita…."

She sits once more, on the very edge of the bed. She cups a hand over his knee. "Since I got here, you're the one who's been there for me. You saved me. You've kept me safe."

"I haven't done anything," Doyle says.

"You have."

It's growing difficult to breathe. "I won't put you in danger," he tells her.

"I'm always in danger."

"You know what I mean."

"I do. But it's just tonight. Only one night."

Not waiting for an answer, not allowing one, Carlita pulls her sweater over her head. She bends forward, so close that her hair brushes Doyle's face, and undoes her jeans and eases free of them. The candle casts her in harsh relief, pooling blackness beneath her breasts, in the hollows of her ribs, between her legs.

She puts her hands upon Doyle's face, holding his eyes with hers. Then she wraps her arms behind his shoulders, drawing him closer. Again Carlita parts her lips, one perfect, one bruised and torn.

This time Doyle doesn't pull away.

*   *   *

Abigail rouses slowly. The tablets will make her groggy, Aaronovich knows.

Aaronovich doubts she can be aware that she's been drugged. Even a healthy child of her age would be unlikely to understand that. Nevertheless, she seems anxious and irritable at first. Half-conscious, she mewls plaintively. After a while, her eyes flicker open, then widen at the unfamiliarity of her surroundings. When she sees Aaronovich, who has placed herself as far from the bed as the small room will allow, Abigail fights feebly against the bedclothes, until Aaronovich is certain she'll tip onto the floor.

"It's okay," Aaronovich says. "Shh. It's okay."

At the noise, Abigail stops struggling and goes still. Abruptly, she puts a hand to her own head and runs stubby fingers across the smooth skin. She investigates every inch of her skull, checking down her neck and around her ears.

Then she begins to chuckle.

It might be the strangest thing Aaronovich has ever heard. It's so undiluted and so inhuman. The one quality explains the other: there's such raw pleasure in the sound. And it's so long since Aaronovich heard anyone laugh like that – or at all.

Bored of her own shaven head, Abigail discovers further details. She holds a hand up to her face and scrutinises, one by one, her newly trimmed nails. She notes the fresh pink skin, where once there had been ingrained dirt. Unselfconsciously, she shimmies free of the bedclothes and inspects her arms and legs, and then the clumsy garment Aaronovich has made for her, holding up its folds and letting them fall back around her skinny frame. She giggles.

Aaronovich stands. She does so slowly, keeping her eyes averted, heedful not to make any movement that might be interpreted as hostile. Yet initially Abigail doesn't even notice. When she does, she whimpers faintly, and watches. Aaronovich goes out into the kitchen, all of her movements smooth, unthreatening.

An expedition the week before managed to retrieve a haul of canned foodstuffs. Aaronovich heats an unappetising slop of greyish meat and unidentifiable vegetables, pours the results into a bowl, and lets it cool somewhat. She fills another bowl with water, puts both on a tray, and carries them through to the bedroom.

Abigail isn't in the bed. For one terrified moment, Aaronovich can't see her. Then her gaze descends, and there she is in the corner of the room, huddled, staring back with those dark-speckled eyes.

Kneeling, Aaronovich places the tray on the floor. She shuffles forward, sliding it in front of her. When she's crossed two thirds of the distance between them, Aaronovich retreats and sits with her back against the end of the bed. She looks aside, at nothing. For no other reason than to relieve the tension in her own mind, she starts to count beneath her breath.

At sixty-three, she hears the scuff of movement. She doesn't look up until she knows Abigail has reached the tray. Abigail is sitting before it on her haunches, appraising the bowls suspiciously, nose crinkling. As she feels Aaronovich watching, she tenses, as though readying to bolt.

"It's all right," Aaronovich says. "It's for you." She doesn't look away.

The seconds slip by. Then Abigail grasps the first bowl with both hands and scoots backward. Having doubled the gap that separates them, she slides onto her rear. She considers Aaronovich again, this time more with curiosity than distrust, and begins to eat, scooping with the fingers of her left hand, keeping the bowl close to her chin. Once it's almost empty, she runs her tongue over the inside.

I'll have to disinfect it, Aaronovich realises, and the thought saddens her.

She had expected Abigail to drop the bowl when she finished eating, as a toddler might. Instead, she creeps forward and replaces it on the tray, exactly as she found it. Noting the second bowl, the one full of water, she picks that up and laps experimentally. Satisfied that it's innocent, she drains it, and replaces the second bowl just as she did the first.

Then, to Aaronovich's total surprise, Abigail scuttles around the tray on all fours and flops into her lap. She yawns cavernously, encircling Aaronovich's thigh with frail arms. Her head sinks down to rest.

Aaronovich drapes her arms about the child, holding her gently. She has to struggle against the tension that threatens to calcify her limbs. She knows that what she told Johnson is true. This small creature is a human child. She knows, too, that she is more dangerous than any child has a right to be. It may take very little provocation to turn her into something deadly, or perhaps none at all. In that sense, it's as if Aaronovich is cuddling a living bomb, not sure if or when it might detonate.

Yet there's more to her unease than mere foreboding. Aaronovich sees herself with sufficient clarity to recognise that here is a boon she's longed for, and that she's already afraid will be taken from her. She's been alone and now she isn't. She's been useless; now she has purpose. Here is what she wants, and she's so likely to lose it. Aaronovich knows that she'll do everything in her power to defend Abigail, from Foster, from Johnson if need be, from her own sickness. But that might not, probably will not, be enough.

It's that knowledge, more than anything else, which threatens to paralyse her. Maybe nothing Aaronovich does can make this child safe, or keep her safe from others. Regardless, she has to try. In this moment, she can feel her choices narrowing to a vanishing point.

Aaronovich sits, as the candle burns to a flickering stump, as cramp makes her thighs smart and throb. And only when she hears the snuffle of soft snoring does she dare begin to relax.

PART FOUR
CONTAGION
CHAPTER TWENTY-SIX

Carlita is gone when he wakes, as always.

Doyle tries to be glad. It's what he insisted she had to do, a rule he set after that first visit. *No one can see you come and go. Silensky mustn't know. You come here when you need to, only if you need to.*

He'd been disgusted with himself for whispering unkind words amid the greying of a new sunrise, when all he'd ached to tell her was that in the night he'd begun to want his life again, for the first time in longer than he could recollect. In her touch, in the drive of her body against his, he'd remembered what it was to care, about someone else and about himself.

He'd thought she'd hate him, with his rules, his lack of tenderness, his packing her off like some cheap whore before the sun was even over the horizon. But Doyle had already given in to weakness once and he couldn't bring himself to compound that error. If he'd let himself, he would have asked her to move in with him there and then, gone out onto the balcony and shouted the news to all of Funland, and dared Silensky and everyone else to oppose it.

Of course, Carlita had no way of knowing that.

He'd felt certain she wouldn't come back. And she hadn't, not the next night or the night after – not for five days. Doyle had been in bed, not sleeping but not willing to waste candlelight when he could think of nothing useful to do. He'd barely heard the knocking at first. When he had, a potent instinct, something like vertigo, had nearly kept him from answering.

Once might be a mistake. Twice was a choice, and there was no returning from that.

This time, she was dressed in jeans and T-shirt instead of the sweater; the night was warm, particularly for so late in the year. She looked like she'd been crying and had attempted to hide the fact. "I'm sorry," she'd said. "You told me to only come when I need you. But I need you now, Doyle, I do."

He could have cried too, with shame. Rather, he'd led her to the bedroom. He'd held her for a long while before they made love, sat behind her with his arms wrapping her waist, her head rested against his shoulder. He hadn't apologised or made excuses for what he'd said. He'd tried to believe she somehow knew already. He'd slept deeply, and hadn't stirred even when she left.

There had been three more visits since then. They didn't talk much. The sex was rapid and desperate, muted because he couldn't shake the fear that someone, through layers of brick and metal and plaster, would overhear. It felt almost like an obligation, and part of Doyle was glad when the deed was done and they lay overlapping in the clammy silence. Yet he knows they both need it, and Carlita perhaps more than him. The months of captivity and isolation have built a terrible energy in her.

But keeping himself in check isn't getting any easier. None of it is getting easier. The feelings she woke in him that night haven't gone away, have only grown stronger. They don't mitigate his guilt and shame, but they make them seem worthwhile.

Doyle drags back the sheets, stale with last night's odours. He has no idea what the answer is. Maybe there isn't one. Maybe the answer is that there's no good end to this, not for them or Funland, and he should be grasping whatever pleasure he can before their fragile existence finally caves in around them. Either way, thinking too hard will make him crazy.

Doyle slides from the bed and washes himself, standing naked and sponging water from the bowl with a facecloth and refusing to wince at its coldness. He can smell Carlita on him, fresh and sharp unlike the sour musk from the bed, and he hates to wash off that scent. Once it's gone, it's gone, till the next time – if there is a next time. If Carlita doesn't decide that Doyle can go to hell, or that ultimately Silensky isn't so bad a bet, that at least he doesn't drive her away, won't expect her to creep like a thief for the barest scraps of attention.

"Christ!" Doyle had meant the word to be only a thought until it slipped from his lips. Why does he feel this need to torment himself? And today of all days. A headache is probing at the edges of his mind, just a promise right now, but Doyle has no doubt that the promise will be kept.

Because today is the day he said he'd talk to Aaronovich. Today is the day he promised Foster he would settle the question of the Sicker child once and for all.

* * *

Kyle gives the ball a hard shove and it tumbles across the tiled floor. His aim is skewed, but Abigail flops onto her side and catches it easily. Batting it toward him with both hands, she rocks back onto her knees.

Abigail never seems to tire of games. It's one of the things that remind Kyle she's sick. She hardly tires at all. She rarely sleeps, and when she does it's in bursts, an hour or two at most.

She loves the ball. It's made of cheap plastic, striped in red and blue, somewhere between a soccer ball and a baseball in size. The game, such as it is, involves Kyle rolling the ball across the floor to her and Abigail rolling it back, an act she performs with surprising precision and clear delight. She struggles to catch the ball, but returning it she manages effortlessly.

The ball came from his dad. Kyle had pleaded with him to bring some toys back, without admitting who they were really for, and had been certain he wouldn't until the moment when he did. Kyle had been so sure his father would let him down that he hadn't known what to say, and before he'd finished hunting through the carrier bag of assorted junk, Ben had slunk away, not even waiting for thanks.

Kyle knows some rupture has occurred between his father and Carlita, but he doesn't know what and doesn't dare ask. His dad has rarely done worse than shout at him, yet there's something in his alienation and in his obvious self-torture that Kyle finds himself afraid to trust. He keeps his distance, wishing he could help, wishing his dad would snap out of it, and recognising day by day that maybe he won't.

Kyle deliberately aims awry. He's getting bored. There are times when Abigail seems to him like a little sister and he feels hopelessly fond of her. There are others when he can only see the sickness. He keeps his distance from her. Whenever she shows signs of anger, or even agitation, he will back off, getting out of the room as quickly as he can. These are rules Aaronovich insists on, and in truth Kyle is glad to obey them. He can only mistake Abigail for a normal little girl for so long, and no amount of familiarity has stopped those surges of insight, the ones that tell him with utter clarity that he's in the presence of somebody no longer absolutely human.

With slightly more effort, scuttling briefly on all fours, Abigail recovers the ball. She doesn't appear to be perturbed that Kyle isn't playing properly. She never is. She shoves the ball back toward him, and her aim is unerring, as always.

On occasions like this, when Abigail's company bores him or else disturbs him, Kyle often chews over how his friendship with Austin has come to nothing. Partly he blames himself. Perhaps Austin really had wanted them to be friends, that night when he'd revealed his hiding place, and Kyle ruined his attempt by letting on how frightened he was. Yet he'd bitten inside his lip to conceal that fear, and Austin hadn't seemed to notice, or to be paying him any attention at all. Easy as it would be for Kyle to make himself accountable, the truth is that there's something terrible going on in Austin's mind, a dark and winding process that he may not even be aware of.

Kyle pushes the ball, not aiming, missing Abigail by a wide margin. She scurries after it, making a weird, high chuckling in the depths of her throat.

If Kyle hadn't already had enough, that would have sufficed. Before she can try and return the ball, he's on his feet and retreating toward the door.

"See you later, Abigail," he says. And she looks round, but at the noise, he thinks, more than from any comprehension of the words.

Kyle is careful to shut the apartment door behind him until the latch triggers. The doctor is sitting at her desk, a large hardback like a textbook open in front of her.

Glancing up at the click, Aaronovich asks, "How is she?"

Kyle nods, knowing she'll deduce that this means there's nothing to tell. They seldom speak, particularly when it comes to Abigail. Her existence is straightforward and follows simple rules, which they both understand. Likewise, there's no need for him to explain to the doctor that he's tired of Abigail. She seems to appreciate intuitively that he has his limits, even though she herself apparently has none.

Aaronovich goes into her apartment, closing and locking the door behind her. Kyle considers going back to his own room, or wandering over to the farm to see if Singh and Torres are interested in help. Aaronovich has persuaded Foster to allow Kyle time off from his responsibilities there, and there's not currently a great deal to do in any case, but he finds that he misses the physicality of the work. Now, though, he's lethargic, for the day outside is stifling and grey, and the glow through the skylight feels like a weight. So instead, Kyle settles in the doctor's chair and stares up at the metal joins that break that heavy light into misshapen diamonds.

After a while, he grows uncomfortable. When Kyle shuffles, he realises what's digging into his ribs. It's Plan John's logbook. He's been carrying it around for days, maybe weeks, without once looking at it.

Kyle takes the book out and lays it before him on Aaronovich's desk. He opens it at a random page. Not quite awake, he stares at the crabbed text, deliberating not so much on its hidden message as at why it should even exist. He saw so little of Plan John; his memories are hazy. Who had he been? Why had he gone to such trouble to create Funland, only to let the place kill him in the end? What secrets did he go to this extreme effort to keep?

Kyle starts when he hears the door open and close. Perhaps he's been drowsing after all.

"She's asleep," Aaronovich says. Then, "What's that?" She pauses behind his shoulder. "Is this that book of Howard's again?"

Kyle wonders why she refuses to call the man Plan John as everyone else does – and at how long it's been since anyone spoke his name at all. These cramped lines of text are one of his last legacies, and they are practically meaningless.

"His logbook," Kyle agrees. He doesn't feel like discussing it.

But Aaronovich remains behind his shoulder. "And you think it's in some sort of code?" Scanning a few stray lines, she adds, "It certainly looks like a code."

"I thought it was going to be easy at first," Kyle admits.

"What happened?"

She's genuinely curious. He isn't going to be able to evade an answer.

"There are paragraphs on every page, you see? Sometimes just one or two, sometimes five or six. I found one I managed to work out. It was really simple." He flicks to that page, where he's scribbled notes in the margin. "See, here? All he did is swap each letter for the next one along. A for B, B for C, like that. I thought, it can't be this easy."

"And it wasn't."

"Yeah. The same thing doesn't work on the other paragraphs. It's not one code. I think it's loads of different codes. What if every paragraph's different? How are you supposed to figure that out?"

Aaronovich takes a moment to digest this. Then she says, "Howard wasn't a man to do something for no reason. Maybe you're just not looking hard enough."

He knows she doesn't mean her observation as a judgement. Still, it's sufficiently close to irritate him, perhaps because, if it *had* been intended as a criticism, it would be deserved.

"What does it matter anyway?" Kyle says. "Plan John had a radio and kept all these notes, pages and pages, and he thought they were important enough to write in code. But who cares? There might be people out there, people who could help us, but no one gives a shit."

His voice has grown shrill. Kyle is disgusted by how much he sounds like a child denied his own way.

It only makes it worse when that's how Aaronovich responds to him, as if he's on the verge of a tantrum and needs calming. "Kyle," she says, "you shouldn't get your hopes up. Johnson tried to use the radio and there was never anything except static. Probably there were plenty of survivors in the early days, but we have advantages they don't. Even if the sickness isn't waterborne, there must have been secondary plagues once the sanitation began to collapse. Typhoid. Cholera. Even flu could be catastrophic without medical infrastructure. In all likelihood, whoever Plan John was talking to succumbed long ago."

She describes horrors so calmly, as though they're hardly significant. Maybe everyone out there is dead, everyone Kyle has known, maybe they're dead and no one is ever coming to help them and this is all there's ever going to be, until the food runs out or the Sickers get in.

Kyle wants to scream. The sensation has been growing in his chest for a long time, building and building like a snowball. This must be how Austin feels always. How does he live with it? How does he keep it in?

Kyle pins his lower lip between his teeth, sealing his mouth against the swell of noise and rage and pain. Slowly, agonisingly slowly, it subsides.

When he's sure he can control himself, Kyle stands, slaps the logbook closed, and stuffs it back into his pocket. "Then I guess we should all just give up," he mutters. And even the hurt and surprise he sees fleetingly in Aaronovich's face only stoke his anger as he storms toward the door.

CHAPTER TWENTY-SEVEN

They hear the sound once more: a gentle rapping like the drumming of rain, which gains in speed and volume to become nerve-janglingly rapid and loud. Then it's gone, and too quickly for Ben to make sense of it. That noise could as easily have been a loose plastic sheet caught in a stiff breeze or the patter of running feet.

"Why don't you go first, Silensky?" Gecko suggests, and seems happy at the prospect.

Ben looks to Oxendine, who holds the sole weapon they were permitted to bring with them, Funland's one remaining shotgun. Ben tries to appeal to him without daring actually to say anything. But Oxendine only shrugs, his features impassive. "I've got your back," he declares, though nothing in his voice implies that he could care whether Ben is alive or dead.

They have explored the main space of the warehouse together, to no avail. There'd been food in the small kitchen once, but animals had got into it, raccoons or squirrels, and the spoiled stench of what was left had nearly made Ben retch. The vodka they'd discovered yesterday, which they'd consumed in an upstairs room of the house they'd barricaded and spent the night in, hadn't helped. Ben had drunk more than he should have, and the other two hadn't seemed concerned. Later in the night, he'd listened to them fucking, briefly, without passion. Everyone found their own ways to deal.

Ben looks at the door. It's painted in chipped and weathered green, and leads, presumably, into offices. He turns the handle, hoping it will be locked, and is disappointed and for a moment mortally afraid when it isn't. Yes, he'll go first. He invariably goes first.

And Ben wonders, as he's frequently wondered, what's keeping him alive.

Luck, maybe — whatever that means. In the wider scheme of things, perhaps usefulness of a sort. If nothing else, he's a pair of hands, and these days even that amounts to a virtue. His death would equate to one less able body, a vacancy in need of filling. Because that vacancy would be at the nadir of Funland's hierarchy, it isn't a position anyone could possibly want.

These expeditions are supposed to be done by roster, partly out of a spirit of fairness but mostly from expediency. The strain of leaving Funland's borders, of going into the world beyond, which every day turns its back further on humanity, takes its toll. And it's only getting worse; since they've looted the nearby towns bare, each excursion now requires that they head out greater distances. Round trips can no longer be made in a day, especially with fall chilling and contracting toward winter. Everybody plays it tough, but Ben knows what the expeditions do to them. He knows because, whoever those other two names might belong to, his will always make the list.

He tried, just once, to complain to Foster, to emphasise the basic injustice. Why should it always be him?

"Tell me," Foster had asked him, "what fucking use are you for anything else, Silensky?"

Ben had no answer to that. He's no use at all. Not to his son, who he can barely look in the eye these days, and certainly not to Carlita. He had left her alone for a few days, as long as he could bear. Then he'd gone and knocked on the door that partitioned her small section of the Big House. There'd been no answer, though he could see the tenuous gleam of her candle under the door. He'd gone back the next night and the next, had knocked as loudly as he'd dared. He'd grown angry, but not angry enough that he might be overheard, because the thought of someone finding out, of what they would do to her, tore at Ben's guts like a wild animal. There were levels of losing Carlita, and that was a level too far.

So maybe Foster was right. If Ben dies here, it will mean little to anyone but him. He pushes on the door, wincing when its hinges complain. Something has fallen upon its far side, and he has to lean into the dinted chipboard, until finally his full weight is against it.

There's the sound again, a pit-a-pat like small feet running, faint yet close.

The offices along the passage, Ben suspects, had been abandoned even before the sickness. A thick layer of grime coats everything; the windows are blackened, staining what meagre daylight creeps through the murky brown of ditchwater. There are four doors off the corridor to the right – all of them wedged open, so that the inadequate light just reaches to lap the borders of the passage – and a fifth door at the end, which is shut. Realising that's where the noise is coming from, Ben feels no surprise. It seems, in fact, inevitable.

He doesn't look for Oxendine. He's there or he isn't. If those clatters of rapid motion represent a Sicker, Ben himself is between them and him, and between them and Oxendine's shotgun. If it's a Sicker then Ben is probably going to die, and whether that end comes from a diseased freak clawing through his face or from a back full of shot doesn't strike him as that important. Better, in truth, if Oxendine keeps his distance. On his own, at least Ben can negotiate the garbage-strewn corridor quietly. There are piles of anonymous mulch everywhere, which he assumes were once the contents of an overturned file cabinet, corroded over the months by damp and mould. But there are other ingredients in there, too; animals have been in here, for the air is redolent with the unsubtle reek of shit and urine. Ben steps with caution.

He's nearly at the door when the noise resumes in an abrupt explosion. It subsides as quickly as it began, and Ben is certain that what he heard was feet, small feet pattering on a hard surface. Yet from the layout of the building, he can tell that the room beyond isn't large, no bigger than the narrow offices to the right. Could there be a back route in? If they'd done this properly, they'd have checked the perimeter before even setting foot inside.

If they'd done this properly, Ben would be the one with the gun.

He can't resist then: he looks round for Oxendine. The big man has set himself up in the farthest doorway, all but cutting off the light from without. He's twenty yards away or more. Close enough to stop anything that comes through the door in front of Ben, too far for accuracy. His disregard for Ben's life is blatant.

Ben reaches for the handle. He'll throw himself to the ground, he decides. He'll hurl himself full length into the malodorous garbage if need be. Maybe no one will grieve his loss, but he doesn't *want* to die. And maybe it's even a good thing that he's forced into positions like this, to be reminded of that fact occasionally.

He levers the handle. The door isn't locked; he knows the moment he tries it. Perhaps, then, it will be rusted, or blocked on the far side as the other had been. But no, it gives freely. Body flat to the peeling jamb, neck craning, Ben shoves with the flat of his hand. His pulse is hammering. Every muscle is shivering with anticipation. He's as ready as he can be for something to lurch at his face, for the thunder of Oxendine's shotgun.

The room is mostly in darkness. A scant glow comes from a small window of frosted glass near the ceiling. The glass itself is opaque with dirt, but one corner is jaggedly broken, and there, drab afternoon sun trickles in. Ben can make out skeletons of metal shelving lining the walls to left and right, piled with decaying cardboard boxes.

The sound comes again: the flutter of padding feet, rising from the darkness. This time, however, Ben sees as well – a blur of white and grey that pinballs around the tiny room, first straight up toward the ceiling and then diagonally across, narrowly missing the shattered window, dipping and rising in a steep parabola and bursting through the doorway in a flurry of noise and motion, to veer up the passage and past Oxendine's head.

"Fuckin' bird," grumbles Oxendine, who had looked as though he might empty the shotgun at close range into the terrified pigeon.

Ben slumps against the doorframe. He knows he should be relieved, but his heart is pounding harder and faster than ever. He gulps great lungfuls of air and grips the frame with one hand until his nails gouge the wood.

When Ben looks up, Gecko is standing over him, considering him with disdain. Gecko turns his gaze on the room at the end of the passage, appraises it briefly, and spits a wad of phlegm into the gloom. He turns away without a word. Oxendine shrugs and abandons his post in the far doorway, heading back into the warehouse.

Ben kneels there for a minute more, until it occurs to him with sudden clarity that they might simply leave without him. Then he clambers to his feet. He spares the storeroom one last glance, and feels vividly what it must have been like to be that pigeon: trapped, battering the walls, too dumb to get out the way it got in.

He hurries back along the passage, and, not seeing Gecko or Oxendine, carries on across the weathered concrete floor and through the gap left by the open metal roller door. There, Ben almost bumps into Gecko, who has stopped on the edge of the loading bay, looking out toward the road. Oxendine is just below him, at the bottom of the short flight of stairs leading down to the asphalt forecourt. He, too, is staring across the road.

For some reason, Gecko had chosen to park on the far verge rather than in front of the warehouse. There's the crusted edge of the road, and then a steep, railed-off decline backed by tightly gathered pines.

On the strip of dirt and tufted grass between road edge and railing, the truck is pulled up. And now, five Sickers are standing around it.

It's an ambush, Ben thinks. He wants to say so aloud, but he can't get a single word out.

Waves of memory are washing over him, rocking him with their ferocity, of the farm and of what happened there. Unbidden, Ben's mind is conflating that time and this, moulding them into a single moment neither past nor present. He watches, as clearly as if it's happening before him, a fist descending upon Houseman's nose, smearing flesh to mush – and then crashing down repeatedly, even though there's no imaginable way to distort that ruined face further.

Only, Houseman is not Houseman but Nando, and the disintegrating glass is a web around his shattered features. Nando is Landser, dying in slow motion. Landser is Oxendine, is Gecko. It's an ambush, and it's happening again.

There are three men and two women. They're strung out in a bracket that pins the truck within its confines. One of the men isn't much more than a boy, surely no older than fifteen. The women are both in their twenties or early thirties, Ben guesses, though rough living has taken its toll. It dawns on Ben that he hasn't once encountered a Sicker he'd have reckoned for over fifty. He wonders what happens to them. Do the others pick them off? Maybe they didn't survive the initial infection. Is it possible there are camps somewhere, Sicker villages full of Sicker babies and Sicker geriatrics?

But such questions are meaningless. Life is short these days, for everyone. He and Gecko and Oxendine, are any of them going to see fifty? Or tomorrow, for that matter?

Oxendine takes a step forward, and, when there's no reaction from the gathered Sickers, another and another. He stops halfway across the loading bay, straddling the faded white line that marks its leftmost edge, feet splayed like a movie western sheriff's. He holds up the shotgun, while still pointing its muzzle in the general direction of the Sickers.

"You know what this is," he says.

There's no response from the Sickers. Ben hadn't expected one; he has no idea if Oxendine did.

Oxendine takes half a dozen more steps. Now he's at the road, equidistant between warehouse doors and truck. Far enough away that if they choose to go for him, there'll be nothing Gecko or Ben can do; far enough that Oxendine might get one or two or even three of them, but couldn't possibly take them all down before they reach him.

Then the shotgun will be lost, just like Houseman's gun was lost. It will all be over. No reaching the truck this time. No last-minute escape; no leaving Gecko and Oxendine to their fate. This time, their fate will be Ben's also.

Oxendine holds the shotgun higher, not quite pressing the stock to his shoulder, not quite aiming. "You know what this is. You know what it does."

Then he does aim. He's picked out one Sicker, the foremost. The man is big, though not as big as Oxendine himself. He's wearing what may have been mechanic's overalls; beneath the grime are patches that perhaps once were dark green. His hair is long and straggling, as is his beard. That's true of all three of the men: they look like trappers come down from a frozen wilderness, the snowbound forest still in their blood and their bones.

"I can't get you all," Oxendine says. To the one Sicker he's picked out, who might or might not be the leader, he adds, "But I can get *you*." Slowly, Oxendine edges his aim to one side, until it rests on one of the women. "I can get *you*." He adjusts again, picking out one of the other males. "And I can get *you*." He returns his aim to the potential leader. "So what's it to be?"

You can't rationalise with them, Ben thinks. He doesn't say it because he's afraid the sound will be the trigger that makes the frozen tableau before him erupt into violent activity. *They're not people, not anymore. It's no good talking to them like they're rational, a group of gangbangers figuring out the odds. They're animals. They're monsters.*

The one Oxendine first picked out takes a step back.

He's standing toward the front of the truck. Step by step, he retreats past its hood. As if this were some unspoken command, another of the men emulates his lead, and then the two women. When all of them are on the far side of the truck, the side nearest the railing, the leader turns. An instant later and he's gone, over the fence, down the slope beyond. In a moment more, the other four have followed.

Oxendine gives it a few seconds and then walks across the road, past the truck, and aims the shotgun over the railing. Apparently finding nothing there to concern him, he turns back and calls, "Okay. Let's go."

Let's go. As though this is a day trip...just out with the wife and kids.

Gecko jumps down from the loading bay, landing easily. He strolls to the truck. Is his nonchalance an act? Even if it is, it's a pretence[1] he's composed enough to make. Ben doesn't comprehend how either of them can feel anything besides petrifying fear. Don't they see what almost happened? Can they not understand?

"Fucking come on, Silensky," Gecko calls. "Unless you really want to give us an excuse to leave your sorry ass here."

With a great effort of will, Ben forces numbed muscles into life. He clambers down from the loading bay, not feeling capable of manoeuvering the stairs. He walks unsteadily across the forecourt and the road, all his attention focused on moving one foot and then the other. A part of him craves to carry on to the barrier and look down – to verify that the Sickers are indeed gone, or else to confirm that they're still there and that his fear has been entirely justified, it doesn't seem to matter which.

Instead, Ben climbs into the truck.

CHAPTER TWENTY-EIGHT

Doyle hesitates outside the door to Aaronovich's office. He's done everything he can to avoid the conversation that lies on its far side.

After much heated debate, Doyle had managed to talk Foster around on the doctor's behalf. To some extent, that had been the hardest part; with Foster on side, the remaining pieces had fallen quickly into place. Foster had put out word that he'd executed the Sicker child, and in a touch of drama suggested by Aaronovich, they had even faked a funeral pyre on the bare ground outside the gates. To most of Funland, that had been the issue settled, a minor crisis simply and rapidly averted. The truth would stay between the three of them, and Aaronovich could work in peace.

But Foster hasn't tired of sidelining those leadership tasks for which he wants neither blame nor responsibility. He insisted that Doyle should be the one to keep an eye on the situation, and Doyle saw no choice except to comply. His one minor victory had been to push for a date far in the future, arguing that there was no point in letting Aaronovich study the child unless they gave her time and space to do so.

On the surface, the arrangement suited everyone. Aaronovich had got her way. Foster apparently had no difficulty ignoring a problem so long as no calamity could be traced back to him; he seemed satisfied by Aaronovich's claims that she could minimise the risks virtually to nothing. And Doyle, well, he'd been spared a decision he had no desire to make, if only for a little while.

That hasn't kept the prospect from grinding at his nerves. The reality is that he'd begun immediately to doubt the sanity of Aaronovich's plan. Silensky's descriptions of that fateful day, when he'd returned with two deaths to report and the Sicker girl in tow, had shaken Doyle badly. If there was so much as a hint of truth in Silensky's story, then it meant that the Sickers had worked in unison, and that raised possibilities Doyle didn't care to ponder. Worse was the insight that had struck him

208 • DAVID TALLERMAN

later; that even if the Sickers were dumber than the dumbest animals, they couldn't be underestimated. That was the mistake Houseman and Landser had made, the one they'd all been making since the start. Maybe, too, it was the mistake Doyle had made by giving in to Aaronovich.

Reminding himself one last time that putting this confrontation off won't make it any easier, Doyle raps hard upon the door. There's no response at first, and he's about to knock again when he hears the doctor's footsteps from within. When the door opens, Aaronovich gazes at him blankly, as if she'd been expecting someone else. Then her eyes widen, and Doyle sees, unmistakably, fear there: fear of him and of what he represents.

"Oh," she says. "Johnson."

"Doctor."

"Can I help you?"

"You'd forgotten," he says. "Our meeting."

"Oh," Aaronovich repeats. She shakes her head dazedly. "No, I haven't forgotten."

"Then can I come in?" Doyle asks, since she's still holding the door half-open, her body wedged into the gap.

Aaronovich edges back, drawing the door after her. "Of course," she says, and almost succeeds in sounding as though she means it.

Doyle steps after her. The pain in his head is gathering like thunderclouds, as he'd known it would. Whatever happens in the next few minutes, whatever decision he makes, he senses that someone is certain to get hurt, for that's the problem with choices that have no right answer.

★　★　★

Aaronovich hadn't realised quite how severely she'd been dreading Johnson's visit until she opened the door to him. Only when she sees his haggard eyes and the hard set of his lips does she understand that every instant she's spent with Abigail has taken place in the shadow of this moment. What she's imagined she was doing – trying to heal, to rehabilitate, to offer a semblance of the life she believes a little girl deserves – has always, on some level, been a sham. What she's really been doing is building an argument that, here and now, will convince this man.

Perhaps she should be comforted that Johnson seems every bit as on edge as she is. Yet she would prefer a calm, clear-eyed Doyle Johnson, one who can be relied upon to make sound judgements when presented with rational evidence, and that's not at all the man she sees before her.

"She's been sleeping," Aaronovich announces. "But I'm sure she'll wake up soon. She never sleeps for long."

She goes first through the reception room and her own private office, making a point of locking the intervening door behind them. That done, she leads the way to the second door, the one to her apartment.

"Wait," Johnson says, "she's in there?"

"Yes."

"Is it safe?"

Aaronovich resists the urge to just say *Yes*. "She'll be nervous of you. Don't make sudden movements. If I tell you to get out, then get out, and lock the door after you. But if you keep your distance then, yes, I think it's safe."

Johnson doesn't appear convinced.

"You've changed your mind, haven't you?" Aaronovich asks.

"What?" His brow furrows with incomprehension.

"About Abigail."

"Tell me what you've found out," Johnson says, "and we'll discuss what happens next."

"That's not an answer."

"Tell me," he says. "Take me through whatever it is you've found. Then we'll talk."

Aaronovich considers him with unveiled distrust. "I think your mind's made up. I hope you'll listen at least."

"I'll listen."

"All right." She doesn't believe him, but even this brief exchange has wearied her, and she needs her strength for what's coming. Aaronovich turns the key in the lock of her apartment door, draws it open, enters, and waits as Johnson follows before closing the door and listening for the click of the latch.

Abigail is indeed awake. She's squatting in one corner, balanced on her heels, arms wrapped tight around her knees, rocking gently back and forth, something Aaronovich often finds her doing when she's been left alone.

Now, though, she looks up. Normally when Aaronovich comes in she will scamper forward, eager for contact, or immediately try to initiate some game. This time she ignores Aaronovich altogether. She sits rigidly in that same position, closed against the world, her gaze locked upon Johnson. It's been weeks since she's seen anyone other than Aaronovich and Kyle.

Aaronovich kneels, careful to make and maintain eye contact. "Abigail," she says softly. "This man is Doyle Johnson, and he's going to be your friend."

CHAPTER TWENTY-NINE

Somehow it's all become twisted. Somehow it's gotten turned backward. It wasn't so long ago that Austin had everything under control, and now....

He no longer feels safe in his hiding place. He blames Kyle for that sometimes, as if the act of allowing someone else in there has made it insecure. He blames Kyle for plenty. Austin had trusted him, and what happened? Kyle had got scared, so scared that Austin thought he would piss himself. He'd told himself that was okay, because hadn't he wanted Kyle to be scared? Wasn't it good that someone was afraid of him? Except, not like that. Not just then. Austin had let slip a little of what he'd been holding inside for so long, and all he'd got in return was fear.

Austin hurries across the yard. There's no one about; still, he feels eyes on him. He fights the impulse to look around, to seek those invisible observers. Austin knows that perhaps they exist only in his imagination, that probably no one much cares what he does. Even his dad doesn't come searching for him anymore. Nevertheless, Austin feels them watching, and refuses to look up, as though by not seeing he can stay unseen. And sure enough, he makes it across without being accosted, with no one shouting to or at him, with the lone sound the tap of his sneakers on the asphalt.

He's going to give Kyle another chance. He's given Kyle plenty of chances, too many, but he's willing to give him just one more.

Who are you kidding?

Austin almost stops short, so furious does the intruding thought make him. He forces his feet into motion, covers the remaining distance to the administrative wing, nearly tears the doors wide, and then, at the last moment fearful of the noise, opens them gently instead.

Does he really need Kyle more than Kyle needs him?

Damn, it's all got so twisted.

Austin has his hiding places. He has his secrets. He knows, for instance, that his father is screwing the woman, Carlita. Austin has heard them in the depths of the night, their grunts of passion echoing through the silver conduits of his kingdom, drilling their ugliness into his mind. He knows plenty of things, but they are no use. Secrets are no good when you're alone.

And Kyle has his own secrets. That makes it worse. He's disappearing for hours, and Austin has no idea where. That ignorance infuriates him. Maybe this time he'll ask, just ask, and maybe he'll even be able to read the truth from Kyle's face, from beneath whatever lie he tries to mask it with.

Austin is afraid that Kyle will be off somewhere right now. He hates making this journey, exposing himself like this, for nothing. But to his relief, Kyle is in his room, sprawled on his bunk, staring at something balanced on his knees.

"What you doing?"

Austin knows the answer: that stupid book. And when Kyle doesn't reply, Austin sidles closer, staring at the pages over Kyle's shoulder.

"I give up," Kyle says. "It's bullshit."

For some reason, this admission of defeat rouses Austin's attention more than Kyle's enthusiasm ever has. "What's so hard?" Kyle flicks between two pages, marking paragraphs with a thumb. "These two use the same code," he says. "A really easy one. Only, it doesn't work for the others. He must have used a load of different codes, and all of them work differently. Figuring them out could take *years*."

Austin considers. "How far apart are they?"

Kyle turns through the pages again. "Um, thirteen...no, fourteen paragraphs."

"So it's something with fourteen. A pattern."

"Maybe," Kyle agrees, without interest. But he moves on a couple of pages, to squint distractedly at the lines of text. Then, abruptly, his face lights. "Fuck," he murmurs.

"Told you." It's so obvious, Austin can't believe Kyle hasn't thought of it. Yet the fact that Austin himself has gives him a thrill of satisfaction the likes of which he hasn't felt in longer than he can remember.

Kyle turns more pages. His smile widens. "Holy shit," he breathes.

Austin lets him check another couple of paragraphs and watches his smile broaden. Then he says, "So…do you want to hang? Unless you're too busy with your secret missions."

Kyle becomes immediately shy, all his excitement evaporating in an instant. "It's not a secret."

"Right."

"I mean…it is. But from everyone. Not just from you."

"Great," Austin says.

The conflict in Kyle's face is plain to see. Finally, his voice dropping to barely a whisper, he urges, "You won't tell anyone?"

Austin shrugs. It hardly seems worth pointing out that he has no one to tell.

"I need to hear you say it."

This is starting to piss him off. "Fine. I won't tell anybody your little secret."

"Okay." Kyle nods shakily. It's clear that he's still in two minds, that whatever this is actually matters to him. "Okay," he repeats. "Well, you remember when my dad brought back that girl?"

Austin is puzzled. What can he be talking about? Then realisation dawns. "The Sicker."

Kyle looks uncomfortable, though he hides it quickly. "Yeah. The Sicker."

"They shot her," Austin says. He recalls the funeral pyre. He had watched from a spot upon the walls, gazing at the flickering brightness amid the dark, all the while wondering what other eyes might be observing from the toothed silhouette of the distant trees.

"No, they didn't."

"What?" This truly *is* a secret, something Austin could never have guessed at.

"They kept her alive. Doctor Aaronovich made them. Abigail…that's her name…she's living with the doctor now, and I help look after her."

That's it? Austin is stunned. A Sicker? That crazy bitch doctor is keeping a Sicker, like a pet? He thinks he'll retch. Who would do that? An image fills Austin's mind with utter clarity: the figure of a man, head tilted in listless curiosity, his posture hinting at brokenness.

How can anyone not see what they are?

"It's okay. It's safe," Kyle says, surely reading Austin's reaction from his face. "We keep her locked up."

"Locked up?" Austin echoes with disgust. As though a locked door can stop a monster.

"Your dad even made the doctor have a gun." Kyle sounds defensive, shaken by the force of Austin's revulsion.

"A gun?"

"I don't think she'd ever—"

"Where is it?"

"It's in her bedroom. But—"

"I need it," Austin says. "I really need it. Just to borrow. Just for a few hours."

"There's no way." Kyle is flustered; his voice has grown thin and quavering. "Look, I'm sorry. I can't. Listen, the door's locked, and Abigail's in there."

"No," Austin retorts, "you listen." But having said that, and with such violence that Kyle actually flinched, he doesn't know if he can continue. He's never told, not any of it. He doesn't know if he has the words, if there *are* words. The memories are like a single noise, a drone too loud to hear.

But this is his one chance.

"My stepdad's out there," Austin begins. He can feel bile rising in the pit of his throat. "He's sick." A recognition: "He was *always* sick."

And after that, there's no turning back. Then it all comes pouring out.

★   ★   ★

Afterward, Kyle can't think about what Austin told him.

He can't even feel sorry for him. And while Kyle understands now why Austin acts the way he does, he feels no gratitude for that insight. He's already regretting agreeing to Austin's plan.

Yet can Kyle deny him what he wants? The chance to revenge himself on someone who made his life a living hell, someone who's barely even human anymore, who would be better off dead? And if Kyle *did* back out, what then? Their tenuous friendship would be over, of course. But more than that, he knows without a doubt that Austin will pursue his plan alone.

Kyle could warn someone. Only, the doctor can't hide the gun, not forever. That it be easily accessible is its entire point. They can hardly lock Austin away, and who would be interested in trying, when even his own father seems to have given up on him? Exposing Austin's plan to anyone besides Johnson would mean revealing the existence of the gun, and therefore the reason for it being in Aaronovich's apartments. More than anything, Kyle must ensure Abigail's safety. If he goes along with Austin, at least he might be able to do that.

It's impossible. Kyle wants to slam his head against the cinder-block wall, to pacify the whirling of his thoughts. It's impossible, this decision that's been forced on him, and there's no right answer.

Then, as though a haze has cleared abruptly from his vision, Kyle sees the logbook resting in his lap. A rush of gratitude flashes through him, mingled with relief. He turns to the last section he managed to make sense of, flips past thirteen paragraphs to the fourteenth. He's sure by now that this paragraph will be the same as the others. Still, he can't help but smile when the words start to cohere. That's one fourteenth of the logbook cracked.

But would Plan John have come up with fourteen different codes? Wouldn't that be too much to remember? On a whim, Kyle turns to the previous page, tracing back five, six, to the seventh previous paragraph. A to B. B to C.

Yes. It works.

Seven. Seven. And there must have been a key; something Plan John could look at easily. Something that wouldn't be immediately obvious to anyone else.

A to B. B to C. And M to O.

As in Monday.

But that would mean that the next paragraph works the same, T to U, and he'd have been able to decode it. Kyle checks, to be certain, and the result is garbage. So if not T to U, then maybe U to T? Sure enough, that produces two words in order: *If they.* For the next paragraph he tests W to E, a migration of eight characters. The word *north* is ample to satisfy him. Next is T back to H, all of twelve characters. *Water.* F to R. S back to A. S to U. It works. And Kyle can imagine Plan John sitting before his radio, staring at a calendar hanging above, running the conversions in his mind, scribbling his gibberish-like notes.

A degree of serious effort and he would have figured the logbook out in no time. He can see that Plan John probably never even intended his codes to be difficult, just to hinder inquisitive glances. Kyle had been so convinced that Plan John had sunk his mysteries deep out of reach, when all he'd done was dig a shallow hole and scrape earth across the top. If only Kyle had really tried, he might have uncovered the logbook's secrets weeks ago.

That thought spurs him on. He's already taken far too long. Now, right now, he's going to work through the whole damn book. If it takes all night, he doesn't care. Better, anyway, than contemplating Austin, better than torturing himself with the promises he's made. But he won't wake another morning without knowing the secrets Plan John buried in this shallow grave.

CHAPTER THIRTY

The Sicker girl doesn't go near him, and Doyle doesn't approach her. Yet Aaronovich plays with her and even at one point holds her, like you would any normal child. *One scratch*, Doyle thinks. *One bite. That's all it would take.*

However, when he looks carefully, he can see that the child's nails have been meticulously pared, and that the doctor is always cautious, always aware of where those small white teeth are in relation to her. She's wearing a lab coat of heavy fabric, sealed tight at cuffs and collar. It's not that she doesn't recognise the danger.

But it's still a risk, he thinks. *Still a hell of a risk.*

After five minutes, Aaronovich gets up from where she's been kneeling on the floor. To the Sicker child she says, "We're going to go away for a little while. But we'll be just outside."

When they're back in Aaronovich's office and the door is again closed and locked, Doyle asks, "Do you think she understands you?"

"Truthfully? I think she mostly responds to the intonation of my voice. Her language skills are severely arrested. Generally she's extremely quiet, far more so than a normal child her age would be."

More of an answer than Doyle had anticipated. He senses that this is a subject Aaronovich is eager to talk about, but also that an edge of panic is threatening to overwhelm her. She's afraid of him, afraid of what he might decide.

Doyle wishes he could reassure her. Instead he says, "She seems healthy. Physically, I mean."

"I've never pretended there's anything I can do for her from a medical point of view," Aaronovich says, catching his connotation. "I don't have the knowledge or the resources. I'm mostly limited to observation, and even then I don't have half of what I'd need to do a proper job. You have to bear all that in mind, Johnson."

"So you're no closer to knowing what it is? Where it came from?"

"How can I be? This is hardly a CDC. Do you want me to guess? Perhaps it was some insane bioweapon. Perhaps it mutated from something else. Does knowing matter in the end? The sickness is here, and it represents the future of the human race. Unless the infected are sterile or too mentally damaged to raise offspring, in which case this will be our final generation."

Johnson shakes his head, feeling as though he's trying to clear it after a physical blow. "Christ," he says.

"Well, what did you expect?" she demands, almost angry.

"No, you're right. It's just, hearing it like that...."

Aaronovich sighs. She sinks into her chair. "I know," she agrees. "Yes."

Doyle considers the second chair, props himself against the corner of her desk instead. "How are they surviving out there?" he asks. "Can you tell me that?"

"Maybe. Yes, I think so. I've given some thought to the question, at least, enough to believe that it's essentially meaningless. Humanity endured perfectly well for millennia with none of the trappings of civilisation. And the infected have basic advantages that, for example, Cro-Magnon man never did. They have domesticated livestock available and buildings to shelter in."

"You think the Sickers are like cavemen?"

"Actually," Aaronovich says, "that may be exactly what they're like. My empirical guess is that that's what the sickness has done, caused such damage to certain zones of the brain as to effectively strip away millennia of development. Is the idea so unrealistic? Society has never existed anywhere but in the human mind, Johnson. Damage that mind sufficiently and society is gone." She pauses, allowing him to digest what she's said, or else because this is the first time she's put these thoughts into words. "Anyway, there's more to it than that."

Doyle doesn't want to hear more. He's regretting this entire conversation; everything she's telling him is disturbing on one level or another. Yet he understands that she needs to get this out of her system, and that perhaps he needs to listen, however he might desire not to.

"Go on," he says.

"Abigail doesn't seem to feel pain, not like we do. I suspect she has a higher than normal resistance to infection, though I can't prove it. Once she tripped and banged her head on the edge of the bed. I had to sedate her to stitch the wound. But she didn't cry, hardly reacted at all. I don't know how it's possible, but there it is."

"So they won't just die out," Doyle says. "That's what you're implying."

"I'm not implying anything. If this was caused by a virus, it may mutate into some more fatal strain. There might be a secondary epidemic; it's hard to imagine that something like bubonic plague wouldn't severely deplete their numbers. On the other hand, they appear to be spreading into the countryside rather than clustering in the cities. Based on the evidence we have, I'd say that, no, they won't die out anytime soon."

Aaronovich stands then, placing hands on hips in a stubborn gesture that seems wholly unconscious.

"I told you I didn't stand the faintest chance of finding a cure," she says. "That's true. Frankly, I don't think the greatest medical minds in the world could have managed it. The sick are irreversibly damaged, and that damage must happen rapidly, within a few hours. They aren't going to get better, and they aren't going to go away. We all know that, deep down. They're the new status quo."

"All right." Doyle feels tired and hollow. He's more than ready for this conversation to be done with, though less certain than ever of what he thinks. In that, he supposes, Aaronovich has achieved her intention. "I'm not saying I necessarily agree with you, but all right. I can see you've given this plenty of thought. So where does your theory leave us?"

"It's simple, Johnson. That *is* my answer." Aaronovich lets her arms drop to her sides, as if she too is afflicted by his lethargy, or as if this has been a physical conflict and not two people civilly discussing difficult notions. "If you want to know why it's useful having Abigail here, why it's worth taking such a risk, then there it is. If we can't beat them, we have only one rational choice left. We're going to have to learn to live alongside them."

★ ★ ★

Aaronovich can't judge if she's getting through to Johnson. Or, no, she's sure she's getting through to him, for there's agitation in that stony face of his, a degree of intensity in his eyes that she's rarely seen there. The question is whether she's *convincing* him. But she has one more argument to try, and she isn't about to let him leave until she's done all she can.

"I want to show you something," she tells him. "Come on."

She leads the way back into her apartment, and when Abigail looks up inquiringly, says, "Just a minute, Abigail," and carries on to her tiny kitchen, closing the door once Johnson has pressed in behind her. She goes to the refrigerator and takes out the plate she prepared before. On it is an anonymous, pink-white slab of flesh somewhat larger than her hand. They cannot, of course, chill food, though the refrigerator remains a useful storage space; meat has become a rarity, and this, from its odour, is already close to spoiling.

"What the hell is that?" Doyle asks, the query pitched between disgust and frank curiosity.

"I've been snaring rabbits," Aaronovich answers, feigning nonchalance. "They get in under the wall. I don't know what they expect to find."

"That's stupid. And dangerous."

"What am I supposed to do? The food Contreras gives me is barely enough for me alone."

"You get as much as anyone," Johnson says.

"Exactly. As any one person. You want me to keep her placid? Starving her won't do that."

"Okay. Point taken."

Aaronovich wonders again if Johnson is being congenial because she's persuaded him, or if his mind is made up and he's only humouring her. She rapidly cubes the meat, talking as she does so: "Like I said, Abigail is extremely quiet, but I'm still optimistic that she might be persuaded to speak. However, she's very resistant to teaching." She holds up the plate to Johnson, who shrinks back at the smell. "*This*," Aaronovich says, "is one way to overcome that resistance."

She opens the door into her bedroom. Abigail has clambered onto the bed and is squatting on her haunches. As before, she gives Aaronovich her full attention – and now, scenting the raw meat, her jaw hangs open and she makes small panting sounds.

Aaronovich sits close to her. She's hoping against hope that, today of all days, Abigail will remember what she's been taught. Not prepared to risk putting her fingers anywhere near those small, chipped teeth, Aaronovich has had to devise an alternative. She places the plate behind her and considers Abigail sternly. Abigail holds her gaze, and Aaronovich is half-convinced that she's forgotten all she's learned when suddenly the child flings both hands out and cups them together. Then, a perfect dramatic flourish, she smiles beatifically. Smiling is something Abigail almost never does; Aaronovich could weep for joy that she's chosen this occasion, with Johnson as witness, to do so.

Still, she makes certain her voice is suitably severe as she insists, "Say please, Abigail."

Abigail's brow creases in obvious frustration. The smile falls away, and a thread of drool works its way down her chin.

"Abigail. Say please."

Again, Aaronovich is ready to lose hope when Abigail makes a noise, deep in her throat. It begins as a low throb, utterly inappropriate to the waifish creature making it, and only slowly takes on form: a single choked syllable. It doesn't sound that much like *please*, more *puz*, but it will suffice.

Aaronovich scoops up scraps of rabbit meat and tips them into Abigail's outstretched palms. In a flash, they're gone, her jaw shuttling back and forth, *slap, slap, slap*, and then the hands are out again.

"Now, Abigail...say thank you."

Once more, Abigail smiles, somewhat shyly this time. "Thaoo."

"Thank you...?"

Visibly, Abigail concentrates with all her might. "Thaoo Kathin."

Aaronovich thinks that her heart will melt. Two clear, whole words.

"What did she say?"

Aaronovich starts at Johnson's intrusion. "Thank you, of course."

"I mean, after that."

It takes her a moment to comprehend. To him she has only ever been Doctor Aaronovich. "She said, 'Thank you, Katherine.'"

"That's...?"

"My name, yes."

She deposits the plate in front of Abigail, and tries not to feel disappointed when the very human expression of a second ago is replaced by raw greed, even cunning. Aaronovich stands, looks away before Abigail can resume cramming wet blobs of flesh into her maw, and leads Johnson out to her office, locking the door behind them.

"You wanted to know if they're capable of behaviour as elaborate as an ambush," Aaronovich says, not looking at Johnson either. "Evidently they are. They may not be entirely people anymore, as we understand that concept, but they're not animals."

"Could they attack us here? Could they coordinate something like that?"

"I doubt it. Moreover, I doubt they'd want to. Maybe during the winter, when other game is scarce, they might begin to reevaluate. What happened with Houseman and Landser suggests they're already working in packs, perhaps based around family units. I thought for a while that Abigail must be related to the ones who attacked them, but from Silensky's account, she was equally as afraid as he was. That's interesting in itself. Anyway, my point is that there's a great distance between what happened then and the possibility of a sustained siege."

"So we're safe in here, but out there we're done for," Johnson summarises. "We're trapped."

"No more than we've always been," Aaronovich observes. "And I have one last thing for you to consider, Johnson, now that you've seen Abigail, seen that she's not a rabid dog that someone needs to put down. Ask yourself: what if, in most cases, the extreme, unfocused aggression is just a phase? An initial reaction, like shock, to the physical symptoms and brain damage the infected are experiencing?"

"Then how do you explain everything that's happened since?" Johnson says. "The Sickers have never done anything but attack us on sight."

Rather than answer, Aaronovich gives him a moment to appreciate for himself the falsity of what he's said. From what Kyle has overheard and passed on to her, Aaronovich knows that in fact there have been no shortage of encounters with infected who've avoided conflict. The general assumption seems to be that they're too crafty to attack without numerical advantage, that they have sense enough to recognise guns, that they're scared. Apparently only Aaronovich herself has thought to propose the obvious. What if they've simply chosen not to?

"Think of it like this," she says. "Neanderthal man and Homo sapiens coexisted once. Oh, that didn't end well for the Neanderthals, but nor were they wiped out in a day. It's perfectly viable for two similar, intelligent species to coexist, at least for a while."

"Now *we're* cavemen?" There's irritation, and more, in Johnson's voice.

"In case you haven't noticed," she says, "or quite absorbed what I've been explaining…we're the freaks now. The infected are the majority, and we can't hide in here forever. If I can find a reliable way to communicate with Abigail, then maybe I'll be able to communicate with them too. If the day comes when coexistence is our sole remaining option, you may be glad of what I'm trying to do. If you need to tell Foster something, tell him that."

Aaronovich leans back, exhausted. A part of her has been formulating these words for such a long time, and she feels as though unleashing them has left a hollow inside her. She regards Johnson with distant curiosity, unable to rationalise to herself why he's still here. She had thought this would be the end; he's clearly been wanting the conversation to be over every bit as much as she has.

Finally, as the silence starts to grow tense, Aaronovich prompts, "So you'll tell him what I've said?"

For a moment, Johnson seems confused by the question. Then he says, "Yes, I'll tell him."

"Thank you. Well, if there's nothing else—"

Johnson stirs. "There is," he says. "I've been getting these headaches. I've been having them for a few months, but lately they're getting more regular."

"Headaches?" Aaronovich asks. He's caught her off guard. It's so long since anyone has approached her in the capacity of patient. "There are plenty of factors that could be causing them. I'd say stress is the most likely. I can run some basic tests if you'd like."

"Tests?"

"Yes. It will take a little while to get the things I'd need together. Can you come back tomorrow?"

"Of course," Johnson agrees. He sounds relieved. "Thank you for your time, Doctor."

And with that, he pushes through the door and is gone.

Doctor, she thinks, *still Doctor.* How long have they known each other? Can there really be only one person in this place who both knows her name and is prepared to use it, and that person a sick child who perhaps doesn't even understand the utterances she's making?

Aaronovich wonders then if she truly believes all she's told Johnson, all the talk of what the sick are, of what they can be. Does she believe a single word? She honestly can't say. But if it was nothing except lies, and if lying is what's required to protect Abigail, she'll do so without hesitation. She'll lie, and if they force her hand, she'll do much more.

CHAPTER THIRTY-ONE

They've driven all day and into the night. That's what it takes now to reach anywhere they haven't already stripped bare. And what they're bringing back isn't worth it: not worth the fuel, not worth the risk they've taken. Not worth facing down five Sickers with one shotgun.

They don't talk about what happened. At first, Ben thinks it's because the other two are as shaken as he is. Then he begins to doubt. Could it be that, for Oxendine, the encounter simply wasn't a big deal? Maybe confronting them, to him, was like driving away a pack of wild dogs. Oxendine wasn't there that day at the farm. He hasn't seen what Ben has seen.

They spy more Sickers on the way, two groups of similar size to the one outside the warehouse and, as they drive through a small town they exhausted weeks ago, a pair that scurry off at the mere sight of the truck. In each case, the infected are at a distance, nothing threatening about them. Yet spotting them sets Ben's teeth on edge. Are there more around, or are they growing in confidence? Or is he just noticing them to an extent that he didn't before the incident at the farm?

At any rate, each sighting draws his nerves tighter. The spells in between he spends in a fugue, hardly hearing. Ben feels that there's something inside him and that it's gnawing toward the surface. Only silence, numbness, blankness can hope to keep it in place.

By the time they get back to Funland, he's barely thinking. He fails to register the clatter of the gate or the sudden stillness of the engine. It takes Oxendine elbowing him in the ribs and growling, "Move it, Silensky," for Ben to comprehend where they are.

He opens the passenger door and stumbles out, legs reduced to jelly by the unremitting hours of immobility. There are figures gathered, out there in the darkness. For one instant, Ben is sure they're sick, until he realises it's only a few of the cons, come to inspect and unload their meagre haul.

With that understanding, a plan of action forms in Ben's mind, a series of steps he can make no sense of but which his subconscious promises will provide what he needs. He hurries around the truck, forcing the flaccid elastic in his legs to comply, lets down the tailgate, and clasps a carton. Then, before anyone can interfere or comment, he hastens across the yard – its surface black and faintly glistening in the starlight, like still water – and past the corner of the Big House, toward the entrance near the stores.

Rather than go inside, however, Ben retreats into the shadows, hunting a spot where he can see the door but not be seen. He drags his jacket tighter about him, huddling in the deep darkness.

Soon others start arriving, bearing sacks and boxes, the gathered spoils of their expedition: canned and dried food, flour, salt, sugar, biscuits, a couple of sacks of rice, and gasoline, though not nearly enough. None of it, really, is enough. Their supplies are running low, each trip providing a little less, and soon winter will be upon them.

As such, not long passes before the last trailing figure drifts into the gloom. Ben waits five more minutes, just in case. Then, satisfied that the ant train between truck and stores has done its work, he gets to his feet and reclaims his carton. Now that his eyes have adjusted, he can make out stacked cans inside, their labels rotted and peeling. Who knows if their contents will still be good? As they've all begun to learn the hard way in these few months, nothing endures forever.

Outside the door to the stores, Ben tucks the carton under one arm and knocks. "One more box," he says, trying his best to make his voice normal, while at the same time unsure of what that might mean.

From the far side comes the sound of something being knocked over, followed by a muffled curse in Spanish. Seconds pass, and then Contreras opens the door a crack. Recognising Ben, he says, "Hell, Silensky."

"One more box," Ben repeats, proffering the carton in both hands. He feels like a bad actor, playing at being a person – playing at being Ben Silensky.

"Sí, sí." Contreras unlatches the heavy chain that holds the door closed.

The moment the gap is sufficiently wide, Ben puts his shoulder to it, shoving past Contreras. "Hey, listen," he says. "I need a drink, Contreras." He drops the carton beside a pile of similar-looking boxes.

"I know you've got a stash. Come on, man, just one bottle. I've fucking earned it."

"Foster says, not without his permission," Contreras insists. "No trouble, Silensky."

"What? I'm not causing trouble. Christ, Contreras! Don't make this difficult."

"You've got to get out of here."

"Screw you," Ben mutters, not knowing if Contreras will hear, not caring. His eyes rove the shelves. There isn't much left: a few dozen cans, some large sacks, bottles of plastic and glass that clearly aren't the sort he's looking for. As he's near to despair, he spies the box stashed carefully in a corner, almost buried beneath bags of rice and flour.

Contreras has followed his gaze, and as Ben paces toward the disguised box, attempts to block his path. Ben places a palm on the older man's chest and shoves, with strength that an instant before he wouldn't have guessed he had. Contreras makes a choking sound, perhaps of pain but more likely of surprise, and stumbles hard against the shelves behind. Cans and packets rain around his feet. By then, Ben is dragging bags aside, tearing leaves of cardboard, clutching the stem of a bottle. For a moment he's entranced by the slosh of gold within. Then he's slipped the bottle inside his coat and is dashing for the door, ignoring Contreras's feeble efforts to regain his feet.

As soon as he feels the cold night air on his face, Ben is dizzied by relief. He's done it. He has the means to get through one more night. He pauses to choose a course – and even that's too long. As he glances in the direction of the administrative wing, he makes out a figure approaching, hunched close to the Big House wall. Ben's first instinct is to run, but what if they should give chase? Probably they'd catch him and he'd lose his prize, which he's gone to such effort for. So instead, he stands his ground, trying to dredge an explanation of his presence from the mire of his thoughts.

Just as he's fathomed that there's something wrong with the figure, that they're not tall enough to be one of the cons, a thin voice rises from the darkness. "Dad?"

"Kyle," Ben says. He should be relieved, but all he wants, badly, is to get away.

"Are you all right?"

"Sure. Only, there's somewhere I've got to be."

"Okay," Kyle agrees. "But can I talk to you for one minute?"

"Kyle—"

"Dad, you remember Plan John's logbook? Well, I cracked it. I haven't finished yet, but...there are other survivors. People out there. People hanging on, like us. Isn't that great?"

Ben grips the bottle within his coat. What's the boy saying? People out there? They aren't people at all. Dumb kid, he has no understanding.

"Silensky!"

The call comes from behind him. Ben spins to face it, hating his son in that moment for this calamitous delay.

"You've got to give that back," Contreras shouts. He has a baseball bat now, one of those lightweight metal ones, and he's waving it in the air. "You give back what you've stolen, or so help me, I'm going to beat you until you can't stand up."

*   *   *

Doyle hears the truck come in, and is glad, not of the fact that the search party have returned, not even of the thought of more supplies to bolster their dwindling stocks, but only of the distraction. The rattle of the gate as it opens and closes, the complaint of the truck as it grinds to a halt in the yard, the fainter sound of voices, excited or disappointed he can't judge – it's a respite to have the night's silence broken.

He'd never appreciated until today how the changing of words could change the thing itself. At the beginning of the day, it had seemed conceivable that he might put down a violent monster. Now he can't imagine executing a sick child. One is a reasonable, if distasteful, step toward maintaining their safety; the other is an abomination.

At the same time, nothing Aaronovich said has reassured him. He believes her when she says that the sick are not about to die out, that probably no defeat will persuade them to relinquish their newfound grip upon the earth. Yet he can't share her faith in the possibility, however distant, of peaceful cohabitation. Indeed, he fears the Sickers more than ever. A day ago they'd been scarcely more than animals. Now they are damaged human beings, of the kind Doyle has spent all his working life around.

He's never entirely accepted the notion of rehabilitation. In so much as he rationalised his work, he had convinced himself that it was enough to keep the scum off the streets for another month, another week, another day. So what do you do when the scum have made every street their own? What do you do about a child who could kill everyone in Funland? And what, tomorrow, is he going to tell Foster?

When the shout reaches him, Doyle is almost relieved. Even trouble will be a diversion. Had that bellowed cry been a name? In an instant, Doyle is on his feet, and is halfway to the door before he remembers the battery-powered flashlight he keeps on his bedside. He rushes on, down the stairs, through the corridors and out. He slices at the night with the flashlight beam until it settles on three figures, near to the stores entrance.

"What is this?" Doyle calls. Rather than run, he starts toward them slowly, pinning them with the light. He recognises Contreras, wielding the bat that Foster gave him, Ben Silensky – Doyle had been right in thinking he knew the shouted name – and who is that with them? He finds himself hoping it might be Austin, that here is a chance to confront his errant son. But no, it's Kyle, Silensky's boy. Is he going the same way as his father? He'd always seemed like a good kid.

"He's been stealing, Johnson. This scumbag." Contreras is choked with rage. "This pathetic *borracho*. Stealing whiskey from me."

Doyle pauses, a few feet from the gathering. If he holds the flashlight high, its beam covers all three of them, confining them like the spotlight on a stage. And what a pathetic little drama this is. Silensky's face is haggard, drawn with sleeplessness and sunken with abuse. Contreras, despite the chill in the air, has his shirt off to reveal his shallow chest, the body of an older man. And the boy Kyle just looks scared, scared for his dad.

"Let him go," Doyle says. "It's one bottle, Contreras."

"Johnson—"

"If Foster gives you shit, tell him I made the call. Get out of here, Silensky."

Silensky doesn't have to be told twice. Before the last syllable is spoken, he's scurrying into the darkness, as though the torchlight is acid on his skin.

While he's still within earshot, Doyle adds, "But next time, Contreras, don't hesitate. If he sets one foot in the stores again, take that bat and cave his goddamn skull in."

"Yes," Contreras agrees. "With pleasure."

"Okay. Now, get back there, will you? Before someone cleans the place out."

"Yes. Of course."

Then Contreras is gone too, leaving only Kyle.

Doyle takes a step nearer, training the flashlight beam away from them, and waits for his eyes to adjust. Kyle's face is pale and anxious. Doyle can see that he's clutching something to his chest.

"It's all right," Doyle says. "You don't need to worry."

"Are you going to punish him?" Kyle speaks the words plaintively, in the manner of a much younger child.

Doyle shrugs. "No. Foster might."

"Will you tell him?"

"No." Doyle hadn't been sure of his answer until he said it. He despises Silensky, but he can't find it in himself to hate the man. Ben Silensky is weak and he's coming apart. Probably he's beyond anyone's help, and if he isn't, who would try? "What's that?" Doyle says, noticing how defensively Kyle is clutching the object he holds.

"Oh." Now Kyle sounds bashful. "It's—"

But Doyle has reached the answer for himself. "The logbook. Plan John's book."

"I figured it out."

"You broke the code?"

"There are seven different codes. But, yeah."

"And what does it say?"

Kyle takes a deep breath. "That there are other survivors. Back in the city."

Doyle realises he's suspected all along, that the answer is practically inevitable. Why else would Plan John have kept the logbook with the radio? Whatever had been occurring in the outside world, whatever last-ditch efforts at self-preservation were being made, he would have been angling for his share.

The issue has never been whether there were survivors, or whether Plan John had been keeping track of them, or why. "When?" Doyle asks. "When was he talking to them?"

The question takes Kyle by surprise. "I've only worked out a handful of pages. And there aren't any dates."

"So all we know is that there *were* others out there. That doesn't mean there still are."

"But...." Kyle protests, the beginning of an argument he clearly has no idea how to progress.

"The logbook might be from the first few weeks," Doyle says. His mind is working quickly now. What would happen to Funland if they stopped believing they were alone? If Foster, for instance, should be persuaded that there were enclaves to be found, with their own food, fuel – with women, maybe. Doyle can see no outcome that won't hasten their end, that won't drive them nearer to the abyss. "There's no point getting anybody's hopes up yet. Who have you told?"

"My dad," Kyle says. "He wouldn't listen. I don't think he even understood."

"Okay. You've done good with this, Kyle. You keep at it. But it needs to stay between us. Once you decipher the rest, come to me and we'll talk about what happens next."

"Right," Kyle agrees. "Sure. I'll do that." Then he too is gone, eager to escape back into the night.

Did the boy believe him? Doyle has never been a good liar. In the long term it won't make a difference; he'll talk Kyle around, even enlist Carlita's help. But in the short term....

Winter is close. Their supplies are running out. Funland is a heap of kindling waiting for its spark. And as much as there's a part of Doyle that could happily stand aside and watch the place burn, it's foolish to pretend that he doesn't have a stake in its endurance.

This thing with Kyle, he'll need to keep on top of it. He'll need to make it a priority. Something else to worry about, as alarming – maybe more so – as the situation with the Sicker girl. Either of them has the potential to be the ember that sets Funland alight.

Only then does that fact give Doyle pause: its strangeness, its absurdity, and for all of that, its absolute reality. Can it really be that, somewhere along the line, two children have become the most dangerous people in a prison?

*   *   *

Ben had planned to make the whiskey last. But the run-in with Contreras and then Johnson has left him more wired than he was already, and as soon as he's around the corner he finds himself gulping from the bottle, the liquid flaring in his throat.

He remembers distantly that he's never liked whiskey, not even the good stuff, which this surely isn't. Strange to think that there was a time, not long ago, when his likes and dislikes mattered. It isn't as if he's come to like the things he once abhorred. But he has learned tolerance, because there's been no other choice.

Perhaps he should resent that. Rather, the simplicity is nearly as comforting as the fire working its way down through his innards. If it mattered that he didn't like whiskey, even this small consolation would be denied him.

Ben hides for a while, in the crook where the Big House and cellblock meet, mindful of the dark. If anyone spots him, they'll take the bottle from him. For the same reason, he can't return to the cellblock. And the night is cold; the whiskey's warmth fades the moment he stops drinking.

When he's confident that Johnson and Kyle have gone, Ben skulks back around the corner of the Big House. There's no one about. Still, he moves cautiously, embracing the bottle as though it's a newborn he's been made responsible for. A brief, mad urge makes him want to seek out Carlita. Ben manages to push it aside. She's speaking to him now, at least. If she sees him like this, she'll despise him, and he'll hate her for doing so, and then who knows what will happen?

But of course they both know, and that's precisely the problem. She's speaking to him. Without that, without the bottle he cradles, he has nothing.

Instead, Ben creeps into the library. As he glances between the high racks of shelves, barely discernible in the meagre glimmer leaking from narrow windows, his position seems almost funny. He had never imagined he'd choose to spend so much time in a library, and a prison library at that.

Ben stops at the first table he stumbles into, finds a chair mostly by touch, sits down, and places the bottle before him. He unscrews the cap and takes a tentative slug.

Yeah, almost funny. But, in the end, not quite.

CHAPTER THIRTY-TWO

He hasn't cried in weeks or months, hasn't cried, in fact, since the first week after they arrived in Funland, when his terror had been all-consuming. But the moment Kyle gets back to his room, he falls onto his bunk and drives his face into his pillow and weeps. Hopelessness could never have done this to him. Only having hope and then losing it so immediately could have shattered him like this.

His dad doesn't care. His dad is a useless, screwed-up drunk. Doyle Johnson, that bastard, he doesn't care either. He just wants to make sure that what Kyle has discovered stays hidden. Kyle hasn't trusted him, not ever, and now he knows he's been right not to. "Bastard, bastard, bastard," he hisses into the pillow, already wet with tears and spittle.

Nobody cares. They're none of them going to escape Funland. There might be people out there, whole villages, whole towns, and those cowards would rather remain here, in a prison, until every last one of them is dead.

After a while, Kyle's tears start to abate, not because he feels better but because he's exhausted himself, and because even crying seems purposeless when there's no hope and no chance of hope. He flips the pillow to its dry side and lies snuffling in the darkness, the logbook still clutched to his chest.

When he wakes, he knows there's someone else in the room. He knows, too, who it must be. "Austin?" Kyle asks the darkness.

"Come on," Austin's voice says. One shadow detaches and approaches the less-black rectangle of the doorway. Halfway there, Austin hesitates. "It's time. Time to do the thing we talked about."

"I don't—"

"You promised. Come on."

Austin's voice, which began as a whisper, is rising now. Foster sleeps in one of the nearby rooms. Aside from Kyle, and the doctor and Abigail of course, he's the only other person living in the administrative wing.

There's a chance that, if Austin raises his voice enough, Foster will hear.

Kyle rolls off the bed. Already fully dressed, he pauses to snatch up his coat. Passing close to where he believes Austin to be, he mutters, "Follow me."

Kyle leads the way toward Aaronovich's office, but at the last moment, rather than turning right, he goes left instead, pushing through the outer doors, ignoring Austin's muted grunt of protest. Kyle keeps going around the building, stopping once they've placed its end between them and the yard. Then he says, "This is a bad idea. Somebody's going to get hurt."

"Just one person. As soon as I get that gun." Kyle can detect no doubt in Austin's words.

"Wait a few more days. We'll come up with a really good plan."

"We don't *need* a good plan. You talk to the doctor, you get the keys. You said she doesn't sleep in her room anymore. You know where the gun is. Get the keys, we get the gun, it's simple."

Austin's right. Phrased like that, it is simple. Kyle even has the perfect excuse to give Aaronovich, a pretext that's hardly a lie. He wishes he'd prepared a better argument, one that might have been convincing.

"Listen to me," Austin says. His voice is different, less obviously hostile, but also somehow less trustworthy. "I know something. About your dad and my dad. About your stepmom."

"Carlita's not my stepmom."

"Whatever. The point is, I know something. Something important. Something you'd want to know. Help me and I'll tell you."

Kyle recalls his dad looking at him as if he was a stranger. There'd been no affection in his eyes, scarcely even recognition. He remembers his visits to Carlita and how she'd talk at him rather than to him, barely registering a word he said. He remembers Doyle Johnson. *It needs to stay between us.*

"I don't want to know," Kyle says. "It's not my problem."

"Fine. Then I won't tell you. I'll tell someone else."

"What?"

"I'll tell Gecko, or Soto. What do you think will happen to your stepmom then?"

Kyle clenches his fists, nails gouging his palms. He wants to say, *Didn't I explain how she's not my stepmom?* He wants to hit Austin, knock him to the ground, smack that arrogant surety from his face. Kyle doesn't even believe him, not really. Nevertheless, he can't shake a sense of accountability, as though the course of the future is being forced into his hands. Going along with Austin is dangerous. Refusing is dangerous too. It would merely propel Austin onto some yet more drastic course.

The choice is Kyle's, but it's no choice at all. He can't avert disaster, only affect its probable course. And, as much as he hates Austin in this moment, it's true as well that he made a promise.

"I'll help you," Kyle says. "But you've got to listen to me, okay? We do it my way."

★　　★　　★

In the dream, Aaronovich knows she's dreaming. She knows, in part, because this dream is familiar. She's had the same one on many, many nights before.

While she understands that this is a dream, and that, if she chooses to, she can wake, Aaronovich allows it to continue. She opens the door as she always does. She's distantly aware that it's her responsibility to do so.

The room is in darkness. But she feels this rather than sees, as if the dark is a presence: she knows it's there, yet it does nothing to restrict her vision. Aaronovich recognises her own bedroom, though not as her bedroom is here. This is her and Daniel's room, from a long time ago or never, for even then the details don't quite add up.

Except it's also like her room now, at least in one detail. Abigail is sitting on the bed, propped on her haunches with hands tucked in her lap, her favourite pose. Noticing Aaronovich, she smiles, and even in the choking gloom, her smile is perfect – despite the mask of blood that cakes her jaw. Abigail leans forward, bending impossibly, to plunge her face deep into the mess of fur and ragged flesh spread out upon the covers before her: what was a dog, maybe, or a raccoon. Aaronovich can hear the slap of her tongue exploring its red cavities, her teeth scratching against ribs. Finally, after much too long, Abigail withdraws her dripping face. She licks her lips. And she laughs and laughs and laughs.

Then, as always, Aaronovich wakes. What she feels is not fear, nor even horror, but cold acceptance, and perhaps that's worse, when all is told. It's a residue from the dream, because in the dream that's what she feels, that and pleasure. In the dream, Abigail is happy, so she's happy.

Staring at a ceiling she can't see, Aaronovich wonders how far she will take that maxim in her waking life, how far she's already taken it.

At first, she thinks the noise is something out of her nightmare. In the infirmary, where she's slept ever since Abigail's arrival, the darkness is all-consuming. She maintains to herself that she's used to it, yet no amount of self-assurance can fully still the whispers of primitive terror it evokes. The steady tapping, issuing from somewhere above, unsettles her where the dream did not.

Then she catches – very faintly, muffled by layers of cinder block and concrete and metal – the sound of a voice. The second time, she's certain. Someone is calling her name.

Aaronovich slips to the floor, fumbling there for the battery alarm clock she uses in lieu of a flashlight. Its pasty glow is sufficient to find her clothes by. She lets the light go out while she dresses and then uses it to reach the first door. Climbing the stairs, she unlocks the upper door. She can hear the knocking clearly now, steady but urgent, and the voice repeating her name, "Doctor Aaronovich," over and over.

As she opens the door, she responds, more heatedly than she entirely intends, "What the hell do you want, Kyle?"

"Sorry for waking you," he says.

"It's too late to be sorry," Aaronovich retorts, not willing to relinquish her anger. "What on earth is so important?"

"I translated part of the logbook," he says. His voice is breathless in the blackness, as though he's been running. "I know what it means. It was Plan John, talking to survivors back in the city. Johnson says they're probably all dead, that probably they died months ago. But what if they're not? What if we can get them on the radio and talk to them and there's a way we can meet up? Maybe they can save us. We're going to die here otherwise, aren't we?"

"Kyle, no, we're—"

"Yes, we *are*. You know it. Everyone knows."

"Kyle...." Aaronovich's brief outrage is all but gone. "I appreciate what you're saying. Still, you're getting your hopes up over a prospect that may come to nothing. As much as it's not what you want to hear, likely Johnson is right. Even if he isn't, it's the middle of the night."

"But I need the last few pages," he says. "I ripped some pages out so

I could look at them without having to carry the stupid book around. I left them in your room before, when I was playing with Abigail. Just let me go and get them."

"My god, Kyle! No, you can't. You'll wake Abigail. You'll frighten her."

"I won't," Kyle says. He's almost sobbing. "I bet she's not even asleep. And she's not once been frightened of me. If she's awake then I'll play with her until she settles down."

This is beyond her. Standing in darkness, arguing with this apparition, Aaronovich longs to crawl back into her makeshift bed. The pall of recent sleep still clings to her, and within its folds is the nightmare, like lice in an old blanket. None of this – Kyle's near-hysteria, his talk of other survivors – seems important, or even wholly real.

"*Please*," he says. "I can't sleep. I'm going crazy. I need to know."

Aaronovich holds out the bunch of keys, relying on Kyle to find them by their soft jingle. His fingers brush hers, and then the keys are gone.

"Make sure you lock the door behind you. And put the keys in the desk drawer in my office. I don't want to be woken again."

"Thank you," Kyle says. His voice is small.

"And Kyle," Aaronovich finishes as she turns away, readying to negotiate the stairs into the profounder blackness of the infirmary, "we're going to have words about this in the morning."

*　　*　　*

Austin can't make out what they're saying. For all he knows, Kyle is telling the doctor everything. Now that they're here, he wants urgently to be elsewhere. Every step of the next few minutes, every potential moment of his future, seems unimaginable. He can't go into a room with a Sicker. If he should manage to get the gun, does he really believe he's going to go outside the walls of Funland? That he'll track down his stepfather, who terrified him even before he turned into a monster?

Maybe it would be better if Kyle is betraying him. Maybe then someone will stop him.

There's the faint scuff of footsteps. The door to the doctor's office opens and closes. "I got them," Kyle whispers.

Austin slides from beneath the desk where he's been hiding. A faint glow emanates from the skylight above, just enough that he can make out Kyle as more than a shape.

"There's a flashlight," Kyle says. He's barely murmuring, yet sounds loud in the empty office. When he opens a drawer, Austin can't convince himself that the doctor won't hear. After all, isn't the infirmary directly beneath their feet? Then, with the snap of a button, a cone of illumination spills across the floor. Kyle moves to the second door, keeping the flashlight beam ahead of him, leaving Austin in renewed darkness. There's the scratch and click of a key turning in a lock.

"You should wait here," Kyle says. "I'll go get it and bring it out to you."

"No. I'm coming." Austin doesn't know why he insists, except that he's disgusted with himself for being so scared. After everything he's endured, everything he's done, he can hardly bear the shame.

He thinks Kyle will argue. If he does, maybe Austin would let himself be talked round. However, all Kyle says is, "Okay. But stay back. Let me go first."

Kyle opens the door and steps through. Hesitating for Austin to follow, he closes it behind them. Then Kyle pans the flashlight's beam steadily across the room. When it reaches the bed, he slows, as though expecting to find some presence there, but there are only the sheets, piled in a tousled mound.

"Abigail?" Kyle asks softly.

He begins to move the beam again, more slowly still. Austin has to fight the urge to wrench the flashlight from Kyle's hand. This, the helplessness he feels, is like something out of a nightmare. All he can see is the small circle that Kyle chooses to illuminate, and even that is distorted by the wan light. The rest is absolutely dark, and in that dark is a creature, lurking.

The light stops, settling on a small figure. Crouched, limbs folded tight, it scarcely seems human; it's more like an insect. How could they have mistaken this thing for a child? It looks up, and Austin observes a small, oval face, ghost-pale. Austin is sure that its eyes flash under the glare, as a cat's would. Then it tilts its head, and for the first time resembles a little girl. Yet also, as much so, an animal: its teeth are bared, those eyes narrowed to slits.

"It's okay, Abigail," Kyle says. "This is Austin. He's my friend. He's not going to hurt you."

Kyle has stopped before a chest of drawers. As he concentrates the flashlight there, the darkness reabsorbs the Sicker girl. Austin had hated to look at her – so nearly human, enough to fool you if you *chose* to be fooled – but not seeing is worse. Kyle is searching through the keys that he holds with one hand, flipping them one by one from the backs of his fingers to his palm. Austin wants to wrestle those keys from him, the flashlight too, wants to so badly that his fingers twitch.

A thin note trembles on the air. It's unlike anything he's heard, and it takes him a moment to understand. The Sicker girl is growling. And the noise isn't coming from the corner of the room where she'd been, Austin is certain.

Kyle doesn't seem to have noticed. He's picked out one key, is rattling it against the top left drawer.

"What are you doing?" Austin asks. He does his best not to sound afraid.

"Just a minute. Dumb key's stuck."

Austin can feel panic rising. He's helpless to stop it. "Hurry," he snarls.

"Hold on. Let me put the flashlight down."

Kyle reverses the flashlight and sets it atop the chest of drawers. Its light spills back into the room, rocking crazily. Austin's gaze follows. All he identifies of the Sicker girl is one foot, disappearing into the shadows beyond the bed. She must have crawled over it on all fours, crept like a bug. That means she's near him, nearer than she'd been – and closer to the door.

"Okay," Kyle says. "I've—"

But before he can finish, Austin has dashed across the distance between them, is grabbing for the gun, is using his free arm to elbow Kyle aside. When Austin's fingers contract around metal, his relief is a dizzying surge. Then the barrel clips the flashlight. It spins, teeters. Austin glimpses the door and flings himself that way, gripping the gun as though he's drowning and it's the hand that's reaching out to save him.

He knows she's close. The flashlight is still spinning, slower now.

As its light slides by, Austin sees her, crouched, jaws open, watching him with naked interest. He flails with the gun, holding it by the barrel, almost losing his grip as the stock strikes flesh.

He hadn't meant to hit her. By the flashlight's stark illumination, it's impossible to make sense of distance. He definitely hadn't meant to hit her so hard. When the pistol's stock slaps her cheek, her head jolts with the fragile helplessness of a doll's. In that moment, again, he recognises her as a child. He has struck a little girl.

Then she bites him.

Her jaw clamps onto his forearm. One hand locks about his wrist, while the other scrabbles at his shoulder. Austin roars, in pain and fear. And more fear than pain, for he can feel how her teeth have broken skin.

The flashlight makes one last rotation. He's at the entrance. With all of his strength, he hoists her, her weight entirely on her jaw and on his perforated arm, and he shoves her at the doorframe, putting his own mass behind. She doesn't let go. Austin tries harder, crunching her small body against the wood. Still she hangs on. Her small teeth only sink deeper.

"Abigail!" Kyle screams.

Then she lets go. Austin gets the door open, falls out, stumbles over a chair. He claws himself to his feet and whirls away and crashes through the second door. He doesn't dare even look at his arm.

He knows that it's covered with blood, with blood and spit.

He knows what's going to happen.

CHAPTER THIRTY-THREE

Even before Aaronovich reached the bottom of the stairs, doubts had begun to intrude. By the time she'd manoeuvered back to her bed by the alarm clock's brittle light and had lain down, not bothering to undress, she'd known something wasn't right.

Nothing is right. She's never seen Kyle in such a state. He'd seemed on the verge of panic. She should have waited and talked to him. She likes Kyle, and more, she needs him. She can't look after Abigail on her own. She can't afford for him to break.

Still, she doesn't get up straight away. The urge to sleep is like quicksand, and with every lapse of concentration it threatens to draw her down. She is so, so tired. It's been so long since she's eaten anything close to a proper meal, since she's slept the whole night.

The sound of an impact is what gets through to her. She isn't even certain she hasn't imagined it, yet suddenly Aaronovich is tumbling from her bed, skidding across the floor, flinging the door open, and taking the stairs so fast that she has to scramble on hands and knees.

She wrenches at the second door and is halfway to the next, the one to her private office, when it springs open and a figure barrels through the opening. Aaronovich cries out. By then, whoever it is, they're past her and gone. For an instant she'd assumed it must have been Kyle, but even in the darkness, she could tell that the build was wrong. And already another shape has appeared in the doorway; a flashlight beam is swinging toward her.

"Kyle?" Aaronovich asks, surprised by the rawness in her own voice.

"You've got to come," he pleads. "Abigail, I think she's hurt. And Austin, she, she...." The sentence dissolves into a wrenching noise, half sob, half retch.

Aaronovich fights the urge to take hold of his shoulders, to shake the words out of him. "What are you saying?"

"She bit him. Austin. She was scared."

"Oh my god," Aaronovich whispers. "What have you done? You've killed her, Kyle."

"No...."

But she's not listening. Aaronovich snatches the flashlight from Kyle's hand and shoves past him, not caring how terrified he looks in its passing glare. She gets as far as the open doorway to her apartment before dread freezes her muscles. She needs all of her strength to raise the flashlight.

She finds Abigail immediately. She's retreated to her corner, as she does when she's afraid. Aaronovich can see that she's shaking, and at the same time rocking back and forth.

"Why would you do this?" Aaronovich demands of Kyle, barely expecting an answer.

"I had no choice."

"What?" She glances back at him, while leaving the flashlight beam trained into the room. "There's *always* a choice."

Kyle shakes his head helplessly. He looks so small, so lost, like the boy he might have been if that other world, the world before, had continued the way everyone had thought it would. "Austin wanted the gun," he murmurs. "He...I couldn't say no."

"And does he have it?"

"Yes."

"Good god." Aaronovich forces herself to consider, though all she desires is to go to Abigail and comfort her. "Do you know where he'd have gone?"

Kyle hesitates. "I think. Maybe."

"Then you've got to get Johnson. Tell him what happened. Tell him where his son is."

For a moment, Kyle looks ready to refuse. Rather, he nods and dashes away.

Aaronovich feels ephemeral relief. She's glad that he's gone and that she has one less thing to process. Then she remembers the awful magnitude of what remains. Here, now, is everything she's feared, the hidden terror she's hardly dared acknowledge since the day she first took Abigail in.

Yet she *has* acknowledged it. She isn't someone who denies her fears. She's planned for this day, and if that doesn't make it less appalling, nevertheless she knows what she has to do.

She shuts the door and locks it, drawing the thick bolts at top and bottom. She goes to the drawer, takes out the box of candles she keeps there, and removes four. Two of these she kindles and places in the bedroom. The others she sets in the kitchen. Then she switches off the flashlight and gives her eyes a few seconds to adjust to the much-reduced light.

Only once that's done does she turn her attention to Abigail. She's still huddled in the corner, whimpering softly. "It's okay," Aaronovich says. "It's okay. It's okay. It's okay." Each time she moves closer. When she's close enough, she kneels in front of Abigail. "It's okay," she vows, and bundles the child gently into her arms.

Aaronovich waits until Abigail has stopped trembling, and then stands, still holding her. She weighs so little, less than any human being should. Aaronovich carries Abigail into the kitchen, returns for the pillows and quilt from the bed. She spreads the quilt on the kitchen floor and wraps Abigail within. By candlelight, Aaronovich checks for injuries. The bruise on Abigail's jaw is obvious, unmissable, already a stain of purple and black. Aside from that, however, she seems unhurt.

As a final thought, Aaronovich returns to the bedroom to retrieve a couple of Abigail's toys, the ball and the ragged cloth dolly she likes to chew and pick at, and takes them to her. She says, "Abigail, I'm going to shut you in here for a brief while. Don't be scared. Everything's going to be all right."

She gets up and goes back into the bedroom, closing the door behind her, trying not to notice how Abigail has begun once more to whimper softly.

Just in time. Abruptly, the apartment door is shaking, at first as its handle is tested, then as a series of blows rain upon it. "Doctor, open this door!"

A pause. Aaronovich sits on the stripped bed and tenses, silently preparing.

"You need to open up. You know what has to be done." Johnson's voice is muffled by the heavy door. Still, she can discern the words clearly. He doesn't sound angry, and that worries her. She feels dimly that an angry Doyle Johnson could be reasoned with, that calm he might be beyond her reach.

Aaronovich walks to the door, stopping a foot away, sufficiently close that her own voice will carry. "I'm not going to open the door, Johnson. And nothing you say is going to change my mind."

She can identify his breathing, even through the intervening plastic and metal. "You told me that monster was safe!"

"She's not a monster." Aaronovich's composure seems to her a sheen of ice just waiting to be cracked. "She's a child. A sick, frightened child."

"That frightened child has killed my son."

Infected, she thinks. *She infected him.* She knows that, in the initial outbreaks, less than one in five of those infected actually died, and a considerable proportion of those deaths were self-inflicted. But this isn't the time to argue semantics, nor statistics. Instead, Aaronovich says, "Your son attacked her. Your son bullied his way in here and stole a gun, a gun *you* forced me to have. I never wanted it. I told you, guns *make* people get hurt, they don't stop it."

"Don't you dare put this on me," Johnson snaps. "You listen to me—"

"No. You listen to me, Doyle. This door is reinforced. You can't break it. And I'm not opening it. Not unless I'm certain that neither Abigail nor I are in any danger. I've food and water for a couple of days. Once that runs out, I have two syringes prepared, one for her and one for me. If we're still in here when that food is gone, I'll use them. Do you suppose I have a single reason not to? Maybe you can't hear this right now, but there's going to come a day when White Cliff needs me, and it's coming soon. You, all of you, need me more than I will ever need you. So you're going to stop this, and you're going to help your boy. Because *he* needs *you*."

Aaronovich ceases then, her breath spent. She presses her cheek against the cool surface of the door and gulps for air, wishing the room were not so suffocatingly warm, while at the same time willing Johnson not to detect her weakness. It seems to her that her fragile body is traitorously undermining her argument.

She guesses at the passage of seconds by the inconsistent metronome of her own heartbeat. She wonders if she'll ever open the door again, and finds that the enormity of that notion defies her current ability to process.

She's heard nothing, has no evidence. Yet she feels sure Doyle Johnson is gone.

★　★　★

Now that Austin knows he's going to lose himself, he can think clearly.

It hadn't been that way at first. As he'd run across the yard and around the Big House, as he'd jumped for the ladder and swung up its rungs, as he'd slid and slithered through the ventilation shafts that he recognises every inch of by touch alone, his mind had been completely vacant.

He'd navigated the ducts in total darkness. But here, in his space within the walls, he has lit a candle. Its quivering light makes the indents between the cinder blocks shudder, and the result resembles a net slowly settling upon him. The candle is the last of the ones he stole. He hadn't tried to get any more. Funny...as if a part of him had anticipated this. Soon that narrow flame will go out, and that's okay, because he looks forward to the darkness. He knows it will be cool on his skin.

He doesn't dare to touch his arm. He doesn't like how the flesh there tingles. It feels like little static shocks, one after another, and like tiny worms crawling beneath the surface. His eyes are sore and gritty. It's difficult to breathe, as though he's lost the rhythm and can't quite get it back: one moment he's panting, the next emitting ragged gasps that leave him dizzy. Austin saw people ill with the sickness, before his mother brought him here. This is the beginning, but there's worse to come.

He hopes there won't be too much pain. He's tired of pain. That might, in the end, explain everything he's done. He'd got so tired of pain that he just wanted to avoid it, whatever the cost. He couldn't have done anything differently. If he could have, he wouldn't have. Nobody makes choices, they only pretend to. That's the difference between him and them, he doesn't pretend.

It's all so clear. He'd never been supposed to live. Not here. Perhaps not ever. Some people are born to be destroyed. Maybe most people.

He's nothing special, never has been, and neither is anyone else. That's why all of this has happened. That's why it had to happen. The time they had was borrowed, and it's been used up.

His thoughts are jumbling. Still there's that sense of clarity, but always, as Austin attempts to examine an idea, to say for sure whether it's correct or logical, it slips away. The sensation is like watching the view go by from inside a train, or watching a train go by from inside the view. Or are those the same thing?

From close by there comes a seismic crack, as if the walls themselves are about to tumble in and swallow him. Normally that would shock him. Now, Austin barely reacts. The noise resounds again, something hard striking against something hard with huge force. Again, again. Austin knows that he should be alarmed, but he isn't. He knows what the noise means. They're coming, coming to get him.

It's okay. It doesn't matter.

It won't be much longer.

★   ★   ★

Doyle swings the sledgehammer, hardly aware of its weight or the jolt as its steel head rebounds from mortar and crumbling cinder block. He drags it back, tips it easily behind his shoulder, and brings it down once more, taking no satisfaction when a block caves in half, feeling only a desperate urgency, and at the same time a desperate urge to fail, so that he won't have to face what lies within.

Kyle helped him to select the spot. Doyle isn't even certain they have it right. No matter. If this isn't the place, he'll start over somewhere else, demolishing every wall in the building if need be, picking through the rubble if that's what it takes to find his son.

His son.

How can you fuck something up so badly? Or someone? How is that possible?

Doyle swings, and the head penetrates with a crash like thunder, dragging fractured hunks of wall into the darkness. Doyle hauls the sledgehammer back with an effort, takes another swipe and another, working at the edges of the hole he's created. Then he drops the hammer, not caring how its impact weaves cracks in the tiles, and begins to dig with his hands. He resumes with the sledgehammer, until it seems the muscles of his shoulders will burst under the strain. Chips of shattered brick slice at his face and arms. Doyle scarcely notices. Again he drops the hammer to work with his hands, clearing rubble, flinging it behind him.

He thinks the gap is large enough. Kyle insisted that he could move around in the space beyond, but Kyle is a foot shorter than Doyle, and lightly built. Still, Doyle pushes through, head and right arm first and then stepping one foot in. Claustrophobia insists there's no way to angle his other arm, no way to turn or back out either, yet he manages to twist, and from there to get the arm in, sliding his left leg after.

Dust scratches at his lungs. Beneath his feet are chunks of broken masonry. Edging sideways, Doyle picks his steps carefully. If he stumbles or twists an ankle, he'll be trapped here. Somewhere in the darkness, he can make out the faintest trembling light, a light where there should be none. He creeps toward it. Trying to judge distance is futile; it's all he can do to see anything. Even with his head to one side, the cinder-block wall scrapes his cheek. His hands are already scratched raw, as are his knees, despite the thick fabric of his trousers.

With the glare from the flashlight he left outside obstructed by his own body, Doyle can make out the flicker of amber light more clearly. It's nearer than he'd thought, a mere few feet away. He pauses, entirely conscious for the first time of what it is he's doing.

"Austin?" Doyle calls, not loudly.

And from somewhere in the gloom ahead, a thin voice, a voice Doyle hardly knows, whispers back, "Dad."

*   *   *

Ben sits, perfectly still, in the darkness. Though he can't say what he expects to hear, though stillness only makes the throbbing in his head worse, he listens with every nerve of his being.

He'd been surprised when the whiskey ran out, surprised and devastated. But the grief had passed quickly, as he'd begun to feel sick, and then violently sick. He had stumbled from his chair to crash through three others, cracking his shins on metal and moulded plastic. Unable to make it farther, he'd had no choice but to drop onto hands and knees and empty his guts down to the last drop. The vomit had been just liquid, meagrely processed by his flagging body. The raw stench of undiluted whiskey had made him want to throw up all over again. Instead, he had crawled like a frightened dog until he could barely smell it anymore. He'd curled around the pain in his belly, warding off waves of nausea. At some point he'd drifted into sleep.

When the noise had started, Ben had imagined the building was crashing down upon him. All his terrors of disaster had risen to choke him, and he'd been certain that this was the end, the catastrophe he'd known for so long was coming. Yet as sleep had sloughed away, he'd realised those steady impacts weren't even near. They were coming from above, and toward the rear of the Big House. Whatever they represented wasn't a threat to him. And slowly, Ben's first, dizzying rush of panic had subsided.

Then he'd noticed the reek of vomit and whiskey. It was overwhelming; he couldn't believe he'd thought he had escaped it. He'd crept on hands and knees, negotiating his way by touch alone past a stack of shelves and a table. Finding a chair, he'd flopped into it.

The noise had seemed endless. Its rhythm was unfaltering, though interspersed with smaller sounds of devastation. Every blow carved a path through Ben's aching head, like lightning searing between one ear and the other. He was very thirsty. He knew there must be some explanation here that he was blind to, but guessing struck him as useless. Nor did he want to leave the library, where he felt instinctively safe.

More than once, the noise – someone working with infinite persistence to break something, he'd concluded – had paused. Each time, Ben counted the seconds until it restarted. The last time, the count got so high that Ben lost track. Then he'd decided it must be over, finally over. Whatever they were doing up there was done.

Now he thinks about trying again to sleep. He thinks about hunting for water, to wash the dryness and flavour of sick from his throat. He thinks about moving, doesn't. Instead, he waits.

Maybe it's only the whiskey. Maybe it's the fear he's lived with for so long that it's grown to be a part of him. But Ben can't convince himself that there isn't worse to come.

CHAPTER THIRTY-FOUR

His father is just a shape, and not a reassuring one. There's something definitely hostile about his outline, something that makes Austin want to kick and scratch and bite, anything to not be trapped in this suffocating cavity with that dangerous silhouette.

He fights the impulse. It's the sickness. The sickness makes you crazy, everybody knows. Except that Austin has been scared of his dad for a long time, ever since the night he executed Plan John. And Austin can only be in the initial stages. Shouldn't it take a day, even two, to get really bad? So maybe what he's feeling isn't the sickness at all.

"Don't come too close," he says. He means to warn his father. The way his voice sounds, though, scratchy and strange, the caution comes out more like a threat.

"I won't," his dad says. True to his word, he stays pressed against the far wall, as far away as the space will allow.

"She bit me." Austin is amazed that three syllables can imply so much.

"I'll make sure she doesn't hurt anyone else."

"Wasn't her fault. It was me. All me."

It seems suddenly important that nobody should take the blame for what he's done. He knows now that he's misconstrued everything. He's lied to himself from the start about every detail, every action – all bar one.

Austin swallows. His mouth feels parched and raw. "Will...will you do something for me?"

"Anything," his dad says. "Let's get you out of here, get you some help. Austin, I know I've—"

"Not that." He doesn't intend to cut his dad off, but his mouth is bone-dry, not a drop of spit to lubricate it, and he fears that it might close up entirely, trapping whatever he has left to say inside forever. "Martin, he...." With the words jumbling in his mind, it's harder to find the right ones than ever. "He hurt me."

"He hit you?"

"Yeah. He hit me." But he wants to explain how that wasn't the worst. How the worst had been seeing that he meant less than nothing in someone else's eyes, and how he'd come, day by day, to view himself the same way. How the worst had been watching himself toughen, trying to grow a skin thick enough to survive inside, knowing that in so doing he was becoming someone unlovable, someone even his own mother seemed barely to tolerate. The worst was losing hope, and beginning to comprehend that he would never have hope again, that somewhere along the line it had been taken and would not be given back.

Many nights, Austin had wished for his dad to come and save him. And always in the back of those dreams had been the fear that, if he did, his reaction would not be sympathy but contempt, contempt for his son's weakness. Doyle Johnson, Austin had felt instinctively, would not be so weak as to let anyone hurt him.

He already feels like he's said more than he can bear. All the waning candlelight shows of his father's face is crude angles, a simplification that betrays no nuance. His eyes are dark hollows. If they detect flaws, shame, failure, there's no way for Austin to tell.

"He's one of them," Austin says. "A Sicker. I saw him. I think he's living out there, in the forest. Maybe Mom too." That possibility hadn't even occurred to him. How could it not have? "He's the reason I stole the doctor's gun. He should die. He really ought to die. I know it won't make anything better, but—"

"Okay."

Austin doesn't understand. "What?"

"Okay," his father says. "Yes. I'll get it done."

Can it be that straightforward? *Okay.* Could he have gone to his dad and told him, and that would have been it, the end of this nightmare, right there? *I'll get it done.*

No. His dad hadn't been there. Not before, not ever. Now he is and it's too late. Now nothing either of them says can matter at all. "Dad," Austin whispers, "I feel really sick."

"I know. We'll get you out of here. Take you to Aaronovich."

"I don't want to be a monster."

"The doctor can help you."

Austin has seen how she's helped the little girl. That isn't the kind of help he needs. "I won't be me." Except that isn't what frightens him. If it was solely that, the notion of continuing in this body but with his thoughts and memories broken or gone, he might embrace what's coming.

No, what frightens him is that he *will* endure.

Austin cradles the gun. Martin took him to a firing range once, a bonding exercise no doubt suggested by Austin's mother. He recalls clearly how, even in those early days, he'd sensed that Martin would have liked to turn that gun on his stepson-to-be. Austin remembers where the safety catch is, so he clicks it off. Guns, he'd learned that day, were simple things. You just point and pull the trigger. Just point and shoot.

He hadn't taken the gun because he believed he would track down his stepfather. Austin appreciates that now. Maybe, on some level, he'd known then. He had only ever wanted it for one purpose. And having come to the crucial moment, he isn't sure he's strong enough. Even if he is, perhaps the sickness will undermine him, will make him weak. Austin cradles the gun in both hands. He thinks about raising it. He knows what you're supposed to do, but the thought makes him gag.

"Dad," he says, so softly that he has no idea if his father will hear. "Do you have your gun?"

He should say it louder. But he doesn't know if he has the strength. He remembers everything he'd been taught that day. So easy. Just point and shoot. Only, he would have to find a way to make his hands comply.

His father's voice is softly spoken and impossibly loud-seeming. "Austin—"

"Do you?"

"Yes."

"Then…there's something else."

"Austin. Please. Put that down."

Austin is holding his own gun up, he realises. "I can't," he says. "Can't keep going. Not like this."

The grip is cool inside his palm. The rest of him is too warm, but the gun at least is cold. Just point. And shoot.

"One of us has to do it. You or me."

Just point….

"And Dad, I don't know if I can."

*   *   *

Kyle delivered the message to Carlita, like Johnson had told him to. He'd knocked at her door and coughed out the brief words he'd been made to memorise: words so important to Johnson, so feeble and absurd-sounding coming from him. When she'd asked him to explain, he'd had no answers. When she'd begun to cry, Kyle had wanted, more than he had already, to be anywhere else. In a pause, as she'd dipped her head into her hands, he had hurried away.

He hadn't made it far. Outside, uncertainty had gripped him. What was going to happen to Austin? Was it his fault? Maybe he should go back and help Johnson, or else attempt to stop him.

Kyle couldn't say which would be worse. So he'd remained where he was, not feeling the night's chill, aware of nothing except the noises from within, the subdued crunch of metal on disintegrating brick. Later, there had come silence. Kyle had tried to imagine what was happening, up there within the walls – had tried not to.

But now, the silence has been broken. All his questions evaporate, rousted by the explosion of a gunshot.

Kyle starts toward the entrance of the Big House, without knowing why. As soon as he observes where his feet are leading him, he stops. There's nothing he can do to help. In fact, if what he suspects is true, if Austin has shot his father, then Kyle should be running. Austin is sick, he was crazy before he got sick, and thanks to Kyle, he has a gun.

The silence is broken once more. This time, it's the rapid sound of feet, punctuated by muffled impacts, as though someone is careening through the lightless corridors.

Could it be Austin? Could he have crawled out of his hole so quickly?

The running footsteps are almost on him, and Kyle wants to run himself, but his body is momentarily unwilling. He's near enough to the doors that all he sees is a shape, before it barrels into him and they're both plummeting earthward. A fist grazes his jaw and Kyle flails to return a blow, striving to drive this other body away from his. He gets one good punch in, by luck more than judgement, and then the dark form cries out, and Kyle recognises that voice.

"Dad?" he manages, still struggling to free himself.

Finally, his father rolls aside, gagging for breath. "Oh shit," he croaks. "Shit, Kyle, it's you."

Kyle gets half to his feet, holding himself up with palms on knees. He touches fingers to his jaw and winces. "Who did you think it was?"

"Hell. I don't know." Ben, too, is clambering to his feet, huffing breaths that mist in the chill darkness. "Jesus, Kyle." He fights for air. "What're you doing out here?" Another gasp. "Did you hear a gunshot?"

"It's Austin," Kyle says, struggling to work the words free through his bruised jaw. "Austin and Johnson."

"Johnson? How do you know?"

Kyle hesitates, unwilling to relive the night's horrors by describing them. "Something bad happened," he says at last. "With Austin. Aaronovich made me tell Johnson; Johnson sent me to talk to Carlita. In case she got scared. In case something...if something bad happened to him as well."

His father's breathing is no longer laboured. "Why the fuck," Ben asks, "would Carlita care if something happened to Doyle Johnson?"

His father's suspicion is clear; suspicion, not knowledge. Kyle could so easily lie.

"Kyle, what message did you take to Carlita?"

He could lie. He could say any of a thousand things.

Suddenly his father's hands are gripping the collar of Kyle's jacket, rough fingers clasping too tight and too close to his throat, and though Kyle has never been afraid of his dad, he's afraid now.

"Kyle, I'm warning you...."

He could lie, but he doesn't want to. Why should he protect anyone, anyone other than himself? "Johnson said to tell her, *I love you and I'm sorry.*"

Kyle knows he shouldn't say it, even as he does. He feels every word, weighty in his throat. He knows it's the worst thing he could have said, the one that might make this night more dreadful than it already is.

Yet in that moment, a tiny part of him is glad. Glad because they haven't cared, haven't tried, and fuck them, Carlita, Johnson, even his dad – *especially* his dad – for letting him down. And with that thought, something cracks inside him. He remembers the secret Austin intended to bribe him with, the one Kyle refused to hear, and wonders to what extent that was because, deep down, he knew the truth.

"Dad," he murmurs, "I think she's screwing him."

Then Ben's hands are off his jacket, no longer near his throat, and Kyle reels back, barely keeping his footing. He's free, and his father is stumbling away.

But Kyle saw his face — for an instant only, though one frozen in his mind's eye. He saw that the words had accomplished everything he'd hoped they would, everything he'd feared. Darkness wasn't enough to hide so much pain and rage.

And even before his father disappears within the Big House, Kyle knows what he's done.

$$\star \quad \star \quad \star$$

Doyle pushes back through the gap in the walls. His hands are shaking and he can't stop them, since they don't feel like his hands. His eyes sting; the stinging blinds him. The headache has become a monstrous presence squatting in his brain, shutting out all else.

Almost all. Not enough.

In his memory he can see an outline defined by the last dying candlelight, growing hazy and then sharp as the flame gutters. A body. Sometime soon, Doyle will have to get him out of there. He'll have to find a way, so that he can bury his son; so that Austin won't be left curled in the darkness, abandoned in death as he'd been in life.

Doyle stumbles over cracked masonry, dragging his feet, hands scraped raw upon bare cinder block. He has no strength, nothing left to keep him up, and his body keeps moving presumably only because that's what bodies do. Vague instincts demand freedom from this crushing fissure, from the nail-varnish stink of cordite in his nostrils. Perhaps when he gets out he'll keep walking, until his body finally agrees to stop and never start again.

The glow from the flashlight is growing brighter. It's as Doyle reaches the hole he made, scrabbles at its edges, contorts his limbs free, that he realises the beam's angle is wrong. He'd left the flashlight on the floor. Now the light is at shoulder height. Doyle reaches uncertainly for the glaring circle of whiteness — and something strikes him hard across the face. He rebounds against the wall, coming up with his arms across his face, so that a second blow hammers his wrists.

"You fucker!"

The voice is contorted by rage into a snarl. Doyle can discern nothing besides the dark and his own raised arms. He tries to return a punch and takes another buffet to the head, redoubling the pain already there. He ducks aside, searching for space and finding none. All the while, the blows keep coming. They're clumsy, flailing, but every jolt is like liquid fire poured across his brain. He can't think, can scarcely react.

Distantly, Doyle is aware that he can't dodge forever. He can't fight back, can hardly see. He's ready to collapse, and it's solely the magnitude of his suffering that keeps him standing, the likelihood of worse that keeps him resisting. If he gives in, his head might crack open, the pain might claw free like a living being, and that thought is too horrifying not to resist.

Then from nowhere comes the recollection of the gun. It's tucked into his jeans, nestling the small of his back. Doyle takes a sharp step away, keeps one arm up, and reaches with the other.

"How dare you?" the voice rasps. "How dare you put your hands on her?"

Silensky. Oh hell. It's Silensky.

When Doyle points the gun, aiming at the outline masked by the flashlight's brutal glare, he has no doubt that Silensky will back off. Even as Silensky plunges nearer, oblivious of the barrel tracking his movements, Doyle doesn't believe for an instant that he'll have to pull the trigger. Only at the very last, as Silensky's knuckles dash toward his face, does the possibility seems real, and by then his finger is already constricting.

The noise is far beyond what his fracturing mind can bear. Doyle drops the gun, doubles up. The punch didn't connect. He tenses for another, but his muscles are barely responsive. Doyle waits, helplessly anticipating a blow that with each moment doesn't come. He gives himself maybe a minute, as the shot's reverberation subsides, hoping against hope that the torture in his head will retreat too.

He has to pull himself together. The shot will bring someone. How can he explain this? How, when he can't make sense of it himself? Doyle fumbles at his feet, picks up the gun. Then he retrieves the flashlight. He swings the beam, hunting for the spot where Silensky went down, as Doyle knows now that he must have.

There he is, a shape with the implication of human form, sprawled in the dust, oily blackness pooling around what remains of a head.

And there, looking up from beside his father's blasted body, crouches Kyle Silensky.

PART FIVE
OUTBREAK
CHAPTER THIRTY-FIVE

The sound of the outer door startles Aaronovich, as it inevitably does these days.

It's hard not to assume that her visitor will be Doyle Johnson, come to exercise his rage. Aaronovich hasn't seen him since the night of his son's death, the night that also claimed Ben Silensky. What she knows of those terrible events Aaronovich has learned in scraps over the succeeding weeks, for Johnson has stayed away and even Kyle visits only rarely these days, saying little when he does.

Kyle, sullen and troubled though he may be, would have knocked. The same is true of Contreras, who sometimes brings her food. Who does that leave? Foster, perhaps. Aaronovich is certain that the events of that night aren't widely known; it's impossible to imagine how word of a death caused even indirectly by infection wouldn't have brought the mob to her door. Foster, however, must at least suspect. And Aaronovich and her ward make for the easiest of targets. It would be a mistake to pretend their presence might have been forgotten.

Therefore, Aaronovich runs hurriedly through her mental checklist as she gets up from her desk. Abigail is safe within the apartment, and the door is locked, the key in its hiding place. Crude precautions with obvious flaws, but then she couldn't have hidden behind her locks forever.

"Hey! Doc!"

The shout comes from the opposite side of the office door. Aaronovich opens it hastily. A man is standing in the middle of the reception room. Aaronovich recognises him, but struggles to remember his name. He's wearing a heavy cotton logger's shirt, no doubt looted from a nearby town. The left arm is ragged from below the elbow, torn into strips and stained. From the fingers of that hand, blood drips in a slow trickle.

Colton, that's it. His name is Curtis Colton.

A patient. And she knows a knife wound when she sees one. Aaronovich has always been surprised that she doesn't have more injuries to deal with. It's a testament to Plan John's social engineering that these men have shown so little inclination to seriously harm each other. Conversely, she supposes that the fact Plan John isn't alive to witness the results of his efforts hints at inherent weaknesses in what he built.

"Wait here," she says. There's no point trying to work in the infirmary; she doesn't even sleep in there anymore. She hurries downstairs, relying on the flashlight to gather the few things she'll need, thinking that she should have moved them to her office long ago. She carries them back upstairs and motions Colton into a chair.

"Who did this?" Aaronovich asks.

"Does it matter?" he mutters gruffly.

Aaronovich shears away the loose-hanging tatters of sleeve. Then she begins to clean the cuts, of which there are four, only one of them particularly deep. Colton doesn't wince at the sting of the antiseptic.

"If I'm going to treat you," she says, "I need to know exactly what happened."

A clear lie. It's obvious that the wounds have been inflicted with a small blade, and their origin makes no difference whatever to their treatment. She's simply curious, starved of information from outside her hermetic world, and she hopes that Colton won't see that.

Then again, maybe he just doesn't care enough to resist her interest. "Was that fuck Silensky," he growls.

Aaronovich pauses, perplexed, wanting to say, *But Ben Silensky is dead.* Finally, she comprehends her mistake. "Kyle did this?"

"Told him his old man was a fucking pussy. He didn't take it kindly."

Aaronovich grits her teeth, thinking how easy it would be to slip. Oh, she could do things that *would* make Colton wince. And though she knows the thought is beneath her, a disgrace to a profession she once valued, she empties her mind until she's wiped away the last streak of crusted blood.

"Should I expect Kyle to be coming in for treatment?"

Colton grimaces. "When I catch the little shit, hell yes."

"I'm going to need to stitch this middle cut," she says. "I'm afraid I don't have any anaesthetic." Another lie, but one she can justify to herself. Her supplies are limited, unlikely to be replenished, and sooner or later there are bound to be worse injuries than this requiring her attention. Still, she's careful not to think of Kyle as she sews a line of four neat stitches, and Colton doesn't flinch.

When she's done, Aaronovich recleans the cuts, applies an antiseptic dressing, and neatly bandages the entire forearm. She steps aside and considers her work, while Colton stares at it in vague disgust.

"Come back in a week and I'll take those stitches out," Aaronovich tells him.

Colton shakes his head, not disagreeing, only expressing his contempt. "Whatever," he says, and is through the outer door before it occurs to Aaronovich that there was a time when patients, even patients like Curtis Colton, would have thanked her.

There was a time when people thanked people. There was a time when people, *some* people, cared for each other. She looks at the splashes of scarlet trailing across the tiles and wonders at how distant and improbable that memory seems.

She has endeavoured to talk to Kyle, on those occasions when he's visited her. Not about his father, not about what happened, just to talk and to draw him out of himself. Yet she has also been distracted herself, overwhelmed − as she invariably is now − by the impossible burden of caring night and day for Abigail. And though she's tried, she hasn't done so nearly hard enough. In her obsessive desire to protect one child, she's been blind to the evidence that another is in grave jeopardy.

She's blind no longer. Of everyone in Funland, Kyle has been the one to support her, asking nothing in return. He has helped her more than she's ever helped him. So there's no way around it: she'll have to do the thing she's been putting off all these weeks, the thing she least wants to do and which has most potential for endangering both her and Abigail.

There's one way for her to help Kyle, and that's by confronting Doyle Johnson.

★   ★   ★

He'd imagined he might lash out at her, or at the very least shout, curse, spit his vitriol. For those reasons and others, Doyle had avoided the doctor. Yet when he'd seen her, there in the passage outside his apartment, Doyle had discovered to his absolute surprise that he'd missed her. It struck him how much he had relied on her calm, her rationality, her ability to be a rock of sanity even when all the world was in flood.

And so he'd been polite and businesslike, and he hadn't mentioned Austin. In fact, for the first time in weeks, it seemed, he hadn't so much as thought of him. Only afterward, when she'd left, had the image that haunted Doyle returned: the curled body, smeared by encroaching darkness. Only then had he perceived what lay behind everything Aaronovich had said. *That boy's going to seriously hurt somebody, or – and I think we both know this is by far the likelier outcome – he's going to get hurt himself.* That she'd stopped there hadn't made her implication any less clear. *Hurt, just like your son.*

Even that hadn't angered him. She was right. Doyle was failing Kyle, as he'd failed Austin.

He'd spoken to Contreras, and to Singh on the farm, passing a simple message. *If you see Kyle, tell him I need to talk to him.* Kyle had gone to ground after the incident with Colton, and as Austin had proved beyond doubt, there was no shortage of places to hide in Funland. But Singh appeared confident he'd return to the farm. "He always comes back, sooner or later."

Now, as Kyle Silensky stands in front of Doyle's open door, it's the morning of the second day after the fight, a couple of hours past dawn. The boy looks nervous and defiant. But he's come, and that's more than Doyle had entirely expected.

"Come in," Doyle says. "Sit down."

"What do you want?"

"For you to come in. We're not talking in a doorway."

"We've nothing to talk about anywhere."

"Then you can listen. Either way, come in." Doyle strives to keep his voice level, while injecting an edge of authority. He can't let this conversation end before it's even started.

Kyle moves past, taking pains not to brush against him. Rather than sit, he walks to the balcony doors and stands there with his arms folded, his back to the room. "Is this about Colton?" he asks, with no hint of interest.

"Among other things."

"I'm not going to apologise."

"I don't suppose he'd accept it if you did."

"I meant to you."

"I don't want your apology," Doyle says.

"Good. I don't want yours either."

Doyle has no answer to that. The conversation is already slipping away from him. Kyle is smart enough to keep this up all day, and nothing meaningful will be said. Doyle lets the silence draw out, sure there must be a way past Kyle's resistance but unable to see it.

He's taken by surprise when Kyle glances toward the door that leads through to Doyle's bedroom and says, "I know she's in there. She might as well come out."

Doyle considers. Then he says, "He's right, Carlita. You should hear this."

There's a pause, a brief tap of footsteps, and the door swings inward. Carlita hesitates in the doorway. "Hello, Kyle."

Kyle ignores her. His eyes don't flicker from the point he's staring at outside the balcony doors. Probably, Doyle thinks, that's all he wants her here for: another diversion, another small blow.

Doyle can tell from Carlita's face that this blow has sunk home. Does Kyle have any idea of how much she blames herself for his father's death? Yet likely he blames her too. It's surprised Doyle that Kyle has held off from revealing her existence. Perhaps, though, he's only saving his most potent weapon for when it can wreak the greatest devastation.

There's no use in stalling. He has just one thing to say to Kyle and maybe just this one opportunity to say it. "You came to me a few weeks ago and told me you'd cracked Plan John's logbook."

Kyle looks at him then. "What?"

"You said you'd deciphered it. That there might be other survivors."

Anger and confusion are warring over Kyle's face. "What are you talking about?"

"Do you still believe that?"

"What does it matter?"

"I asked, do you believe it?"

"And I said, what does it matter whether there are survivors or not? I don't care. You don't care. No one does." Kyle's voice is rising. His cheeks are flushed. "Is that what this is? Do you think I give a shit anymore?"

Here, then, is the moment of truth. "Yes," Doyle says, "I think you do."

It's as if Kyle is a balloon that Doyle has stuck a pin into. All the fight spurts out in a gust and in an instant he seems to deflate. "You shot my dad. What does some stupid book matter? We're going to die here."

"Yeah," Doyle says, "we are."

Once more, Kyle looks straight at him. And again all he says is, "What?" This time, though, there's the barest suggestion of real interest in the question.

"We'll all die, sooner or later. Probably sooner. Probably *real* soon. I get that now. Nothing I do or anyone else does is going to change that. But I was a fool for not taking you seriously when you told me about the logbook and about breaking the code."

"Out of everything," Kyle says, "you're apologising for that?" He sounds genuinely astonished.

"It's the only thing I can do something about."

"Really? How's that?"

"We can go to the city," Doyle says, "and see what's there."

From beside him, Doyle hears Carlita gasp. Kyle looks bewildered, utterly off balance.

Good. That's how Doyle needs him. He's been going over their situation for weeks, testing answers in his head, and every path seemed to lead closer to the abyss, every one but this. He doesn't dare interrogate the reasons for that too intently. Because once the prospect of leaving Funland, even briefly, had embedded itself in his mind, he had felt as though a weight had lifted, setting him free.

"You know I hate you?" Kyle says. There's no aggression in the words, just numbed indifference.

"And you know I can't let you run around stabbing people. We can't afford to lose even a maggot like Colton. We can't afford to lose you either." Realising that isn't an answer, Doyle adds, "This is the best chance you'll have to get to me. If that's what you decide. And, to answer your question, yes, I think you care. You want to find out if you were right."

"I *was* right. I finished the translation weeks ago. There were survivors there when Plan John died."

"Then come with me and prove it."

Kyle shakes his head, but uncertainly.

"Fine," Doyle says. "Take some time. Figure it out, Kyle. Deep down, I think you know this is the thing to do."

★   ★   ★

Reaching the yard, Kyle is unaware of where his feet are leading him. He should be watching out for Colton, but he isn't. He had been so sure he was beyond anyone's ability to harm, and now Doyle Johnson, of all people, has stripped away his most basic defences.

Everything had been under control. Until this morning, everything had been simple.

Hellish, but simple. Kyle's world had spun between two poles, hate and revenge. If rebellious emotions had threatened to intrude – sorrow, guilt, loneliness – he had subdued them with fortitude that bordered on religion. All that mattered was his hatred for Johnson. All that mattered was the thought of one day hurting him.

Hate has made Kyle stronger. It's stifled his fear. He thinks sometimes about Austin, about the things that must have sustained him. He has tried to emulate them, but he won't hide the way Austin did, for he's seen how that ended.

The general belief, in as much as anybody discusses the subject, is that Austin killed himself. Kyle, though, is positive that Johnson was the one who pulled the trigger. It's one of Kyle's two great secrets, along with the existence of Carlita, her relationship with Johnson, and his conviction that Johnson murdered his father to secure his hold on her. Many nights, Kyle has gone to sleep swearing he'll reveal one or the other the next day. He's never certain what stops him. So what if Austin had been infected? So what if Carlita's affection for his dad had faltered long before they'd come to Funland? Kyle refuses to accept that it's an urge to protect her that holds him back. Weakness is all that binds his tongue, and night after night he vows to find more strength.

Now, however, even walking straight feels like an unreasonable challenge. It's as if his life is a house caught in a mudslide and all the furniture is tumbling past him, impossible to grasp.

There's only one thing he's sure of. Kyle knows he can't refuse Johnson's offer. Because the prospect of revenge is no longer a distant fever dream, it's real and at hand. Yet also, and as thoroughly as Kyle despises himself for the admission, the thought of opening himself to something besides anger is appealing. The logbook brought him the closest to happiness he's been since they left the city. He's never forgotten what he found there, the anticipation it brought. Johnson was right about one fact: Kyle *does* care, whether he wants to or not.

Everything that had been simple is hopelessly tangled. Where there'd been only revenge, now there's also hope. And between those two, how can he be expected to choose?

CHAPTER THIRTY-SIX

Doyle tells Contreras first, and the conversation is a brief one.

"I'm going outside for a few days. I need you to look after things while I'm away. I think I can persuade Aaronovich to take care of Carlita, but I'd like you to keep an eye on them both, as much as you can."

"Doyle, are you serious?"

"It shouldn't be more than half a week. If it is, I guess that means I'm not coming back."

"You are. You're serious. Doyle, what is this?"

"Can you do it? There's nobody else I trust."

"You can trust me. Of course you can."

"I know, Tito. That's why I'm asking."

"Then…yes, Doyle, of course. Of course."

He doesn't like it, putting Contreras on the spot that way. He doesn't like it at least partly because he knows he can't be completely relied upon. Doyle has even considered keeping Contreras in the dark, to avoid any possible repeat of the incident with Plan John. However, he has no other options, and necessity makes difficult decisions straightforward.

Or so Doyle assures himself. The conversation with Carlita is harder.

"It's just for a few days. I've talked to Contreras. I'm going to talk to Aaronovich. They'll take care of you."

"I don't want to be taken care of." She's sitting on their bed. She must have known this was coming; he's never been good at keeping secrets.

"Still. They will. Until I come back."

This time, she doesn't answer. She isn't even crying anymore.

"It's the only way," he presses. "I can't protect you here. You or Kyle or anyone else."

She looks up at him. Her eyes are red and fierce. "You can't protect anybody. God, Doyle, haven't you learned anything? We're going to die here. You said it yourself. This is all that's left. There's nothing out there, no one coming to help us, no cure, no miracle. *Nothing*. And that's okay.

As long as there's us, right up until the end. I accept it. Why can't you?"

He wants to say that he can. But it wouldn't be true. He wants to tell her he loves her, but he knows that love doesn't mean the same thing to them. He can't love what he can't protect, just as he refuses to keep protecting what he doesn't love.

He wants to say, *because of Kyle*. That would be less untrue. Probably they *will* all die here, perhaps that end isn't even far off, but Kyle's time is running out faster, and as a result of crimes not his own. Doyle has reconciled himself to the fact that Kyle's part in Austin's death had been entirely unwilling. In truth, of everyone in Funland, he has done least harm.

So, because of Kyle. Not untrue, not wholly true either. This Doyle realised in the night, lying beside Carlita, sleep at an unattainable reach: he *wants* to go. He wants to get out of Funland. Even if it's hopeless or worse than hopeless, dangerous and irresponsible, he has to try. He can't stand living inside walls any longer, or inside his head. He can't bear the fog of grief he moves about in.

"I have to do this," he says. "For you. For me. Maybe, I don't know, maybe more for me. But I have to."

Carlita looks away, down toward last night's rumpled bedsheets, piled like driven snow. "You won't come back."

"I'll do my best to."

"No. *No*." Eyes still averted. "That's not good enough. You tell me you're coming back."

"All right."

"Not 'all right.' Tell me."

"I'm coming back," Doyle says.

Then she looks at him again. Once more, she's crying; tear marks track her cheeks, curving about her jaw. Yet something has changed. Her hostility is gone, or lessened. Doyle sits beside her, and when he puts his arm around her and draws her close, Carlita doesn't resist.

⋆   ⋆   ⋆

"I have two conditions," Aaronovich says.

The look Johnson gives her conveys with abundant clarity that she's in no position to be making conditions.

Too bad. If he needs her help then Doyle Johnson is going to hear her out. Aaronovich is amazed, really, by how clear her thoughts are, how they've crystallised from murmurs into definite intentions in the time it's taken him to explain what he's asking of her.

"Firstly," she says, "I want to check you over. When we last spoke, you told me you were suffering from headaches. Headaches can be a symptom of any number of things, or of nothing much at all. At the very least I can help you manage the pain."

"They're gone," Johnson replies. "It's not a problem anymore."

"I don't believe you. And I don't care. That's condition one. Kyle's going to be relying on you out there, and if you're not in a fit state, you'll put him at even graver risk than you are already."

"You don't think I should do this?"

Aaronovich sighs. "I see that you think you have no choice."

"I *don't* have a choice." And sure enough, there's no hesitation in Johnson's voice.

"I won't argue with you. Right or wrong, it doesn't change the facts of what I've said, just as my opinion won't change whether you go or not."

"Fine," he says. "Check me out."

"Good—"

"But," he adds, with unexpected force, "if there *is* a problem then it stays between us. I want your word, Aaronovich."

Why does the man have to be so damned headstrong? "You have my word."

"Whatever the results."

"Whatever the results," she agrees.

"Okay." He nods. "Your second condition."

She'd never really doubted he would submit to the checkup, or imagined that her medical opinion could have any bearing on his decision. At least it puts one small but nagging part of her conscience to bed; often she's recalled their conversation that day and been troubled by the prospect of Johnson suffering needlessly.

More than that, though, Aaronovich had needed a lead into her second demand, the one she can't bend on, the one she's certain he'll deny. "I can't take care of Abigail anymore," she says. She'd thought she had control of herself, but her restraint comes close to cracking as she speaks those words. She pauses, summoning calm. "I can't. Even if I could, she's not safe here. This place is not safe. You know as well as I do, it's not going to last."

"I know," Johnson allows. "Just like you know that one diseased child is nowhere on my list of priorities."

"Yes." Aaronovich holds onto her forced tranquility, with all the resources at her disposal. "But she *is* mine. And I haven't looked after her to watch her die here. So my second condition is that you take her with you, far away, to somewhere where there are other sick – preferably women of childbearing age – and you leave her there."

For a moment, the rage in Johnson's eyes is dangerously near to release. She sees in that instant a passage to the molten core of him, to the pain swirling inside, and for the first time, she's afraid. If that flood of white-hot emotion were to come out then she can't envisage what he'd do, or if he'd ever again find a way to contain it.

Yet his voice is, while not steady, at least controlled as he asks, "Are you insane?"

"It's my condition."

"Absolutely not."

"It's my condition."

"That thing killed my son."

"That's not true. And even if it was, it's *still* my condition."

"How do you know I won't just put a bullet in its head the minute we're out the gates?"

"Because," she says, "I choose to trust you. Because I know that, when it comes down to it, you're a decent man. And, beyond all that, because Kyle won't let you."

Johnson shakes his head, and if she'd believed him when he claimed the headaches were gone, the manner in which the muscles in his neck knot at even that slight movement would have betrayed the lie. "No. It's impossible."

"It's not," Aaronovich says. "It's what has to happen. If you want me to look after your girlfriend then you have to take care of my—" She almost says *my child* and catches herself, but can think of no alternative. "You have to do this for me. I can't do it myself. Take some time to consider if you need to. But Doyle, this is what has to happen."

"All right," he says.

That catches her entirely off balance. "Excuse me?"

"Yes. You're right, it needs to be done. It means we're no longer keeping an infected child inside our walls. It means you're not distracted with this, which, frankly, we can't afford."

"All right," Aaronovich echoes. "Good."

"You want to do those tests now?"

Not understanding, bowed beneath the weight of her reflection, Aaronovich looks at Johnson uncomprehendingly.

"The tests," he repeats, with patience.

"Oh. Yes."

He's agreed. And she hadn't let herself think, not until this moment, about what that would portend. She hasn't thought about the possibility of giving up Abigail. Everything she said is true: she has reached the limits of her ability to care for the child, and all her instincts as a doctor tell her she's doing more harm than good, that she has let her feelings interfere with the wellbeing of her patient.

But this? Releasing a little girl into the wilderness, like a wounded animal nursed back to health?

She'll deal with it. She will have to deal with it. Not now, but she will, somehow, because there's no choice.

"Yes," Aaronovich says, more firmly – though unsure, suddenly, of just what question she's answering. "Yes, let's get it over with."

CHAPTER THIRTY-SEVEN

They leave before dawn, huddled in heavy coats. The Sicker girl is bundled within a too-large jacket lined with fake fur, and Aaronovich has insisted on providing the quilt from her bed, in spite of how the child doesn't appear to notice the cold at all. She seems frightened, agitated, and Doyle senses that only Kyle's presence is keeping her anywhere near calm. Doyle hopes that will suffice until they can get rid of her, though he has scant faith. As he takes his place behind the wheel, he feels as if he's trapped in the vicinity of an unexploded grenade, the pin already pulled.

Contreras lets them out. The inmates have long since disabled the electric gate mechanism, not willing to be contained by a system that relied on the virtually defunct generator. These days, all that restrains the gate is a heavy chain and a padlock, which Foster holds one key to, Doyle – and so now Contreras – the other. Contreras has strict instructions to hand that key on to Aaronovich. Should the worst happen, at least she and Carlita won't be trapped within these walls.

There's no one else around. *Like thieves in the night*, Doyle thinks. They take the jeep, the least preserved of Funland's three remaining vehicles. It's a badly scuffed matt black, with *White Cliff Penitentiary* decaled across its sides in white, and has gone neglected in favour of the larger trucks, presumably explaining why it's been left with the key in the ignition. Evidently someone has been maintaining the vehicle, though, for it starts on the second attempt.

Only as they pass through the gate does Doyle recollect that, in theory, Funland possesses one more means of transport. The ambulance that brought Carlita, the Silenskys, and Contreras's nephew still rests on its side, close to the wall. Doyle recalls with perfect, unintended clarity the sight of Carlita as he first saw her, perched upon its flank, blood and rain matting her dark hair. The memory is almost enough to make him turn back right then.

Instead, Doyle takes it slowly, practically coasting. It's been a long time since he's driven, and feels like even longer. Also, he wants to put off the discovery of their absence. He has no idea what the consequences will be, but there will be consequences. Rather than think about that, he concentrates on the twin cones of yellow hovering before him, which acknowledge a triangle of road amid the deep gloom and reject all else.

Once they break the edge of the forest, Doyle speeds up, while still driving cautiously – until they come to the wreck of the SUV. It has struck a tree, so hard that the entire front is scrunched to one side like balled tinfoil. Both front doors are open. Beside it, brilliantly white in the headlights, moulded by decay into the asphalt, lie dislocated segments of a human skeleton. Whatever happened there happened months ago. The SUV's seats are mostly gone, their stuffing probably absorbed into a hundred nests and animal homes. The nearby bushes have begun to reach inside, as though assimilating the ruined vehicle by slow degrees.

Doyle stops the jeep and gets out. He considers the bleached bones, many of which are missing, to leave only the abstracted semblance of a human form. "Rachel," he says. It surprises him that he can look at the final remains of his ex-wife and feel nothing at all, not anger or pain or grief. Then again, the thought of their relationship is now unnavigably distant, not even like remembering another life but like remembering a film of that life watched long ago.

Kyle, in the rear with the Sicker child, has opened his window. "What did you say?"

"Rachel," Doyle repeats. "My ex-wife. Austin's mother. That was her new husband's vehicle. Austin's stepfather. His name was Martin." He pauses, and more to himself than Kyle, adds, "There's something I need to do here."

"Then do it," Kyle says.

"When we come back."

Doyle gives the skeleton one more glance, pondering if he should bury it, understanding the futility of such an action. He climbs into the jeep and pulls away again, careful to give the SUV a wide berth, contemplating the vehicle in the rearview mirror until a turn steals it from view.

They are high up, heading downward, and the sun is rising invisibly behind them, giving the impression that they're sinking out of darkness into light. There's little to see, just the road, the trees to either side, and a granite sky supported by columns of weak illumination. It's a numbing view, and after so long having his reality constricted by four walls, one that makes Doyle faintly agoraphobic. Whatever has motivated him to do this, whatever he'd hoped to feel, he can't find it in himself.

By degrees, his driving experience returns. He settles into his seat, working the wheel with the heel of one hand. Increasingly his concentration drifts to the rearview mirror, and to the back seat. He watches Kyle and the girl. Though work on the farm has hardened his body and grief has erased any softness from his face, Kyle still looks young – like a child, or at least not like an adult. The Sicker girl seems to have relaxed; she's comfortable in his company. For a brief while, she slept. Now they're rolling a ball to each other across the fake leather seat, and every time it comes to her, she chuckles.

She killed my son, Doyle thinks. But he can't altogether bring himself to believe it.

He turns his regard back to the road. He must have driven this way often, yet nothing feels familiar. The surface is frequently cracked and pitted, particularly toward the edges, where in places the asphalt is crumbling apart in petrified waves. Apart from causing the jeep to buck on the worst patches, that deterioration doesn't concern him greatly, though in another year or two this journey may be impossible.

No, the problem is where branches and even whole trees have come down in the recent storms. Older obstructions show signs of having been partially cleared by one of the expeditions, but the trips out have been less frequent of late, the last was almost a week ago, and there were high winds a couple of nights before. For the first hour, Doyle manages by driving around or pushing through the lighter foliage. Eventually, however, they come upon a beech tree fallen from verge to verge, and it effortlessly resists his attempts to nudge it aside with the bumper.

Doyle pulls up. He doesn't shut off the engine. Prior to climbing out of the jeep, he reaches into the glove compartment for the gun he has stashed there.

He doesn't like this. Rationally, the obstacle makes perfect sense. Irrationally, it feels too much like a trap.

★   ★   ★

Having watched Johnson scrutinise the fallen tree, Kyle turns his attention to Abigail. She's squatting on her haunches, shifting to gaze first through the side window and then the back, all the while making a strange chuckling deep in her throat. She seems uneasy, and oblivious to his presence. Kyle wonders if he should try to calm her, suspects that she won't let him. Reaching a decision, he instead opens his door and slips out.

Johnson has moved around to the trunk. Seeing Kyle, he holds up a saw in one hand, a pistol in the other. "Which one?"

The enforced stop and Abigail's behaviour have frayed Kyle's nerves, and the sight of the gun sets them further on edge. "Are we okay here?"

"Maybe. Best to be wary."

Kyle considers the gun. For a moment his craving of revenge surfaces, only to be submerged quickly by the reality of their situation. He doesn't want to be out here alone, not like this. "I'll saw," he decides.

The tool is a small hacksaw, ill-suited to the task at hand. Up until about its middle, the tree's bole is thicker than his leg. Kyle strives to calculate the farthest place he can cut and still leave room for the jeep to get by. Picking his spot, he makes a few experimental strokes and then begins to work steadily.

He realises quickly, the saw is no good, and he's taking too long. Should he suggest they trade jobs? But he's not trained to shoot the gun. This is all he can do. Except that he can't even do this, because he's too damned slow.

"Kyle…."

Kyle stops sawing and turns. Johnson isn't pointing the gun. Rather, he's holding it ready with both hands, arms outstretched at a diagonal to his torso. He has his back to the jeep. He isn't looking at Kyle but directly ahead. There, two figures, a man and a woman, are standing just within the forest.

"Behind us," Johnson says.

Kyle looks. Two more are farther up the road, and a fifth stands amid the trees on the far side. He doesn't know which of them Johnson was referring to, or whether he's seen them all. "Five," he reports.

"Five," Johnson confirms. "Don't stop. But when I say go, *then* you stop, drop the saw, and get over here. Okay?"

"Okay."

Only, Kyle's palms are sweating. It's difficult to get a good grip. As soon as he starts, he finds that the blade is jamming in the wood, where it hadn't before. Is Johnson going to leave him behind? Even if he doesn't, there's nothing he can do about five Sickers.

Kyle struggles to focus. Back and forth, back and forth, smoke of sawdust in his eyes, cringing whenever the blade jams, as it seems to do now on every second or third stroke. He shuts out everything else, but even that won't steady his hand or put new strength into numbed biceps. Back and forth, on and on. How far through is he? Maybe two thirds, three quarters, yet when he puts his weight on the shorter section, it doesn't give. So there's no choice except to keep sawing, despite the screaming pain in the muscles from his fingers to his shoulder.

"Go," Johnson says, not loudly but firmly.

Kyle almost does as he was told. At the last instant he can't bear the thought of leaving the saw, and wrenches it free. Then he turns. The two Sickers on this side of the jeep have advanced, though currently they aren't moving. They're outside the forest, at the bottom of the bank beside the road.

Johnson has his back to the jeep's flank and has the driver's door open. Kyle crosses to him, walking rather than running. The two Sickers don't advance, but he can't see the other three. They could be very close.

"Get in," Johnson tells him. "Climb over." He edges aside to make way. At that, one of the Sickers, the woman, takes a step forward. Kyle tries to calculate if he can get into the jeep before she reaches him, and if in that time Johnson could shoot her – and if the second Sicker should go for Johnson, what would happen then. And there are still the others. He feels that they're near.

Kyle backs up as far as the wedge of space within the open door. He knows without doubt that, the moment he enters the jeep, one of the Sickers is going to go for Johnson. They'll go for him, and if they get through him they'll come for Kyle. Glass windows won't stop them. Nothing will stop them. Clear in his mind, he plays the scene: Johnson going down and glass showering like snow, hands dragging him out the splintered opening, tearing, gouging, digging....

Kyle hears the sound of a door opening.

He doesn't want to turn to look, but he can't help tracing the female Sicker's gaze. There, crouching beside Johnson, is Abigail. Her mouth is open, and only then does Kyle comprehend that the noise he's been barely conscious of, the low hiss like air escaping a tire, is coming from her. It shifts pitch, rises higher – becomes a snarl. Abigail moves farther forward, in front of Johnson. The Sickers observe, heads tilted. They seem more fascinated than hostile.

The woman is the first to retreat, hesitantly for a step and then with determination. The man follows, edging backward with confidence. Kyle feels with certainty that the other three are withdrawing too, as though a storm has passed and now the pressure is tangibly lifting.

"Get in the back," Johnson says.

Kyle edges around and slithers inside. He watches as Johnson slips into the driver's seat.

"Shut the door," Johnson says, as he drags closed his own.

"What?"

"We're going. Shut the door."

Kyle sees, finally, what Johnson is intending. "No!"

"Yes."

"She just *saved* us."

"She's better with them."

"No."

"Shut the door, Kyle."

"She just saved your life!" He's almost shouting. He doesn't like the thought of shouting, with the Sickers so near. But he can't give in. In that moment, it doesn't even matter that Johnson might be right. The sense that has come over him is primal and he has no resistance.

"Abigail," Kyle says. "Come on. We're going."

She turns her head. The look in her mottled eyes makes him afraid. There's no affection, no recognition, nothing he can identify. *Yes*, he thinks, *she's better with them.*

"Come on," Kyle says again. He shuffles back, clearing space.

When she moves, it's in one swift motion. She seems to flow across the asphalt. Then she's on the seat, curled, arms tight around knees, a pose he understands well enough to associate with fear. Kyle reaches over her to catch at the door and haul it closed, though in that instant, their proximity and the strange scent of her terrify him.

Johnson is already reversing. Only when he slams on the brakes and accelerates does Kyle grasp his intention, by which time it's too late to do more than brace against the seat ahead.

They strike the end of the tree with juddering force.

It slows them, but doesn't stop them. With a catastrophic crack, the tree's entire summit snaps free. They carry it with them, wedged upon the windshield, the road altogether concealed by tangled foliage, until Johnson hammers the brakes again and it tumbles out of view.

Then he backs up, accelerates, throws the wheel hard right, and they're past.

CHAPTER THIRTY-EIGHT

It's inevitable, Aaronovich realises. Not because Doyle Johnson is crucial to the integrity of Funland, though maybe in some strange way he is, but because Funland as an organism has grown so utterly resistant to change. While Foster isn't stupid, he possesses no inventiveness or ingenuity. He's tried to preserve what Plan John built without appreciating any of its complexities, to freeze it in place even as decay corrodes its edges. Aaronovich pictures a great and ugly machine of clockwork: it isn't perhaps that Johnson is a vital cog, only that he's a cog at all, in a mechanism that no longer allows for redundancy.

Thus, Aaronovich isn't surprised when Foster comes, nor that he's angry. His anger, in fact, makes the encounter easier. So, strangely, does her grief. It's like coolant running through her veins, like lubricant that makes the untruths slip easily from her throat.

"Johnson? No, he hasn't spoken to me. Why would he?"

"If you're lying to me, Doctor...."

She feigns confusion, indignation. Both come effortlessly. "What possible reason do I have to lie?"

"Oh," says Foster, "I can think of a few." Yet she can see that his anger is burning itself out in the absence of anything he can identify as a valid target.

"Has something happened?" Aaronovich asks, more softly.

Foster's scowl cuts deep into the lines of his face. "He's gone."

"Gone where?"

"Fucking Christ," he says. "If I knew that, would I be talking to you?"

"And," she asks, patiently ignoring the outburst, "is it a problem? I mean—"

"Yes." She recognises it in his eyes now, the fear. "Yes, it's a problem. How long do you think they'll take to start wondering, to get suspicious? For someone to decide that Doyle Johnson's bailed so clearly

Funland's finished? What the hell do you imagine is holding this place together, Doctor? I tell you, it's spit and fucking duct tape."

"I see," Aaronovich says.

"You see?"

"Yes." And she does.

"Well, great." As Foster begins to turn away, a thought holds him. "You still got that Sicker here?" he says. His gaze drifts downward, toward the infirmary invisible below.

"Abigail? Yes. She's sleeping."

Foster nods. "I can't have that. Not any longer. Never should have agreed to it in the first place. You've got until tomorrow, Doctor. Say your goodbyes or whatever the hell you feel the need to do, because then I'm coming back here."

Foster turns again, and makes it all the way out of the door this time, leaving Aaronovich staring into the morass of her own thoughts. He can't, of course, harm Abigail. He probably will hurt Contreras, knowing that Contreras and Johnson often talked, and Contreras will likely give up his secrets. Maybe he's learned enough sense and courage to keep Carlita out of it, but there are no guarantees.

In either case, it won't matter, because, on one count at least, Foster was right. Johnson's absence will be the spark that sets off the incendiary Funland has become. The fuse is already lit and burning. Foster's coming to her just now is a sure sign of its progress toward the inevitable. She can't wait for him to return, to discover Abigail's absence and so expose her lie. She can't wait for Funland to disintegrate around her.

Still, she *will* have to wait until nightfall. That gives her the rest of the day.

Aaronovich destroys anything that might be dangerous. Given the nature of the infirmary's contents, that doesn't leave much. She burns all of her records, taking them down into the darkness and feeding them steadily into a metal wastepaper bin. Once the blaze gets going, the flames lick almost to the ceiling, taunting the long-dead smoke detector. They light the walls a grimy, flailing yellow, and cast huge shadows. When the ashes in the bottom of the bin are white-hot, enough to make the metal itself glow dully, Aaronovich starts dropping medications in there, those that could be addictive, poisonous, or readily abused. Of the remainder, she takes whatever she'll be able to carry easily, leaves the rest.

She knows she's breaking a pledge. Not, perhaps, her Hippocratic Oath, but a deeper version of it, something she formulated herself and has held unspoken, practically unthought. She'd told herself she would look after these men, regardless of who or what they were, regardless of what they did. She'd told herself she would continue to do so until someone took over her responsibilities or, as seemed infinitely more plausible, until they cost her life.

It's hard even to say what has changed her mind, only that her mind *has* changed. Her previous existence and the death she'd promised herself both now resemble martyrdom. Aaronovich no longer wants to die a martyr. Maybe it's entirely that simple.

When she's burned everything that needs burning, she takes off her smoke-reeking garments, leaves them at the bottom of the stairs, goes back up to her apartment and dresses in cleaner clothes. She packs a few things, including the medicines and a small bag of equipment, and then, in a separate bag, what little food she has that won't quickly spoil. She makes one last, hurried check of her apartment and office, and pockets a pack of batteries, a pen and paper, other small items. She checks that the key Contreras passed on to her that morning, the one that will open the main gate, is safe. She finds herself wishing she still had the firearm that Johnson insisted she take.

But that is her sole regret. She feels nothing at the prospect of leaving this place, which for so long has been her home, nothing except a tug of sorrow at the thought of Abigail's absence, which she forces herself to rapidly stifle.

There may come a time for grief. But more likely, there will be no time at all.

CHAPTER THIRTY-NINE

Now that the adrenalin has subsided, Kyle feels only exhaustion.

He fingers the knife in his pocket, not thinking about Johnson or his father, just grateful of its presence. If he considers one man or the other, the two swim together in his tired brain, a self-murdering chimera that horrifies him more than anything.

He can't understand why his mind would play such vicious tricks on him. Perhaps it's that this journey draws him back so strongly to its reverse, the days they spent travelling to Funland. He'd arrived there with his father. He's leaving with his father's killer. How can he be expected to make sense of that?

Since it's impossible, Kyle rejects thinking altogether. Sunk in half-awareness, he hunches into his seat and lets the world slide by.

Only when a familiar detail catches his attention does Kyle begin to come out of his fugue. He sits up and stares blearily through the dust-darkened window, trying to remember the significance of what he's seen: a turnoff and a signpost, the name stirring faint memories.

Of course. It's the town where they stopped, all those months ago. He recalls the woman in the store, the man with the gun, how they'd left him on his knees in the street. What's become of those people? Are they dead? Probably they are.

Kyle is reminded of Fernando then, for the first time in weeks, and feels a sharp pang of remorse at having all but forgotten someone who was so good to him. He remembers what Carlita said on that last night in the city, her voice taut with shame and anger. *Your father's been arrested. Uncle Nando is going to pick us up.* If not for Nando, they never would have made it out. He'd saved their lives, and sacrificed his own. Fernando, his father, Austin…the truth is that Funland has taken more from Kyle than the outside world ever has.

Yet two of those people died at the hands of the man sitting in front of him, and perhaps Nando would still be alive if Johnson had played things differently. So maybe Funland isn't the problem.

The day wears on, the sky sliding through shades of grey – slate to almost white to slate again – the sun never quite penetrating, the clouds never quite surrendering to rain. Johnson doesn't talk, except for when they stop to eat a brief lunch out of cans and a perfunctory exchange when another fallen tree compels a short, nerve-jangling stop. Afternoon wears into evening, and Kyle wonders if Johnson plans to sleep at all.

When the sun splits over the horizon, a little colour finally enters the sky, peach, fleshy pink, and faded lilac. They've driven through two towns already; a third, with its ageing, untreated clapperboard homes and badly weathered stores, brings with it more reminiscences of that long-ago day. Kyle thinks again of the man with the gun and how he'd threatened them. It takes him a moment to dredge up the reason: his father and a pocketful of stolen candy bars. He can't help but be ashamed, and the shame brings guilt. His father, after all, had been trying to feed his son and girlfriend.

Or was he just looking out for himself?

The thought feels like a betrayal, and Kyle stifles it, though not quickly enough. It's tied to too many other thoughts, other memories, and a tug on one thread sends the whole web shivering. He wants to doubt. He wants his resolve to weaken. That's all this is. Doubt is the way out of what he needs to do, but only if he allows it to be. Once more, Kyle empties his mind of everything and stares into the growing gloom beyond the windshield.

There's no room for weakness. Johnson killed his father. He has to kill Johnson. Nothing can be allowed to change that.

*   *   *

By evening, Doyle's legs feel bruised from ankles to thighs, and the small of his back as if someone is rhythmically sliding needles through the muscle there. Unaccustomed inertia has hardened his shoulders into a solid bar of pain.

Still, he stubbornly resists the urge to stop. While they're moving, they're safe, or so his instincts tell him.

Also, there's no need to talk. Doyle is ashamed of himself for admitting it, but there it is: now that they're out here, all of the things he'd intended saying to Kyle, all the carefully judged words that might have drawn the boy back from this path he's on, have vanished. Any argument Doyle can come up with seems melodramatic and absurd, or else banal, dismissive of the weight of horror and bloodshed between them.

As darkness starts to fall, however, as the torment of unaccustomed hours behind the wheel exceeds the point of discomfort and the silence shifts from strained to ominous, so it becomes harder to deny that he's risking a terrible mistake. The deteriorated road has already slowed them to a crawl, and still Doyle keeps snagging dips and cracks in the asphalt, drawing creaks from the suspension. In the rear mirror, the Sicker child looks dangerously tense. Kyle appears merely drained and anxious. The boy will never ask to stop, regardless of how badly he might want to.

It's Doyle's call to make. Yet only as he accepts the need does he begin to speculate, too late, at the feasibility. They'll be easy prey on the roadside, and he wouldn't dare risk entering a building, even if they could find one that looked suitable in the mounting darkness.

It's more luck than he feels he deserves that a solution presents itself. Ahead, a low gorge looms from the twilight, spanned by a bridge of stained concrete and metal barrier rails. A dirt track breaks leftward from the road, and on a flash of impulse, Doyle crosses to follow it. The trail leads down the slope, tucks under the struts of the bridge, and then, inexplicably, peters out. The headlights fall upon a muddy strip of river crawling through the gorge bed. On the near bank, an overturned supermarket shopping cart and a couple of battered plastic crates lie amid other assorted trash.

Doyle manoeuvers the jeep so that they're facing toward the trail. Satisfied, he leans back, stretching cramped limbs. A groan, half of discomfort and half of relief, slips free before he can contain it.

When he glances at Kyle, the boy is gazing at him, bleary-eyed from tiredness but with evident distrust. "Why here?" he asks.

"It's as safe as anywhere."

"What if Sickers come by?"

"Then it's still as safe as anywhere."

Kyle considers. "Can we take a walk?"

Doyle doesn't like the idea of letting the girl leave the jeep. He reminds himself that she's been out before, that in fact her presence might have saved his life. But it's hard to make the thought stick. "Keep close," he says.

He watches them for a minute, Kyle pacing stiff-legged and the girl scurrying back and forth around him, holding her arms always as though she isn't certain what to do with them, making chuckling sounds that never come near to being words. Then Doyle makes a start on a fire.

The river has washed up scraps of wood, and he's brought firelighters and matches and a small sack of barbeque coals from the stores. Altogether, it proves easier than he'd expected. Once the fire's going, Doyle prepares a sparse dinner of beans and dogs. He doesn't need to call the others back; the smell of cooking food draws them. Doyle and Kyle sit on the overturned crates, the gun stashed at Doyle's feet. The girl eats rapidly, scooping with her fingers, oblivious of the heat. She's heedful to waste nothing. Afterward, Doyle washes the plates and pans in the river, and empties his bladder into the murky flow. He walks to where Kyle is waiting beside the flagging fire and says, "You can sleep in the back. I'll take the front. The girl can have the trunk."

Doyle unpacks the blankets he's brought. There are even a couple of stiff, yellowed pillows in there, a suggestion of Carlita's. Doyle carries the bedding around and tosses it through the open side doors. He returns to the fire. "We should bed down before it gets any darker."

"I'll help Abigail get settled," Kyle agrees.

Doyle would like to say more, something that might cement this hesitant peace between them. No words come to him. He scuffs the leftovers of the fire with a heel, paces back to the jeep, and climbs into the front, locking the door behind him. He settles the gun in the passenger footwell, lies down in his clothes, pulls the blanket to his chin, and bundles the pillow in the angle where seat meets door. He closes his eyes and listens as Kyle strives to make himself comfortable.

Tiredness settles over him, a weight that draws at his whole body. Doyle was convinced he wouldn't sleep, but the notion seems absurd now. He feels like cement sinking into dark water.

However, when sleep comes, it's sullen, fragmentary, a smothering presence beyond which he can perceive the waking world. He dreams unsettling chunks of dreams. Once, he's certain Sickers have gathered round the jeep, but when Doyle forces his eyes open, there's only the darkness. The third time he wakes, it's with the awareness of a nightmare he's forgotten even as he reaches for the memory, and with unease that has nothing to do with Sickers. He knows what's caused it, though not how he knows. And as he wonders, Doyle hears the slightest creak of the seat backs.

He doesn't open his eyes. Nevertheless, Doyle is suddenly, entirely awake. He isn't afraid, but there's a pressure in his mind and limbs that's almost paralysing. "Kyle," he says, so softly he can scarcely be sure he's spoken.

Again, there comes a fractional noise, or else a change in the quality of the silence. Yet all Doyle feels is that overwhelming weight.

"You can kill me anytime," he says. "Why not see what's in the city first?"

The moment stretches. He begins to doubt himself. Then, once more, there's an impression of motion, and Doyle knows that Kyle has moved away. He knows as well that in the morning he'll remember this as if it had been a dream, as if he'd never woken or spoken. He knows that as much as he feels he won't get back to sleep, he will, and that it will be better sleep than the night has offered so far.

Doyle settles against his knotted pillow and lets himself sink.

CHAPTER FORTY

She doesn't know what time it is, except that it's night. Aaronovich can hear raised voices from the direction of the cellblock. Just raised voices, and yet they must be very loud to carry such a distance, even in the still air.

That air is cool rather than cold, but the cold will surely come soon. Aaronovich, finding herself thinking of Abigail, pushes the thought aside before it can take hold. The cold doesn't bother Abigail. If there's anyone she should be concerned for, it's Kyle or Doyle Johnson – or herself.

Aaronovich keeps close to the administrative wing, merging her silhouette with its darkness. At the corner, she hurries across the gap to the Big House, already regretting the weight of the bags she's packed. She's not a young woman. She won't be able to get far burdened like this. However, if she wants to survive for more than a day or two, then, sooner or later, she'll need all that she's carrying.

And she *does* want to survive. Of everything she's realised in the last few hours, that is perhaps her greatest revelation. She's not willing to let Funland take her life as it's taken so much else.

She slips through a door and, only once it's shut behind her, flicks on her flashlight. Aaronovich has spent so little time in the Big House, or anywhere outside of her offices, that she's hardly familiar with these corridors. But Doyle made her memorise the route to Carlita's rooms, and it isn't complicated. She knows she's followed his directions precisely when she comes up against a locked door; few doors are kept locked in Funland these days. She taps lightly, and when there's no response, more firmly. Though she would like to call Carlita's name, it seems just plausible that someone might be listening. Nothing can be trusted or assumed.

Aaronovich waits. Even the prospect of knocking again makes her anxious. If circumstances should get out of control, the Big House is the first place they'll come. It's a symbol, and don't revolutions thrive upon such things? Yet she finds that she can't imagine what has begun in those terms, as a rupture with the past intended to resuscitate the future. No, what Aaronovich envisages when she thinks of the events occurring at this moment in the cellblock is the last frantic spasms of a dying animal.

Aaronovich senses rather than hears movement on the other side of the door. "Carlita?" she murmurs.

"Doctor?"

"Yes. Will you open the door?"

There's a pause, and a palpable air of hesitation. Then comes the click of a lock turning. The door opens a sliver. There's candlelight beyond, but Aaronovich can't see Carlita's face, merely the shape of her, outlined.

"What are you doing here?" Carlita sounds apprehensive, as if even Aaronovich could be a threat, or at any rate the harbinger of danger.

Which indeed she is. "We're not safe," Aaronovich says. Because that's too much a statement of the obvious, she adds, "Foster came asking about Johnson. He's afraid he's going to lose control. He's right to be. Maybe he'll be able to keep them in check and it won't come to anything. But even if he can...." *Even if he can, I think it's all over. No, I know it is.* "We need to be ready. To plan for the worst."

"The worst?" Carlita echoes, as though testing the concept.

Aaronovich gives her a moment to reach the same conclusions she herself has, which are the only conclusions possible.

"My god," Carlita says. "You really mean it."

"I don't know how long we have. Likely not long at all. If they find out what I've done in the infirmary—"

Carlita's eyes widen. "What did you do?" But nothing in the question suggests that she expects an answer. Perhaps she's already read what she needs to in Aaronovich's expression.

"So can I come in?"

This time, she allows an edge of forcefulness into her voice. She doesn't take Carlita's reluctance personally. They're both aware that along with Aaronovich comes everything she represents, an irreparable puncture in Carlita's hermetically sealed reality and hard choices with no correct answers. Still, every instant she spends in the corridor makes her feel more exposed.

Then Carlita steps back, drawing the door after her. "Yes," she says. "Of course."

CHAPTER FORTY-ONE

Johnson was right about one thing. There will be other opportunities. As grey light seeps around the edges of the bridge, that's the only thought Kyle can find any comfort in.

He'd lain, not feigning sleep because he knew Johnson couldn't see him, but staying perfectly still. All the while, he'd kept one hand in his pocket, gripping the hilt of his knife. He'd planned to wait for Johnson's breathing to level out, but it never did, and Kyle had decided that must simply be how a man slept when he had so much guilt on his conscience.

Kyle could perceive a narrow stripe of sky past the bridge, and he'd watched the stars glimmering there. The night was clear, the moon brilliant and sharp. The astringent light had made him think of Aaronovich's infirmary. He'd fallen asleep just once, despite himself. He'd dreamed of that first night in Funland: he and Carlita together after the crash, the doctor tending to their injuries. In the dream, however, Austin had been there, and he'd been sick. Initially, Kyle had been afraid, until he'd come to comprehend that all Austin did was cower in the corner, whimpering with steady terror. Kyle had roused feeling not frightened but troubled, and for a moment the frigid moonlight had made him question if he'd really woken.

By then, he no longer doubted that Johnson must be sleeping. Kyle had slipped the knife out of his pocket. He'd shifted to his knees, flinching at every slight creak. For the first time, he'd considered how he would do it. He'd have to lean through the gap in the seats, holding the knife outstretched. Yet there was no way he'd be able to apply enough pressure like that for a clean cut. His sole hope would be that surprise would buy the second or two he needed.

He hadn't thought until then of Johnson struggling, of there being blood. But Johnson would struggle. There would be very much blood. Kyle felt bile swelling in his throat. Regardless, he'd leaned into the gap between the seats, the knife held out before him.

And Johnson had begun to talk.

Nothing could have horrified Kyle more. It wasn't the words themselves; perhaps it was only how Johnson remained so completely immobile, as though speaking out of sleep or even death. Still, Kyle had kept control of himself. He'd moved back slowly, as slowly as he'd ever done anything. He'd lain down, by the smallest degrees. He'd pulled his blanket over him, willing the coarse fabric into silence.

That was how he'd spent the rest of the night. It's how, with eyes gummed by tiredness, he greets the colourless morning.

If he had merely been deterred then he might have slept. What bothers Kyle isn't that he was discovered, it's the sure knowledge that he could never have gone through with his plan. He'd realised the truth in the instant before Johnson spoke, had known with cold and absolute certainty. Whatever it would take to drive a knife into a sleeping man's throat was nowhere to be found in him.

That doesn't mean Johnson gets away with what he's done. Nothing can diminish for one moment the fact that he shot Kyle's father to death, that, when he lets himself, Kyle can still feel the warm spatter of blood on his cheek.

What it means is that he can't use the knife. Probably not a gun, either. But there are other ways to kill a man, aren't there? Out here, there must be. All he can do is wait to see what possibilities this desolate new world has to offer. Maybe it will kill Doyle Johnson of its own accord, and all Kyle will have to do is watch.

★ ★ ★

Doyle stirs soon after dawn, chilly and stiff-limbed. He isn't surprised to find Kyle already awake. Doyle considers suggesting that they have some breakfast, but the thought makes him queasy, he'd rather not push their supplies, and the notion of building a fire strikes him as somehow riskier now than on the previous night. In the end, he shares around a packet of cookies. Of the three of them, the girl seems to be the only one to have had any sleep. She's alert, full of nervous energy, too much so for Doyle's liking. He's glad when

Kyle walks with her along the river's edge, allowing him to pack the bedding and bundle it into the back without constantly feeling the need to keep her in view.

At no point does he mention what happened in the night. It isn't that he's trying to protect Kyle. Doyle just has no idea what he can say.

When Kyle returns, the Sicker girl is calmer, a portion of her vitality burned off by the exercise. She's behaving better than Doyle had dared anticipate. He has to remind himself that's absolutely not a reason to trust her, any more than he'd trust a trained wolf. Doyle pauses until Kyle has her settled in the back before he takes the driver's seat, wincing at the prospect of a second day behind the wheel. He builds speed on the brief flat stretch beyond the bridge and then guns the engine, as the jeep struggles upon the loose-surfaced incline. The tyres slide and spit gravel, and Doyle is grateful when the dirt track resolves to asphalt.

He'd been expecting Sickers. In his imagination, they were waiting on the bridge, or back up the road maybe, watching cold-eyed as buzzards. That they aren't there perturbs Doyle. A threat that behaves according to his expectations is one he stands a chance against. People that act like monsters he can understand, he's seen it all too often. He doesn't want to have to think about Aaronovich's theories, which even now nudge the edges of his mind. He doesn't want to wonder if she might be right.

At first, the roads are much the same as yesterday, cracked and pockmarked and littered with debris. The going gets easier when finally they leave the back roads for the highway. There, at least there are no fallen trees, though in places refuse has blown across the lanes: in one spot a battered billboard, in another a sheet of polythene, snared on the central reservation and flopping like some obscene jellyfish.

With six lanes, these hazards are easy to avoid, and for whole stretches the highway is utterly empty. It's ten minutes, even, before Doyle spies the first vehicle, a flatbed truck painted in military colours, pulled carefully to the side of the road and clearly abandoned long ago, for the windows are shattered and the green is nearly grey with plastered dust. After that, there are others: once an eighteen-wheeler on the far shoulder, a couple more military vehicles, but very few cars.

Here, too, there's no sign of Sickers. Doyle has to caution himself not to relax. Not seeing them doesn't mean they aren't around. Yet, rationally, there's no doubt that the highway has little to offer; with no traffic, there's nothing, not even roadkill, to draw them. It makes sense that they should keep to the country, where they have shelter, water, and the possibility of food.

By early afternoon, Doyle has grown so complacent that, when the jeep crests a rise and the dip beyond reveals a half dozen Sickers spread across the lanes, his immediate reaction is to stamp the brake rather than to speed up. It's crazy, stupid, but in that moment they look so normal, it's easier to accept the illusion than to convince himself they're a threat.

They're crossing between the banks, the road now just another terrain to them. Spaced across the blacktop, their presence conjures the absurd impression of a mother duck trailed by her ducklings. Doyle counts four adults and two children, scantly covered despite the cold.

One of the children – a boy in his teens, perhaps Kyle's age – is first to look round. He cocks his head at the low rumble of the engine. His thin pale face is suspended in a rat's nest of black hair that hangs past his shoulders. His eyes are wide open, as though in shock. He takes a step toward them, and at that the others turn as well.

Doyle has been observing rather than driving. In the back, the girl is growling, a constant rumble from the depths of her throat. The jeep is hardly moving. Doyle goes for the accelerator, grazes it, and the engine makes a strangled sound. He wants to pound his foot upon the pedal. Instead, he forces himself to work it gently.

They're too spread out. There's no way around. If he tries to break through, how will they respond? A human body, even emaciated like these are, is a heavy thing. Doyle prefers not to learn what one would do to their windshield. And six Sickers, working together, what could they achieve? Or should he be counting seven? The girl is still growling, an insistent, off-key note such as a damaged machine might make.

The line isn't moving. Doyle doesn't slow, doesn't accelerate either. They're all of them watching, heads tilted, mouths hanging open, in idiocy or hunger. He has aimed at the children, a decision based entirely on body mass and worst-case scenarios. Neither shows any reaction.

Only at the last moment do they step aside, unhurriedly moving sideways, backward, as if possessed of some capacity he lacks. Doyle fights the urge to speed up, though it's close to overwhelming. The woman's face passes by, inches from his. Dark, mottled eyes regard him without emotion.

When he checks the rearview mirror, they've resumed walking. And he appreciates then why his mind went so eagerly to the image of a mother and her ducklings. For it's one of the females leading them, clambering gracelessly up the bank that will return them to the wilderness.

★   ★   ★

Johnson gives it a few minutes, until the Sickers are far behind them, and then asks, "Are you okay back there?"

"Sure," Kyle says.

He had been. He hadn't even been afraid. The Sickers had seemed not terrifying, not monstrous, but familiar. Their presence had been much less strange than the sight of empty lanes of highway stretching without interruption.

Now, against his will, he recalls once again their journey so many months ago in the other direction. Kyle and his father, Carlita and Nando: two of them are gone, one half of that briefly formed family dead and buried. Only then does Kyle understand what he'd experienced as he saw those six Sickers spread across the blacktop, moving in awkward synchronicity. What he'd felt was jealousy.

"I didn't get it at the time," he says. "How close we came." He hadn't meant to speak. His thoughts have bypassed whatever part of his brain gets to make such decisions. He can scarcely recognise his own voice; it's so thin and weary. Kyle hates to show Johnson this weakness, but he can find no strength in himself anywhere. "The army wouldn't let people use the road. They were keeping everyone together. We wouldn't have got out without the ambulance."

"That was Carlita's cousin's idea?" Johnson queries.

Johnson must know. Carlita will have told him everything. Therefore, Johnson is encouraging Kyle to talk, and he should be resentful. Yet the need has built to such a point that he can no longer restrain himself. "Fernando. Yeah. It was all his idea. He saved us. My dad...." Kyle doesn't want to finish the sentence, but the words are there, already queued up. "My dad tried something. It didn't work out."

Except that Johnson knows what his dad tried and failed to do. So the only person Kyle's fooling is himself. He presses back in his seat, no longer looking at Johnson, implying by posture alone that he's said more than he intended to.

Late in the afternoon, the city finally comes into view. They break the brow of a hill and it's there in the bowl of ground below, a disorganised sketch of drab shapes spread with no clear objective over the landscape. Even from a distance, its outlines don't look right. The last few months have not been kind to the city. Whole blocks, whole boroughs have been ravaged by fires, some probably begun by Sickers in the first waves of madness, but most, Kyle guesses, simply nature running its course.

As they draw nearer, he's struck by the bizarre sensation that, moment by moment, they are moving back through time. The highway has suffered a degree of damage but, devoid of traffic for months, has weathered well for the most part. The city, in contrast, is a relic of an ancient age. Its buildings are falling into the earth, the earth all too ready to claim them. Though such patient decay can likely go on for decades, Kyle finds it hard to imagine any sign of civilisation surviving another five years.

That sight, the feelings it brings, reopens the sinkhole of emptiness inside him. Here is the difference between knowing everything that was once his life is gone and seeing in irrefutable detail. He can feel his silence slipping, can feel more words rising, exactly like vomit. And staying silent seems practically disrespectful, because Kyle remembers this spot. Ahead, where the access road trails off to meet the overpass, a large arrow sign remains, hoisted on poles set into concrete. Round about are scattered temporary blinker lights mounted on plastic orange pillars, all long since tumbled over, the orange a dull brown and the lights themselves extinguished. When he looks carefully, he can make out dints and scuffmarks where the heavy military vehicle rested.

"This is where they were taking them," he says.

Johnson slows the jeep.

"The refugees. The ones that got out. There was a camp, something like that. They were herding them; they wouldn't let them onto the highway. Not without knowing if they were infected or not."

"A quarantine zone," Johnson says.

"I suppose." They're almost upon the junction. It occurs to Kyle that, all this while, Johnson has been driving in the wrong lanes. "I'd like to see," he says.

Johnson slows the jeep yet further, to a crawl. "You think there might still be people?" There's evident doubt in his voice.

"No, I just...Johnson, I need to see."

Johnson hesitates. Then he says, "No you don't."

"What the hell do you know? You—"

"Calm down."

But Kyle can't calm down. Suddenly he can barely control himself. "I need to see!" he blurts. "I need to know what happened. There were people trying to get out, hundreds and hundreds of them. Some of them were sick. Maybe the soldiers were sick. They were all trapped there together. And that...it could have been us!"

Johnson gives him a few seconds, long enough for the strangled note to leave Kyle's breathing. "But it wasn't."

All the answer Kyle can manage is a shapeless mumble.

"What?"

"I said, we should do what we came here to do."

Johnson's response is to pick up speed once more. He keeps on until they're on the verge of entering the city, then slows again and this time stops altogether, there in the middle of the highway. From behind, Kyle watches him curiously, distrustfully. Perhaps it's only the tension radiating off him, but Kyle divines that whatever Johnson is doing has long been planned.

Yet when Johnson speaks, his words don't sound premeditated.

They sound, in fact, as though they're being wrenched from out of him. "There's something I need to talk to you about," he says. "Before we go in there. I should have told you before we set out. You deserve to know. I should have and I didn't. Then I convinced myself there'd come a point when you might be willing to listen. There won't, I get that now."

"You're right," Kyle says. "Nothing you tell me is going to change anything."

"I get that. But like I said, you deserve to know. The truth is...." Johnson's whole body tenses, shoulders bunching, fingers wringing the steering wheel. Then he sags. "Truth is, I'm dying."

Kyle hears the words. He can make no sense of them. He stares mutely, attempting to read the logic that language has failed to provide from the sliver of Johnson's face revealed by the rearview mirror.

"I mean," Doyle continues, "we're all dying. Chances are I'm just dying sooner. I've been getting headaches for a long time. Real bad headaches. I talked to Aaronovich; she thinks it's a tumour. On my brain. She says, under normal circumstances, it might have been treatable. But these aren't normal circumstances and she can't fix me. Probably there's no one left alive anywhere who could."

Now Kyle understands – more than he wants to. Still, his thoughts are a lightning storm. It would be impossible to pick an emotion from that flickering delirium and claim with certainty that's what he's feeling. All Kyle can do is grasp for the easiest, the most obvious reaction. "What do you want from me, Johnson?" His own voice sounds thin, watered down. "You killed my dad. And you didn't have to. Maybe if you'd done things differently you'd never have had to kill anybody."

"I realise that."

"Then what? What did you think I was going to say?"

"The reason I'm telling you," Johnson replies, "is that I don't know what might happen. Aaronovich doesn't know what could happen. Or when. Or how long I have. But when it gets bad, really bad, I can't do much. So I need to be sure you can cope. And that if you get back and I don't, you'll take responsibility. Whatever you believe, none of this is Carlita's fault."

Kyle is shocked by the threat of tears in his own laboured breathing. The unfairness of this is almost beyond his ability to process. He'll have no revenge. Nature has beaten him to it. But he can feel no satisfaction at the prospect of yet another death, only a gaping sensation of loss. Prior to setting out, he'd imagined he was faced with a choice between hope and revenge. In truth, both will be denied him. The world as it is now has no place for such things.

"I'll need to know how to drive," he says. To his surprise, his voice is calm again, calmer, perhaps, than before. "My uncle let me drive a little. I learned the basics. I just need you to show me enough to get back on my own."

"Fine," Johnson agrees. "But out here, not in the city."

Of everything that's happened in the aftermath of the sickness taking hold, what follows is feasibly the strangest part. Johnson lets Abigail, who has been growing steadily more restless since the incident with the Sicker pack, out to play upon the embankment. There she scurries to and fro, her gaze rarely leaving the vehicle. Then they spend an hour trundling along the same brief stretch of road, practising simple manoeuvers, Kyle crouched intently over the wheel and Johnson reeling off instructions, with greater patience than Kyle would ever have expected from him.

It's nowhere near enough. But Johnson must be conscious of their fuel supplies and of the dwindling daylight, and Kyle is a fast learner when he needs to be. By the end of that hour, he feels like he might have a chance of making it back alone – at least until he envisions what that would actually entail, for then his mind clamps shut and terror takes the place of all coherent thought.

When Johnson gets out and opens the rear side door, Abigail scampers up without encouragement and flops onto her side, tongue poking between her lips. Kyle scoots over, for the first time taking the front passenger seat rather than sitting in the back with Abigail.

"From now on," Johnson tells him, as he slides in behind the wheel, "whenever we leave the jeep, you keep the keys. If anything happens to me, you get out of here. Keep yourself safe."

"You don't need to worry about that." But Kyle finds that he can't say it with the conviction he intends.

"Whatever happens. You keep safe."

"All right."

"Okay."

Johnson starts the engine. He drives through the gap in another barricade, this one reinforced with two police black-and-whites, their windows long since caved in.

And just like that, they're within the city.

CHAPTER FORTY-TWO

They sleep in shifts, as well as they can, for the night is far from quiet.

There's much shouting, audible from the cellblock even through the intervening walls. The gunshot comes soon after dawn. Carlita is on watch, but the noise wakes Aaronovich, immediately and entirely. She gathers her bags, and Carlita her few possessions. Having carefully erased any trace that her rooms have been occupied, they go up to the roof by a narrow staircase Carlita knows of, one clearly unused in months or even years.

After the gunshot, there's silence for a long while. It must have been Foster who fired, Aaronovich thinks: a gamble, a ringleader put down. Perhaps it will work. Perhaps order can be restored with a single bullet, at least temporarily.

They huddle in blankets, sheltering amid arches of ductwork, agreeing by mutual consent to stay in the open. The air is cold, the wind colder. Aaronovich can smell a promise of snow; it brings with it fractured memories of her childhood that never quite coalesce. They talk occasionally, in low whispers. But there's so little to be said, and most of what there is they covered during the night. They have plans, and contingency plans. The common element of them all is surviving, until Johnson and Kyle return or, though they've not admitted as much, until it becomes apparent they never will.

The second gunshot comes around lunchtime. It's followed in close succession by a third, and a minute later, three staccato bursts. After the initial shock has passed, Aaronovich decides that Foster is dead, or if not yet then soon to be. At any rate, there's no doubt in her mind that the final rattle of gunfire was aimed at him.

From then onward, the tempo of the distant commotion changes. Whatever disagreement has been working itself out through the night, it's done now. The new note is one of celebration, but with a manic energy, which feels to Aaronovich every bit as dangerous as the preceding conflict.

For the first hour, the revellers confine themselves to the cellblock. From the sounds she hears, they are smashing things, as if destruction is some long-withheld privilege. It's strange, Aaronovich thinks; with a few exceptions, these aren't violent men. The crimes that placed them here weren't crimes of violence, for that had been an underpinning of Plan John's ordered society. Have they always had this in them? Has Funland changed them? Or is this simply how men behave after a world has ended?

Whatever the case, when they've broken everything they judge needs to be broken, they move on to the stores.

Aaronovich has already discussed with Carlita the possibility of warning Contreras. Carlita argued in favour of it, yet in the end, Aaronovich's reasoning had won out. Securing Tito Contreras's safety would compromise their own. If the convicts don't find him where they expect him, they'll go looking. She and Carlita can't hide long from a sustained search. Perhaps it will come anyway, when they investigate Aaronovich's offices, but even then they'll focus their efforts on the administrative wing, at least at first.

As they listen to the tumult of the stores being overturned and to Contreras's brief, muted cries, Carlita won't meet Aaronovich's eye. Afterward, Aaronovich listens to them moving out the supplies and carrying them into the cellblock. It takes a little over an hour. They laugh and joke throughout, and she wonders if Contreras is alive. Can men who've just killed without reason laugh like that? Probably they can.

After that, there comes quiet, broken only occasionally by the drift of raised voices. When she's sure there's no one below, Aaronovich gets up to stretch cramping muscles and walks a huddled circuit of the roof. Then, though her appetite has all but vanished, she opens a can of fruit from the supplies she's brought and shares the contents with Carlita. Still they don't talk. She can't ascertain if Carlita is angry with her about Contreras or merely exhausted. Maybe all Aaronovich senses is her own desire of silence reflected, for she feels she's passed the point where conversation can serve any useful function.

Is this what happens to the infected? Have they crossed some internal Rubicon that renders their old existence obsolete, that makes words futile and necessity plain to see? And she thinks of Abigail, of where she might be, of whether or not she's safe. Aaronovich considers these questions for the first time without sadness or guilt, because wherever Abigail is, it's likely safer right now than Funland.

When night has fallen completely, Aaronovich gets to her feet once more.

Carlita, who had appeared to be drowsing, opens her eyes and looks up. "What are you doing?" she asks, her manner almost accusatory.

"I'm going to check if Contreras is alive," Aaronovich tells her. "And if he is, I'm going to help him."

CHAPTER FORTY-THREE

It looks to Doyle as if a war has taken place. Probably one has. Two buildings at the opening junction show gaping holes on their upper floors, as though somebody has conducted clumsy surgery to display their insides. No window anywhere is unbroken. Half a dozen overturned cars lie like fumigated insects. There's rubble piled along both sides of the street, in scabbed heaps already turning green with grass and weeds.

When the Sickers begin to reveal themselves, it's like a trick of the eye. For each one Doyle sees, another appears. At first, there's a couple in a window far up the street, gazing out at this intruder that has ruptured the stillness of their home. Even as he registers those, a flicker of movement drags his attention to a gang on the opposite side, four – no, five – gathering around a torn-out double doorway. And there are more sidling from the darkness.

"Hang on," Doyle says.

He urges the jeep forward, and for a moment it seems the Sickers will be content to stand watching. Then Doyle catches a flash of movement in the side mirror. The creature coming after them looks too old to be running as fast as he is. His spittle-flecked mouth is the only feature visible through a mane of vile grey hair. Doyle actually finds himself believing that the old man might be able to catch them, though they're doing fifty and still accelerating. But at last the man trips and goes down in a cyclone of flailing limbs. He hasn't got up again by the time Doyle turns from the road.

"Can you navigate?" Doyle barks.

"I guess," Kyle mumbles back. He sounds shaken.

"There's a map in the glove compartment." Doyle turns left at the next junction. Far ahead, a Sicker sprints across their path, hardly sparing them a glance.

Not taking his eyes from the road, Doyle hears Kyle click open the catch, draw out the map, and unfold it over the dash. Doyle already knows what Kyle is currently realising. There's plenty of city between them and the circle of red ink that marks their destination.

"All right," Kyle says, "I think I've got it."

Farther ahead, another Sicker makes three quick steps into the street and turns to glare at them, a woman with dark skin and deeply black hair, scrawny and off-kilter as a scarecrow. She raises her arms, as though she'll be able to stop them. From the rear, Abigail chatters anxiously. Doyle can feel her motion through his seat, as she scampers back and forth, clawing at the side windows like an animal in a moving cage.

"It's okay," Kyle tells her, his tone soothing. "It's okay, Abigail."

Doyle eases down on the accelerator and they pick up speed again. There's less garbage in the street here, but the surface is bad, and immediately the jeep starts to bounce. The woman stares at the oncoming vehicle with neither fear nor interest. With maybe ten feet still separating them, she scurries aside, into a doorway. It belongs to a small convenience store, and as they roar past, Doyle spots more figures crowded in the gloom. He can't see their eyes, but he can feel their gaze.

"Which way?" he asks.

The question draws Kyle back to reality. "Take the next...no, the second left," he mutters. "Stay on there. I need time to work this out."

Doyle does as instructed – and slams the brake, flinging them both to the limits of their seat belts and drawing an indignant yelp from the girl. The street, a residential district of four-storey brownstones, is blocked not far ahead by two police cars, sunk down on flattened tires. The gaps between them and to either side have been cemented with furniture, everything from armchairs to a wood-framed double bed. There's no possible route through.

"Can we turn around?" Kyle says.

Doyle's eyes flicker over the mirrors. "Yes."

"Then go back. Take that last left."

Rather than turn, Doyle reverses at a furious pace, slams on the brakes just past the junction, and noses in. This way is clear, and a turnoff farther up returns them to the original road, a few feet past the barricade. There are signs that this entrance had been blocked as well, but only the parked cars remain, with a sufficient breach for the jeep.

By then, Kyle seems to have his course figured out. His next directions are delivered with more confidence. Within a minute, they're onto a major road, which leads into an affluent district of apartments and offices in multistorey towers. Here, there's room to manoeuver. The Sickers they see keep their distance and appear to be travelling alone, as though these citadels of glass and steel intimidate them. Those who stayed in the city were the ones unable to evacuate, which meant those too poor to find a means of escape. Doyle suspects they're keeping to the areas they knew before.

A turn later, things go wrong again. The road Kyle proposes is cut off diagonally by an armoured personnel carrier, and the signs of destruction beyond imply that it wasn't abandoned without a fight. One building in particular has been torn like wet paper and now droops into the street, held together by who-knows-what.

"We can go right," Kyle suggests. "Get around that way."

But the detour is nearly as bad, a return to the narrow thoroughfares Doyle had been hoping to avoid. The hum of the jeep's engine is already drawing out Sickers; they tumble from doorways, visibly arrested between fight and flight. Doyle starts to speed up.

"Left," Kyle says. "Next left, then the right straight after."

They get through the left okay, but the right is impassable. Fire has devastated both blocks, leaving them as a landslide of grey sludge.

"Left," Kyle yells. "Now, left!"

Doyle's last-moment swerve carries them onto the sidewalk and inches from a wall. The tyres squeal in protest. Behind, Abigail takes up the note, keening in alarm. More houses here, windows at street level gaping, stairs ascending to torn-open doors. The jeep begins to roar, their speed inappropriate to the cramped space. Are there Sickers everywhere or only a few, multiplied in his mind by adrenalin? In that instant, Doyle feels that the city is purposefully dragging them from where they need to be.

"That alley." Kyle points. "Do you see it?"

"Hell!" Doyle protests.

Still, he goes for it – a second too late. The jeep comes up hard this time, throwing them left, metal melding into brick. The alley is barely wide enough to hold them and thick with ancient trash, the stink foul even through closed windows. Doyle knows instinctively that the sick have been feeding here. It's in their expressions, their slack-jawed perturbation – and, now that he looks, one is clutching a rag of bloodied fur in both hands, another licking smeared crimson from its lips.

Trying to wrestle the jeep free brings a screech of scraping metal. Their front-right corner has compacted against the wall, and his efforts appear to be worsening the damage. Doyle can feel the wheels spinning helplessly beneath them. The Sickers shift, uncertain.

Doyle gives up on accelerating, slams them into reverse. Only the pitch of the metal-tearing sound changes. The nearest Sicker is a dozen feet away. Its mouth is open, displaying gobbets of half-chewed rat.

"Johnson," Kyle chokes, "please…you've got to—"

"Calm down," Doyle says.

The Sicker advances, his mouth turning up in a dripping smirk. From the rear seat, Abigail keens a steady, piercing note. Doyle switches back to accelerating. But the jeep still isn't moving. The metal-on-brick shriek merely changes its tempo again. The Sicker is regarding them with fascination. He wipes one filth-dark hand across his lips, seemingly oblivious to the stripe of red he leaves.

Doyle reverses. The jeep screams, an awful dying-animal noise. They move fractionally and stick. He drags the wheel down, and with a lurch the jeep finally comes loose, to shudder backward.

Just briefly, for Doyle is accelerating, into the alley and toward the Sickers. They have an instant to measure this new development, and then they're running. Doyle has no desire to plough through them. All else aside, the jeep can't take many more hits. He revs the engine, staying close upon their heels, until they tumble together into the open. One, however, he inadvertently clips as they break the mouth of the alley: the man who was nearest, the rat-eater. He spins like a dancer, once, twice, before he tumbles to the asphalt.

Doyle swings left, onto the new road, leaving their entourage rapidly behind. "Where are we going?" he asks. His own voice sounds leaden with forced composure.

Kyle's answer is a wordless croak.

"Kyle, *where are we going?*"

"Ah…."

Doyle manages to catch his eye. "Get it together."

Somehow, that's enough to draw Kyle back. "Keep straight," he says, only a little shakily. He takes a moment to consider. "We'll hit a junction at the end. Turn right, and two thirds of the way down there's another right. That's where we want to be."

This time, thankfully, the route is clear. They encounter nothing worse than wreckage that Doyle can manoeuver easily around. Nor, as they turn onto the final street, is there any difficulty in identifying the building they seek. It's large and distinctive, three floors done out in mock-renaissance style, with an elaborate first level of white stone distinguished by a grand portico yielding to storeys of red brick and plainly framed sash windows. A sign over the door reads 'Alexis Hotel', but it's chipped and faded, a relic of an age long passed. There's no means to guess at the building's function in the years since, if it's had any at all.

Its role in recent months, though, is unmistakable. Its obvious purpose in the face of the sickness is the reason they couldn't have missed it, for what was once the Alexis Hotel has become a fortress.

CHAPTER FORTY-FOUR

She descends in darkness, nor daring to use the flashlight. Is it possible they would have set guards? Aaronovich can think of no reason for them to do so, but then she can think of no reason for the destruction in the cellblock, or the overturning of the stores, or for assaulting Contreras. She has already decided that she will no longer expect rational behaviour from anyone besides herself.

With that in mind, it doesn't surprise her when she hears soft footsteps upon the stairs behind her.

Aaronovich pauses to let Carlita catch up. At the bottom of the stairwell, she realises she can go no farther without a light. The blackness is absolute. She takes the flashlight from her pocket, uses it to find the door, and flicks it off once more. However, the passage is every bit as dark. It's one thing to imagine the convicts might have left someone on watch, but that anybody would be waiting in this obscurity is sheer paranoia. Aaronovich cups her palm around the flashlight and turns it on again.

Like that, she makes her way toward where she believes the stores to be. She can hardly remember the route, and doubts Carlita will be any help. Aaronovich has to fight the impulse to vacillate, the fear that she'll get lost in these passages and have the two of them wandering all through the remainder of the night. It's simply a matter of keeping her head. Everything from here onward will come down to that. She has to be the person who stays calm, because there's no one else.

And she isn't lost. There before them is the back door into the stores. It doesn't surprise her to see it left wide open. Aaronovich places a hand on Carlita's arm – *Go slowly* – clicks off the flashlight, and creeps forward.

At first, she can discern no light beyond the doorway. It takes a moment's adjustment to register the slender windows high in two walls, filtering moonlight that smudges black to deepest grey. Only then does she make out the dim form curled upon the concrete floor, apparently too small to be a person.

"Contreras?" she whispers.

The figure shudders.

"Contreras, it's Doctor Aaronovich."

"Doctor?" His voice is fragile.

"Can you walk?"

"What?"

"*Can you walk?*"

"Walk? Where to?"

Contreras seems bewildered. Her initial thought is that maybe he has a head injury, that he doesn't understand. Her second is that, in fact, it's a reasonable question, and not one she has a sensible answer to.

She kneels beside him. "Upstairs," she says, deciding as the words form on her lips. "Somewhere safe."

Contreras sits slowly. Even in the darkness, his movements speak eloquently of pain. When he's halfway to his feet, Aaronovich offers him her shoulder, wrapping an arm about his waist. He's light as a bird, lighter than any grown man should be.

"It's going to be all right," she tells him.

Carlita takes Contreras's other arm and together they support him. Once they're well clear of the stores, Aaronovich clicks the flashlight back on, no longer able to shield its beam with her hand. She's confident that there's no one to see. The convicts won't return tonight. Soon, tomorrow perhaps, they'll begin to search the Big House methodically. Plan John's former rooms will prove irresistible. But it's plain from the way they've left Contreras that, in the meantime, they have little concern for security. Surely they know by now that Johnson is gone, and without him, who is there to secure against?

The stairs prove most difficult. Contreras is regaining some of his strength, but she suspects that he's concussed. He finds the narrow steps inordinately complicated. Exhausted, feeling no triumph, Aaronovich stops at the summit and, with Carlita's help, lays Contreras down. Supine, he takes up much of the space within the tiny rooftop shelter. Aaronovich doesn't like the idea of staying inside the Big House, but it's cold and getting colder, and adding exposure to Contreras's maladies will help nothing. Having made him as comfortable as is possible, Aaronovich inspects his injuries by the glare of the flashlight.

They've beaten him extensively and randomly, with no evidence of mercy: not trying to kill him, perhaps not in any meaningful sense trying to hurt him, only inflicting violence for its own sake. Strangely, that reassures her. It makes everything she's done in the last forty-eight hours seem more rational. She's glad that the ones who did this will never have the resources of her infirmary. She's glad that their final use should be here and now, in attempting to repair the damage those men inflicted.

"Can you help him?" Carlita asks.

"I think so."

"And then what?"

"Then," Aaronovich tells her, "we see what happens."

Yet as she says the words, she knows they're untrue. There's one course remaining and it's perfectly clear, like a silver thread unravelling through the night.

The only one way left to them is the way that leads out of Funland.

CHAPTER FORTY-FIVE

Johnson makes a U-turn past the entrance, chooses his spot with care, and cuts the engine. There are no Sickers visible as yet, but it seems to Kyle a safe bet that the noise of the jeep's arrival will draw attention.

The doors of the hotel have been reinforced with metal plating and ringed with a gunner's nest of sandbags and broken furniture, while the majority of the first- and second-floor windows boast thick wooden boards. "What now?" Kyle asks.

Johnson is scanning the mirrors and Kyle's gaze follows his. This time, he does spy Sickers, though a good distance behind them.

"You're sure you want to chance this?" Johnson says.

"Of course I'm sure."

"Okay. Then we're getting out and onto the roof. We're directly under an open window. I think I can hoist you up. Once you're in, you need to find a way back down here. Got it?"

"Got it."

"Then go."

Kyle pushes through the door of the jeep, pulse beginning to race. He can distinguish the Sickers clearly; they're keeping their distance, just watching. Kyle clambers onto the hood and from there to the roof. As Johnson indicated, two of the second-floor windows, including the one above, have been knocked out and left unboarded.

Moments later, Johnson is alongside him. He's carrying the rucksack that contains all of their remaining food and water, and Kyle notes the grip of the pistol poking from his jacket pocket. Lacing his fingers, Johnson leans closer to the wall. Kyle takes one deep breath and places his right foot in Johnson's hands, flattening his palms against the boarded first-floor window.

"On three," Johnson says. "One…two…."

Kyle is unprepared for how strong Johnson is. On *three* he's practically flung upward, and he barely manages to clutch at the ledge before his head and shoulders are through the gaping window. He pins a forearm over the frame, and then Johnson's hands are grasping both of his feet and shoving, and Kyle has no choice but to scrabble until weight and momentum give him the leverage he needs.

Kyle tumbles onto bare floorboards, unsettling billows of dust. Taking a moment to catch his breath, he looks back out the window and downward, at Johnson perched upon the roof of the jeep. Johnson is holding up in one hand the rucksack containing their food supplies, and in the other the pistol.

Leaning, Kyle takes the rucksack, hesitates over the gun. "What about you and Abigail?"

"We'll be safe in the jeep."

Kyle is doubtful. Then again, the gun has done them no good so far. Reaching, he takes that as well.

"Be quick," Johnson tells him. "Get those doors open."

Kyle ducks back inside, peers around to get his bearings. He's in a long corridor, with behind him the windows, most of them boarded and two knocked clean of glass, presumably for exactly the purpose that Kyle has just taken advantage of. Ahead of him are a series of doors, marked with faded brass numbers that increase in sequence. A hotel, then, like the sign says, but the general air of decay makes him think that the place was vacant long before even the sickness.

Farther along the passage is a sign to stairs. Kyle follows it and, sure enough, beyond the next door is a stairwell. The first floor is much like the second, except that the carpet remains, striped in blue and grey and badly scuffed, and of course the numbering on the doors is different. Also, the corridor he's come out in is considerably shorter, ending in a diagonal wall and another door.

That deposits Kyle in what must have been a lobby, a fact betrayed by its general shape and a darker stain where the front desk once sat. The room has been thoroughly gutted, more so than the hallways, as if redevelopment work was begun here and hurriedly abandoned.

It only occurs to Kyle as he looks toward the double doors that they might be locked. His heart lurches at the prospect of having to explore alone. But the doors are secured in far simpler fashion: brackets have been fixed to either side and a thick bar of timber laid between. The beam is extraordinarily heavy, surely never intended to be moved by one person. Kyle merely needs to shove it aside, however, and that at least is possible. The beam strikes the floor with a tremendous crash, loud enough that he has no doubt Johnson will have heard from outside.

Kyle drags the leftmost door open, carving an arc in the thick grime. As he'd supposed, Johnson is there ready. Behind him, Kyle can see the Sickers he noticed earlier, still grouped far down the street, though perhaps nearer than they'd been before.

"No problems?" Johnson asks.

Kyle shakes his head. "Place seems empty."

"No reason not to be careful." Johnson's eyes stray to the pistol Kyle is clutching.

Kyle hands back the gun, grateful to be free of its weight. In return, Johnson presses something into his palm, and it takes Kyle a moment to understand that it's the key to the jeep.

"Johnson...."

"This is the deal," Johnson says, no room for argument in his voice. He pushes past, into the foyer, and it dawns on Kyle that Johnson has no intention of going back for Abigail.

"Wait." Kyle looks in the direction of the jeep, where Abigail is squatting on her haunches, observing through the gap in the seats. "We can't just leave her."

"She's safer there," Johnson tells him.

"No, she isn't. And she's going to draw attention. You know I'm right." Belatedly, Kyle remembers that Johnson has given him the key. He dashes toward the jeep, squeezing around the edge of the barricade. He expects at any second to feel Johnson's hand hauling him back. But it doesn't come, and when Kyle glances over his shoulder, Johnson hasn't moved from the doorway. Ahead, in the near distance, the Sickers are watching him. He counts six, all men, none of them older than about thirty.

Kyle opens the rear-side door of the jeep. Abigail cowers away, her eyes flickering between him and the distant Sickers.

Kyle takes a step back, giving her space. "Abigail," he says, and at the sound of her name, her gaze settles on him. "Why don't you come out? We're going to explore. It'll be fun. And we won't let anyone hurt you."

Abigail tilts her head, as though weighing her options. Then she slides onto hands and knees. When Kyle takes a further step back, she scampers past him. She hesitates, eyes interrogating the street in sharp jerks. But when Kyle starts toward the open doors, she hurries after, moving upright now.

Johnson edges aside to let them pass, shoves the door shut, and considers the crude mechanism on its interior. "Help me," he says. He doesn't seem angry that Kyle defied him.

Together they manage to manoeuver the beam back into position. Once it's done, Johnson inspects the empty foyer. "Is everything like this?"

"The next floor isn't so bad," Kyle says. "But I don't think anybody's been there in a while."

"Then we'll work our way up to the top," Johnson decides.

Kyle leads. Out of curiosity, he chooses the opposite direction to the one he arrived by. The corridor beyond is a mirror image, and there's another stairwell at the end. He's intending to carry on upward, but Johnson hesitates at the first landing. He pushes through the fire door, into the passage that runs the length of the building's front.

Kyle follows, keeping as close as he dares to Abigail. She's evidently anxious, but at the same time curious, and he senses that obvious attention will make her skittish. It occurs to him, too, that she's very different from how she was in Aaronovich's apartment; that much of her apparent tameness has worn off during the drive, as though the wilderness and the desolation of the city have exerted their influence upon her.

Most of the doors are shut, but halfway along, one lies ajar. Johnson pauses to look inside, leading with the gun barrel. It's a wasted precaution. Kyle sees that the space is as empty as could be. Only lighter marks on the dark green carpet hint at where furniture has stood: a bed and bedside table, a wide cabinet with rounded feet. However, there's also a window in the far wall, and that strikes Kyle as strange, for he remembers from the map that no road runs there.

When he goes to look out, the view from the window is a genuine surprise, so much so that Kyle finds himself staring longer than is necessary, as if to test its reality. It's clear now that the building is actually a hollowed rectangle, longest on its front and rear edges. The inner area, which is substantial, was most likely a garden back in the hotel days.

More recently, it's been put to a new and quite different purpose. The farm beneath them is smaller than the one in Funland, but better planned. Among the tangled undergrowth are remnants of wood and wire fences, raised beds and other signs of diligent cultivation. There's even a sort of shanty greenhouse, the plants within running riot, struggling to force their tendrils through what few mottled panes of glass have endured.

Johnson, who has come to stand beside Kyle, lets the silence drag out. Finally, he says, "I think this place was some kind of a commune. That garden's too well established to have been started after the sickness. But the way the front's been defended, that points to an altogether different mindset. Someone knew what was here and realised they could make use of it. Probably they drummed out the squatters, if they hadn't already got sick, that is."

"Why do you think that?" Kyle asks. "I mean, that they'd have driven them out?"

Johnson shrugs. "It's what I'd have done."

Kyle wonders about that as he recrosses the room, about how he doesn't believe Johnson, and whether Johnson believes himself. He wonders, as well, why what Johnson revealed to him before they entered the city has so alleviated his hatred. Is it only that he imagines himself unburdened of the responsibility he's carried since the moment of his father's death? Even if he's surrendering to weakness, doing so feels right.

He's first into the passage, with Johnson close behind. Kyle stops there, caught by sudden doubt, though not certain why. Then he comprehends.

"Abigail!" he calls. His raised voice sounds weird and too loud in the desolate corridor.

She hadn't accompanied them into the room. Now she's nowhere in sight. How long has it been? Not much more than a minute, yet she can move quickly when she wants to. Scrutinising the dusty boards for some clue, Kyle can make no sense of the muddle of overlapping footprints there.

"Abigail!"

Johnson brushes past him and looks left and right, as though Kyle might somehow have missed her presence. "There's no way out," he says. "Either she'll catch us up or we'll find her when we come back this way."

Kyle would like to argue. Johnson's logic doesn't hold. Perhaps Abigail is lost, perhaps she's scared. They don't know what dangers lie within these walls. But he can see that Johnson isn't going to be swayed.

"You promise?" Kyle is willing to be convinced. When Abigail behaves predictably, it's easy to trust her. When he has no idea what might be going on in her head, it's harder. He doesn't want to contemplate searching for her alone.

"I promise," Johnson agrees.

When he starts toward the stairwell, Kyle falls in behind. *She'll be okay*, he assures himself. Only, that isn't what has stirred his feet, it's the suspicion that Abigail has understood more than he's dared to suppose.

Maybe, after all, this is what she wants. And maybe it's even for the best.

*   *   *

This time, Doyle leads.

That way, his face can't betray how the Sicker girl's disappearance has unsettled him. That way, Kyle won't guess at his first thought, the one he now can't escape. *Perhaps she knows something we don't.*

Doyle follows the stairs up to the next floor. From the moment he pushes through the door, he feels a difference, though it's difficult to place. It's as subtle as a change in the air, but he's sure that people have been here recently.

As below, the stairwell stands at the junction of two corridors, one running along the front of the building, the other retreating along its shorter side. The front corridor boasts more brass numbers, presumably representing yet more shabby hotel rooms. In the opposite direction, however, a pair of double doors stands open, beneath a faded sign that reads 'STAFF ONLY'. Half crescents in the dust suggest that these doors have been used in the recent past, and so it's that route Doyle chooses. He levels the pistol before him, moving with renewed caution.

If he'd had doubts that this was the section the survivors had chosen to make their home, they're dispelled as he enters that doorway. The doors have also been reinforced and fitted with brackets for a bar, like the main entrance. There are the tight rows of beds beyond, too, surely salvaged from the nearby rooms. The exactness of their arrangement dismisses any possibility that this could be the work of squatters, as do the clear signs that this large dormitory was once divided into smaller chambers. Doyle can see where walls have been knocked through, where doorways have been bricked up. Everything speaks of a disciplined, coordinated effort, favouring security always over comfort.

The other unmistakable fact about the room is that it's abandoned, and has been for some time. The same is true of the next he checks, a storeroom from the racks of shelving and rectangles of crushed carpet, and the one after that, a long kitchen.

Doyle refuses to give up his caution. He keeps the gun held ready. Yet he's conscious that he no longer envisages finding anyone, at least no one alive and uninfected. When he glances at Kyle, the boy's expression is desolate. Perhaps he's concerned for the Sicker girl, but Doyle suspects it's more that this place is rapidly dashing whatever tatters of hope he had left. Doyle tries to look inside himself, to identify similar disappointment. What had he expected, coming here?

There's nothing. He came because he said he would, because doing so was the only way he could conceive of to divert Kyle from his path of self-destruction, or maybe just for the most selfish of reasons, because he needed to be free of Funland's walls for a little while.

They travel the length of the next corridor, passing room after room, the recent purpose of each plain but their inhabitants long gone. Ahead, the passage meets the corner of the building and veers left, past which point, Doyle assumes, will be more empty guest rooms. There's one remaining door, closed and unmarked, so he pushes it open. The space within was clearly an office back in the hotel days. Since the sickness, it's perhaps been used for a similar purpose; the dust on the desk is a fine sheen.

Then he thinks, no, not an office. Upon the chipboard desk is a wide rectangular stain, whitened like scar tissue on the brown, laminated skin. He recognises that shape from Plan John's apartment, enough to have a hunch what object left it.

Not an office but a radio room.

Doyle spares the desk the briefest of glimpses. For above it is a whiteboard and on the whiteboard is writing, two long numbers in precise strokes of blue permanent marker, both split with decimal points and the second preceded by a minus sign.

"Coordinates," he says. The word sounds strange to his own ears. This is more, far more, than he'd ever foreseen them finding. "They're map coordinates."

Kyle stands beside him. "You think that's where they went?" His voice is small, reverential.

Doyle doesn't answer, knowing there's no need. Somehow these people were convinced to pack up and set out, and he can imagine only one reason, when they were safe here with their garden, their order, their locked doors and barred windows: the prospect of something better.

"Can you read it?" Kyle asks. "Could we get there?"

"With the right maps. Yeah. We can get there."

"And will you?"

Rather than answer, Doyle searches the drawers. Mostly they've been cleared out, but in the bottom of one are a few yellowed sheets of paper with Alexis Hotel letterheads and a pack of cheap disposable pens. He writes out the coordinates twice, at top and bottom of a page, tears the sheet in half and folds each half in four. One he slides into a pocket. The duplicate he hands to Kyle.

"In case we get separated," he says. "Come on, it's time we started back."

For the sake of completeness, Doyle opts for the direction they haven't explored. As he'd predicted, the rear of the building consists solely of vacant hotel rooms. At the next corner is what he supposes to be a stairwell, the entrance bricked up. Around the turn, along the fourth side, yet more bedrooms are interspersed with offices, these locked, and a small laundry. Halfway along is another reinforced doorway. When he passes through, Doyle feels an unexpected pang, a distant echo perhaps of what those who dwelled here experienced as they moved from the security they'd carved out into the dangers of the outer world.

He's almost at the corner stairwell when he discerns the noise from below. It's the sort of sound, neither interesting nor distinctive, that would have passed unnoticed if not for the deep silence that lies upon the city. A moment after it's faded, Doyle can no longer decide what it had been, a tapping or a scraping. Only an effort of will stops him from mentally filing it as meaningless. Doyle tilts his head, trying to recreate the sound in his mind.

A creaking. From below. In the street? No, not the street. Floorboards.

"Johnson…." Kyle murmurs.

"I heard it."

"Is it Abigail?"

The possibility hadn't occurred to him. Doyle had all but forgotten about the girl. "Come on," he says.

He begins to move again, walking fast rather than running. He slows to descend the stairs, taking pains not to trip; so often it's the stupid mistakes that get you. Doyle moves his body like an engine, gripping the gun as if it's welded to his palm. Whatever this is, and he knows that it's not the girl, he will find a way to deal with it.

He pushes through the door into the second-floor corridor. Though he isn't surprised to see them there, he can't resist how his heart leaps in his chest. The Sickers are clustered between the stairwell doorway and the window where Kyle clambered up. What had ever made Doyle assume they couldn't follow? He ought to have reparked the jeep. Their sickness doesn't mean they can't think, can't climb, and no doubt this building has been a longstanding source of fascination to them.

"Listen to me," Doyle says. "You're going to go downstairs. Go out the front. Get in the jeep and drive."

Kyle only looks at him.

"Take care of Carlita. The doctor. Do what you promised me you'd do."

"Johnson, wait—"

"Shut up. Go." When Kyle still doesn't move, Johnson grips his arm, spins him around, and shoves hard against his back. "*Go!*"

This time, Kyle doesn't resist. He staggers through the door, and Doyle can hear the clatter of his shoes upon the metal-edged steps.

At that, some of the tension goes out of him. Doyle looks back at the Sickers, the six of them clustered in the narrow passage, watching him without expression.

Now it's him and them. Just as he needs it to be for what comes next.

CHAPTER FORTY-SIX

Aaronovich wakes early. Opening the door a sliver, she can see a parallelogram of grey-white sky, spattered with flakes of cloud that make her think of desiccated skin.

She can't say what disturbed her. She has a distant memory of shallow sleep, of troubled dreams. She can hear wheezing snores and knows they belong to Contreras. A part of her mind studies his anguished respiration for evidence of a cracked rib, a bruised lung, and is satisfied that it represents nothing of the kind. Contreras's breathing might be harsh, but it's steady, another reassurance that he hasn't sustained any serious or lasting damage.

Aaronovich listens, then, for the noise of Carlita's breathing – and sits with a jolt. She needs only an instant to confirm Carlita's absence. And she recalls what woke her: the faint squeal of untended hinges.

The morning is cold, much colder than the day before. Even within the shelter of the prefabricated walls, even wrapped in her fleece-lined jacket and the blankets she brought, Aaronovich can feel its bite. Winter is coming, hour by hour, or so it seems. What possible reason could Carlita have to abandon this relative warmth? Aaronovich struggles to her feet, rubbing sensation into chilled muscles. It isn't solely concern she's experiencing but also distrust. Might Carlita conceivably have decided she'd be safer with the others? That her loyalty lies with those formerly imprisoned and now made free?

And in the crudest terms of survival, Aaronovich thinks, *would she be so wrong?*

But she's jumping to conclusions, letting the hunger, the tension, the sleeplessness, sway her. She slips through the door, careful not to rouse Contreras. As she assays the roof space, Aaronovich acknowledges how unlikely it is that Carlita has betrayed them. For if she had, she would of course have gone downstairs, into the Big House, and from there to the cellblock.

So, what? With each slight movement, the cold strikes at Aaronovich like an open-handed slap. She can scent snow on the air. What could have tempted Carlita out here?

Then she catches the sound, a glutinous rasp. At first she has no idea what it could be, though she's heard the same often enough throughout her professional life. Finally understanding, she follows. There's a shaded area, cut off by a barrier of the ductwork, in the corner that faces toward the administrative wing. Once Aaronovich knows where to look, she can see Carlita's back quite clearly. She's crouched, leaning forward, and her shoulders are heaving.

Aaronovich, too, stays low, so as to be invisible from the yard below. After a while, she perceives that Carlita has sensed her presence. Yet Carlita waits until her own heaving breath has settled before she wipes a palm across her lips and turns.

"How long?" Aaronovich asks her.

Carlita shrugs. She looks weak, deflated. "A couple of weeks. Three, maybe."

"It might not be—"

"No," Carlita agrees. However, what she's left unsaid, what's apparent in her face beneath the dull morning light, is more eloquent: the balance between hope and terror.

"Does Johnson know? I mean—"

"No."

"You don't think he deserved to?"

"He'd still have gone," Carlita says, and there's certainty in her voice, certainty mingled with defeat. "Even if he'd known, he'd have gone."

Aaronovich wants to argue Johnson's case. She can't. That last time they spoke, she'd seen the expression in his eyes, the utter surety. Could even this have introduced doubt into that sealed-off mind of his?

"You should rest," Aaronovich tells Carlita, and then notes how the sentiment sounds. "We *both* should rest."

"Are we safe?" Carlita wonders.

She seems dubious. Yet it's equally clear that she has no qualms about submitting to Aaronovich's authority. She trusts her judgement, not merely as a doctor but as someone with the right, even the obligation, to make decisions on her behalf.

Perhaps that fact should frighten her. A part of Aaronovich questions why it doesn't, and how the rest of her can look so calmly on the responsibility she bears. Maybe the reason she wants to defend Doyle Johnson is that she, too, has set herself upon a course she can no longer deviate from.

"A couple of hours more," Aaronovich says. "Then we'll see."

CHAPTER FORTY-SEVEN

Doyle feels that he understands them now, in a way he never has before, in a way that perhaps he couldn't understand people who weren't sick.

They're defending their territory. They haven't come looking for a fight. But if Doyle runs, they'll pursue, because if he runs he'll be prey. And they'll get both him and Kyle, because he doesn't have enough bullets to stop them.

Five left. Who would have guessed that ammunition would be the first resource they ran out of? Something else he's kept from Kyle. Doyle has never been a good liar, but it occurs to him that he has a talent for lying by omission.

They're approaching cautiously. He suspects that they recognise the gun for what it is. Their eyes are on him, not on the doorway through which Kyle vanished. So long as that's the case, Kyle has a chance. But there are only five bullets. Five bullets, six Sickers. He can't get past them. He has no means to stop them. So this isn't likely to end well.

Doyle starts walking toward them, for no other reason than that it seems the last thing they'll expect. They stop advancing, the front two even backing up a pace. All six are male this time, none of them too young or too old, and that makes the prospect of what's coming easier. They're not a family, not a tribe, they're a hunting pack. He realises then how much he's been itching for a situation this straightforward. These are just people, sick people. Everything Aaronovich told him was right. But here, now, they're a direct threat. If he runs, they'll give chase. If he doesn't, their weight of numbers and his intrusion upon their territory will make it impossible for them to back down.

There's a dozen feet between them. Advancing any farther will lose him the one advantage he has, which is range.

Doyle shoots the nearest Sicker squarely in the chest. The man is wearing the tatters of a logger's jacket; the rotted fabric bursts into confetti. He doesn't get even the barest murmur out, just jars backward like he's on a piston. He bowls down one of the others, and Doyle feels momentarily good about his chances.

Then they're coming. Doyle takes two steps back and fires, aiming left. The result is another chest wound, off-centre but good enough to suit his purposes. He's going for damage, for chaos. He needs their undivided attention.

Had he really believed they wouldn't be able to follow? Or, on some level, had he anticipated this?

One more rapid step back, the last he'll get, and Doyle fires again. The shot goes higher than he intends; a face erupts, spewing teeth and gobbets of meat. Its owner leers appallingly, staggers, but doesn't stop. There's no distance left between them, and only now that it's too late does Doyle want to turn and run.

They don't attack as people would attack. They get close straight away, limiting their own offence. Nor are they quite like animals. But the assault is effective. It leaves him few options. All Doyle can do is slide one hand into a pocket, grasping the object he's stashed there, and at the same time fling his gun arm up in defence and give way, so that their momentum carries him toward the ground instead of smacking the air from his lungs.

He lands roughly. The weight of them is almost enough to paralyse him, half-starved though they are. A mouth gnashes inches from his eyes, filling his nostrils with a reek of putrid meat and halitosis. In picturing this as a fight to the death, he hadn't considered infection. He'd thought that they might kill him, like his own body is killing him. He's reconciled himself to that, but sickness is a different prospect. It appalls him as death never has.

Doyle resists, pushing harder, lest they bury him. Hands clasp the gun; the four of them might as well be one creature. He flails the pistol, not hurting them, only trying not to lose his hold. His other arm he manages to tear loose from his pocket, fingers still gripping cold plastic. Already, both arms ache. They'll soon wear him down.

Sure enough, the gun goes first. Something unseen — a shoulder, a knee — crunches on his wrist, and the pain is impossible. He can no longer feel the muscles of that hand, but he's aware of the absence against his palm and fingers. Then his left arm comes free, and so Doyle jabs for the nearest neck.

The Sicker directly on top of him arches back, scratching at the yellow plastic handle that juts from his throat. Doyle discovered the sharpened screwdriver beneath Plan John's desk, on his initial day of searching the apartment. At the time, it had been one more mystery, but he'd kept it, because a weapon was a weapon. Now, whoever the shiv once belonged to, it's saved his life, at least for an instant. Doyle jams a suddenly uncovered leg into a Sicker's chest, kicks with every bit of strength he has, and the whole knot of them roll aside, finally giving him space to slither free.

Doyle lurches back to his feet. Three of them are up also and already circling warily. When they come again, he won't be able to stop them. His arm is numb, darting pain through his shoulder. Doyle looks for the gun, can't find it. There are just two bullets left anyway, not enough to end this.. But surely he's done what he needed to; surely Kyle has got away? If only he could be certain. Everything that's happened might have taken seconds, and so he has to keep going somehow, to buy a little more time.

Much too late, Doyle perceives that the three still standing aren't even looking at him. Simultaneously, he becomes aware of a tendril of noise, rising and falling. He's heard it before, though he requires a moment to identify it: an animal sound, but not issuing from any animal throat. He doesn't want to turn his back to the Sickers. Instead, he edges against the wall, placing them on his right, and steals a glance.

The Sicker girl is stooped over, virtually on all fours. Her gaze holds the three beside him, as their dark-specked eyes are focused upon her. She's approaching in fits and starts, scurrying a pace or two and then hesitating. And close behind her is Kyle.

He must have traversed the front of the building on the first floor, have come back up by the opposite staircase. Maybe he saw Abigail and chased after her; maybe he returned deliberately. In the end, the details hardly matter. Doyle has sacrificed himself for nothing.

"Get out of here!" he roars, sure that the commotion alone will trigger the remaining Sickers.

Yet they scarcely seem to notice. Nor does Abigail, who's scampering nearer, on two legs but hunched like the werewolf in an old movie. Only Kyle looks at him, with brief disregard. He's gained a weapon from somewhere, a length of wood that might once have been a chair leg. He's hurrying to reduce the gap between himself and Abigail.

Then everything is in motion, too fast to interpret, bodies blurring, noises collapsing together. The impact as one of the Sickers goes for Doyle tears him off his feet, and he distantly registers the fact that Abigail has flung herself at another.

In a gap of whirling limbs, he snatches a glimpse of Kyle, close enough to be sucked within the gravity of the exploding violence. "Go," Doyle spits through gritted teeth. "Kyle, just go!"

He can't say more because an elbow punches into his stomach, sucking the wind from his lungs. He almost loses his grip on the body against his, and whatever glimmer of energy he's using to keep the Sicker from gouging his throat out. Doyle manages to hold him back, but not to shove him away; he hasn't the strength for that. He's stalling, playing for seconds, and at any moment this will be over.

An earsplitting crack engulfs the garbled confluence of sound. Half deafened, Doyle can make no sense of the eruption; not until he sees that one of the Sickers has reared back, not until he sees the blood. It's the gun. Kyle has the gun. The shot wasn't a good one, but at that range he couldn't have missed. And now Kyle is looking at Doyle, his eyes desperate. "Come on, Johnson!"

He can't. There are still two of them on their feet, two that will follow if he moves, that will be quicker than Doyle can possibly be. "Throw it to me," he says.

Kyle does as he's told. The throw is a good one, thankfully, slow and underarm, better than the shot. In a flash Doyle has the gun up, trained on the remaining Sickers. Even while they're registering that, he's moving, edging through the gap in their ranks. He doesn't dare look toward Kyle. The slightest faltering, the slightest hint of distraction, and they'll be on him.

"Kyle," he says, "you can't wait for me. Get out, with the girl. Do it. Right now."

Nor can he look to confirm whether the order is being obeyed. However, he can hear the scamper of feet. Abigail, at least, has retreated. Doyle aims at the crowd of Sickers: two watching him warily, a couple motionless and likely dead, and the last two nursing wounds, though still unquestionably threats. Doyle tries to keep the gun on all of them.

He has one shot left, but they have no way to know that. Yet there *is* knowing, he thinks, in the eyes of the two that are staring at him, knowing and terrible self-assurance.

Doyle takes a step back, keeping the gun up. When one of them shifts, he snaps the barrel to them and the man pauses. Doyle keeps backpedalling, his free arm raised to feel his course along the wall. The second uninjured Sicker takes a half step, and Doyle pins him with the gun, daring him with all of his will.

Except that they aren't people, and he can't predict them. So maybe they'll chance it. And Doyle is halfway to the unboarded window, that he's sure of. They won't just let him walk away like this. It's gone too far for that.

Doyle turns and runs.

No, he'd been wrong, less than halfway. The distance appears much farther. He should have used that last bullet, should have put one of them down. Now they're behind him, and they're faster than he is. If he delays to aim, they'll be on him. So Doyle drives all the strength he has left into his legs. He lopes along, feeling as though the window is somewhere far above and he's crawling against the weight of gravity.

Only as he comes close does the impression of speed return, and then only as he realises what lies beneath him. Not the jeep as he'd expected, for this isn't that window. Below is nothing but distant asphalt. And even as he sees, Doyle is hurling himself over the sill, comprehending perfectly what's coming, hoping it won't be his head that hits first.

It isn't. His right arm takes the impact. He hears it snap, a jagged crack. There's no pain as such, but the promise of pain to come swaddles Doyle's whole body. He thinks his head is in one piece. He wouldn't lay bets on anything else. The thought of what's happened to that arm makes acid vomit bubble in his throat.

Something unfeasibly heavy comes down on him and rolls aside, hammering his chest and sending the first real burst of agony shrieking through him. A second Sicker lands just inches away; the man's ankle bends like a drinking straw before the rest of him crashes into the road. Twisting onto his back, Doyle spies a third poised in the window above, frozen by indecision. He's the one Doyle shot in the face, and his cheek is a charred patch of torn muscle and black blood. He shouldn't be moving at all, yet his gaze is cool and collected.

Then Kyle is standing over Doyle, reaching out a hand. "Come on."

Doyle can't communicate that the arm Kyle is grasping for is broken. In that moment, the anguish is all-consuming. The fear of contact is sufficient to get him to his feet.

Kyle stares at him, eyes massive, not understanding. "Come on!" he repeats.

The girl, Doyle sees, is already in the jeep. He starts toward the vehicle, dragging his feet as best he can. Kyle darts ahead, flings the passenger-side door open, and shuffles into the driver's seat. Doyle tumbles in after. He has to contort to use his good arm to haul the door shut, and the torture of that is monstrous, enough that he can hardly believe he hasn't blacked out.

He isn't certain if the motion he feels is real or his battered mind tilting reality about him. Then he glimpses the side mirror, and in it the hotel, the Sickers, the entire scene receding. In another instant, a corner has erased the Alexis from view.

Doyle knows then that they've made it. Against all his expectations, he's alive.

CHAPTER FORTY-EIGHT

Aaronovich can't guess why the convicts would have come back for Contreras, if indeed they have. Maybe they were just passing en route to other business. Maybe they're tying off the loose ends of last night's violence. Either way, they don't seem pleased at his absence.

"Hey! Contreras! Where the fuck are you?"

She thinks that's Stokes, though she can't be sure. Even with such a relatively tiny population, Aaronovich has only ever been familiar with those few inmates she's treated.

Then comes another voice, the two of them — or is it three? — conversing. Aaronovich is unable to make out words. It sounds, however, as if they're arguing, and it's easy to theorise about what. Aaronovich wonders why they should care where Contreras is, decides they probably don't. It's an irony of having any sort of power, she supposes. Suddenly you find yourself forced to worry about things that once would have meant nothing. Funland is theirs now — she assumes the new regime is basically egalitarian, as revolutions tend to be until the moment when they're not — and they can't have one badly beaten former guard wandering on his own. Also, no doubt, there will be issues of blame and responsibility. She doesn't envy them, being the bearers of such news.

They make a cursory search. From the rooftop, it's easy to track their movements within the building; they don't try to be quiet. Ten minutes have passed, or less, before they give up and start back toward the cellblock. Aaronovich still can't discern words, but there's clear tension in their voices.

She returns to the shack that surmounts the stairwell. Contreras is resting, with Carlita tending him, which, given the limitations of their resources, means little more than keeping him company. Aaronovich can see from their faces that they too have been anxiously following the brief hunt through the building below.

"It's time to go," she says.

Contreras is stronger than he was the previous night. Not only is he able to stand without support, he seems surer of himself. Perhaps, like her, he's simply more comfortable with a situation of transparent crisis, as opposed to the grinding dread of recent months. Whatever the case, Aaronovich dares hope that his presence may be a benefit rather than a burden.

Even by daylight, the Big House is thronged with shadows. Aaronovich leads the way to the entrance in the back right corner, which happens to be farthest from the cellblock. Outside, she glances along the building's flank, half expecting inmates to be approaching from the other direction. But there's no one. Maybe Contreras isn't that much of a priority, or they're just busy arguing over their next step. Still, sooner or later they're bound to come, and there's no time to waste.

Aaronovich points toward the administrative wing. "I'll need you to take my bags," she says. "If you cross here, you'll mostly be out of view. Go around the back. Wait as near to the gates as you can and be ready to run. If you see a chance, take it."

Carlita stares at her in horror. "What are you doing?"

"I'll catch up," Aaronovich tells her.

"Whatever you're planning," Contreras says, "let me do it."

In that moment, the temptation is all but overwhelming. Because when she looks at Tito Contreras, at the bruises blackening his face and the dried blood where they've split his lip and eyebrow, she knows exactly what these men will do to her if they should catch her. Yet that's the wrong lesson to draw from his injuries, for the damage to Contreras's ribs, to his right thigh and calf, is much worse. He's in no shape to run, should running be what's needed.

And is she? Perhaps not. Regardless, the less time they waste here, the less likely she'll be to have to find out. "No," she says, "absolutely not." She probes a pocket, withdraws the key that Contreras gave her the day before, and presses it into his palm. "This isn't debatable. Please, do what I've asked."

At first, she's certain they'll both argue on. Then Contreras grasps the rucksack she's holding out, slings it over his shoulder, and takes the second bag she proffers. He puts his free hand on Carlita's shoulder and says, "Come on now."

Having watched until they reached the near end of the administrative wing, Aaronovich goes back inside. She knows where the generator is; among the instructions Johnson drummed into her, he'd insisted she have that knowledge. She makes full use of the flashlight, for speed is her only priority. She knows they'll be coming soon. Indeed, she's counting on that. What can't be controlled can at least be manipulated.

The generator is smaller than she'd imagined. The room is a nondescript box of concrete, claustrophobic even under the restrictive beam of the flashlight. She checks the oil and gasoline levels as Doyle instructed, finds it fuelled just as he'd said she would. She hunts for the starter key, takes a trembling breath, and turns it. The machine chuckles petulantly and then settles to a steady rumble.

The instant she's positive it's working and will continue working, Aaronovich begins to run.

She's never considered herself to be in bad shape for a woman of her age. Not in bad shape is one thing, running for her life is entirely another. By the time she's reached the far end of the Big House, Aaronovich can still clearly hear the generator's dissonant roar. Has it always been so loud? It seems like thunder. Amid the deep silence of Funland, the sound carries to an improbable degree.

The main gates are in full view of the entrance to the cellblock. Carlita, Contreras, and her, they can't simply walk out. Hence, this becomes necessary: a diversion, suspicious enough to demand investigation but not so dramatic as to create widespread alarm.

Once more she leaves the Big House through the easternmost entrance. Once more she feels certain someone will be out there, hurrying toward her, and once more there's no one. Then again, across the yard is by far the quicker route from the cellblock – which means that, if anyone is coming, they're sure to see her as she crosses to the administrative wing. It's half a minute's fast walk, or if the fire in her chest subsides, perhaps a fifteen-second run.

Aaronovich leans upon the wall, fighting for air. She tries to tell herself that she's accepted what may well come next, that she's evaluated and consented to it. Of the three of them, she's the one most valuable to the inmates alive and intact. They might hurt her, but not so badly that she can't do her job. If there aren't already wounded in need of her services, she has no doubt there will be soon, and that she isn't the only one aware of that fact.

All these things Aaronovich assures herself of. But they're not easy to believe.

She can't get a proper view of the yard without exposing herself. Therefore, it makes sense that she should be moving, so that at least she'll be ready to run. Again, even if she can't dispute her own logic, her every instinct rebels against it. Nevertheless, Aaronovich starts walking. Being still feels too much like waiting for the inevitable.

She's taken a dozen steps by the time she clears the corner of the Big House and sees: there are four of them crossing the yard.

She recognises Nguyen, Farmer, Baptiste, and Oxendine. Other than Nguyen, they're all big men; they're heading out in force. That posse seems excessive for a woman doctor in late middle age and one recently beaten guard. Then she understands. This isn't for them, or not solely. The convicts don't know where Doyle Johnson is. They don't know why he's disappeared, if he's disappeared at all. And Johnson, the man who defied and eventually executed Plan John, who killed Ben Silensky, is a genuine danger.

She doesn't run. She doesn't run because they haven't spotted her, and if she does then perhaps they will. It feels absurd that they shouldn't be looking at her, and more so when she compels herself not to look at them either. But their attention is on the Big House and on the rumble of the generator, which even now she can hear as a fluttering vibration on the air.

She's past the halfway point. She can't resist a glance. They're closer, but only because they're closer to the front of the Big House. They aren't looking her way. Why should they? There's no reason. So she can't run, though it would be easy to.

Aaronovich returns her gaze to the asphalt before her. She watches her own feet, the dust they stir. Five steps. Ten. She mustn't look. Fifteen. She passes the corner of the administrative wing. Abruptly, the strength deserts her. Her legs give up, and dashing out a hand for support is all that keeps her standing. She feels the cool, uneven surface of the wall, absorbs the reality of it. Yes, she's made it this far.

Aaronovich releases the wall, and is relieved when the world doesn't spiral away from her. Up is up, down is down. She can stand, and so she can move. She puts one foot in front of another, and then doing so becomes easier and she's walking almost normally. Past the next corner, once she knows she's hidden by the administrative wing, her breathing begins to steady.

She had hoped, though, that Contreras and Carlita might be waiting here. The next corner will be the nearest point to the cellblock where they could have hidden out of sight. That they aren't there is either a good sign or a terribly bad one, and as she approaches, Aaronovich's pulse mounts.

But it's a good sign after all. When she peeks around, she can see them clearly. They're in the doorway of the tower beside the gate, the one Doyle Johnson made his own, in what seems a vanished lifetime. Carlita raises a hand in greeting. Contreras leans out, sneaking a glimpse of the cellblock. Satisfied, he scurries to the gate and reaches for the heavy chain and padlock that bind it shut.

If anyone was looking from the front of the cellblock, they couldn't miss him. If anyone were to leave now, he'd be directly in their line of view. There *are* two inmates outside – Silas and Cousins, Aaronovich thinks – but their attention is directed the opposite way, after the four who set out toward the Big House.

If either of them should turn…. But such thoughts will only paralyse her, so Aaronovich resumes walking. She hugs the outer wall, as though its ash-grey expanse might camouflage her. Ahead, Contreras has the padlock off and is hefting its weight in one hand, as he tries to unravel the chain with the other.

That's his mistake. One-handed, it can't be done quietly. She observes the realisation on his face, the dread, even as she hears the clank of metal against metal. Aaronovich's eyes drift mechanically to track the two by the cellblock.

Yes. One of them has turned. And yes, it's Silas. He sees Contreras first. "Hey!" He reaches to slap his companion hard on the shoulder.

The second man – not Cousins, no one she can identify – turns too. "What the fuck?"

She doesn't slow down. Nor does she run. She's near to Contreras, nearer than they are. She motions to Carlita, suddenly afraid that she won't come, certain she finds hesitation in her face.

Then Carlita is hurrying toward them, and Aaronovich has reached

Contreras, and Contreras has the chain off and on the ground, is gripping the gate with both hands. Aaronovich joins her strength to his. She feels the chain-link shift. A gap is all they need, but Silas is halfway to them. If he'd run, he might be on them by now. He looks confused, irresolute.

Aaronovich slips through. Contreras follows, snatching up the chain as he passes. Silas is close. Carlita is closer, and out in time for Contreras to drag the gate shut after her, for Aaronovich to wrap the chain in place and to snap the padlock shut.

Silas clings to the knotted wire with both hands. He's inches away, yet he might as well belong to a different world. "What is this?" he growls.

To Aaronovich's shock, he seems more frightened than angry. In his eyes she recognises the look of someone faced by the incomprehensible.

She takes a moment to consider Contreras and Carlita, to confirm that they're both all right. She takes another to put herself under the same scrutiny. Yes, she's out of breath and her heart is racing, but those are temporary symptoms and they'll pass.

"Come on," Aaronovich says. She starts up the road, toward the distant fringe of forest.

"Where are you going?" Silas asks. His voice is choked.

Maybe they have a key for the padlock. If Foster is dead then likely they will have. If not, they have tools, should they choose to use them. She can't assume they won't get the gate open, and so she walks as fast as she's able. But somehow, she knows the three of them have made it.

"There's nothing out there," Silas calls after.

Yet through the words, Aaronovich is sure she can detect his doubt, the doubt that says, *There's nothing in here either.*

CHAPTER FORTY-NINE

The night is the longest of Kyle's life.

The worst moment, the point when he's certain he'll lose control, comes about midnight. The needle has been hovering in the red for an hour, and there's no choice but to stop and refill the gas tank from the can stored in the trunk. Even on full beam, the headlights merely cut a sliver from the pervading black. As Johnson stands over him, propped precariously against the jeep's flank, the flashlight he holds only makes the night feel more vast and unforgiving, and it seems to Kyle that, at any second, the darkness might flood in to drown them both.

Later, he's forced to take other, brief breaks. He has never been so exhausted, never imagined it possible. Early in the morning, soon after sunrise, Johnson insists that they stop properly, so that Kyle can eat and rest. Kyle can't argue. His driving is becoming erratic, and more than once he's come close to veering off the road entirely.

Abigail has dozed in fits and starts, curled upon the back seat and sometimes mewling softly to herself. Johnson, so far as Kyle can tell, hasn't slept at all. He's been taking painkillers, but the listless manner in which the muscles of his face droop suggests they're doing little good. They share a can of beans and one of hot dogs between the three of them. After that, Kyle can't help but sleep. Oblivion comes over him like the wave of darkness he'd feared, and he's helpless to resist.

When he wakes, the light has hardly changed. He feels sick, distant, and no less tired. Johnson is watching him. His eyes are hollow. "Can you drive?"

Kyle nods. Yes, he can drive, since there's no choice.

Soon after that, Johnson finally slips from consciousness. Kyle, confident in his direction and having no desire for company, leaves him to whatever tortured rest he can get. Occasionally he sees Sickers at a distance, and their presence unsettles him. They feel like a threat now in a way they didn't before. Even Abigail's presence is constantly drawing at his nerves. He recalls that she saved their lives, however his exhaustion twists that remembrance into something frightful.

He's glad, really, when he begins to mistrust his course. It's an excuse to wake Johnson, and that in turn becomes the justification for another hour's unsatisfactory rest, another rudimentary meal. Yet Kyle feels no better for either. He knows objectively that there must be an end, that this interminable drive can't go on infinitely. But, as he slips back behind the wheel, with Johnson's gaze showing concern amid the ever-present pain, Kyle can't convince himself. His gut tells him that they'll never arrive because there's nowhere to go. They've been absent from Funland less than three days and already the memory of it seems unreliable.

Then – and Kyle can't say what time of day it is, or how long they've been travelling – through the tiredness he feels a vertiginous tug of familiarity. At first, he puts it down to imagination, for this stretch of road is identical to any other. The forest hemming them close to either side is no different from other forests they've passed. Only as he rounds the next bend does he understand. Ahead is the crashed SUV, which once belonged to Johnson's ex-wife or to her husband.

"Stop here," Johnson says.

Kyle slows. "Why?" He doesn't like this place. And they're so nearly back. He could refuse; he feels powerfully that he should.

"Stop, Kyle."

There's an imperative in Johnson's tone that he finds himself unable to resist. Kyle brakes and draws up to the side of the road.

For a minute they sit in silence. Through every moment, Kyle wants to restart the engine and pull away, Johnson be damned. Instead, he stares at the wheel, and at his own hands gripping its curve. Kyle only looks round when he becomes aware of movement, but it's just Johnson rubbing the fingers of his good hand across eyes bruised by fatigue.

As though with that gesture he's arrived at a decision, Johnson draws the pistol from his jacket pocket. He places the weapon in his lap and considers it.

"I need you to wait here," he says. "There's something I have to do." Uncertainty flickers across his features. "To try and do," Johnson corrects, with doubt Kyle has never before heard in his voice. "If I'm not back in an hour, or if you think you're in danger, then go."

"What are you talking about?" This makes no sense. They've done what they needed to, and it's been a success, it's been worth the risk.

They're alive and, for the first time in forever, they have a chance.

"Park up near the gates. Contreras should be watching out."

"What? No."

"Kyle. I have to do this."

"Then I'll come with you."

"No, you won't."

Kyle can feel himself drawing close to panic, the nightmare sensation of passively enduring a terrible occurrence that he's unable to prevent. "Johnson, this is insane. This is fucking crazy. Please, don't do this."

"I've no choice." Yet Johnson sounds so unsure that Kyle is certain he's about to change his mind, until the very moment when he opens the passenger-side door. With one arm useless, even climbing out is difficult for him. His jaw is clenched tightly. His eyes are compressed to slits.

Kyle gets out too, almost falls out, his limbs numbed by driving and his brain by two days without proper sleep. He leans on the hood and hisses at Johnson, "You asshole. You murdering asshole. What is this?"

He can feel that he's crying. That only makes him angrier, and more helpless, for Johnson has already descended the bank beside the road and is within the verge of the forest.

Kyle knows he should go after him. He should go after and drag him back, literally drag him if that's what it takes. He knows that's what he should do, and can't comprehend why he doesn't. He can't explain why he watches, motionless, as Johnson's shape becomes smaller amid the trees, and as the shadows thicken around him.

Then, abruptly, Johnson is gone from view.

Kyle sags against the hood of the jeep, feeling its distant warmth through the tips of his fingers. From the back, a noise makes him start: faint scratching. When he looks, Kyle is briefly horrified to see Abigail clawing at the glass with her stubs of nails. She glances his way, dark eyes expressionless but mouth turned down in a scowl of anxiety. He can discern her faint whimpering.

The sound reminds him of Sickers, and suddenly the nearby trees don't feel safe. The trunks are like bars. They've shut Johnson away, and who can predict what else they might conceal? Kyle gets into the jeep. Abigail is still making nervous noises in her throat, and he wishes he could do or say something that she'd be comforted by. However, his presence alone seems to settle her. She gives up on the window and moves to crawling back and forth upon the seat, till she tires of that too and curls at one end. A minute later and Kyle thinks she's asleep.

Kyle envies her. He feels agonisingly tense, yet his eyelids are intolerably heavy. He doesn't want to close them, but he has no say in the matter. He knows he can't possibly sleep. His body is dead weight, his mind also. He tries to find anger at Johnson. He lacks the strength. He's adamant that he can't sleep, until he does.

There's no question that what wakes him is a gunshot.

Just one, far off. Nonetheless, he's convinced of what he heard. Kyle sits rigid, expecting a second shot, or shouts, something, *anything*. But now there's only silence, heavy and blanketing, as though it's a component of the encroaching dusk.

How long since Johnson left? While he can't say for sure, he thinks perhaps half an hour, enough for late afternoon to slip into evening. Half of the time Johnson told him to wait. Kyle peers at the rear seat. Abigail is still sleeping, or appears to be. If the shot disturbed her, she gives no sign. Kyle settles back, forcing the tautness out of his muscles. Yet he can't close his eyes again. His tiredness has retreated to a point of focused pain behind his forehead.

Time passes.

Kyle wonders distantly what he's doing. Here is every opportunity he'd dreamed of when they set out. Here's the revenge he sought. What's changed since then? He stares toward the edge of the forest. The shadows are lengthening. The sun is out of view. It's been at least an hour, probably longer. There's no wind and the trees hang still, with hardly a twig stirring. If there were movement, even in the half darkness, then he would see.

More time has gone by, he thinks, since the gunshot than before it.

And he's growing afraid of the encroaching night, of what the dark might bring. Regardless, if it were only that, Kyle feels certain he'd stay. He's grown used to fear. It can't control him the way it once did. That isn't what's undermining him, but the conviction, beyond his ability to explain, that Johnson won't be returning – and that he never meant to.

Kyle spares the forest one more glance. There's nothing but the shafts of trunks, row upon row receding into blackness. For a moment he wants urgently to dare those dark spaces, to trace Johnson's steps, to find him and bring him back.

Instead, Kyle starts the jeep's engine.

CHAPTER FIFTY

She thinks she hears an engine. But the distant hum resolves to nothing, and afterward Aaronovich can't be sure.

The minutes wear by. She doesn't intend to sleep. It's a gunshot that wakes her. Carlita and Contreras are both already looking in the direction from which it came, gazing helplessly into the thick foliage as the echoes abate.

Aaronovich is on her feet by then, anticipating a second shot. There isn't one, and eventually she sits once more, her back against the bole of a tree. She's cold and tired and she aches, deep in her bones. She's not cut out for this. And now this fresh alarm; it frustrates her. What could it mean? A single gunshot, out here in the forest?

She knows they should be discussing it, but she can't bring herself to speak, and Carlita and Contreras don't seem inclined to either. Aaronovich tells herself that it's because they don't want to risk drawing attention. There's a slender chance that Funland will have sent out search parties, especially if they've discovered that she's taken the last of the medical supplies. There's a more significant likelihood of infected being close at hand.

She wishes she could say with certainty that she'd heard the engine, and that the sound had come from the nearby road. If that were the case, perhaps it would be worth their setting out on foot. Maybe Kyle and Johnson have had an accident. Conceivably they might need help. Yet, without knowing for a fact, the hazards involved in scouting for them would be too great. Aaronovich has already decided that they should wait until nightfall before moving on, as that's the earliest time by which Johnson had hoped to return.

She is only beginning to realise how absolutely she's believed in him. Somehow it had scarcely occurred to her that Johnson wouldn't make it back. Now, here in the dark woods, that blind faith seems absurd. But she has nothing to replace it with. If Johnson and Kyle don't come then they'll have to decide: either accept whatever fate awaits them in Funland, or take their chances in the wilderness. The prospect of making that decision horrifies her almost more than the options it represents. She hasn't allowed herself to think this far. If she had, she might never have dared act at all.

She looks for the sun, though it's out of view behind the trees. The shadows are substantial and artificial-looking, like painted stripes of darkness. Aaronovich wears no watch. She can't say with certainty when the shot was fired, or how long has elapsed since. She picks out one particular shadow and follows its crawl across the ground, over black earth jagged with discarded pine needles.

When it touches that root, I'll make a decision. Twenty minutes, thirty at most. When the shadow touches the root, I'll decide. And it will be my responsibility, whatever comes.

Then she hears it. This time she's positive: an engine. And it's drawing nearer.

Aaronovich listens, as though in a trance. She doesn't look at Contreras or Carlita, but she has no doubt that they're staring toward the noise, unmoving, hardly breathing, just as she is.

At last she snaps herself free. She's sure. An engine. The jeep. They're coming back.

"Come on," Aaronovich says, hoisting her pack onto her shoulder and already moving. "We need to get to the road."

★　　★　　★

Kyle has parked some distance from them. Aaronovich was surprised, in the first moment, to see him there behind the wheel. Yet, as she looks closely, he seems older to her than when he left. Little remains of the child she knew even a few months ago.

He appears, too, utterly exhausted. However, while she feels for him, Kyle only commands Aaronovich's attention for an instant. Her eyes are drawn past him, to the figure hunched in the back seat. Then she's hurrying, abruptly desperate to cover the intervening distance, and then she's scrabbling at the door handle.

Abigail half falls, half leaps into her arms. A distant part of Aaronovich's mind warns her of the danger from teeth, nails, saliva,

340 • DAVID TALLERMAN

but she can't attend to it, or else finds she can ignore it. She grips Abigail and the child gurgles and laughs, and Aaronovich laughs as well, for all that she's every bit as near to crying.

She appreciates now how it's wounded her to let this small and fragile human being out of her sight. She recognises the hole it's torn, to do what she thought was necessary — what *had* been necessary.

Yet this, too, is necessary. This moment is as vital as any she's known.

But it can't last. Barely has she caught up Abigail when Aaronovich hears the scream. She thinks at first that Carlita must have seen the men from Funland, finally hunting them, or Sickers perhaps. But this isn't that sound, not a howl of fear. It's an outpouring of raw, torn grief.

Only as she lowers Abigail to the ground does Aaronovich register Doyle Johnson's absence.

"Kyle," she says, forcing calm into her voice because it's apparent that once more she's the one who will have to be calm, "where's Johnson?"

Kyle is out of the jeep, hovering at the verge of the road as though he might decide at any second to flee. "He...he went into the woods," he says, not looking at her or at Carlita. "He took the gun. He said there was something he needed to do. I tried to go with him—"

Carlita takes three rapid steps, halving the distance between her and Kyle. "Liar!"

"No." But he seems uncertain. "He said to wait. He didn't come back."

"How could you let him, Kyle? How could you let him do it?"

"I tried to tell him—"

Even as he speaks, Carlita has taken three more steps, and before he can finish, she strikes him, open-handed, across his cheek, hard enough that Kyle rocks on his heels.

"My god," Carlita spits, the words garbled with horror or disgust, "did you hate him so much?"

Aaronovich hastens to grasp Carlita's hand, where it hovers ready for another blow. "Don't."

Carlita doesn't look at her. "You talked him into this," she says.

"This stupid, whatever this was, this *bullshit*. This useless bullshit. When we were safe. You dragged him out here, just to die. And it was all for nothing!"

Aaronovich places herself between them. "This isn't helping."

Carlita turns away, though not, Aaronovich thinks, because of anything she herself has said. She stumbles across the road to the far verge. Contreras, who has been hanging back, appears as if he might try to comfort her, but when he glances to Aaronovich for confirmation, she mouths, *Leave her.* She's seen enough of grief to know that Carlita is beyond consolation.

Aaronovich returns her attention to Kyle. He's shaking his head spasmodically, and repeating something over and over, a brief phrase, but one she can't make out. Sensing her attention, Kyle looks directly at her, and this time she can separate out his words.

"It *wasn't* for nothing," he says.

She doesn't understand. All that's happened in the last few minutes is a jumble that her mind is only now attempting to piece together.

"It wasn't for nothing!" Furiously, Kyle hunts in his pocket, yanks out a scrap of paper, and holds it up. "Look...look! We found this. Johnson found it. It's somewhere safe, maybe, if we can get there."

Aaronovich considers the paper in the dying daylight, striving to deduce its significance. There are two numbers, punctuated, written in large scrawl. Coordinates perhaps? But she doesn't know how to read them.

"It's where they went," Kyle says. "Somewhere better."

So yes, coordinates. A destination, if they can interpret and follow them, and if they can remain safe in the meantime. That thought brings home the fact that they're standing talking in the road, with night coming on fast. Aaronovich turns back to Carlita and Contreras. "We can't stay here," she says.

To Aaronovich's surprise, that's enough to snap Carlita out of her grief. She nods, the motion mechanical and not entirely human-seeming. "Yes. We can still find him."

And Aaronovich doesn't have the heart to say that isn't at all what she'd meant.

⋆　　⋆　　⋆

Ten minutes later and Kyle is pointing out the spot where he last saw Doyle Johnson. It's easy to identify from the SUV crashed there, a mystery Aaronovich has no desire to decipher.

The sky is almost fully dark by then. Carlita insists on getting out, and walks past the edge of the forest, in the direction Kyle has indicated. Aaronovich is ready to go after her, is trying to judge whether she and Contreras together will have the strength to force her to come back if she should resist, when Carlita turns and hurriedly retraces her steps.

"I know what this is," she says. "I know why he did this." She speaks the words without anger, but with a note in her voice that Aaronovich thinks may be despair. There's nothing there, however, to suggest she believes Johnson is going to return – or that he's still alive.

Aaronovich opens her door but, wary of unsettling Abigail, doesn't get out. "We can wait a little longer," she proposes. "It's not quite night."

Carlita looks down at her. Her eyes are expressionless. "He was dying," she says.

"Yes, I know."

"Oh. Of course." Carlita nods thoughtfully. "That was why I couldn't tell him." She touches the fingers of one hand to her belly, perhaps unconsciously. "Because it wouldn't have been fair."

"No," Aaronovich agrees. She had wondered if Johnson had shared her diagnosis with Carlita. Here's her answer.

"But," Carlita says, "he didn't have to die alone."

"We can wait," Aaronovich repeats, not knowing how else she can possibly respond.

Carlita only shakes her head and climbs back inside.

Kyle doesn't start the engine immediately. He's staring into the fathomless rectangles of gloom between the trees. A minute passes, and another. Then, unprompted, he rouses the jeep to life and pulls away.

Aaronovich watches the SUV until a turn in the road steals it from view. She feels no pain, no sadness for Johnson's loss. Perhaps that will come later. Or maybe it won't. She knows now that she has always respected him more than she's liked him, and that on some level she feared the man more than either.

The jeep is ample for the five of them. It was designed, after all, for people of a different age, one recent and unimaginable, beyond her ability to recall in any detail. They aren't those people. They need less space. Even with five of them, the vehicle seems roomy.

After a few minutes, Contreras offers to take over the driving, and Kyle grudgingly accedes. Within seconds, he's fast asleep, and for the first time Aaronovich can see some trace of the boy she met all those months ago. In the back, Carlita presses herself to the very edge of the seat, as though with effort she might squeeze her body out into the night. For a short spell she cries softly, and then she's quiet. Aaronovich takes the farther side and holds Abigail near, the child drowsing on her knee.

Aaronovich realises she's no longer afraid to be this close to Abigail. There's no more that the sickness could do to her. Whatever she can be turned into, she's been turned already. She's become some entity that grew inside the desiccated shell of her old self, a being she doesn't recognise, or even feel the need to examine.

None of them talk. Except that once, a couple of hours after they've left the crashed SUV behind, and apparently speaking to no one but himself, Kyle says, "What if it's something worse?"

She'd thought he was still sleeping. Maybe he is. The question sounds like part of an internal conversation revealed by accident, and Aaronovich doesn't suppose for a moment that it was aimed at her. Nevertheless, she tells him, "It won't be."

She's not trying to reassure him. She doubts he would even understand her meaning; she barely understands herself. Only that, whatever's ahead of them, it's something new, and for them at least, something unprecedented.

What's out here?

Freedom, for a while anyway. A world without walls. Danger, certainly, and death. The sick – since it's their land now, their time. Perhaps other survivors, people better and worse than those they've known. Change. And therefore hope.

Aaronovich shuts her eyes, runs her fingers through Abigail's tangled hair, and lets the sense of being in motion lull her into peace.